The
Dewey Decimal

The
Dewey Decimal
System of *Love*

JOSEPHINE CARR

NEW AMERICAN LIBRARY

New American Library
Published by New American Library, a division of
Penguin Group (USA) Inc., 375 Hudson Street,
New York, New York 10014, U.S.A.
Penguin Books Ltd, 80 Strand,
London WC2R 0RL, England
Penguin Books Australia Ltd, 250 Camberwell Road,
Camberwell, Victoria 3124, Australia
Penguin Books Canada Ltd, 10 Alcorn Avenue,
Toronto, Ontario, Canada M4V 3B2
Penguin Books (N.Z.) Ltd, Cnr Rosedale and Airborne Roads,
Albany, Auckland 1310, New Zealand

Penguin Books Ltd, Registered Offices:
80 Strand, London WC2R 0RL, England

First published by New American Library,
a division of Penguin Group (USA) Inc.

First Printing, September 2003
10 9 8 7 6 5 4 3 2

 REGISTERED TRADEMARK—MARCA REGISTRADA

LIBRARY OF CONGRESS CATALOGING-IN-PUBLICATION DATA:

Carr, Josephine.
The Dewey decimal system of love / Josephine Carr.
p. cm.
ISBN 0-451-20971-0
1. Women librarians—Fiction. 2. Middle aged women—Fiction. 3. Conductors (Music)—
Fiction. 4. Philadelphia (Pa.)—Fiction. I. Title.

PS3553.A76323D49 2003
813'.54—dc21   2003044158

Set in Garamond
Designed by Ginger Legato

Printed in the United States of America

With admiration and endless love,
this novel is dedicated to my mother,
Jo Carr,
the paragon of a passionate librarian.

ACKNOWLEDGMENTS

I wish to offer my love and gratitude to Elliot and to our children, Rachel and Daniel, as well as to my father and mother, King and Jo. I am forever proud of them.

My thanks and devotion to other family members: Jean, Este, Becky, Josephine, and Cecilia; George and Sarah; Jackie, Artie, Stuart, and Rich; Allan, Karen, Lewis, Esther, and Laura.

In the book world: I send my heartfelt appreciation to my agent, Stephanie Kip Rostan of the Levine Greenberg Literary Agency. She is a guiding light to me, and I am grateful beyond words. My new editor, Ellen Edwards, and the entire team at NAL have baptized me in their waves of enthusiasm and intelligence.

In the library world: I cheer the Allentown Public Library, with its dedicated and brilliant leader, Kathryn Stephanoff. To my fellow board members of the Friends of the Lehigh Libraries, my thanks for your many votes of confidence.

To the community of Lehigh Valley Hospital and Health Network, I thank you for your kind and constant generosity.

Finally, to my readers: may you continue to honor the extraordinary literary heritage found in our free library system and the librarians who help us discover its enduring wealth.

1

*For questions about love, and, more particularly,
inappropriate love, go to the 306.7s (e.g., The Single Woman–
Married Man Syndrome, Addicted to Adultery, Affairs,
Secret Loves, Keeping The Love You Find, etc.).*

Aleksi Kullio, the new conductor of the Philadelphia
Philharmonic, strode onto the concert stage with quick,
small steps, like a boy who hadn't learned to match his
stride to the new length of his legs. I knew he was married. In fact, I could just glimpse the back of his wife's
head, where she sat in the front row. Blond, of course.
The *Philadelphia Inquirer* had devoted a front-page story
to his arrival. We learned that after a dreamy childhood in
his native Finland, he'd attended Harvard as an undergrad-
uate, then the Curtis Institute of Music. His conducting
style was described as "buoyant" and his wife as "gorgeous." The color photo showed a handsome, interesting,
and vaguely cruel face. He was perfect and he was married and I was not.

Something happens when you hit forty and you've never
been married. It begins to feel permanent. You convince
yourself that you never wanted to be married *anyway*

because otherwise surely you would have been by now. Your friends have stopped fixing you up and you completely forget that a penis can be anything other than God's joke. Your therapist talks in an ever so gentle voice about the value of solitude. Flannel nightgowns and sheets, down comforters, and multitudes of pillows call your name with a low urgency that is positively sexual.

So picture me, a librarian spinster, falling in love with a married man I didn't know and had no chance of ever knowing. I would have doubted it myself except that the body tells you when you fall in love. My body sure did. Simultaneously, I felt like I was going to throw up, pass out, and have a heart attack.

My best friend, Suzanne, sat with her husband to my left. Her elbow poked me seconds after love had so unceremoniously grabbed me.

"What?" I hissed.

"Nothing."

"Why'd you nudge me?"

Her voice skipped from low to high. "He's a doll."

"You're married, remember." It wasn't often that I got the opportunity to make her feel sorry for being married and I certainly wasn't squeamish about making the most of it.

Applause resounded through the hall, a gracious, enthusiastic welcome to the new conductor.

Suzanne turned her head and looked at me with an inappropriately stern expression. I hated it when she got bossy. "So's he," she said.

I stuck my nose into the air. "I have no interest in a man's physical appearance. You know that."

"Give me a break." She sighed. "He could look like a toad and there'd still be something marvelous about him."

Aleksi Kullio turned away from us and in so doing gave the musicians a sweeping glance, lifted his baton, paused, and then lowered the baton. Mozart danced.

I took a deep, shaky breath and exhaled slowly. The brief conversation with Suzanne had calmed my heart's palpitations, but I still felt like throwing up. I had to admit that I was no stranger to nausea. I was one of those thin, vaguely anorexic-looking women who didn't quite eat enough. Nothing major, just a mild distaste for food. I'd last eaten a bag of potato chips at four o'clock in the afternoon while I read a biography called *Georgiana: Duchess of Devonshire* in my aforementioned bed. Now, she was a woman who *lived*. That is to say, she lived and loved. (Look it up in Biography, *Devonshire*.) Perhaps the duchess was responsible for my state. I think she'd made me jealous and oddly uncomfortable in my den of pillows and down. Had I gone soft?

You're probably thinking that I'm using the term *falling in love* too loosely. Surely this was just a desperate crush, not much different from when you're fourteen? But it wasn't. I watched his arms wave like the wings of a bird fighting the turbulent air currents of a coming storm, and my crowded feelings jostled for space in my chest, shoving and pushing to breathe more freely. This was love, inexplicable and absurd and utterly pointless. My silly heart beat fast with the joy of it.

Gordon Albright, director of the Free Library of Philadelphia, was my boss and my best friend at work. Whereas with Suzanne I shared the feelings of my life, Gordon and I shared the facts of our lives. We met on the following

Monday morning in the small back room where a coffeemaker, refrigerator, and square table were squeezed together, thus making us an unusually intimate library staff. He'd just finished adding too much sugar to his coffee and turned his strong, handsome face toward me. I knew enough, just from the way his hair poked up at the back of his head, not to ask about the weekend. A love affair lost or some such thing.

His bored eyes shot open when he looked at me.

I was so surprised that I made a little involuntary gasp. "What?" I gulped.

"Your hair is great today."

My long auburn hair was tucked into its usual french twist, no different from any other day at work during the last fifteen years. "Don't be ridiculous," I snapped.

"It's all poufy and shiny."

"Oh."

"And your cheeks are pink like little flowers!"

"Jesus." I picked up my Bryn Mawr mug and poured out some coffee, fighting the temptation to be pleased.

"You're in love," Gordon said triumphantly.

I whirled around. Then I grabbed a sugar and dumped it in the mug of coffee.

"See!" He pointed triumphantly.

I don't use sugar.

We stared at each other, and he seemed to re-collect himself. We might talk about sex (his) and dates (his), but love was off-limits. Gordon rubbed a hand over his head, discovering and smoothing the errant lock of hair that made him look like a naughty boy.

Somehow, right from the start, we'd never strayed into

thinking of each other romantically. He was an attractive man, but just not my type. Untrustworthy was how I figured it early on, and judging by the vast numbers of women he dated—and never married—I'd been right. It goes without saying that I wasn't his type. Too thin and muscular, with tiny boobs and small brown glasses hiding my green eyes. Suddenly, feeling his attention drilling into me, I felt like Queen for a Day. I found myself standing straighter. Was I almost beautiful?

Women know that we each have our moment. Clothed and out in the world, I was a discreet woman, just the sort you'd imagine behind the reference desk of your local library. But take off my clothes in the safety of my own apartment and I changed into a glittering, gleaming creature with white, silky skin, hair tumbling around my shoulders, and my taut body like the spine of a beautiful book with gold-embossed lettering. Only I saw this other creature and I couldn't pretend that I truly believed in her. She was my fantasy.

"Any problems over the weekend?" I asked.

"Ed created the usual difficulties, but the police handled things quickly."

Like all public libraries, we were plagued by the homeless, but Ed was our greatest challenge because he was smart. He fell asleep for a short period of time, usually about twenty minutes, and then he leaped to his feet and approached the reference desk to request five obscure articles in ancient journals. The worst of it was that he read and took notes from the journals until he fell asleep again, then leaped to his feet and started all over. Every day, he carefully folded the pages of notes and placed them in the trash can as he left the library. On the weekends, he tried to get a more substantial rest by sleeping in the far corner of the 600s. He drove us round the bend.

"I just wish he'd stop researching serial killers. I know he does it to make us nervous—" I muttered.

"I'm going to see if there's anything we can do."

We gulped our coffee. Yvonne, from the circulation desk, wandered into the room holding a carton of yogurt she would leave in the refrigerator until lunchtime.

She began chattering to Gordon, clearly enamored. Silently I wished her caution and made my way out to Reference. It was only eight thirty in the morning and we didn't open our doors to the public until nine o'clock, so I had time to straighten up my desk. I was the head of the Reference Department, which meant that in addition to helping people find answers, I also advised Acquisitions of our major reference requirements. It required an enormous amount of reading and a good memory.

I scooted my rolling chair around the reference area, where we had three desks (mine was behind glass walls in the back) and many of the more obvious materials were placed on deep shelves backed by a walnut half wall. After the weekend, things were always in a mess. I loved the act of cleaning up. It made me almost as happy as reading in bed or eating a piece of homemade vanilla cake.

As I bustled to and fro, the chair squeaking faintly, my mind circled around an idea that I couldn't quite hold on to. Something pleasant, I was sure, because my stomach fluttered a bit. Then I remembered. There had been an interesting review of a Stravinsky biography in *Publishers Weekly* and I happened to notice that Aleksi Kullio had

scheduled Stravinsky's *Rite of Spring* for a concert sometime during the fall season. I returned to my desk, looked
up the review, and read it again, this time more carefully. I
hadn't put a check mark next to the title, not even a question mark, so I'd obviously decided that such a massive,
detailed biography of a classical composer wasn't necessary to our collection. It was a starred review. Quickly, not
allowing myself to dwell on the rationale, I made a large,
determined check mark. I would order the biography.

The red pen dangled from my fingers as I imagined
writing a note to Aleksi Kullio, a professionally warm little
note, pointing out that, should he be interested, the Free
Library of Philadelphia owned the newest and most defin-
itive biography of Stravinsky. My unfocused eyes rose from
the desktop and stared through the glass walls, beyond
the reference section, and into the main reading room. A
few people ambled about, and I realized that the doors
had opened to the public.

A woman's blond head bobbed about, coming closer to
our reference area. I blinked. For a brief moment, I
thought I'd seen Aleksi Kullio's wife.

I looked again.

She marched toward our walnut divider. Huge gold
hoop earrings dangled from small ears. The blond hair fell
in graceful swoops to her shoulders. It occurred to me
that she—unmistakably Aleksi Kullio's wife—looked like
the perfect bakery birthday cake. Her icing was sleek,
with rosettes of flowers, and she clearly made mankind
drool with hunger. Of course, bakery cakes taste like
nothing at all.

An enormous desire filled my chest with air. I rushed

out of my office and over to the walnut divider, the air puffing my small breasts into little mountains. I wanted to blow out the birthday candles on her cake. Instead, I let out the air in a swoosh just as she reached me. Her face made a small moue of displeasure, which she almost immediately covered with a large, fake smile.

We shared a too-long moment of silence until it occurred to me that I was supposed to say something. Actually, I'm not sure what Miss Manners would advise about this. Is there a correct way to decide who speaks first?

"May I help you?" I said at last.

Her turquoise eyes danced around, searching the other members on duty in the Reference Department. She obviously wondered whether I was up to the job.

I spoke in a frigid tone, mimicking the chair of the English department at Bryn Mawr who, though otherwise brilliant, had had the unfortunate need to sound like British royalty. "I am the director of the Reference Department."

Her eyes settled back on me. "I'm researching a novel," she said, "and I need some sort of resource describing little-known poisons."

I nodded curtly. "Right this way." Now I sounded like a saleslady at Neiman Marcus. I led her down a row of library shelves, the number 615s buzzing in my ear. I stopped at a section of books, slid a finger along their spines, and then grabbed *The Poisons and Antidotes Sourcebook*. "This is just a start," I explained. "There are many other possibilities, but the bibliography should give you ideas of where to go next."

I glanced at her. It was possible, I thought, that he'd

married her for her pretty face and great body, not her intelligence. I hoped that even wondering this would cause my love to wither. No such luck.

She took the book, turned her back, and marched over to a table.

If you work in a library, you become used to the bad manners of the public. I don't mean to argue that it's forgivable, because it's not, but the lack of gratitude, the downright meanness and hostility, was an inevitable fact of life. Still, sometimes it bothered me. This was one of those times. In fact, I rapidly became engulfed with fury. I wanted revenge.

I walked briskly back to my office, head held very high, and I sat regally on my rolling chair. Of course, I knew why I wanted revenge. I was hopelessly and foolishly in love with this blond bombshell's husband. Aleksi Kullio had never met me, would never *want* to meet me, and would never fall in love with me. Why, after fifteen years of hard-earned celibacy, why, oh, why was I doing this?

Quickly I yanked out an order form and filled in the Stravinsky particulars. I would write that pleasant little note. Maybe I could personally deliver the book to him? Ridiculous, I moaned. It wouldn't make any difference. I stared at the wife. She was bent over the book so that the blond hair, which could be entirely natural, fell forward and hid her face.

She was writing a novel and she was researching deadly poisons? My chin rested in the palm of my hand. She wasn't taking notes and she sure didn't look like a novelist. The *Inquirer* hadn't mentioned anything about a writing career. The long red fingernail of the wife of Aleksi

Kullio flipped a page. I watched her for exactly four minutes, when she suddenly stood up and strolled out of the library.

Naturally she did not replace the book on the shelf. In fact, she left it open on the table, still turned to the *A*s. Her research hadn't been exactly extensive. I wasn't surprised.

2

*For questions about sexual dysfunction,
go to the 613.90s (e.g., Inhibited Sexual Desire, Sexual Healing,
The New Male Sexuality).*

*D*id you notice how I slipped it in that I'd been celibate for fifteen years? Bet you did. Hard to miss. I was
hoping to pretend that fifteen years wasn't such a big deal
by simply inserting it, no fanfare, into the text. I see now
that that won't wash. You want to hear the gruesome details. Have I got excessive vaginal dryness, perhaps? Do I
have an odor problem? Did my father abuse me and do I,
therefore, hate men?

Uh, no, no, no.

Men kind of scare me, if you really want to know. I can
deal with boys, and old men, but the in-between guys
make me nervous. The last date I went on was four years
ago. He was this man who came into the library every
Tuesday from one to two o'clock in the afternoon. He
wasn't good-looking and he wasn't bad-looking. I think
he was probably fifty years old, with a slim body, silky
brown hair, and enormous eyes. He always checked out

exactly six books of fiction, usually chosen from the New Books section out front. After about four months, I found myself expecting him. Then one week, he didn't come. And then he came again.

Isn't this exciting so far?

With a worried little scowl on my face, I'd left the reference area and nosed around the new books.

"Are you looking for something?" he'd said.

The librarian's supposed to ask the patron, not the other way around. "Isn't that my line?" I asked.

His big eyes were chocolate brown, darker than his hair. A slow smile stretched his lips wide and I caught a glimpse of clean teeth. "I'm a librarian, too," he said.

I was flabbergasted.

"At Hahnemann—a medical librarian."

My eyes were glued on the title of a book in the nonfiction section, *Choosing Your First Puppy*. Why the hell had I ordered a book with such a dumb title?

This was the moment when I would always get scared. I could tell that he liked me and I certainly liked him. He might ask me out.

"Obviously a medical establishment doesn't have fiction," he said.

I nodded my head and kept my eyes trained low.

"What do you read?" he asked.

I know, I know. He was the perfect match for me. You don't have to tell me. His shoes were big brown walking shoes, the kind you expect to find on Irishmen tramping about bogs and mogs. Is there such a word as *mogs*? If I hadn't mentioned it, I bet you would have said to yourself, *I must look that word up in my OED.*

"I read widely."

His head bobbed up and down. I risked a quick look. That was all the encouragement he needed.

"Would you like to go out to dinner?" His right arm bundled the requisite six books close to his chest, but his left hand actually moved through the space between us and touched my shoulder.

"Sure," I whispered.

"Saturday night?"

"Okay."

Four years later, you already know that the date was not a success. I don't really want to talk about it. Maybe I will, in the future, if I find you're trustworthy.

Not having sex can become a habit, just like smoking or drinking. A bad habit, I must admit. Not having sex probably won't give me cancer or a heart condition, but I'm sure it doesn't help my state of mind, and the medical establishment is gung ho on how the mind and body talk to each other. When I'd go out on a date, my mind would say things like, *Touch me right there and I'll never ask for anything else!* I'd be in constant begging mode. *Please, please, please?* Then, my body actually receives a touch— like it did four years ago—and it screams, *Leave me alone!* That's a lot of backing and forthing. Not good. Not healthy.

So what I think is that maybe I just haven't met the right man. It might be an unlikely explanation, but it's possible.

It's not that I woke up one morning and made the declaration, "I'm going to be celibate for the next fifteen years, by golly, as God is my witness!" I will admit that I made a conscious decision about it the first year. I was twenty-five years old and I'd just started as a children's librarian in the Free Library of Philadelphia. To say that there weren't many opportunities to meet men would be an understatement. I wore corduroy jumpers decorated with barnyard animals to the library every day, and most of my friendships were with three-year-olds and their socially aggressive mothers.

Nevertheless, I met a man.

When we finally started to have sex, I was traumatized by his desire for, well, anal sex. Maybe the barnyard animals gave him the wrong idea? I showed him out of my apartment, double-locked the door after him, and retreated to my painfully single bed with its thin white bedspread from JCPenney. I decided to try celibacy for one year.

Obviously, celibacy suited me, since I stuck with it for another fourteen years. I'm not in the least bit apologetic about it. So don't start.

On Friday night, I called Suzanne. By sounding weak and sad, I got the desired invitation to dinner. She and John live out on the Main Line, very close to the Haverford College campus, where John teaches embarrassing courses like "Gender and Sexual Orientation." I guess he's in the sociology department, but, for obvious reasons, I try not to delve too deeply into his work. Suzanne, once upon a time a corporate attorney, had her second child six months ago and she's at home with both kids.

I changed into blue jeans and a hooded gray sweatshirt. In my Mazda Miata convertible (a virginal white, of course), I zoomed out of the underground parking garage and onto the parkway. On an early evening in early autumn, I was surprised by the nip in the air. At the first red light, I yanked up the hood of the sweatshirt and tied it tightly under my chin. Nothing would make me put up the car's top except pouring rain. I made it out to Haverford in a near record twenty-three minutes.

Their miniature Main Line mansion glowed with lights and I smelled woodsmoke as I slammed the car door. Alison, the three-year-old, pressed her nose against the screen door as I climbed the front steps.

"Hey, Ally," I said.

"Ally," she said back.

My namesake.

I knelt down and stared through the screen door into her dark eyes. Blink, blink.

She started to giggle and I touched her nose through the screen. "Can I come in?"

"Yeth," Ally shouted. With a whoosh, she disappeared and I opened the door to let myself in.

"Where is everybody?" I yelled.

"In the living room," Suzanne called.

She was nestled into the corner of a large, saggy couch covered in faded chintz, breast-feeding the baby, Charlie. I plopped into the opposite corner with an exaggerated sigh. Suzanne's thick, unruly eyebrows rose in question.

"I'm in love," I said.

Her wide mouth curled into a grin.

"Don't get all excited." I took off my glasses and carefully licked both sides of the lenses, then polished them with the tail of a white undershirt I wore beneath the sweatshirt.

John strolled into the living room with Ally in his arms. "Would you like something to drink?" he said by way of greeting.

His tall, angular body seemed almost to touch the ceiling of the living room, though he always stooped with that quintessential academic slouch.

"Yes, I would."

"The usual, I presume?" When I nodded, he looked at Suzanne.

"A beer will put this guy to sleep," she said, glancing down at Charlie's small head where he nuzzled into her chest.

"So have a beer," John interrupted.

"Breast-feeding is the strangest thing," I said after John left to fix drinks, Ally still clasping him tightly around the waist with strong legs.

"You only think so because you don't have boobs."

Each hand rose to clasp a breast. "That is such a lie." It really was, too. I was only an A cup, but an exuberant A cup.

Suddenly Suzanne offered Charlie to me. "Try it."

Laughing, I waved my hands frantically. "That's sick."

"Don't you wonder what it feels like?" She stood and walked the length of the couch with Charlie offered to me like a tray of hors d'oeuvres. "John tried it."

"John breast-fed Charlie?!?"

"Yeah," she said. "He wanted to know what it felt like."

"Couldn't you have simulated the sensation for him?"

"But then it would have been sexual, and breast-feeding isn't sexual."

John inched into the living room, a martini glass balanced carefully. "I should shake and pour in here," he grumbled.

"Tell Ally to try breast-feeding," Suzanne said.

"It's an incredible feeling." John put my martini down

on the coffee table. "Just make sure he's pretty much finished feeding so he doesn't get mad."

"You guys are serious?" I reached for the martini and swung it to my lips without spilling a drop. When I'd replaced the glass on the table, Suzanne tumbled Charlie into my lap and arms.

"It was a lot harder for me," John said. "I had to smash his poor face into my chest."

Charlie's head had turned toward my stomach and he was rooting around like a small, attractive pig. "You should've called him Wilbur."

"Want me to leave the room?" John asked.

"Definitely."

He turned on his heel and dashed out of the room.

I sighed and ached for another sip of the martini.

"Just pull up your bra," Suzanne said.

"What bra?"

She gave a little shrug. "I'm going to get that beer."

I stared down at Charlie and listened to the dim sound of her sock feet swishing across the wood floor as she headed down the hall toward the kitchen.

Obviously I didn't have to do it.

I yanked up my sweatshirt and T-shirt, cradled Charlie in the crook of my arm, and pressed his plump cheek against my breast. He turned and clamped his mouth over my nipple. An electrifying sucking sensation erupted. I thought my little Wilbur was going to swallow the damn thing whole.

I yelled.

He let go and turned his face up. I swear he gave me the evil eye.

"That was too hard," I lectured him. "You need to learn some manners."

Both John and Suzanne ran into the room.

I stood up and handed Charlie to John. "Thank you for that educational experience."

He peered at me with what I call his soft expression. There had been times over the last five years when I thought John liked me in some obscure way. It wasn't so much that his interest was sexual, but more loving. I'd imagined a conversation during which he and Suzanne concocted a plan for John to end my self-imposed celibacy.

I didn't find John attractive, though I couldn't have said why. There was nothing wrong with him except, perhaps, his lengthy limbs, which reminded me of a huge tree in winter. Anyway, I wasn't desperate enough to find my best friend's husband desirable. I wasn't desperate at all. I liked my solitude.

Suzanne glugged her beer and then spoke with her mouth still circling the bottle's mouth. "Will you make the salad?"

"Sure." I picked up the martini and headed for the kitchen. I always made the salad.

The Crock-Pot sent dazzling smells into the air and I peered through the glass top to see a stewy concoction of chili bubbling gently. The kitchen was old, with wrinkled Formica countertops and a wavy linoleum floor. Piles of unread mail battled with the Crock-Pot, toaster, coffee-maker, and radio. The radio's weekly Celtic hour of music rollicked through the mess.

Over dinner in the dining room, I told them about

Aleksi Kullio's wife searching for a reference book on poisons. Alison's plump lips hung like ripe strawberries as she listened attentively.

"Suspicious," Suzanne murmured.

"Maybe she is writing a novel," John said.

"Right!" declared Alison.

"I don't mean to generalize, but she doesn't look like a writer," I said.

"What does a writer look like?" John asked.

I scowled at him.

"Hey, writers come in all shapes and sizes."

"She looks like a deb," Suzanne said. "Remember, I stood in the line for the women's room right behind her."

John shook his head. "I'm ashamed of you—just because a woman is beautiful, you assume she has no intellect."

Suzanne and I stared at each other and then burst out laughing.

"What?" John said.

"If a woman's beautiful *in that way*, a reasonable assumption can be made that she does not have a lot of smarts," Suzanne said.

"John, you have no idea how much time it takes to look *that way*," I said.

"It could be entirely natural," he interrupted.

"Define *natural*." I scooped up a large spoonful of chili and stuck it in my mouth.

While I chewed, Suzanne jumped in. "Even if she's a true blonde, her hair was layered with highlights."

"Highlights?" John said.

Alison pointed her baby spoon at the ceiling fixture

that blared white light onto the table like a foghorn. I could never get Suzanne to dim the damn thing and light candles.

"She goes to the beauty parlor for a one o'clock appointment." I looked into John's eyes. He seemed positively mesmerized by the conversation. "You with me so far?"

"Yeah." He picked up a beer and took a quick swig.

"Her hairdresser separates strands of hair—about five or six in a bunch—lays them ever so carefully onto a piece of aluminum foil, picks up a small paintbrush, dips the brush into a bowl of white gunk, paints the white gunk onto the hair, puts down the paintbrush, folds the aluminum foil over and over again so that the hair is thoroughly encased, and then the hairdresser begins all over again."

"I don't know—" John began.

"Highlighting," Suzanne interrupted, "takes the entire afternoon."

"You can hold down a job, but then you have to devote your Saturday to it," I said. "And we haven't even discussed the full-body waxing, and the pedicures and manicures."

"Maybe she listens to Books on Tape during these beauty sessions." John smiled wryly. He'd become addicted to audiobooks in the last six months.

"Don't let me forget," I said, "I've got *Madame Bovary* in the car for you."

Alison slipped off her chair and ran around the table to her father. "Read, read, read!"

"If you put her to bed," Suzanne said, "we'll clean up."

John rose and hoisted Alison into his arms. Watching the way she climbed on him like a little monkey gave my heart a tug. For a moment I was in her place, my legs locked around a man's waist, and his strong arms holding me. Aleksi Kullio stirred me up, no question.

We cleared the table and I stationed myself at the sink to rinse and load the dishwasher. A Chopin piano concerto from the radio jumped over the sound of rushing water. Behind me, gathering dirty pots and wiping counters, Suzanne danced.

"You think there's something fishy about his wife?" she yelled.

"I do and I don't."

"Uh-huh."

"I could just *want* to believe she's up to no good." I tackled the Crock-Pot with steel wool.

"You have sound instincts about people." Suzanne leaned against the lower cabinet next to the dishwasher so that I could hear her better. "It might be interesting to do a little digging into her background, see what's what."

I glanced at her. "You could do it when Charlie's napping—you're more experienced at that kind of research than I am."

"Could do."

"How come you're not yanking my chain about Aleksi Kullio?"

"Anything that gets you turned on, I'm all for it."

I upended the Crock-Pot on top of a dish towel, swiped the sink clean, and turned off the water. "You've been telling me for years that you admire my dedication to being celibate."

"I admire happiness," Suzanne said. "You've been happy—you didn't mope around complaining about how lonely you were—"

"I'm not lonely," I interrupted.

"That's what I mean. You were content."

I picked up the dishrag and squeezed it dry. Then I folded it into a perfect rectangle and draped it over the faucet. Suddenly the faucet reminded me of a half-erect penis poking out of a pair of underpants.

This was not good.

3

*For questions about the science of smell, foul or fair,
go to the 612s (e.g., The Compass in Your Nose and Other
Astonishing Facts About Humans; The Secret Family: Twenty-four
Hours Inside the Mysterious World of Our Minds and Bodies;
The Natural History of the Senses, etc.).*

On Monday morning, the library smelled bad. I often imagined that people chose to become librarians because of their obsessive love for the odor of books. Maybe it was one of those quirky gene things where a certain chromosome on the genome went off like a gun at the first scent of paper, bindings, and print. In much the same way, a person working in a gas station loved the smell of gas, and people in hospitals had a thing for disinfectant.

It smelled pukey, as if an unconscionable number of people had vomited throughout the building. I rushed to Gordon's office and found him holding a handkerchief over his nose and mouth while simultaneously speaking loudly into the telephone receiver.

"What the hell is that smell?" I bellowed.

I am somewhat overly familiar with the condition of nausea, and this odor wasn't helping my precarious stomach.

Gordon hung up the phone and stared woefully at me over the top of the white handkerchief. "We don't know." His voice was nasal, as if he was holding his nose.

"Who did you call?"

"The police—I think it may be vandalism."

"Vomit vandalism," I said.

"Not funny."

"Are we going to close the library?" I wanted the day off.

"I don't think so," he muttered. "Custodial is trying to locate the problem; then we'll have the police check it out, and finally, we'll eradicate the odor."

"How do you eradicate the smell of vomit throughout an entire building?"

"You're the research librarian—go research the subject and report back in thirty minutes."

"Do you happen to have another handkerchief?" I asked.

He shook his head.

"Do you think a paper bag over my head would help?"

Gordon didn't deign to answer.

I headed for the kitchenette and started rummaging around until I found a forgotten dish towel stuffed in the back of a drawer. I tied it around my head so that my nose and mouth were covered, and then took an experimental sniff. Not great. I opened the refrigerator and peered in, searching. Yup, there was a jar of dill pickles. I stuck my finger into the pickle juice, lifted the dish towel, and smeared the juice under my nose. Another test sniff. Success.

The library staff looked like a herd of bandits. Virtually everyone wore some kind of mask around their lower face. It occurred to me that we ought to film this because we could win the ten-thousand-dollar first prize on *America's Funniest Home Videos*. One look at Gordon storming past the New Books collection and I decided not to make the suggestion.

I went right to the 648s to search for a solution and immediately happened on *How Do I Clean the Moosehead? And Ninety-nine More Tough Questions About Housecleaning*. The title may have been amusing, but the guy (note: *guy*) sure knew his stuff. Odors that are organic in nature (vomit, excrement, etc.) used to pose a huge problem because their smell actually becomes worse when bacteria grow on them. Seems you have to fight "organic with organic" and now we've got cleansers called *bacterium/enzyme digesters* that "feed on the source of the odor and stain."

Who knew?

Certainly not I.

Although the day was cool, we opened every possible window and door. The automatic doors at the front had to be disarmed, but security even managed that, so desperate were we for relief. The public began to trickle in. They'd make it about twenty feet inside the door and then get this very peculiar expression on their faces. Yvonne quickly made a sign written in red ink.

> **Please excuse the pungent odor. The police are investigating and we hope to successfully expel this noxious smell just as soon as possible.**

I thought Yvonne could have used a study break with Strunk and White's book on writing.

A few hearty souls persevered, but most skedaddled out. One of the few remaining, a teenage girl with a cloud of angelic hair, sat reading in a semicomfortable armchair (if you made them *too* comfortable, people stayed forever).

I wandered over to the circulation desk. "That girl seems oblivious to the smell," I said to Yvonne.

"She comes in a lot, even on school days," she said. "I've been meaning to ask whether we're supposed to call the board of education, or somewhere, to report a possible truancy?"

I squinted at the girl. "Maybe she's older than she looks—I certainly am!"

Yvonne perused me with a glance that managed to combine innocent pity with disbelief. Pretty deadly.

Embarrassed, I said frostily, "Try and find out her age."

Ed, our resident homeless man, arrived just then, at his usual time of ten a.m.

"Let's see if he acts suspicious," Yvonne whispered.

It was hard to hear each other because our masks muffled our voices.

"What?" I yelled.

She shot me a furious look and then rolled her eyes toward Ed.

"Ed didn't do this," I said loudly.

I saw Ed's backbone uncurl and straighten. As I'd intended, he'd heard me.

My voice dropped to a whisper. "Ed drives us crazy in more sophisticated ways—this is too sophomoric."

"It may be sophomoric, but it's extremely destructive." Yvonne's bandanna—trust her to *have* a bandanna— slipped off her nose.

She was having trouble because her nose was singularly long, pointed, and thin, like the blade of a knife.

"Maybe somebody genuinely got sick, and it happened to be near a heating vent, so overnight the smell kind of got baked like a cake and then permeated the whole venting system, which in turn spread through the building." I was pleased with this explanation, but the expressions on everyone's faces made it abundantly clear how absurd it really was.

"I bet you can buy an aerosol can of something called Vomit Smell," I continued, "and some practical joker sprayed it all over the place, without realizing that it would be quite so malodorous."

Gordon had walked up as I was speaking. "Can you be serious about this?" His right hand smacked the countertop.

"I am serious—I'm almost positive I've heard of an item like that." To redeem myself, I quickly explained all about bacterial enzyme cleaners.

"For them to work we need to find the source, right?"

"Yup."

He stared at me, his blue eyes almost magnified above the white handkerchief, as if somehow I should be able to tell him where to find a pile of puke. I decided to take refuge in my office.

With the office door closed, the smell was potent but not deadly. The phone rang and I snatched it.

Suzanne's deep voice launched into a conversation as if we'd already been talking for an hour. "There's not much about Michelle Kullio, just the usual kind of stuff, date of birth, graduation from college—"

"She went to Harvard, I presume?" I interrupted.

Suzanne whistled. "Summa at Harvard—she's no slouch."

"The grade inflation at Harvard is disgraceful."

"Her senior paper was called 'The Rhythm and Beat of West Indian Literature.'"

"How multicultural of her." I made a hand gesture and knocked off my dish towel. The putrid smell of vomit struck me in the face like someone's fist. I let out a moan.

"What's the matter?" Suzanne said.

I took a few minutes to tell her about what we were dealing with at the library before returning to the much more interesting topic of Michelle Kullio. "So she majored in English literature?"

"Yeah."

Long silence. Michelle Kullio *could* be writing a novel.

"She's a very annoying person," I said.

"We went to Bryn Mawr," Suzanne said in a small voice.

"Please."

Gordon opened my door and made a desperate waving motion with his hand. I said good-bye and hurriedly disconnected.

"They found small, broken ampoules at the mouth of the main heating duct," he explained. "Looks like a practical joker used a stink bomb."

"Can we do anything?"

He shook his head. "We're going to put some powerful deodorizers in the same spot, but meanwhile I'm closing the library."

"This is going to be an irresistible story for the *Inquirer*."

"And the television networks." He rubbed his eyes. "If they call you, please say, 'No comment.'"

We walked toward the entrance. "It's kind of amazing that a measly smell can force us to close a public institution," I said.

"This isn't measly."

"Still, you don't usually think of a smell as having such power."

"Lucky we're not dogs—we'd be howling and running around in paroxysms of pleasure."

"You're a bit of a dog," I teased.

He threw back his head and let out an extremely realistic dog howl. Four staff members, heading out the door with coats on, whirled around.

I joined in with a howl that sounded like a Scottish terrier to Gordon's Great Dane. Together we kept yipping and howling. "We're dogs being driven mad by the marvelous odor in here," I explained to the others.

Gordon grinned. "Go home," he said to us. "I want to revel in my dogginess all alone."

I pulled on my corduroy jacket and left the building with them. Just outside, we ripped off our masks and gulped at the fresh air before noticing that three television cameras were filming everything. I am proud to report that every staff member dutifully claimed, "No comment," before leaving the scene.

I crossed the Benjamin Franklin Parkway and walked down Twenty-second Street. The air, absurdly pleasant and sweet-smelling, made me drunk. At the corner of Eighteenth and Delancey, close to Rittenhouse Square, I climbed the three flights to my apartment at the top of an old mansion that had been chopped up twenty years earlier. When I bought it ten years ago, I ripped out the shabby walls that had been slammed in place and made the fifteen hundred square feet into one glorious space. Two fireplaces, each of which had been in a former maid's room, now framed the room at either end, with six windows across the front and back. That's *twelve* windows.

I opened the door and took a deep breath. It smelled of me.

But what, really, does that mean? Houses and apartments always carry their own singular odor. I remembered going to my best friend's house for a sleepover when I was eight years old and having to call my mother at midnight. "Come get me," I hissed into the telephone receiver. When she duly fetched me home and asked what was the matter, my answer made complete sense to me. "It smelled funny." Meaning foreign.

The smell of me, besides being utterly familiar, was a heady combination of books, old draperies, ashes, and oranges. In front of each window was an orange tree, carefully pruned so that it never became too large for its container, framed by one of twelve different kinds of velvet drapes I'd found in antique stores on Pine Street.

Admittedly, the smell of me was not particularly fresh.

Cautiously, I lifted my arm and sniffed at the corduroy jacket. If I was a carrier of vomitous vapors, I didn't want to infect my home, but my smell was of the city air on an October morning. I threw off my jacket and went right to the telephone book, where I looked up the Philadelphia Philharmonic. Then I dialed the number and asked to be connected to the office that coordinated volunteers. After I explained who I was and that I wanted to usher for no pay, the woman patiently told me that there was a waiting list of 150 people who wanted to usher for no pay.

"Oh," I said in a wee voice.

"But if you really want to help—" she added.

I thought about whether I really wanted to help.

"Sure."

"You work at the library?"

"I'm the director of the research division."

"The Philharmonic's archives are a mess," she said. "Perhaps you'd be interested in talking to the head of Volunteer Services about putting the archives into some kind of order?"

I made an appointment for four o'clock that afternoon. Then I took off all my clothes and placed them carefully over a chair so that they wouldn't be wrinkled when I needed to get dressed for the meeting. My bed, conveniently unmade, beckoned. I climbed between the soft flannel sheets. This was where the smell of me was most prominent, caught in the folds of my blankets and crumpled pillows. Before dropping heavily into sleep, I wondered what Aleksi Kullio smelled like.

Maybe like me.

4

*For questions about nuns and the celibate life, go to the 255s
(e.g., The Cloister Walk) or the 239s (e.g., Virgin Time: In Search
of the Contemplative Life).*

𝒴ou do understand that I'm not a virgin, don't you? I wonder if saying you're celibate implies an active sex life prior to the celibacy. No, of course not. Nuns are celibate and it's certainly conceivable that a goodly percentage of nuns are also virgins.

I'm not, technically, a virgin.

I'm awfully interested in virginity, however.

I feel as if the last fifteen years have, in some obscure way, remade me as a virgin, though I understand that the whole concept of virginity, its true essence, implies that you simply can't go back. Once lost, lost it will always be. Which isn't fair. Lost equals found, if you know what I mean. If you are lost, you can be found. If found, you might be lost. Yet I am a virgin, methinks. For proof, I call upon my skin. I do not look forty years old. In fact, I probably do not even look thirty years old. Just a year or two ago, I was carded at an airport bar when I ordered a dry martini. I laughed in the bartender's face, thinking he was joking, but he just glared at me with this look that said, *Don't even try to fool me.* When he saw my birth date on my driver's license, he refused to charge me for the martini.

Sex is supposed to give you a fulsome glow, as if you've been to a spa and opted for some rare treatment called Crushed Pearl Rub. When I look around at all the other women my age, the ones with an active sex life—or so they claim—they really resemble lab mice. I'm not being mean. Look, I went to Bryn Mawr. I am a champion of women. But truth's truth. The thin ones have this terrible pinched quality to their faces, with eyes that burn. The fat ones look like inflated beach balls, their stretched skin composed of plastic or rubber. No wonder I don't feel in any hurry to lose my virginity . . . again.

I will say that I held out as long as possible, despite my glamorous mother's arrangements for me to visit her gynecologist when I turned eighteen years old. I was fitted with a diaphragm, one of the most repulsive objects I've ever seen, and was thereby deemed ready to rumble. I don't know for sure, but I think that diaphragm essentially sealed my fate. If sex and love meant inserting that device inside my body, then I opted out.

On the morning of the Great Smell, I woke from my strange midmorning nap and lay in bed thinking about all of the above. I was terribly happy. My gaze, profoundly myopic, roamed to the ceiling and then around the room. Shapes were undefined and amorphous, shifting into whatever my imagination came up with. The branches of the orange trees blended into a mass of greeny gray and if I squinted, I could just see dots of orange. Moments like this made me determined not to have LASIK surgery. Why would I want to lose the ability to see the world as haze and dream?

I was always a fanciful little girl, but especially after I'd learned to read when I was four years old. Real life just couldn't compete with the stories in books, though I never really gave life a chance, anyway. Books were too delicious and far-reaching. You could curl up in a corner of the couch and travel to other worlds, be other people, feel every emotion ever invented.

Suddenly the phone rang. I understand that most people leap when their telephone rings; they seem to assume that a ringing phone implies a ringing popularity. I am not popular. Given. The phone is simply an interruption in my life, usually an interruption of reading. At this moment, the peremptory ringing sound interrupted my befuddled state of mind, half asleep and half awake. I thought about not answering. Maybe fifty percent of the time, I let the machine get it, but since it could be Suzanne with more to report on Michelle, I picked up the phone.

I always know it's my mother before she utters a word. She lets out a loud sigh, as if to express her essential, deep unhappiness with me. My mother's a sex bomb. She divorced my father, an oboist with the Boston Symphony Orchestra, when I was five years old and she came into her inheritance. We moved back to her hometown of Philadelphia so that she could attend medical school. She is a sex bomb doctor, actually, with a specialty in urology.

I doubt I have to tell you what that means, but I will anyway. She spends her days examining penises. This was why I went to a women's college.

Finally, she spoke. "I didn't expect to get *you!*"

"We had an emergency at the library and had to close."

"Goodness, what kind of an emergency?" she said. "The hospital has been quiet."

"Not exactly a medical emergency." I explained what had happened, and as I had feared, she began to laugh.

She doesn't just *laugh*. I could handle a good, hearty laugh. She roars and guffaws at first, then rapidly moves into a hysterical giggling phase. But today she outdid herself. I could tell she was about to pee in her pants, which I thought was exactly what a sex bomb urologist deserved. A loud clunking noise. She'd dropped the phone.

"Mom?" I yelled. "Are you still there?"

I heard faint gasping sounds.

I hit the disconnect button on my cordless and carefully put it under the pillow. Throwing back the covers, I stood up on my bed, arms raised to the ceiling. The muscles in my arms stretched and pinged.

So much for exercise.

I jumped off the bed and headed down the room to where a makeshift kitchen fit between two windows. The refrigerator held two apricot yogurts, milk, orange juice, and a lot of lettuce. Actually, four different kinds of lettuce (iceberg, arugula, romaine, red-leaf). I could eat a yogurt or a bowl of cereal, or take the long way around and make myself a salad. The freezer was stocked with frozen Stouffer's dinners. I peeked at their little red boxes all lined up. Well, some of them were white Lean Cuisines, which I only ate because they were different from the regular ones and I liked them. I don't watch my weight because watching my weight is so instinctive that I eat very little and, therefore, don't have a weight problem.

Which is to say that I watch my weight all the time, though, again, I hasten to assure you that I am a perfectly respectable weight. No one has *ever* claimed I was too thin. I wish.

Abruptly, I decided I was starving to death and I yanked out a macaroni and cheese. The phone rang. Mom again. I ignored it. She'd already seriously compromised my happy mood from fifteen minutes earlier.

While the frozen mac and cheese cooked in the microwave, I went to my CD collection and found the Mozart Oboe Concerto in C Major conducted by Ozawa in 1984, with my father as soloist. The music poured through the room like sunshine and I let it beat into my heart. I imagined that Aleksi was conducting.

Kullio's style reminded me of a ballet dancer more than anything else. His arms and upper torso poured through the air, and his long fingers swathed the baton like a pure white bandage. Of course, the audience mostly watched his back—the thick white-blond ponytail curling against the black jacket of his tails—while the musicians saw his face and eyes. I envied them. I wanted those eyes.

I entered Liberty Music Hall, on Market Street, from a side door. Inside, the building teemed with a heady combination of anxiety and anticipation. I remembered the rare weekends when I'd take a Friday off from school to visit my father in Boston; he could never meet my train because of rehearsals, so I would take the subway to the orchestra hall and make my way quietly backstage. Usually there would be an empty, rickety chair where I could sit and listen. A living, breathing orchestra still clutched at me, its grip a taunt and a promise.

The director of volunteers, Jeffrey Owens, was a tall African-American. He undulated around his desk and held out a languid hand.

"A librarian," he drawled. "I'm so excited."

"If you tell even a single librarian joke, I'm outta here."

One arched eyebrow lifted. "Testy, aren't we?"

My gears were shifting madly. I'd expected a patrician woman wearing a pleated blue skirt and cashmere twin set, with sleek white hair done in a discreet pageboy.

He smiled broadly, reading my mind. "I love being a surprise."

As we wound our way below ground, following a long hallway carpeted in deep red, we chatted about the archives. He explained that a significant number of scores and papers had been donated to the Albrecht Music Library at the University of Pennsylvania, but in more recent years the orchestra had made it a priority to hold on to their documents. The recently opened Liberty Music Hall was still so new that even their basement looked good. We strode along quickly until I saw light spilling from an open door at the very end of the hallway.

"Goodness, someone is actually in the archival room," Jeffrey said.

Nausea assailed me. I knew who that someone would be.

Jeffrey turned through the open door. "Good morning, Maestro."

I crowded behind Jeffrey, trying to peer around him.

"Mr. Owens, good afternoon."

Aleksi Kullio's voice was light and airy, neither masculine nor feminine.

Jeffrey walked farther into the room and I followed, stepping sideways as soon as I could.

He was sitting cross-legged on the floor, dressed in old blue jeans and a black turtleneck. A score was open in his lap. "I was curious about Stokowski's notes on Mahler's Ninth."

"Of course." All the loosey-goosey quality had drained from Jeffrey's body. Clearly, the maestro already exerted authority.

Then Aleksi Kullio looked at me.

Remember who you're dealing with here. I wore a long gray skirt and a white, high-collared blouse. My brown hair was braided and wrapped into a bulbous bun stuck to the back of my head with long pins. Reddish tortoise-shell glasses with thick lenses leaped out of my colorless, thin face. I certainly didn't look attractive, much less pretty, and I don't think I even looked interesting.

And so, I felt compelled to interest him.

"I'm sure you know that his Ninth Symphony was about impotence," I said.

Jeffrey made a *ta-da* gesture with his left hand. "May I introduce Alison Sheffield? She's going to try and bring order into this place."

Aleksi nodded. "Well, it certainly could use some help," he said. "I'd be most appreciative if I could easily find whatever I was looking for, and whatever I wasn't looking for, too."

Jeffrey, puzzled, kept his smile turned on.

But I'd understood. "Grazing can be fun," I said.

He rose to his feet in a single, fluid motion, like the froth of a beer on tap. "I'll study this back in my office."

He was taller than I'd expected, at least six feet, and his slender shoulders beneath the turtleneck extended like wide, dark fins. He looked at me with an equally wide grin centered on a broad face. His coloring was almost as pale as his hair, and blue eyes twinkled. "I shall try and think of impotence as I conduct—I just hope my conducting isn't . . . impotent." As he spoke, he raised his right hand, pretending to hold the baton, and then let it droop.

I burst out laughing.

His eyes flashed.

I tried to say something more before he scampered out. I did try.

"So, this is the situation," Jeffrey said, arms flapping toward the wide shelves piled with papers.

I walked over and carefully lifted a score. Hindemith's Clarinet Concerto. Scribbled marginalia dotted the opening measures.

Jeffrey peered over my shoulder. "That's Ormandy's handwriting."

"Is this room climate-controlled and fire-resistant?"

"Oh, yes, we managed at least that when the building went up."

One finger stroked the handwritten notes. "You should have a professional archivist," I said sternly.

"Absolutely, you're quite right," Jeffrey said, "but do you have any idea of the financial plight of orchestras? We're lucky to have this new venue, since it's brought in new subscribers. I'm sure Maestro Kullio will do well, but he's young and untried. He wasn't the board's first choice. It's a question of money, my dear."

"I can do some organizing, but I work full-time at the library—"

"We would be grateful for whatever you could manage."

"I thought Kullio was quite brilliant last week," I said, rankling at his statement that Aleksi hadn't been the board's first choice.

"I would tend to agree with you," he said cautiously, "though I found the second movement of the Mozart dragged."

"It's supposed to be slow."

"Are you a trained musician as well as a librarian?"

I smiled. "My dad plays first oboe with Boston, but I am not a musician."

"You must have learned an instrument when you were a child."

I shook my head and then replaced the score where I'd found it. Circling the room, I peered at various piles in an attempt to discover some intrinsic order. "Did you?"

"Of course—guess my instrument." Jeffrey folded his arms across his chest, easy and confident.

I turned around completely so that I could look at every part of him, from the top to the bottom. Finally I said, "Flute."

His arms dropped. "How the hell—?"

I shrugged.

"What's made you interested in helping out the orchestra?" he asked.

"I'm not sure, but it probably has something to do with

seeing Kullio at the opening of the season." I turned away so that he couldn't see my face. "I was inspired."

I glanced at him and watched his slow nod.

"Maestro Kullio has something, a charisma, that's for sure—it could be great for us."

"Have you met his wife?"

"God, she's so gorgeous!" Jeffrey's mouth pulled into a pout of pleasure. "And she's wonderful to talk to . . . intelligent, gracious, cultured."

His anxious eyes did not seem to agree with his words.

"They don't have children, right?" I said.

He shook his head and then checked his watch. "Whoops, I have to get a move on. Can we finalize things a bit? We ask that our volunteers commit to a certain level of activity—it can be anything, but we find a formal commitment allows us to determine expectations and plan accordingly."

"Uh-huh."

"What do you think you could manage?"

"How about three hours every Saturday morning?"

Jeffrey fingered his lower lip. "Well, that's the busiest time, but you'll be out of the way down here."

He held the door open for me, and when I'd passed through into the hall, he closed and locked it behind him.

Naturally I'd deliberately chosen Saturday morning because I knew that would be prime rehearsal time and I'd be able to sneak around during the bustle of activity and sound.

We shook hands at the elevator and he sent me on my way, but I felt his awareness of me, perhaps even puzzlement, as the elevator doors closed. Instead of waving or calling out a cheery good-bye, I folded my hands and gazed serenely into space. I savored the hint that Jeffrey had unwittingly given about the Kullios' marriage, a muted rumble of trouble, a distant flash of lightning, a tiny hope for me. I felt the calm and serenity of a nun.

I defy any woman to claim that she hasn't, at some point in her life, flirted with the idea of becoming a nun—and that includes Jews and Muslims. In fact, that sets me to wondering. Why don't Jews and Muslims offer convent life to women? Although the Muslims, I believe, have monks, they have nothing comparable to a nun. A retreat into the virginal, celibate way of life seems to me so utterly and universally desirable, although I admit that much of the allure was lost when nuns stopped wearing those wonderful garments.

I was particularly conscious of this as I walked down Walnut Street, toward Rittenhouse Square, passing one incredible clothes shop after another. The whole business of dressing oneself, as a woman, simply confounded me. I would have liked nothing better than to be sweeping along the sidewalk in rustling, starched robes, my veil drifting behind me like a vapor.

Come on, admit it—you feel the same way.

My mother dresses me. She arrives with bags and bags of clothing about twice a year. I can't complain. She's got my number, no doubt about it. Lots of librarian blouses with high necks, like I'm wearing today, but made of heavy silks and thick linens. Somehow she finds long skirts that cling to my hips and then flare out below the knee. She accepts that I want my body covered up and she never argues with me. I appreciate that.

What I don't particularly appreciate is how *she* dresses.

She's now sixty-three years old and has never remarried. She is free and unfettered, as she likes to say too often, and therefore her hems are two inches above the knee. Like me, she's a petite size, but she makes the most of it. Tight turtlenecks and short little jackets that nip in at the waist. She's always saying that things "nip."

To nip is to bite. It's hurtful, which is why the Allies used it as slang to refer to a Japanese person. Actually, the word comes from Nipponese, which was what the Japanese called themselves. We obviously mistook the word as derogatory because it could have, in our definition, such a nasty connotation.

I turned into a Starbucks for a massive latte and managed to grab one of the window stools. It was rush hour. People and vehicles poured down the street like water rushing over a rock-strewn river. My life was often like this, in direct opposition to the rest of the world. When others were in a hurry, I sipped coffee and thought about words like *nip*. I added two packets of fake sugar to the coffee and stirred with a wooden stick.

Opposites attract and you couldn't get much more opposite than Aleksi Kullio and me. It suddenly occurred to me that an aggressive stance on celibacy might be considered to be quite the opposite of what I'd always thought. Perhaps, just as the strong emotion of hate can actually imply love, my dedication to a nonsexual life actually implied . . . a sexual life. I gulped at the hot latte. Was I, in fact, secretly obsessed with sex? I didn't like that the answer to my question came without fanfare or opposition. No?

No.

Yes.

5

*For questions about the psychology of loneliness,
go to the 152s (e.g., Loneliness and Love; Alone, Alive, and Well;
etc.).For the sociology of loneliness, go to the 304s
(e.g., Lonely in America), and for the science of loneliness,
go to the 616s (e.g., The Broken Heart: The Medical
Consequences of Loneliness).*

$\mathcal{I}$ sniffed. If anything, the library smelled too clean. I prayed that they hadn't wiped out the odor of old books while obliterating the vomit vapors. I'd have to quit my job and find another library.

Other than the lone janitor dusting in the main reading room, I was the first staff member to arrive. Though I was the type to get in early, seven thirty in the morning was extreme even for me. I hadn't slept well, probably because of that long nap the morning before. Or the latte at five o'clock in the afternoon. Whatever, it felt like I'd been awake all night. I'd finally showered at five a.m. and then gone out for a huge breakfast at IHOP. I know, disgusting. And it really was. My stomach looked like it was about to hatch an egg.

I caught up with paperwork and piddled around my office until Gordon arrived an hour later. He saw my light on and came over right away.

"Do you smell anything?" His nose twitched like he had a cocaine habit.

"I've been here an hour and there hasn't been a whiff of vomit."

We walked together to the kitchen, where I made a pot of coffee. "Did the police come?" I asked as the coffee dripped with a wonderful *kerplunking* sound and the odor of coffee began to dissipate the odor of Too Clean.

"So much for the course of true love," he said, staring at me and ignoring my question about the police.

I gave him a look meant to shrivel testicles, but I guess at this point I don't have to tell you that Gordon's testicles were too vigorous for one look by me to have any effect.

"Yesterday you looked like you were in love, and today the lover appears to have dropped dead," he continued.

I cocked my head and smiled sweetly. "I think this coffee is about ready."

We each poured a mug of coffee, seasoned it, and sipped a little.

"How's your love life, Gordon, darling?" I asked.

"Fun."

Still mulling over questions of virginity, I blurted out, "When did you lose your virginity?"

"Ally, it's Tuesday morning, for God's sake."

I just stared at him. Since the vomit calamity appeared to have been resolved, his eyes had regained their normal bright, perky blue.

"I was twelve years old," he said. "You?"

Yvonne came into the kitchen at that moment. "What happened when you were twelve years old?" She wore a skirt and blouse that nipped all over the place.

"I lost my virginity," Gordon said.

She turned bright red and I thought it exceptionally interesting that I, the essential virgin in the bunch, didn't blush at all.

"How about you, Yvonne?" I said.

I swear, her ears started to tremble and hives crept up her neck.

Both Gordon and I gazed at her, unperturbed.

"When I was in college." She went hunting for a mug in the cabinet, though there were clean mugs turned upside down on a dish towel.

I decided now was a good time to leave, before they started asking for my own "how didja lose your virginity?" story. I was probably the only virgin in my graduating class at Bryn Mawr accepting a diploma on that spring day in May. Even the lesbians had experimented enough to know for sure that they were interested only in women. I ultimately lost the big V when I was twenty-two years old. Obviously, given my history, it didn't go well.

Looking back on it, I probably shouldn't have planned on losing my virginity with another twenty-two-year-old virgin named Joel, but at the time it seemed like a good idea. He was a fellow graduate student in library science and, I confess, a bit nerdy. Hunched shoulders, thin chest, bandy legs, and a nasal twang in his voice—he didn't make me feel as if I particularly wanted to have sex. But I was getting uncomfortable with my situation.

I'd lied to Suzanne during our second year at Bryn Mawr by pretending to have had a sexual relationship with a guy over the previous summer. Since her family lived in Massachusetts then, I got away with a magnificent fantasy. I've wondered since whether I really did fall in love with my make-believe man and no one could ever be as suitable for me. I pretended that he broke up with me right before school began in the fall and that I was crushed. Thereafter, I faked a lover every summer. Suzanne probably knew what I was doing. More importantly, I knew what I was doing. I felt compelled to prove myself.

While Joel and I were helping each other with an assignment on the Dewey decimal system, we managed to reveal our mutual secret. As I recall, we were supposed to locate all possible sources for information about gefilte fish, which led to carp, rhyming with harp, suggesting angels, who are virginal. Well, put two library students together and these things are apt to happen. We're just not ordinary.

Nor was sex between us.

I will spare you the gory details. I'm pretty sure I actually did lose my virginity, but I can't be certain. It was that hit-or-miss. You understand.

"Hi, Mom, sorry I didn't get back to you last night."

"I was out, anyway," she said. "Does the library still smell like vomit?"

"Nope."

"How's my friend Ed?"

I'd told her stories about Ed's escapades in the library, and she'd taken an inexplicable liking to him.

"He's been awfully quiet. I think this vomit business upstaged him."

"Poor baby."

Now, I have to tell you that when my mother says *poor baby*, she sounds like she's about to seduce anything and everything, including the telephone itself. I had this feeling that she'd been trying to seduce *me* all my life, to no avail. I used to claim I was unseducible.

"I called to ask if you wanted my tickets to the symphony next Friday night—you know it's with the new conductor, Kullio, but Phil Altar invited me to the Metropolitan Opera and—"

"I was at the season opening last week," I interrupted.

"You *were?*" she said. "What did you think?"

"Fabulous."

"That's what I've heard from everyone. Good for you to be at his first concert."

She was thinking I might have gone with a man. She was thinking that I might have worn the fall suit she'd delivered a month ago, a suit that even I had to admit was beautiful. It was a terra-cotta wool and silk that hung in straight, gorgeous drapes (no nipping, none whatsoever). She was full of hope.

"I went with Suzanne and John."

"That's so nice—did you wear the new suit?"

Actually, I did. But I wasn't sure I wanted to tell her so.

"I know I thought about wearing it," I hedged. "So I'd love the tickets."

"Great." She yawned right into the phone. "I'll stick them in the mail to you."

After I'd hung up, I got a message from Carol that one of my reference librarians had called in sick, which meant I'd probably have to join two others in covering the reference desk. Five minutes later, as I was standing there, Ed ambled up.

He slid a slip of paper across the desk, with a list of five periodicals he wanted from the bowels of the library. I don't know what came over me, but I'd suddenly had enough of wasting our time finding him periodicals we knew he asked for just so that he wouldn't be kicked out of the library.

I picked up the piece of paper and my eyes rose to meet his. "Good morning, Ed," I said.

"Morning."

"What do you need these periodicals for?"

"Work."

"Work on what?"

"This is a free country—I don't have to tell you."

I leaned over the counter so that I drew quite close to him. It took him by surprise since most people wanted to be as far away from him as possible. "I'm not going to lie to you or play games, Ed. I can see you're an intelligent man and I'm going to treat you as an intelligent man."

He blinked and licked his dry lips.

"I am weary of finding you obscure periodicals when I know that at the end of the day, you will simply toss the notes you make from them." I smiled broadly. "It feels fruitless and it makes *me* feel as if my job was a waste of time."

We kept staring into each other's eyes. It was quite disconcerting, which was, of course, what I intended. But then, as I kept my eyes fastened on his, an interesting thing happened. I saw that he wasn't crazy. We'd always assumed, because he was homeless and odd, that he was probably schizophrenic or in some other way mentally ill. If only we'd really looked at him instead of letting our gaze falter.

I leaned even closer, still staring, and spoke in a whisper. "Hullo, Ed."

"Hello?" His voice rose and turned the greeting into a question.

"I have an idea."

"What kind of an idea?"

"How would you like to work for me?"

His skin erupted with a red flush. "I could," he said. "I've got a Ph.D. from Harvard."

"Holy mackerel!"

He laughed. Ed actually laughed. One of the other reference people glanced our way, nervous.

"How would you like to be my periodical point man?" I said.

"Uh, sure, but I'm not clear on—"

"You'd be in the basement, and when one of the reference librarians brought down a request for a periodical, you'd find it," I interrupted. "Then you'd reshelve it when it's returned."

"I could definitely do that."

"I can't offer any pay—this would have to be a strictly volunteer position."

His face clouded, but I understood Ed now and I realized that his pride was wounded.

"I'm volunteering my Saturday mornings at the Philadelphia Philharmonic," I said. "It's a very cultured gesture to give your time as a volunteer. The library would be in your debt."

"Can I start right away?"

I nodded. "Let's go down there and I'll show you around."

After a tour and an explanation of how it would work, I

stayed with Ed until he got his first request, just to make sure he was comfortable. As he scooted off to find the desired periodical, I confess to some self-congratulation. The problem of Ed was solved.

I didn't get home until seven o'clock that night, after a day crammed with disagreeable library patrons. If you ever suffer from the "Aren't People the Greatest?" syndrome, spend a day working in a library. In fact, that gives me an idea. We have "Bring Your Child to Work Day" and "Spend the Day with a Nurse/Doctor." Why not a national event called "Laboring with a Librarian"? In my zest for alliteration, that sounds like a librarian about to give birth, but you get the gist of what I mean.

The windows of my apartment shone dark and glittery when I snapped on the lights. Quickly, I pulled all the mismatched velvet drapes closed and lit a fake fire log in one of the fireplaces. When it had caught, I threw on two real logs. Slumped in the ungainly sofa stuffed with tired goose down, I stared at the flames.

I was lonely.

You think, *Well, of course she's lonely. . . . I would be, too.*

I am often alone, but I am never lonely.

I wandered over to my stereo system and selected a CD of Sir Neville Marriner conducting Mozart's *Prague* Symphony. As the first movement began, I found myself on tiptoe. My right arm rose slowly, and pretending to hold a baton, I conducted. Frustrated, I rushed to the kitchen and scrambled around for a shish kebab skewer, then leaped onto the couch. Concentrating, I truly tried to conduct. But my beats were off. I could feel that I was either just behind or just ahead. Never right on time.

With no warning, tears slid down my cheeks. My baton slashed at the air, jabbing to the winds while I placated the strings with my left hand, urging the percussion, then curling into myself, the baton tracing tiny movements. Always off.

I was so damn lonely. And it was the fault of Aleksi Kullio. He'd made me feel this. *Why?* I asked, tears streaming. *Oh, why.*

6

For questions about querying publishers and agents, go to the 029s (e.g., The Writer's Market; Literary Agents: A Writer's Introduction; Writer's Guide to Book Editors, Publishers, and Literary Agents; etc.).

• •

"Gordon!" I flung open his office door.

He placed a hand over the receiver of the telephone. "This is a private call."

"My office smells of farts," I yelled.

His eyes widened and he spoke quickly into the phone. "I'll have to get back to you."

"Just my office." I turned and led the way.

I unlocked my door and stepped aside. Gordon walked in and I followed, but only for a brief visit. The smell of one fart can be pretty bad, as we are all regrettably aware. Multiply that by a thousand.

Gordon slammed the door shut as we propelled ourselves out of there, breathing heavily.

"What on earth?" I gasped.

"A practical joker."

"But why me?" I tried not to whine, but failed. "Why not you, for instance?"

"You must have an enemy."

"I am the nicest person in the world."

His face was starting to regain its original color. "My mother is the nicest person in the world."

"Your mother is a total bitch." The words flew out of my mouth, astonishing me and Gordon. I swallowed. "Sorry, that was uncalled for."

"Why did you call my mother a bitch?" he asked. "Really, I'd like to know."

"She's the reason you're a serial womanizer."

It was as if the overwhelming fart smell acted as a truth serum.

"And you call yourself the nicest person in the world?"

I clapped my hand over my mouth and refused to say another word. I hoped my desperate eyes would speak for me.

He placed an arm around my shoulders for a quick hug. "Okay, okay," he murmured. "You're absolutely right—I *am* a serial womanizer. No hard feelings."

I nodded, still sending him beseeching looks and my hand still clasped over my mouth.

"Any bright ideas about how to get rid of the smell?" he said quietly.

Finally, I spoke. "I'll go out and buy a bunch of those odor-eating candles."

"Fire hazard," he murmured.

"Fuck the fire hazard," I said too loudly.

"Right." He let me go and turned to glance through the glass walls into my office. "I'm going to try and figure out if there's a way to catch this jokester."

Two hours later, I was able to enter my office and do

some work. My colleagues said the candles flickering all over the place looked like a wake.

I lost myself in paperwork and barely heard the knock on my door. "What?" I asked, looking up to see a reference clerk sticking her head in.

"Someone's asking for you," she said, slamming the door shut again.

Maybe I was getting used to the smell.

Michelle Kullio stood behind the reference counter. One polished red nail tapped impatiently as she waited.

I was in no mood for her. "Yes, can I help you?"

"The *LMP*, please," she demanded.

She was referring to *The Literary Marketplace*, a reference guide to publishers and agents. We kept it behind the desk, and she could have asked any of the clerks to give it to her. For a moment, I debated saying just that. I was so annoyed by the day thus far that I welcomed an opportunity to put someone in her place. Without a word, I found the *LMP* and plunked it down in front of her.

Unexpectedly, she gave a huge smile. "I'm so excited," she said.

"Why is that?" My tone was flat, but polite.

"I'm ready to submit my novel."

"That is wonderful." I paused. "What's it about?"

"A mystery set at a major, internationally known orchestra."

My heart thumped. It felt as if it might leap out of my chest and begin doing the Hokey-Pokey.

Put your left foot in. "Who's the unlucky victim?" I asked.

"The first cellist."

Put your right foot in. "Let me guess. . . . The last cellist is the murderer?"

She laughed at my deficient imagination. "The *next* murder is of the conductor."

And shake it all about. "Oh," I said weakly.

"Do you know anything about querying publishers?"

Despite the red fingernails, she looked less fake today. Her blond hair frizzed into small, attractive curls around her face and I couldn't see any evidence of makeup. The baggy gray sweat suit and Polartec jacket hid her body.

"No, I'm afraid I don't, but there are a number of helpful references on that subject."

"Where would those be?"

I got her settled at a table with three guidebooks. Since she had no paper with her (this woman went to Harvard?), I gave her some. Then I retreated behind the reference desk to watch her scribble information for about fifteen minutes, at which time my curiosity compelled me to amble over and then speak to her.

"How are you doing?" I smiled a false smile.

She smiled a false smile back. Just reward. What goes around comes around and all that jazz.

"Okay." One perfect eyebrow arched upward.

I held out a hand. "I don't believe I ever actually introduced myself when we were talking before. Alison Sheffield, the director of the Reference Department."

Her fingers brushed mine with such a tepid response that I felt humiliated.

"Do you enjoy being a librarian?" she asked abruptly.

I hesitated. It was an odd question. "Yes—I always wanted to be one. I think most librarians feel that way."

Her mouth puckered. "So I've heard."

She moved her face around as if the various parts belonged to a machine that didn't quite go together. I decided she probably had a personality disorder.

She continued. "I can't say *I* ever wanted to be a librarian."

"We enable writers." I waved airily. "You give us our fix."

"Librarianship as addiction—fascinating concept." Her mouth gaped with a massive yawn, which she made little attempt to cover.

I couldn't figure out why we were wandering through the maze of librarians' career choices. "I'll let you get on with your work," I said a little lamely. When I got to my office door, I peeked quickly over my shoulder and saw that she'd abruptly slammed the books shut. Without a glance my way, and leaving the books right where they were, she left.

"Joan," I called to my colleague, "I'm taking lunch out of here today."

"Can't say I blame you." She grinned.

I grabbed my purse from my desk drawer and fairly ran. Outside, just in time, I saw Michelle's blond head disappearing around a far corner. I trotted to catch up, staying a good half a block behind her, though I wasn't worried that she'd be aware of my surveillance. A woman so supremely egotistical probably expected to be followed, even if her followers were usually men.

We headed up Benjamin Franklin Parkway and I remembered that the *Inquirer* had reported the Kullios' purchase of an apartment in one of the new luxury buildings in the art museum district. A fresh wind blew off the Schuylkill River, carrying the smell of water, and my unbuttoned coat flew open. I relished the fingers of chill skipping over my body, since it felt as if the odor of farts had infiltrated my every pore.

Sure enough, she turned into the grandiosely named Rodin House. I strolled along, uncertain what to do. Much as I would have liked it to be true, I had no reason to believe that Aleksi Kullio's wife was up to no good. Yet I smelled something rotten in her. She was like an overripe peach growing mold on its skin. I found a bench in the park across the street from her building, close to the museum, and sat down.

Thin sunshine scattered through the autumn trees, and the breeze from the river was still strong. I buttoned my coat, wrapped my arms across my chest, and hunkered down, strangely unwilling to move. A kid walked by eating a hot dog and I wondered whether I could risk going to the corner to buy one. But I didn't get up. Apparently I couldn't take the risk. I drifted into a vaguely hypnotic state, my eyes unseeing and my heart slowing to a clippety-clop pace.

I forgot who I was. Moments later, when I came alive because Michelle Kullio tore out of her building, I briefly wondered whether I'd ever really known who I was. If I try to concentrate on myself, position my body and mind in the particular time and place of *now*, I feel myself skittering away. But enough philosophizing.

There went Michelle Kullio and there went I in pursuit. She rushed down dozens of streets. The sidewalks moved in a blur under my feet and I became horribly breathless. We crossed the Schuylkill River and headed deep into West

Philly. Just as I thought I'd have to drop out of the race, as it were, Michelle turned into a small shop at Fifty-second and Walnut. I crossed the street in order to see the sign.

Special Treats of the West Indies

In five minutes, she tossed open the door and emerged onto the sidewalk. I turned my back, but not before noticing that she dangled a small paper bag from one hand. She retraced our steps, back toward the center of downtown Philadelphia. I fell farther and farther behind, no longer quite so insane as to keep up with her. I had to get back to the library, anyway.

I was whipping through the library's main floor, intent on getting to my private office and calling Suzanne, when Yvonne's hissing whisper circled through the air like a lasso, drawing me in.

"What?" I demanded, panting from my long walk.

Her smile widened and revealed crisp white teeth. They looked sharp and scary. "We're giving Gordon a surprise birthday party next week."

"Whose idea was that?"

"Mine!"

I shook my head. "He hates his birthday—I wouldn't advise it."

"It's a done deal," she declared. "And, anyway, I find that people who claim to hate their birthdays are really delighted when their friends remember and celebrate with a party."

"How old is he going to be?"

She flushed. "I don't know."

"Yvonne," I said in my best chiding voice.

"He'll be forty-nine."

"Why don't you just take him out behind the building and shoot him?"

"I'm going to make my famous sour cream chocolate cake," she burbled.

"I guess I have to come."

"Don't you dare tell him, Ally!"

As I passed through the reference section, I suddenly remembered Michelle sitting at one of the tables and studying the guide to poisons. When I'd retrieved the book from where she had so unceremoniously left it that morning, I'd seen that she only got as far as the *A*s. Now I found the book on the shelves and carried it into my office, where the lingering smell of farts blending with the flora and fauna of scented candles nearly overpowered me. I opened the book to the *A* section. With a practiced eye, I ran down the poisons. I turned the page. And there it was.

Akee.

I reached for the phone.

When she answered, Suzanne sounded like an old-fashioned windowpane made of watery glass.

"Are you all right?" I asked.

"Yeah . . . I guess I fell asleep while Charlie was nursing."

"I have news."

"Tell me," she said. "I promise I'm awake now."

I described everything—the fart smell in my office, Michelle Kullio's arrival, the plan in her mystery to kill off an orchestra conductor, my following her, and the shop in West Philly where she made a purchase.

"Uh-huh."

"Don't you remember the title of her senior paper at Harvard?"

"Oh yeah—it had something to do with the West Indies."

"Keep that in mind as I elaborate."

"Right, I shall keep that in mind."

"When Michelle came into the library and used one of our references to look up poisons, she didn't put the book away when she was finished."

"Doesn't that drive you wild?"

"Normally, yes." I waved my hands around, trying in vain to dissipate the fart odor. "This time it's okay because when I went to close the book and then reshelve it, I happened to notice that she was close to the beginning, still in the *A* section."

"Uh-huh." Suzanne sounded as if she was falling back to sleep again.

"Akee is a vegetable eaten in the West Indies that is highly poisonous."

"Then how do they eat it?" She had perked up. "Or, let me guess, they eat it, die, and then magically come back to life, proving that there is a God?"

"Cool your jets," I said. "You can eat akee when it is ripe, but if you eat it unripe, or overripe, it kills you. The Jamaicans eat it in between all the time!"

"So you think—"

"Michelle bought akee at a West Indian market in order to poison her husband!"

"Listen, I'm a lawyer and my legal mind says you're jumping an awful lot of fences right in a row."

"I know it's conjecture."

Indeed, you're probably thinking I'd jumped over the moon. I will admit that I was indulging in some dramatics here, but so what? I'd been rational my whole life, and frankly, I was sick of it. Part of falling in love is being irrational. I wanted to wallow in the deep, warm, liquid heart of love. I imagined a tub of hot mud, used in some obscure beauty treatment, and I was lowering myself into it. Warm mud lapped in thick ripples over me. Only now, miraculously, the mud had changed into chocolate!

Suzanne interrupted my daydream. "We need to follow her some more—try to establish a pattern or routine, just to verify it," she said.

"We?"

"John and I had a big talk last night and we both agreed I have to get out of the house more."

"Are you going back to work part-time?"

"First I'm going to follow Michelle Kullio all over town."

"Who will look after the kids?"

"My mom."

"You vowed never to cede control of your children to her!"

"I changed my mind."

"Changing your mind is a sign of maturity."

"Right," she said, doubting herself, which she rather tended to do.

"Look in the 153s."

"I warned you about that." Her voice, though teasing, held a sliver of seriousness.

Over the last ten years or so, I had started to exhibit signs of an unusual illness. Suzanne called it the "Dewey decimal disease" because whenever we talked about anything, and I mean *anything*, I recited where in the library, using the Dewey decimal classification of knowledge, you could go for further reading or information. I understood why it drove her bonkers and I admit I had become quite tedious.

However.

Okay, okay, I won't go into a riff about the beauty of the Dewey decimal system. If you want to pursue the subject on your own, go to the 027s. I won't say another word about it.

"I can't believe you're actually going to do this," I said.

"Yup—she lives at Rodin House, right?" Suzanne's voice vibrated up and down when she was happy, and since she was happy about this turn of events, I was happy with her.

"Maybe you could even chitchat with the doorman and stuff, do some real sleuthing."

"I am totally psyched," she said.

After we hung up, I sifted through my phone messages and checked my E-mail. A gaggle of small administrative duties presented themselves and I set to work. Like many librarians, I enjoyed a sense of order and I was happy when I could bustle around creating that order. The downside of being anal is well documented, but there *is* an upside. Or so I would argue if it were the kind of argument you could win or lose. It isn't.

As my reward for being good and accomplishing a laudable amount of nitpicky work, I wrote a note to Maestro Aleksi Kullio. Brief and professional, it welcomed him to the city and mentioned that the library would be acquiring the newest biography of Stravinsky, which had been favorably reviewed in a number of journals and periodicals. I enjoyed my handwriting's appearance on the white paper, rather like the spiky footprints of a small prehistoric animal after being buried a million years beneath Santa Fe, New Mexico. I didn't really expect an answer from Aleksi, and perhaps that was why I felt comfortable sending the note in the first place.

Gordon suddenly opened my office door, jumped inside, and slammed the door closed behind him. "How's the Queen of Farts?"

"You better be nice to me."

"Why should I be nice to you?" He was on the alert immediately.

"Because."

He cocked his head and stared at me. His thick hair grew bushier and bushier as the afternoon wore on, and by now he looked more like a schizophrenic than Ed. He waggled his finger at me. "You're in love again."

"Oh, for heaven's sake."

"Pink cheeks, dewy eyes, swollen lips."

"Swollen lips?"

He nodded.

I ran my tongue over my lips, tentative. They did feel kind of puffy. I decided to take a coffee break, since I'd never had any lunch, and amble by the 138s. Physiognomy.

In case you wanted to know.

I felt Gordon's eyes on me and I ducked down an alley of books just to avoid his stare. Even I couldn't miss the fact that my putative pink cheeks, puffy lips, and dewy eyes were making him aware of me. Aware, not of the me me, the one you know. I mean the me no one knows, including myself. The me of the body, the me of desire, the me of fantasy . . . okay, the me of sex. It was true: I wanted sex with Aleksi Kullio. But, and this was the kicker, the me of sex still existed hand in hand with the me of my mind. And my mind wanted love.

7

*For information about how to try to make the perfect martini,
go to the 641.87s (e.g., Trader Vic's Bartender's Guide,
Bartending for Dummies, etc.) or look in Fiction
under F for Ian Fleming, chapter 7 of* Casino Royale.

It was annoying to have to wake up early on Saturday morning. If I hadn't volunteered at the Philharmonic, I would still be asleep. I could hear the ping of raindrops against the windows and the thrum of a steady downpour on the roof. A wonderful morning to stay in bed and begin a rereading of *The Forsyte Saga* (if you haven't read it, I pity you—it's in the Fiction section, under *G* for Galsworthy). I plumped up several of the dozen feather pillows scattered around and put on my glasses.

The long room had an unfinished quality because the night before, I'd deliberately pulled back half the windows' curtains with the idea that the morning light would wake me up, while at the same time, the other half were closed so that the streetlights didn't keep me awake during the night. Okay, make up your mind: do you want to sleep or do you want to wake up? Neither, nor. Either, or. I have a strong disaffection for this sort of thing and I was forced, nausea or not, to leap out of bed and dash about yanking back curtains. Then, in a fit, I also made my bed.

When I purchased the linens to decorate my bed, I imagined a queen's bed in Elizabethan England. Hence, the massive mahogany four-poster bore a gold velvet dust ruffle and matching pillow shams, a Jacobean woven coverlet, silky feather pillows in a rainbow of rich colors, and a ruby red satin comforter folded at the end of the bed. Not to brag, but it was luscious. Making the bed was exhausting, though. All those pillows had to be thrown on the floor, the comforter shaken and refolded, the coverlet yanked back in order for me to pound and sweep the sheets clean, and then the whole business reassembled. I figured making my bed counted for a full day's physical exercise. Really. It made me quite breathless.

Panting, I put the kettle on for hot water and simultaneously began running a bath. With the walls knocked down, the old iron tub was fully visible in the room, so I'd painted it a deep eggplant color. An antique brass light, fixed to the wall at the head of the bathtub, angled out like an old person's arm, all cranky and knobbly, giving me the light to read in the tub.

As I ground the coffee beans and measured them into my battered French press coffeemaker, I stared out the window. A genuine rainstorm was going on. Trees bent and twisted, leaves whirled into miniature tornadoes, and my view was the color of sop (look it up). The water in the teakettle shrieked and I filled the French press, then quickly plunked myself into the bathtub.

You probably think I'm a clean freak, given my propensity for order and tidiness, but the truth is that I rather revel in a certain degree of personal grubbiness. I've always figured it was one of the beneficial by-products of being a born-again virgin. And since my baths were invariably long overdue, it made the business of getting clean so much more pleasurable.

This morning served to prove my point: if I hadn't been going to the Philharmonic, I would not have had a bath. Frankly, I wasn't all that yucky. I'd been exceptionally clean on Thursday . . . actually, excuse me, right before bed Wednesday night. Normally, I would have waited until at least Saturday night, when I had my ritual bath and martini and shrimp cocktail.

Now everything would be thrown off. Saturday night loomed large and threatening. I always cleaned my apartment on Saturday afternoon, to the rollicking accompaniment of the Rolling Stones; then I peeled the shrimp that had been steamed at the grocery store and arranged them decoratively on a glass plate, with a cut-crystal bowl of cocktail sauce in the center. As the bathwater filled up, I piled the logs onto the fire and popped the martini glass into the freezer, next to the vodka.

After a reading bath marathon that usually lasted ninety minutes, I'd wrap up in my gigantic terry cloth bathrobe, throw more logs onto the fire, and finally make myself the perfect martini. Sweat would drip down my face from the heat of the bath and fire while the glacial combination of vodka and vermouth shivered down my throat.

Instead, here I was cleaning what wasn't dirty, and doing it in an insane hurry so that I'd arrive on time, whatever on time meant. I could obviously show up whenever I wanted. This decision to involve myself at the Philharmonic felt like a mistake and I toyed with the idea of calling Jeffrey to make an excuse. While the water drained, I stood up in the tub and grabbed a thick towel to drape over my shoulders. Suddenly I let the towel fall open and I looked down at my body. White and goose bumpy, but not too bad. Small but, to my mind, flawless breasts, flat stomach, funereal thighs. (No, I don't have a clue what *funereal thighs* means—maybe thin to the point of sadness?)

I intended to stand there the rest of my life, damp and clean and scared. I didn't want to step out of the tub, I didn't want to go to the Liberty Music Hall, and most of all, I didn't want to want. Aleksi Kullio had turned me into a wanting kind of person. I did not, philosophically, approve. I'd been raised a lackadaisical Presbyterian, but I'd nevertheless developed a severe notion of ethics. I did not believe in desire because desire could cloud your judgment and make you choose to behave in a wrong way.

At any rate, I did put on my glasses, just to see more clearly, and what I saw was the coffee steeping in the French press coffeemaker. With all the damp chill around me, inside and out, I suddenly developed a craving for that hot coffee. Where would all this wanting lead?

Look, I know full well that I'm not particularly normal, though how to define *normal* is a fair question. We're told that passion and zeal are laudatory emotions.

But I don't see why I have to conform to society's definition of *laudatory*. I happen to think it's laudatory to be me. And it's not that I'm without ardor. I am ardent about books. I made a choice in high school, when everyone else started zinging around from one activity and sexual partner to another, like out-of-control pinball machines, that I wasn't going to bebop all over the place.

I wanted to sit still. And I wanted to read. I'd been cradled by the act of reading from the moment I learned how. If you look at a book lying open on its back, it forms an ark for holding. Books held me, and without their embrace, I would be held by no one.

Liberty Music Hall burst open to me like the juicy segments of a ripe orange. Bright fluorescent lights, the constant buzz of telephones, people seesawing up and down the halls, and the distant hum of an orchestra tuning up— all this created a cacophony of sensation that felt both claustrophobic and irrepressibly alive. If Jeffrey hadn't spied me immediately, I might have rushed away. He steered me along and introduced me to other members of the Office for Volunteer Services before showing me where the key to the archives was kept.

My heart beat fast and my fingers itched when I switched on the lights in the archival storage space. I wanted to leave this death of a room and dash back upstairs, but I realized that if I got some work done, I might be able to listen to part of the rehearsal. I'd brought empty boxes with me, and I immediately began tossing clearly dated material into various boxes, each representing a given year.

An hour later, I discovered a letter from Stokowski to

Stravinsky himself, with a question about the performance of the *Rite of Spring*, which was premiered in the United States by the Philadelphia Philharmonic. I nearly yelped with delight. This was obviously the beginning of an extensive correspondence between the two. I began a separate pile but didn't take the time to actually read any of the material.

So lost was I that Jeffrey's voice made me jump.

"What?" I said.

"I just asked how it was going." He sounded amused. "You certainly don't mind getting dirty."

I noticed the black streaks of grime coating my hands.

"You could take a break and have a cup of coffee," Jeffrey said.

"Given the dirt, I'll probably keep at it." I sneezed. "Is there a bathroom down here?"

"Keep going to the end of the hall." He stepped back.

I continued. "Listen, at some point we're going to have to get something to store this stuff in—I was thinking clear plastic bins, with lids that I could label."

"When you're ready, let me know, and I'll arrange it."

"Okay." I turned to reach into the back of a shelf and pull out more papers.

I quit two hours later. The bathroom mirror revealed a satisfying sight: I looked like a chimney sweep. No worry that someone would think that I was actually *interested* in Aleksi Kullio. I cleaned up a bit with paper towels, but I still managed to be singularly unappealing.

I took the elevator to the second-floor balcony level and walked purposefully to a closed door leading into the concert hall. I slipped through the door and behind the darkened rows of seats. I stood very still, listening and watching, frozen by the sight of Aleksi Kullio on the podium. Then I heard his voice.

"Strings, you're building the crescendo much too quickly. Slow like molasses." He tapped his baton. "Again."

Up the baton rose and then it came swinging down into the measure. The strings sounded okay to me, but not to Maestro Kullio. He stopped and shook his head. I held my breath, terrified. His gentle tone coaxed them and I let out a deep sigh. I had been frightened that he would chastise them; that, somehow, would have been unbearable to me. I slowly lowered myself into a seat. He never raised his voice or showed anger.

I had been watching for about thirty minutes when I felt a monstrous sneeze building. I stood up, trying to leave before it exploded.

I didn't succeed.

My sneeze reverberated and echoed. The music stopped and I saw Aleksi Kullio whirl around to peer into the dark pits. His head tilted back and one hand covered his eyes as he gazed to the balcony.

"Who's there?" he called out.

I swallowed and then announced in my normal speaking voice, "I'm nobody."

Without missing a beat, his voice shouted, "I'm nobody, too."

"That makes a pair of us."

The entire orchestra burst into laughter.

I turned and fled. At the elevator, I hit the button for the ground floor, waited nervously to descend, and finally rushed out of the elevator and down the hall to Jeffrey's lair. I managed to hang up the key in the unusually quiet office and leave without notice.

The rain poured down, and belatedly, I remembered my umbrella, left to dry in the offices. I didn't dare return. I stooped over like the wretched woman I was, trying not to get wet. Half a block on, I straightened and allowed the water to go where it would. My glasses steamed up so badly that I took them off. Emily Dickinson's poem rattled in my head as my feet splish-splashed through gargantuan puddles.

> *I'm Nobody! Who are you?*
> *Are you—Nobody—Too?*
> *Then there's a pair of us!*
> *Don't tell! they'd advertise—you know!*
>
> *How dreary—to be—Somebody!*
> *How public—like a Frog—*
> *To tell one's name—the livelong June—*
> *To an admiring Bog!*

Of course, Aleksi Kullio didn't have a problem with telling *his* name.

The rain pummeled me and I began to hum a tune to the sounds of traffic, my clomping boots, and the rain, the rain, the rain. As usual, my voice was out of tune and rhythm with the rain. In the entrance to my building, I collected my mail and waited a few minutes so that the worst of the wet could puddle around my feet.

My apartment, still as pessimistic and lonely as when I'd left it that morning, was dark except for the blinking red light on my telephone answering machine. I had this insane thought that Aleksi Kullio might have called and left me a short message in which he quoted the rest of the poem.

"Hi, sweetie. This is your mama. I know it's last-minute, but I haven't seen you in ages and I wondered if you could come to a dinner I'm throwing tonight? I understand you don't normally like parties, but I had a cancellation and I'm too many women short—it's embarrassing! Please come and help your poor mother out! And let me know right away!"

If it were socially acceptable, I have no doubt, my mother would have dinner parties consisting entirely of men and one woman—herself. I waited for the second message.

"And wear that silk dress I bought you this fall from Saks, the blue. Bye-bye!"

I began peeling off my clothes while wondering whether I could get out of the dinner. I hadn't seen her for at least eight weeks, but I never let guilt dictate my decisions. Stark naked, I pulled on the big terry cloth robe and cleaned my glasses by running them under hot water and using three tissues.

When they were again in their proper place, I saw the dismal, damp apartment even more clearly. A fire would cheer things up, I knew, but I suddenly realized that I wanted to go to a dinner party. I wanted to wash my hair and wear a little makeup, and most of all, I had to admit that I desperately wanted to wear the blue silk dress from Saks.

Want, want, want.

You see?

I called my mother and promised to be there. Then I curled up on my massive Victorian couch, covered in dark brown velvet, switched on the light, and began to reread *The Forsyte Saga*.

My mother nearly swooned when she opened the door to admit me later that evening, and her beautiful, rouged face flushed even redder. "You look lovely!"

"Thanks." I held up my dripping umbrella and raincoat.

"Are you dumping wet things in the bathtub?"

"There are coat hangers on the curtain rod in the guest bath, where you can hang them up."

My mother's modern apartment in the Society Hill district of Philadelphia was a good twenty blocks from mine in the Rittenhouse Square area, but I'd walked fast, trying to work off my self-imposed agitation at having agreed to attend her dinner party. She'd moved downtown after I left for Bryn Mawr, so this apartment was nothing like our home in Swarthmore, and for that I was grateful. Her decor, pale woods and an obsessive use of white, suited a sex bomb urologist, not a virginal librarian daughter. After I'd hung up my raincoat and propped up the umbrella in a corner of the bathtub, I headed back down the long hallway and into her living room.

Acres of black glass glittered with the city's lights and a view of the harbor as well as the reflections of the flames of dozens of candles. The effect would have been chilly except for the intoxicating odor of coq au vin and the music of someone playing her Steinway. The grand piano shone black like the wet night through the windows.

And a man with white blond hair was playing. He turned his head to smile at my mother and my heart caught. The man was clearly of Nordic ancestry, but he was not, as I'd momentarily and insanely hoped, Aleksi Kullio. He stopped playing and rose to follow my mother. They came toward me.

He was short, but handsome. Better looking than Aleksi.

"Ally, I'd like to introduce Peter Nobel."

I held out my hand. "Hi, Peter."

His lips smiled, but not his eyes. "How do you do?"

"Peter is a landscape architect," my mother said, "doing the design work for the hospital's new building—you remember I told you there would be a courtyard and exterior space for roaming about."

I fought a terrible urge to throw myself at him. I wanted to touch him, to know him. I turned away abruptly. "I need a drink," I said loudly.

"Ally," my mother murmured.

I plowed toward the opposite end of the room, where a bartender in a short white dinner jacket stood behind a white-skirted table crowded with bottles of liquor. The doorbell chimed and suddenly the room behind me filled with people, their voices chattering and squawking in a hideous discord.

"Please, a freezing cold Grey Goose martini, very dry, shaken and not stirred, with one olive," I said to the bartender.

"Certainly," he intoned.

"While you're at it, I'll have the same." Peter's voice came from behind me.

I cautiously turned my head and smiled. I knew I'd been rude to him, and I wanted to make amends, but my usual tongue-tied disposition had taken hold.

"You are Mary's daughter, is that right?" he asked.

I nodded, my eyes riveted to the bartender's fluid movements.

"I believe she mentioned that you are the director of the research department at the library."

"Yes." I held out my hand for the martini.

"I didn't know librarians drank martinis."

I turned, making room for him to take the second glass. I struggled to find something amusing to say, or to say anything at all. A horde of people was headed our way and I would be saved soon. "They do," I said.

He threw back his head and laughed. I hadn't meant to be so funny.

The people arrived and I melted away.

My mother's best friend, Jerome, waved to me from across the room. Tiny and impish, he wore his bald head like a marvelous hat. I sped over and gave him a hug.

He held me at arm's length, checking me from head to toe while he made clicking noises with his tongue. "Something is different about you!"

I shrugged. "People keep saying that."

"Men people or women people?"

"Men mostly, except Mom."

"Oh, she's a man, honey."

I laughed. "How are you? Last I heard you were in love."

He didn't smile, just shook his head lazily from side to side.

Jerome was a nurse in the ICU of the hospital. He could manage all the grief and brutality of that environment like a workhorse, but in his private life, a life that meant being a man loving other men, he periodically fell apart. My mother was always there to put him back together. Years ago, I'd been jealous of their relationship, until I realized that he made it possible for me to survive as her daughter.

My mother gave up trying to change me only in the last five years. Until then, it was fairly relentless. Even when she eased up, it was *obvious* she was easing up—I felt as if a timer were ticking, ticking, ticking, and at any moment the alarm would scream.

Until I started high school, I was pretty indistinguishable from all the other kids. Maybe a little quieter and less athletic, but I had plenty of girlfriends—all you were supposed to have at that age—and Mom liked my mania for reading. She's a reader herself, and it was a quality she respected. Then high school happened and I opted out of the whole game. Looking back, I swear my grim memories of those years reflect the unfortunate truth of how it really was. So let's just say that without Jerome's interference, she would have tried to devour me and then spit me out—a second birth—in her image.

Jerome went to get a drink and I wandered over by the windows, staring out at the night. Rain streaked and dripped in thin lines down the glass. I wanted to go home.

When dinner was announced, I was seated next to Peter Nobel. So much for my hope that he was intended for my mother, a hope I'd indulged in even though I felt sure he was closer to my age than hers.

My mother made a toast that struck me as somewhat incoherent, though I didn't dwell on it because I was too busy worrying about how I would manage to talk to Peter. An older gentleman I'd met at another event, seated to my right, had already plunged into rhapsodic conversation with the woman to *his* right. Silent, Peter and I watched as our salads were served. I stabbed a piece of lettuce and then stared at it. I was never hungry at dinner parties, which was one of the reasons why I found other people's enthusiasm for them so inexplicable.

I absolutely had to speak.

"Do you read books?" I asked.

His mouth had just opened wide to receive an enormous lettuce leaf. He chewed assiduously while I poked at my salad.

"I love to read, of course," he said finally.

"But what I meant was, do you read *books*?"

His fork speared an unidentifiable object and he held it midair, contemplating it.

"I think it's a parsnip," I said.

"A parsnip in a salad?"

"Maybe a radish?"

"Probably a white radish." He popped it in his mouth and masticated in a dramatic fashion. "Radish, yup."

I sorted through my salad until I found a piece of radish. It took several tries before I managed to pierce it with the tines of my fork.

"I read almost entirely nonfiction, I regret to say." He glanced at me, appraising. "You're undoubtedly a fiction lover—most women are."

Actually, this was categorically untrue.

"As a research librarian, I read widely, including nonfiction, fiction, and children's."

"Why children's?" He opened his eyes wide to make sure that I understood how absurd I'd sounded.

"I started out as a children's librarian, but I continue to read children's literature because it's damn good."

"That right?"

He smiled charmingly, only I wasn't charmed. It had taken me a while, but I'd finally come to the conclusion that Peter Piper hated women. Some men disguise it better than others, but a women's college graduate can always, ultimately, sniff 'em out. That's one of the many valuable assets that goes along with attending a women's college, in fact. I think the Seven Sisters should advertise this quality much more aggressively.

Something like

Our 100% Guarantee: A Women's College Will Teach You How to Flush Out the Men Who Hate You

It needs a little work, but you get the idea.

The waitress hired for the evening took away my salad plate. I straightened my remaining silverware and refolded the napkin in my lap. I found that I was experiencing a brand-new emotion, and it was a bit disconcerting. I was suddenly bored silly with always being shy. It was such a snore. I might as well plunk my head down on the table-top and go to sleep.

I noticed a man across the table from me, which felt like miles away because of the flowers and candles and paraphernalia, but I decided to go for it. I said, "Do you think it's acceptable to use real historical figures as fictional characters?"

Silence hit that dining room like a torpedo. I ducked.

And then the conversation took off, everyone arguing and interrupting and pontificating about Virginia Woolf, Michael Cunningham, and the nature of literary fiction.

I sat back, fat and happy, though I hadn't eaten that radish and I still wasn't exactly hungry.

Well, maybe a little.

8

For questions about dreams, and particularly flying dreams, go to the 154.63s (e.g., Dreams and Dreaming, Our Dreaming Mind) and to Reference 133s (e.g., Man, Myth, and Magic).

"I flyed last night," Ally said.

"Flew," I corrected.

"I flewed last night."

Give it up, I thought. "Did you fly in an airplane?"

She tilted her head at me from where she sat in my lap, with an expression of disdain and exasperation. Silky hair stroked my chin.

"I flewed by myself." Her arms stretched out straight, impersonating wings.

I reached and grabbed each hand to make giant flapping motions with her arms. "Like this?"

Ally wrenched them away and leaped off my lap. She ran pell-mell across John and Suzanne's backyard, arms still held at rigid, ninety-degree angles; then abruptly, the arms zapped to her sides and she became a little rocket about to take off.

Only, of course, she didn't. I could tell from her de-

jected walk back that not launching herself, as she'd undoubtedly done in her dream, had been a disappointment. I figured I'd better distract her. "You want me to
read to you?"

"Yeah, just a minute, just a minute," she said, scurrying
to the house. She looked back, checking that I wasn't
going anywhere and would still be there when she returned.

No, I wasn't going anywhere on this glorious, autumn
Sunday afternoon. The ground squelched underfoot from
the torrents of rain the day before, but I was sitting in a
chair on the flagstone terrace. Harsh sun punched the top
of my head and I felt weighted in place.

Suzanne had already made her report to me, based on
one morning of trailing Michelle Kullio. At ten o'clock in
the morning, she had entered a large upscale grocery
store and purchased five bags of dried prunes.

"Prunes?" I said. "Are you sure?"

"I was right behind her in the checkout."

"Did you ask whether she had a constipation problem?"

"Of course not." Suzanne sounded disgusted with me.
"Although I admit that the cashier and I caught each
other's eye and almost burst out laughing."

I paused to think. "I've got it—she's stewing all these
prunes to disguise the presence and taste of rotten akee!"

"Maybe."

"It's perfectly plausible."

"It's not necessarily even plausible, much less *perfectly*
plausible."

"How do you explain it, then?"

"She's blocked."

"Oh."

"She has that blocked look."

"I know what you mean." Since I tended to the opposite problem, I felt comfortable with this comment.

I sighed.

Suzanne said, "You could be right; we'll just have to wait and see what else happens."

"You're not giving up?"

"Nope—I trust your instinct on this. I do think there was a creepy connection between those poisons in the *A* section of the reference book and then Michelle traipsing all that way to buy something in a West Indian store."

"Also, it's weird she didn't take a cab."

"As if she didn't want a record of her going there."

We'd left it that Suzanne would try some more sleuthing again on Monday morning.

Ally came outside pushing one of those toy grocery carts, overflowing with books.

"Got enough books?" I asked.

Her face creased with a frown of worry.

"I'm just kidding," I reassured her, since she was about to turn around and go back for more.

Busily, she maneuvered the cart to its proper position next to my chair, climbed into my lap, and leaned over to select a book from the top of the pile. She thrust it into my hands.

Before beginning to read, I whispered into her ear, "You'd make a great librarian, Ally, just like me."

Suzanne and John didn't have to know that I was using subliminal advertising techniques on her.

I read to her for over an hour, until Suzanne finally yelled from the kitchen window that dinner was ready.

We ate in the kitchen with *The Mikado* playing loudly

from the stereo system in John's office, a former maid's room located off the kitchen.

"Are you teaching a course for freshmen this fall?" I asked John.

He nodded while chomping on the tuna noodle casserole. His mouth always attacked food, even when the food was something soft and malleable like tuna noodle casserole.

"'The Matriarchal African Model,'" he said, swallowing hard and glancing at me to gauge my level of comprehension.

Since my level of comprehension was nil, he explained. "African society developed with the matriarch as leader because the woman grew the food."

"What about us?" I wolfed down the casserole, which I found breathtakingly delicious.

"Oh, we're obviously patriarchal," John said. "I doubt that will ever really change."

"Neither one nor the other is *better*," Suzanne said. "It's determined by the dictates of weather and land, that's all."

"Are your students intelligent?"

Though John's plate was clean, he ran a single searching finger along the edge. "Every year I notice a small decline in their overall preparedness," he said. "Television is ruining us."

"TV?" Ally said, looking from mother to father, and back again.

"TV is yucky." I pulled a terrible face.

Her eyes opened wide, but I knew she didn't believe me. None of us owned a television.

"Ella la vio en la casa de mis padres" ("She saw it at my parents' house"), Suzanne said.

"Eso iba a ocurrir algún día" ("It was bound to happen someday"), I answered.

"They're speaking Spanish so that you won't understand," John explained to Ally. "You should learn Spanish as soon as possible. I could understand French and read Latin, but I had to learn Spanish when I married your mother—otherwise, she would have kept secrets from me."

"Suzanne tells you everything," I said. "It's so annoying!"

John blushed and smiled.

They were the greatest love affair masquerading as marriage that I could ever have imagined, even in my most feverish, hallucinatory moments. I adored them for giving me the gift of watching it happen. It didn't make me envious or bored. It made me believe.

In love.

Ally threw open her hands and yelled, "Jambo!"

"Jambo!" Suzanne yelled back.

"Where on earth—"

"A lovely Kenyan couple joined the faculty, and they have a daughter Ally's age," Suzanne said.

"Cool." I stood up and began to clear the table.

At that moment, from the stereo speakers Yum-Yum began to sing "Here's a how-de-do!" I piled plates next to the sink, then rushed to sweep Ally into my arms. We danced and I sang along.

> *Here's a state of things*
> *To her life she clings!*
> *Matrimonial devotion*
> *Doesn't seem to suit her notion—*

Burial it brings!
Here's a state of things!
Here's a state of things!

John and Suzanne laughed as the meaning of the words, particularly applied to me, registered. Scorning them, I whirled more wildly and Ally screamed with delight.

Dusk clung to the trees and houses as I drove home, the top down on my Miata despite the bite of the night air. When I got on the Schuylkill Expressway, the wind tore at the scarf I'd tied around my head and I thought it might blow off. "Here's a state of things, here's a state of things!" I yelled into the dark gale, then threw my head back and laughed maniacally.

Suddenly self-conscious, I looked to my left where a sleek silver Mercedes sedan was in the passing lane. A man in the passenger seat grinned at me and waved. I waved back, gay as Yum-Yum. His grin widened and I could actually discern a set of extraordinarily white teeth. I wondered if they were real. His flamboyant white hair soared like geese taking off for their winter holiday.

I stared straight ahead and concentrated on driving, but my peripheral vision clued me in to the fact that the Mercedes still rode alongside. I dared to sneak another look.

A piece of paper with big letters scrawled across was plastered to his closed window. I wasn't sure whether to be nervous or charmed. I gazed straight ahead, but curiosity was killing me. I peeked.

DRINK?

Here's a how-de-do, indeed!

I smiled, though I tried not to. I knew all about being careful (go to 362.88, *The Gift of Fear: Survival Signals That Protect Us from Violence*, by Gavin de Becker), and I was somewhat annoyed with myself, especially since I have to admit that the Mercedes may have been an influence. A stupid one, I grant you. Now I scowled with my face forward, but I had a suspicion that this fellow knew a faker when he saw it. I tried to move my eyeballs left without turning my head and giving away the game. If you wear glasses, you already know my problem. I could see, but I couldn't *see*.

Perhaps it all came down to glasses, my big thick glasses. What all, you ask? The all of me being revirginified. My glasses were keeping me from the world, like a viscous barrier, or an armor made of some living, breathing stuff that shifted from an opaque—and this was the most tantalizing—to nearly translucent. Nearly, but never entirely.

I pounded my fists on the driver's wheel. LASIK surgery! I'd tried soft contact lenses on three separate occasions, back when I made periodic attempts to distract my mother by occasionally giving in, and I was hopeless with them. The ophthalmologist thought I was allergic to the intrinsic composition of the contacts. Recently, Mom had offered to pay for me to have the LASIK procedure. Her proposition had, of course, guaranteed that I would initially refuse, and I remembered that only last week I'd been gratified by my hazy vision. Funny how the very thing you cling to one week is what you're ready to trash the next. I guess you cling because, in some obscure way, you understand that life is going to require that you give it up.

The Mercedes pulled inexorably ahead, and I gave my head a quick left twist. The man stared at me with two fingers pulling the corners of his mouth into an exaggerated frown. And then he was gone, just as I noticed that he had obviously turned prematurely white, since he looked quite young. Not as young as I, but still. Did I mention that he was good-looking?

Come on, even the most eccentric among you would not have followed two strange men in their car to a bar. This is just the sort of thing to give women a bad name. What if you had agreed to follow them to the bar, and what if they slipped a drug into your drink, and what if they took you somewhere to rape and murder you? Huh? Then where would you be? You'd be very dead and the last thing you'd think would be, *Everyone's going to say what a stupid fool I was to trust men who picked me up on the Schuylkill Expressway. Furthermore, they will never solve my murder, and no one—and that includes my mother—no one will ever know that I followed them to the bar because they drove a Mercedes.*

I zipped into the left lane and wove onto Vine Street. Thinking about murder and rape had made me nervous. I took the first exit on Twenty-second Street, pulled over, and quickly jumped out of the car to pull up the top. I looked around, scared that parking would prove to have been a fatal mistake. Leaping back into the car, I locked all the doors, latched the top in place, and put up the windows. My heart beat fast and I took several deep breaths to settle down.

Safe in my fourth-floor apartment, I yanked the velvet drapes closed and turned on all the lights. The long room glowed like a golden honeycomb and I felt almost beeish as I buzzed about. On with a Bach cantata, I didn't care which one. Off with all my clothes, folded, and put away. On with a worn flannel nightgown, the first of the season.

I pulled down the coverlet and pleated it to lie flat and neat, exposing the soft pillows. I placed a large glass of plain water on the bedside table, with a coaster to catch the sweat and drips. Buzz, buzz, buzz. I now switched off all the lights except the one next to my bed. I found *The Forsyte Saga* hidden in the couch cushions and carried it to the bed. I took a very long pee, as I am wont to do. I did not look at myself in the mirror, even as I brushed my teeth, because I wasn't interested in what I looked like.

I was interested in going to bed.

It was eight o'clock in the evening and I wanted to sleep.

Have we discussed sleeping?

All women love to sleep. That isn't to say all women are successful at sleeping. I believe I would put a bullet through my head if I were a serious insomniac. However, you've probably guessed that I'm a gargantuan sleeper.

I have a theory about why I'm so good at sleeping. Maybe you've figured that one out, too. I am utterly and blissfully alone. But that's not all; that's not the entire philosophy. There are a lot of parts to this. Because, you see, I'm not really alone. I've got books. Not just the physical presence of books, though they're obviously attractive and warm. I mean the people, the stories, the active intelligence of whatever I'm reading.

Finally, I don't have a television, and this is the crux of

the matter. People who go to bed alone often have a TV playing. They say it keeps them company, assuages the pangs of solitude, but in fact, it doesn't work that way. When you read a book, you fully and completely enter a universe. Your mind is an energetic participant in the written language. It cannot be otherwise. But when you watch television, you cannot enter that world. You always remain on the outside looking into the screen, and the screen is the wall blocking your entrance. And so the television makes you horribly aware of the very thing you wish to escape, your loneliness.

Bottom line: if you're an insomniac, throw out the television set.

I often hungered for sleep, hungered for it in much the same way I imagined more normal people desired sexual intimacy. Which is strange, when you think about it, because the bed is where most people *have* sex. Their beds must be so fraught with tension, with wanting and not wanting, with loving and not loving, with hot thighs and icy toes. Quite, quite exhausting. Almost enough to make me think twice about sex with Aleksi Kullio.

I climbed under the covers and lay back against the multitude of pillows. My gaze drifted straight out, all the way to the end of the room where in the darkness I could barely see the gleam of the kitchen sink. Bach's cantata minced the cool air of the apartment—the heat hadn't been turned on yet—and I smelled the orange trees almost trembling in their fervency.

I pretended Aleksi was here with me. I mean, I really pretended. I gave myself to the dream and I made it real. I turned to him in the bed, lying sideways, and I reached out to touch his eyes. They closed, and so I, too, closed my eyes. Could I hear his breathing? Almost, though he wasn't a heavy breather. Did he desire me? No, not at the moment. We were friends in bed together, breathing rhythmically together, murmuring words together, softening together like butter.

Did I dream that night?

You tell me.

9

For questions about the penis, go to the 612.61s
(e.g., A Doctor's Guide to Men's Private Parts), and for
explicit, colorful drawings of the penis,
go to Reference 611 (e.g., Atlas of Human Anatomy).

⦿ ⦿

*Y*ou noticed.

No sex.

I was in bed, I was fantasizing, and there was *no* sex. I guess I've just forgotten what it's like. I try to imagine a penis and all I come up with are things that look like penises. The actual contraption makes me squirm and feel silly. I agree with you and I understand your frustration. This whole endeavor, loving Aleksi Kullio, is starting to seem hopeless. You are losing faith in me. *I* am losing faith in me, but that's how, in essence, the times they are a-changing. I never used to have any faith to lose.

I should see a therapist—that's what you'd like to suggest. No thanks. The concept of therapy, talking about myself and explaining everything to an actual person, is too anxiety provoking. Anyway, I have you, don't I? Even if you are growing impatient with the slow speed of my forward movement, you have to concede that I *have* moved. I am moving. I will move. Promise.

On Monday morning, I had seven E-mails waiting at work for me to read. I recognized every name except one: kuku. I almost deleted it, since the risk of a virus had seemed particularly intense after the library's experience with foul smells, but the *ku* combination made me hope that Aleksi Kullio might have replied to that charming note I'd written to him about the library's intended acquisition of the Stravinsky biography. I hadn't really expected an answer, but at the same time, I was well aware that my library notepaper gives my E-mail address.

Dear Ms. Sheffield:
Thank you for the kind note concerning the Stravinsky bio. I actually read it in galleys because I had been asked to do a blurb. Not that I usually blurb, but Stravinsky is hard to resist. When you receive the book, I believe you'll find my comments quoted on the back cover. I hope to find the time to visit the library soon. Since my mother was a children's librarian in Finland, where I grew up, you can imagine that the library is like a second home to me. Again, thank you for the perspicacious thought.
Best wishes, Aleksi Kullio

I stared stupidly at the E-mail. His mother was a librarian, and not only that, but a *children's* librarian. My heart pounded so hard I thought I'd crack a rib. I called Suzanne immediately.

Before I could explain what had happened, she started chattering.

"Ally, I'm sorry I couldn't get in to follow Michelle today. I was all set and walking out the door when your dear namesake, Ally, vomited all over my mother's new sweat suit. I know it's not pleasant to be puked on, but you'd think a sweat suit was haute couture by the way she hollered. There was no way I could leave after that, plus I had to take Ally—your dear namesake—to the doctor because she just kept on vomiting."

"It's perfectly all right," I said, wedging my way into her manic word flight. "How's Ally? What did the doctor say?"

"Oh, it's just a twenty-four-hour bug." Suzanne sounded exhausted. "The next phase, which we have most assuredly begun, is diarrhea. I parked her on the toilet with a basket of books next to her. You have never seen such a god-awful mess in all your life! She must have gone through five sets of underpants before I—"

"I get the picture," I interrupted. "Can you talk for a few minutes? I have very important news."

"She's totally fine on the pot and I'm on a cordless so I'm right with her—now TELL me!"

Was there something about infants and toddlers that made parents talk with almost constant exclamation marks? I'd noticed in the last couple of years that everything happening in Suzanne's household was of life-or-death stature. *She pooped for three hours straight! He screamed for ten hours! He smiled for the first time! She read a word in her storybook! He's adorable! She's gorgeous!* It was no wonder, despite the exclamation marks, that Suzanne always sounded either drugged or drunk. Today was a unique combination: drugged *and* drunk.

"I got an E-mail from Aleksi Kullio," I said. "Let me read it to you."

When I'd finished, Suzanne was silent. "What do you think?" I said, impatient for her response.

"It's an omen," she declared in a soft voice.

"That's what I thought."

We breathed in and out together, sharing a sense of significant serendipity.

"Ms. Sheffield?" Ed cracked open my door so that I would be able to hear his voice, but I could see him clearly through the door's glass panel.

"I have a visitor—I'll call you later, okay?"

"As soon as possible!"

I held the receiver away from my ear. "Yup."

I hung up and waved Ed into my office. "Yes?"

"Uh, could I speak to you for a minute?"

"Of course—please come in."

He shuffled into the office and gingerly closed the door behind him.

I sat down and gestured to the chair off to the side, but he remained standing, one finger of each hand touching the desktop.

"I need some help with Mr. Albright's birthday present," he said.

I'd forgotten about Yvonne's party plans, scheduled for tomorrow, and I was troubled to think of Ed's considering it a requirement that he purchase a gift.

"Ed, you don't need to—"

"I work at the library," he said firmly, "and I want to get him something. I had the idea of a shirt." He glanced at me tentatively, gauging my response.

"A shirt would be fine," I said.

"But not great?"

"He likes shirts—I'm sure of it."

"What are you going to give him?" Ed said.

"Well, I hadn't quite figured it out."

"You better—there's not much time."

"That's true."

"You could give him the pants to go with my shirt."

"I'm not sure that pants would be quite"—I paused— "appropriate."

"I know!" His body straightened up with excitement. "*You* give him the shirt and I'll do the pants. That would be just right."

I stared at him and could think of nothing to say. Other people might easily get out of such a predicament. I am aware that I tend to be softhearted. If I had had the time to formulate a good reply, I might have managed, but I didn't have any time whatsoever. Ed looked at me with eyes that reminded me of myself, and I had to agree.

"Okay, how about we go shopping on my lunch break?" I said.

Ed's smile resembled one of Charlie Brown's infrequent, wobbly smiles, the one where his mouth goes up and down in jagged little peaks.

As he left my office, I followed behind him, to check on how things were going out on the front lines. Yvonne, on loan to Reference from the circulation desk, stood at attention behind the long counter. She brought a certain military stature to librarianship, perhaps because she wasn't a professional librarian at all.

"How's it going?" I nudged her with one shoulder, trying to force a slump. She made the rest of us look bad.

"All right."

She was still standing tall, despite my jolt.

"I've been meaning to ask you about something," Yvonne said.

I glanced at her, trying to be receptive. Not easy to do with Yvonne.

"Remember that girl I mentioned to you?"

"The one you were going to report for truancy?"

"She's been coming in *after* school, so that's not the problem." Yvonne shrugged.

"Okay." I waited.

Yvonne said, "She never checks out books—it's so weird."

Bored, my gaze left Yvonne and ambled around the reference section. That's when I saw the back of her head. You know, the head. Blond hair in a sleek helmet. I'd know that head anywhere.

"How long has she been here?" I asked Yvonne, forgetting about the teenage girl we'd been talking about.

"Who?" She looked around with open curiosity.

I put a hand on her arm to shush her. "The woman at the far table with her back to us. Blond hair."

"Oh, you mean Michelle," Yvonne said with a big smile. "That's the new conductor's wife, Michelle Kullio."

"I know." I raised my eyebrows.

Recollecting my original question, Yvonne said, "She's been here all morning—she's writing a mystery novel and I helped her scope out some possible ways to murder someone. It was great fun."

Among Yvonne's unfortunate traits was the small measure of obsessive-compulsive disorder she possessed. Her eyelids began opening and shutting like the lens of a camera operated by a three-year-old child.

I was cursing myself for missing the opportunity to interact with Aleksi's wife and, at the same time, wondering why she'd told me last week that she was ready to submit the novel when she hadn't even finished figuring out the story. Still watching Michelle, I asked Yvonne, "Did she tell you what it's about?"

"Obviously she wouldn't tell me 'whodunit,' but she did say who would be murdered. You'll never guess—"

"The conductor of a major orchestra," I interrupted.

Her pointy chin wagged like a dog's tail. "How did you *know*?" she said.

I put my finger to my lips in the traditional librarian's lament and Yvonne had the good grace to blush. "So she hasn't figured out yet how the murder will take place?" I asked.

"Nope," Yvonne said.

"I think I'll check and make sure that she doesn't need any more help."

Yvonne's face, already pink from my shushing her, turned turkey red.

Great, I had hurt her feelings.

I approached Michelle from behind, exploring every nuance of her posture and appearance as if I were a private detective. There wasn't much to deduce. Her hair was immaculate and fake-looking, even if it *was* real, and her pale blue cashmere turtleneck sweater clung to her sinewy arms. I rounded the table so that I could smile at her before I spoke. "Excuse me, I'm the director of the Reference Department—I believe we met last week? Have you found everything you need?"

Her eyes rose from the thick reference book and gazed at me. She didn't say a word.

I waited.

Her eyes were wintry, like a city's dirty slush the day after a snowstorm.

I waited some more.

"I'd like to do my work without your constant interruptions," she said at last.

I felt the hot flush of humiliation on my cheeks. "Of course—I apologize." I turned and walked back to the reference desk, where Yvonne stood watching me with an open mouth threatening a drool spill.

"She was nice to you?" I asked.

"Delightful."

"Well, I wasn't so lucky," I said. "She told me to bug off."

Yvonne, troubled, hunched her shoulders.

"I know you handled things beautifully—it was my fault for being nosy," I said.

"We could plan a murder mystery that happens in the library," she said, trying to make me feel better.

"Only the victim can't be the director of the research division."

Yvonne gave a sly smile. "How about the head of the library?"

I gave her arm a slap. "You're bad."

"No one would want to murder Gordon, anyway," Yvonne said with a dreamy expression.

"Except for one of the three zillion women he's dated and dumped." *Someone* had to be responsible and warn her to cross Gordon Albright off her list of eligible bachelors.

"I don't know." She shook her head doubtfully. "They keep coming to the library and flocking around him, like they have no hard feelings."

"How does he manage that?"

Yvonne leaned forward on the counter, resting her chin on folded arms so that her face was hidden behind a computer terminal. "I have a theory," she whispered.

I crouched over. "What?"

She gave me a look meant to imply a need for total secrecy.

"I won't tell anyone, promise." My eyes opened wide with sincerity. "Come on, you *know* I can keep my mouth shut."

Her whisper was so low I thought I misheard. I had to ask her to repeat it.

"I *said*," she hissed, "that I don't think he sleeps with them."

I clapped a hand over my mouth to keep the guffaw from escaping, turned, scuttled back to my office, slammed the door, and screamed with laughter. Behind me, the door opened and slammed shut again.

Yvonne bent over double, gasping with laughter. Tears streamed down our faces.

"I really *mean* it!" she howled. "He doesn't have sex so they don't get mad at him!"

I collapsed onto the floor, rocking back and forth, arms wrapped around my waist. Obscene snorting noises spurted out of my mouth and nose like a fireman's hose gone berserk.

We didn't even hear the door open, so Gordon's bemused voice came as a shock.

"What's so funny?" he asked.

We shrieked.

Gordon clasped both hands over his ears. "A fancy lady just marched out of here like she was ready to kill—can you get a grip and tell me what's going on?"

I hobbled over to my desk and groped for the tissue box. Yanking out several, I handed the box to Yvonne. We honked and mopped, working to get a grip, as requested.

I sank into my chair and dropped my head to the desk, where I beat it gently, moaning with painful merriment. When I next managed to get control of myself, Gordon's subdued expression sobered me.

"A little joke," I whispered.

Yvonne decided to skedaddle out of my office.

"I love a good joke," he said.

I grinned. "Not this one, baby cakes."

He cocked his head sideways and said, "Exactly *what* has gotten into you?"

I was beginning to wonder the same thing, but I segued into an entirely different subject by telling him about Michelle Kullio. As I developed her character, I started traipsing around the office on my tiptoes, as if I were wearing high heels, with my hips swishing from side to side. Quite unlike Michelle Kullio's gait, if I were honest. Then I unfastened the top three buttons of my blouse, pretended to light a cigarette, and blew smoke in Gordon's eyes.

He blinked.

"She's a foxy lady and she's got something foxy going on—I'm sure of it." I glared at him and plopped into my chair.

Gordon walked around my desk and put his large hand on my forehead. It felt like a hot blanket. I almost fell asleep right then and there.

"You're acting very strangely," he said. "I thought maybe you were febrile."

"I am febrile; you were febrile; he/she/it will be febrile," I intoned.

He ambled back around my desk and toward the door. I noticed his rear end, which was, frankly, as terrifically appealing as Aleksi Kullio's tiny ass.

Gordon was right. I never even think of words like *ass* and yet I felt perilously close to saying the word aloud. *You have a nice ass, Gordon. You are an ass, Gordon.* And the thing was that, in fact, he did have a particularly nice ass, and furthermore, he wasn't an ass.

"Maybe you should have a long lunch break." Gordon stood with one hand on the doorknob.

I looked at his crotch, then hurriedly back to his face. I had suddenly been gripped by the need, the irrepressible need, to see a penis. He was an old friend, a colleague, and I trusted him. Couldn't I ask him to do me a little favor? I swallowed, about to speak, and then swallowed again.

"Lunch," I murmured. *Penis à l'orange? Roasted penis with fennel? Penne and penis?*

"I think a longer lunch is in order," I agreed with Gordon.

"How are you and your mom getting along these days?" he asked, probing.

"The usual. I made a mistake and went to one of her dinner parties on Saturday night."

Gordon leaned against the doorjamb. "Why was it a mistake?"

"She seated me next to some guy, a landscape architect, and it was obvious we were supposed to hit it off."

"I guess you didn't." He grinned.

"The guy was an asshole, a handsome, smart asshole, but an asshole nonetheless."

"You think all men are assholes."

"I absolutely do not."

Gordon lifted one foot off the floor and gave it a little swing. "Yeah, you do—it's 'cause you resent your father not being around when you were a little girl."

"That is utter bull—"

He interrupted, "Last week, when you said I was a serial womanizer because my mother was a bitch, I accepted your statement. I didn't get all defensive."

"That's because I was right and you couldn't deny it."

"And I'm right this time, but you always refuse to acknowledge any painful truths about yourself." He grinned again, as if he didn't care whether I believed him or not.

I didn't.

"I like you," I said, triumphant.

One of his eyebrows cocked (yes, I know I'm still on penises). Then he actually dropped his head against the doorjamb, like a little boy who's been embarrassed by the attention of a little girl.

"Gee, you do?" he murmured.

That was when it happened. Like a camera flash exploding in my head, I saw it! A penis! Clear as clear. There it was in all its dubious glory.

No wonder I'd forgotten what a penis looks like.

Something in my face must have registered my aesthetic judgment on the beauty of a penis. Gordon straightened up, gave a little cough, and made a quick exit.

After he left, I swung around in my chair and pressed the space bar on my keyboard. The computer burst with light, and Aleksi's E-mail emerged. Without stopping to think, I clicked on the REPLY button.

Dear Aleksi,

How nice to hear from you! I will certainly look forward to seeing your words on the back cover of the Stravinsky biography. I do want to mention that I met you briefly last week when I was getting a tour of the archives, where I am working to organize and categorize the orchestra's papers. While putting in a few hours on Saturday morning, I found correspondence between Stokowski and Stravinsky concerning the United States premiere of the *Rite of Spring*. Perhaps you'd be interested in perusing it?

I am gratified to hear that you'd like to visit our library. We have enjoyed helping your wife with research on her novel and we would, similarly, welcome you. Has your mother retired from her duties as a librarian? Well, enough rattling on. Let me know if you'd like to see the correspondence mentioned above.

With my very best wishes, Ally Sheffield

I pushed the SEND button and almost immediately checked to see if I'd received an answer from Aleksi. I swung my chair around until I was facing the wall, where I stuck both feet flat against the wall, like a climbing spider. I tried to call Suzanne back, but I got her voice mail. Terrible body juices were probably hurling through the rooms of her house. I thought about why Michelle Kullio had been so rude to me. Frankly, I got no closer to understanding her behavior, beyond deciding that she was a terrible person, and therefore, I didn't have to feel awkward about pursuing her husband.

I stuck my arm out and hit the space bar. Nada. Then I grabbed the phone and called my ophthalmologist. Using my mother's name (I think they were once lovers), I managed to grab a cancellation for a week from Friday for LASIK surgery. When I hung up the phone, a scant five minutes later, I checked for E-mails.

"Kuku" pulsated and glowed.

Dear Ally,
I would be extremely interested in the correspondence you mention! How can I get my hands on it?
Best wishes, Aleksi
P.S. I didn't know my wife was writing a novel.

I wrote back immediately.

Dear Aleksi,
I'll leave the correspondence with your personal secretary later this afternoon. I thought you'd be intrigued. Your wife seems to be writing a mystery novel. I hesitate to say more.
Yours sincerely, Ally

After I pushed the SEND button, I let out a small scream of excitement. Then I had one of those moments.

One of those moments packs a million moments into one, as if your entire childhood, all the bad moves and good moves of your life, every blessed part of you, suddenly coalesces into a sphere of incredible promise and

beauty. It's a moment where everything and anything becomes possible, when you know that you can achieve
whatever you want. Bliss bubbled in my blood even while
I shook my head at my own blindness: it was all in the
wanting.

I grabbed the phone again and dialed my father's home
number in Boston.

"Hi, Dad," I said.

I don't call my father often, or really ever.

His voice was puzzled, but warm. "Ally, how are you,
sweetie?"

I didn't seem to mind the *sweetie*, though it had driven
me nuts for twenty years. "I'm great—listen, I'm calling on
the spur of the moment, but you know Aleksi Kullio
began his first season last week?"

"I read the *New York Times*'s review on Sunday."

"The opening night was terrific—"

He interrupted, "You were there and you didn't call to
report?"

"Sorry, it's been busy."

I told him about the smells in the library and that I'd
volunteered to clean up the orchestra's archives. "Mom
gave me two tickets for this Friday's concert. They're
doing that Bruch symphony you love, so I was wondering
if you might want to come down and go with me." My enthusiasm had started to give out, like a balloon losing
buoyancy. "Maybe you're working, though."

In truth, I felt more positively about my father than my
mother, but that simply transformed antagonistic feelings
into lukewarm ones. You could not dislike Joseph Sheffield.
Mildness pervaded his identity, from his slight, nondescript body, to his graying brown hair, quiet eyes, and

gentle voice, and even his love for music. One assumed that as a professional musician, he loved music, but he never expressed that love. What he exhibited was more like affection, and I'd always wanted to see enormous excitement or joy.

"I'd love to watch Kullio tackle that monster of an orchestra," he finally said.

"Do you want me to call for a reservation at the Latham?"

"I'll take care of it."

We made arrangements to meet for dinner, and triumphant, I slammed down the phone. You may well ask what I was feeling triumphant about. Don't ask me. I'm notoriously unreliable.

10

For questions about librarians featured in erotic literature,
you will find absolutely nothing
in the public library.

"You'd look good in this." Ed held up a blouse the color of germs.

We were at Vintage Clothing Company on South Fourth Street, where Ed figured we could find an interesting pair of pants and a shirt for Gordon's birthday. Frankly, I found it hard to believe that I was actually shopping with a homeless man named Ed, even if he did have a Ph.D. from Harvard. Normally, as you know, I don't shop, much less with a man, ditto with a man named Ed for another man named Gordon.

"Uh-huh," I said. I resolutely thumbed through the racks of shirts. I hadn't a clue what kind of shirt to get Gordon. When I tried to define his style of clothing, I went cold all over. "Concentrate on pants for Gordon," I ordered Ed.

"Okay, but you could dress better than you do," he muttered.

Yeah, you, too, Mr. Ed. I yanked a shirt away from its

mates and stared at the brown windowpane design on thick yellow cotton. Phew. Ugly. I checked the price tag. Cheapo. I desperately wanted to buy this shirt for Gordon.

"No way," Ed said, appearing next to me again. "It's got to be silk."

"Are you crazy?"

He grinned, suddenly boyish. "Maybe."

Embarrassed, I shoved the shirt back.

"I want to get him these black pants," Ed said, holding them up for my inspection.

They were nubby and handsome, with some kind of inexplicable way of hanging, almost as if they came ready-made with real legs inside.

"Only silk goes with these," Ed added, now understanding that he was dealing with a fashion fool.

I sighed. "How come you're so knowledgeable about clothes?"

"I have a well-developed aesthetic sense," he said casually. "My Ph.D. was in theatre, with a focus on the history of costume design."

I stared at him. "Really?"

He looked down at his own clothes, as if to apologize. "When I get a job and stuff, you'll see."

"Are you searching for employment?"

He shrugged. "I hope to start looking soon—my wife won't let me see our daughter until I get some work."

"Ed, I didn't know you were married and had a child!"

"I meant ex-wife." His face gleamed red.

For a moment, I saw the little boy in him. "I wish I could promise you something at the library, but the Commonwealth of Pennsylvania keeps slashing our budget, and—"

Ed interrupted, "I wasn't suggesting anything."

"When you feel ready to get serious about a job, let me know, okay?"

He nodded, still embarrassed.

The silk shirts, needless to say, cost twice as much as the ugly one I'd picked out. They were also cool. Talk about drape. They practically slunk off the hangers and tangoed around the store.

I could just imagine Aleksi Kullio in this purple one, his right arm raised with the baton in hand. The sleeve would float in the currents of the air, drifting this way and that. I dangled and then danced the shirt, mesmerized by the fabric's motions.

Suddenly Ed grabbed the shirt and held it up against the black pants. "This looks great!"

"I'm not buying Gordon that shirt." I pulled it away from him and returned it to the rack.

Unperturbed, Ed rifled through the rack. He selected a dark gray silk woven with flecks of black and burgundy.

Since the shirt didn't tango, I bought the damn thing. I don't even want to tell you how much it cost.

Out on the street, I turned to Ed. "Listen, I have to run an errand at Liberty Music Hall, so I'll see you back at the library."

"I'll come with you," he said.

I tried the old trick of looking straight into his eyes, but he didn't seem to mind. He just stared back at me until I noticed that he had brown, endlessly deep eyes. I think he started to hypnotize me. My hands grew heavy and twitchy and far away. I clutched the bag with the shirt. "That's not necessary," I whispered.

"But I want to."

"I have to pick something up in the archives and then get it to the maestro's office—I don't think they'll let you in, even with me."

"I'll wait for you outside."

Ed turned and began walking toward Liberty Music Hall.

Since I didn't know what to do, I'm sure you've figured out, I did nothing. Like a meek little lamb, I ran to catch up.

We passed a florist and Ed glanced at the dazzling window full of flowers. "What's your favorite flower?" he asked me.

"I don't have one."

He threw me a look and I had to laugh.

We walked on a few paces. "Aren't you going to ask me?" he said.

I stared down at my feet. I was feeling more and more disembodied from the situation, simply because I could not believe I was *in* this situation. "What's your favorite flower?" I asked. I did not sound particularly interested, I can assure you.

"Pansies."

Okay, so it was a cute answer. "Umm," I said.

"You're like a pansy."

"I am?"

"Your face."

We turned right at Broad Street, neatly ducking around the lunchtime crowd.

"You look like a little pansy—I mean your face does," he said again.

He *must* be mentally ill, I thought. He has a rare disease called pansyitis, which causes him to believe everyone looks like a pansy. I glanced at him. His skin was mottled and colorless. He looked nothing like a pansy. More like a dilapidated daisy caught in a summer storm. It began to occur to me that I might have a wee problem on my hands.

Outside Liberty Music Hall, Ed got comfortable on the steps. He spread out like a hugely obvious grizzly bear sleeping off a night on the town, and I felt guilty for foisting this image onto the front stoop of the Philadelphia Philharmonic's cultivated home.

I rushed to Jeffrey's office, waved to the one person on phone duty during the lunch hour, and dashed out again. The Stokowski-Stravinsky correspondence was right where I'd left it in the archival room. Back upstairs, I returned the key and headed down the hall to the musical director's office. I was fairly confident that Aleksi would be eating at some restaurant like Le Bec-Fin, schmoozing with the Beautiful People who give millions of dollars to symphony orchestras. Part of his job, though I knew he hated every minute of it. Still, I tried to slink in without drawing attention to myself.

I wasn't avoiding him, I promise! It's just that if I was truly pursuing this man, I must look my best. I needed to get the LASIK surgery, have my hair cut, and maybe even wear some makeup. Okay, so I know it was a long shot, given the aforementioned Beautiful People, but this was an intellectual man who—let's not forget!—had a children's librarian for a mother. It was not out of the realm of possibility that he might have a "thing" for librarians. After all, librarians are a major image in pornographic literature (e.g., *The Lusty Librarian*). They're right up there with nurses and nuns and military personnel (see "Librarians in Pornography" at www.riverofdata.com).

His secretary's outer office's lights were on, but no one was around. I grabbed a pen from her desk and wrote quickly on a yellow Post-it.

Maestro Kullio asked to see these right away.
Thanks! Ally

I left the papers smack-dab in the middle of her tidy desk and skedaddled out of there. My heart pounded too hard for such a small skirmish, especially since you couldn't call it a skirmish at all. But it sure *felt* like one.

Ed lolled on his back, face tilted to catch the autumn sun. I paused, considering whether I should escape his company by tiptoeing down at the farthest end of the stairs. Enough was enough. I had to put an end to this. I marched over and nudged him with my shoe.

He woke with a jump, and I jumped away.

"Ed," I ordered, "please stand up. I have something to say to you."

He rose to his full, apologetic height and stared at me. Was that defiance in his eyes?

"I prefer to walk back to the library alone." My loud voice didn't appear to faze him.

"Okay." He turned and trotted down the steps.

I waited for a few minutes, checking the direction he took so that I would not end up following him. Then I walked slowly, enjoying the solitude, until two blocks along when I felt the first stirrings of hunger. I hadn't had anything to eat since seven o'clock in the morning. I bought a pretzel from a street vendor, squeezed too much bright yellow mustard over it, and began to eat with a napkin clutched just below my chin to catch the drips, the bag holding Gordon's shirt crammed under my arm for safekeeping.

Just as I was dabbing at my chin for a final swipe, my eyes roamed the people on the sidewalk and landed on that fellow librarian from Hahnemann Hospital—remember the one I had a date with four years ago? He was sitting on the stoop of a brownstone converted to a violin-making shop and he was actually playing a violin. You might find him a picturesque, appealing sight. I admit that I didn't know he could play the violin, though even watching his bowing from this distance showed poor technique. Strictly an amateur.

Not that I could do any better, but I certainly wouldn't force my poor playing on the innocent public as they tried to have a pleasant midday break. Even so, females gathered round him, smiling and tapping their feet to whatever rhythm they thought he was keeping. I know I sound rather shrewish, and I'm sorry for that because I don't believe in holding a grudge. You may imagine that the failure of that date had to do with me and my ongoing, odd penchant for celibacy. Nope. I'll take the blame for a lot of things, but not that one.

It was an icy Saturday night four years ago this winter. During dinner at Avenue B, we talked easily. We'd both had a martini, and then he also drank a glass of white wine with dinner. I never go beyond one martini and I never drink wine. Boring of me, I know, but drinking too much is a worry. My personal opinion is that my mother drinks more than she should. I don't want to go that way. Anyway, when you eat as little as I do, one martini packs plenty of punch.

Intelligent and patently kind, he was a gentleman. I liked him, which is to say I didn't dislike him. My mood was neutral but edging toward the positive because he was a librarian, this despite my unfortunate experience with that fellow librarian graduate student when I was twenty-two years old. Since then, I'd never been involved with another librarian, and it was slowly becoming a logical idea: why wouldn't a librarian be perfect? His face dimmed and I was only vaguely aware of his mouth moving silently. My fantasy ripened.

He would turn out to be independently wealthy, so after our marriage we would purchase a mansion on Rittenhouse Square where we would daringly transform an entire floor into a library to house our collection. *Architectural Digest* would do their lead story on our home, and the librarian, as archetype, would suddenly grab hold of the country's collective psyche. Soon, there would be an explosion of films and books with the Librarian Character as hero and this, in turn, would build on children's budding love of books, begun when Harry Potter captured their hearts.

I came back to earth and listened to him for awhile. He had many interesting stories to tell, since he worked in a hospital, but I began to notice a tiny flaw. He was a bit dry. I didn't find myself smiling, much less laughing. Nevertheless, I was truly trying to give him a chance, what with my wonderful fantasy and all, so I lectured myself.

You're not exactly a laugh a minute, so maybe he's like you, a little shy and uncertain. Maybe you should cut him a break and get to know him. And just maybe you should make him laugh, instead of expecting him to do all the work.

I gripped my hands in my lap and concentrated, trying to find a place to jump in and be funny. It was hard and a little worrisome that absolutely nothing came to mind.

The bill arrived and we split it, even though he had invited me. I always offer and it seems as if my offer is always accepted. I tried not to be bitter. You see, I was really giving my all. And that was why I invited him up to my apartment. I admit that I couldn't conceive of kissing him, and that he might get quite the opposite idea because of my invitation, but that was the measure of my effort.

He roamed all over my apartment, murmuring appreciatively about one thing after another, fingering the leaves of the orange trees, cupping a tiny green orange in one hand, stroking the pillows of my couch. A creepy-crawly sensation tiptoed up my arms. I know. You're thinking, *Get a life; what's wrong with a nice guy being appreciative of your home?* That's exactly what I lectured to myself.

I set the kettle to heat for tea and put on some music. I have to admit, I'm not above feeling boastful about my dad, and I therefore chose one of his solo performances, hoping for a question about the piece so that I'd be able to mention him. Instead, he asked whether I had any ballroom-dancing music.

I perched on the opposite end of the couch, maniacally sipping the mug of hot tea I didn't want. "I'm not sure."

"May I check?"

I nodded and then started begging the Powers That Be to spare me from what I knew was coming.

"Hey, this works," he exclaimed, holding up the Broadway musical *A Little Night Music*. One of the CDs I'd been meaning to chuck.

Without asking, he abruptly cut off my father's solo and put it on. I watched as he listened, his back to me, while his regrettable butt began to sway. He turned, dancing in place, and held out his arms.

I smiled mightily. "I don't dance."

Apparently deaf, he danced forward. His eyebrows leaped up and down so violently that I suddenly visualized him as a puppet with his various parts controlled by strings tied to God.

"I can't dance," I reiterated.

"Sure you can," he said, swaying.

I tried not to fixate on his hips, but it was hard to control myself. I have to admit that there was something vaguely attractive in his movements. Okay, more than that. I suspect that the back-and-forth motion hypnotized me, and the sensation was so unusual that it persuaded me to open up with the truth.

I whispered, "Actually, it's not that I *know* whether or not I can dance." I glanced at his half-lidded eyes and saw only what I read as compassion. "I've never even tried to dance."

His eyes opened slightly, and he reached to grab my hands.

"I don't know how," I protested even as I let him pull me to my feet.

Without a word, he put my left hand on his right shoulder and curled his fingers around the fingers of my right hand. I recognized the classic dance pose. He was moving slightly and I was terribly conscious of those hips of his, still swaying like a wild animal.

I couldn't move at all.

"Feel the music," he whispered in my ear.

My eyes closed and we started to move together.

"On the count of three, step out with your right foot."

My eyes shot open and I said, "My right foot?!?"

"One," he said.

I tried to remember which was my right foot. I am not being facetious. My inability to quickly determine my left from my right is unusual, but not unheard of. There are some famous people who suffer from this syndrome. When I remember who they are, I'll let you know.

"Two," he said.

His hand seemed to be spouting damp spots, like patches of mold.

"I step forward or backward?" I said.

"Forward," he said, "and three!"

My left foot stepped backward.

The Gulf of Mexico opened between us.

He dropped me, swirled to the left, swept across the room, and jabbed at the stereo's controls. The music stopped.

I started to smile and apologize, until I saw the rage on his face.

"You certainly can't dance," he said.

"I told you—"

He interrupted, "What kind of woman can't dance?"

I found myself folding and crumpling, like a piece of paper that's been wadded up.

He leaned toward me, his chest and chin jabbing. "You know what they say about people who can't dance."

"No," I whispered.

"They're lousy in bed!"

I don't think I answered. I wish I'd had the balls (I use that term advisedly) to find the words that would wither him. Even now, I can't really imagine what to say. I guess I prefer that words nurture, and in the end, I would rather not be the kind of person who knows how to be withering. That's the only bit of solace I have.

I told you I'm always off the beat. No rhythm whatsoever. I wish I knew why.

Four years later and he's playing a violin on the streets of Philadelphia, with hordes of admiring women clustered around him. In those four years, I hadn't seen him because, needless to say, he must have begun using another branch of the Free Library of Philadelphia system.

I turned down a side street to avoid him. So much for fantasies.

11

*For questions about the art of conducting,
go to the 781s (e.g., The Compleat Conductor, The Elements of
Conducting) and the 927s (The Great Conductors).*

"I hold you responsible," Gordon hissed in my ear.

I whirled around, slinging lemonade in a slow arc. We both leaped backward. "I told Yvonne not to do it!"

"You should have forbidden her." His face, white and tremulous, looked like the portrait of an ancestor.

"She likes you," I said in a singsong voice.

Blue eyes rolled.

I wagged my finger. "You really have to develop more responsibility for the effect you have on women. It's just not fair to be so handsome and charming."

"You sound like my mother."

I gave him my back and waded through the dozen library personnel crowded into our conference room.

To my surprise, his voice again whispered in my ear. "*You've* never fallen for me."

I cut a second piece of sour cream chocolate cake,

larger than the first. Yvonne was right about her cake-baking abilities.

When my mouth was full, I turned around and chewed ostentatiously.

"And how come you can eat like a horse and never get fat?" He sounded genuinely aggrieved.

I swallowed and glanced down at his admirably taut belly. "Celibacy keeps me trim."

Blue eyes widened.

Should have kept quiet.

"You don't really mean *celibate*, do you?" Gordon grabbed a plate and cut a thin sliver of cake.

Suddenly I couldn't imagine finishing mine. It looked like a fake cake, something made of plaster as a practical joke, enticing you to try to eat it.

I couldn't let Gordon Albright intimidate me. "It's the secret of life," I intoned.

"Some secret—you just told me."

His cake had disappeared in two bites.

"I told you, but I haven't convinced you. That's the secret part. Until you try it, you don't understand." I dumped my paper plate and the piece of cake into a trash can.

When I looked at him, he had that ancestral appearance again. I could almost see the dried, cracked oil of the painting in his haggard skin, and I momentarily wondered whether Yvonne might be right. Was it possible that he didn't actually sleep with all those women he dated?

Gordon plunged both hands into his pants pockets and with practiced insouciance sauntered over to five female library clerks. Gales of high-pitched, nervous laughter erupted.

Of course he slept with them. Pathetic Yvonne had let her crush dislodge all reason.

The E-mail icon on my computer screen blinked, signaling that I had mail. I hadn't been surprised at not hearing from Aleksi Kullio since dropping off the Stokowski-Stravinsky correspondence the day before, but that didn't mean I was happy about it. Hope sent shivers through my stomach and chest.

"Kuku" beckoned.

Dear Ally,

The papers you discovered have been extraordinary! I have decided to pursue quite a different sensibility, based on Stravinsky's comments to Stokowski, one which I believe is indicative of Stravinsky's original intent. You may be aware that the question of interpretation by a conductor is a hot button these days. I believe that the composer's vision is the primary one, and that the job of a conductor is simply to discover and support that vision. Not everyone agrees, including the majority of the orchestra players and board of this symphony. So, it will be interesting to see what happens when rehearsals begin Saturday afternoon. Perhaps I will be in Philadelphia for only one season . . . !

I am grateful to you, and I was wondering whether you would care to attend the opening night of the Stravinsky performance? You probably know that we're honoring the seventy-fifth anniversary of the Philadelphia Philharmonic's premiere of the piece with a gala black-tie party. I would be pleased if you could attend. My secretary will hold two tickets for you.

Finally, I would appreciate it if you could continue to let me know about some of the more interesting documents you discover in the archives, particularly those that might be valuable. They should be locked in a safe.

I'm off to the lions, otherwise known as musicians. I hope they don't devour me!

Best wishes, Aleksi

I immediately reread the E-mail three times. It was thrilling to be invited as his guest to the gala, but even more exciting and interesting were his comments on the dilemma of conductors interpreting a composer's score. He had confided in me concerning a subject that, to him, was more important than any personal story. I could see that he was scared, and I knew without a doubt that he had confessed his fear only to me. The responsibility felt like the anchor of a ship, pulling me inexorably into the sea's depth. And at the same time, it was a kite on a windy day, yanking me into the blustery skies. I printed out the E-mail and read it again. Then I picked up my pen and drafted a reply by writing the old-fashioned way, on a piece of paper.

Dear Aleksi,

I am very happy that the correspondence has been so important. I do understand the dilemma you face, both in deciding how to interpret Stravinsky's original score and in leading the musicians to a place where they've never been. But that is your job and that is why you've been chosen. You will do what is right, even if it is hard or criticized by those who resent change. I know this because I have seen you conduct.

I will be sure to let you know of other significant scores and correspondence that I discover.

I look forward to the gala and I appreciate your thoughtful gift of two tickets.

I wish for you a clear vision and steadfast arm. Perhaps you should just let the baton do what it will? All the best, Ally

The result was somewhat eccentric, but I was hardly one to argue with eccentricity. I retyped the letter into my computer, as an E-mail, and pressed the SEND button.

I wanted to call Suzanne to get an update on her sleuthing from that morning, and to tell her about hearing from Aleksi, but we were short on staffing as Gordon's party flowed into the afternoon. Instead, I went out and relieved a newly employed clerk so that she could get a piece of cake and, probably, flirt with the birthday boy. She was young enough to be his daughter, but that was about right for Gordon.

During the next two hours, I hurtled from patron to patron, powered by the joy of Aleksi's E-mail. When Gordon's party finally died, and the various clerks returned to duty, I rushed to my office to check whether Aleksi might possibly have answered. I knew it was unlikely, but I'm sure you understand. I'd discovered faith, and like all the newly faithful, I was possessed by it.

An E-mail from "kuku" waited for me.
I almost crowed.

Dear Ally,
You understand.
Aleksi

I could feel my heart hammering inside my chest, quick
bangs of *rat-a-tat-tat*. It was as if he'd reached a hand
through the computer and actually touched me. Even the
way the words were positioned on the screen reminded
me of a poem, not to mention the terseness packed with
untold emotion.

I had hooked him.

The door to my office opened and Gordon's voice interrupted my reverie.

"Ally, have you seen Ed today?"

I looked up from the computer screen, but I know I
didn't really focus on Gordon. "Huh?"

He snapped his fingers a couple of times as he crossed
the office toward my desk. "Wake up, sleeping beauty."

He swam into focus. "I'm sorry, that cake must have—"

"I asked whether you'd seen Ed today," Gordon interrupted.

I thought about the question for a while. "No, I don't
think so."

"It's odd that he gave me a present, but wasn't here for
the party."

I didn't say anything.

"Thanks for the shirt," Gordon said. "It's very handsome."

"You're welcome."

"First time you ever gave me a present."

"Everyone was bringing a present, Gordon. I couldn't exactly stiff you in front of the whole library staff." I grinned.

He wandered into my office and sat down. I don't think he'd ever plunked his butt in one of my chairs before. I was nonplussed. Then I looked at his face and saw the worry hovering there.

"Are you okay?" I said.

He rubbed a hand over his cheek. "I'm not crazy about my birthday—it's stupid of me."

"A lot of people have trouble as they get—" I stopped talking when I realized that I'd neatly put myself into a corner.

"Older." He grimaced.

"It's a fact of life," I said.

Gordon stared at me. "*That's* the best you can do?"

I spread my hands wide. "Hey, I'm just not invested in aging—I don't mind getting older."

"I don't want to be around when you hit menopause."

"Are you kidding? I can't wait!"

He dropped his head into his hands, shaking it back and forth dolefully.

"You try bleeding from you-know-where every month," I said.

He stood up and headed for the door. Over his shoulder, he called, "I'll pass!"

"Happy birthday, Gordie," I said.

He waved one hand and didn't quite slam the door behind him.

Oops. Maybe I'd gone too far.

I gave him a few minutes and then went out to the

612.6s in the reference section for a quick peek on the subject of male menopause.

When I was ready to leave for the day, I wandered past his office. His lights were off. At the front desk, I stopped to congratulate Yvonne on the great party and her cake.

"Looks like we must have worn out Gordon," I added, "since he's already gone home."

"I feel kind of bad," Yvonne said. "I don't think he liked the party after all. I know you warned me."

"Actually, I was going to say that you'd been right—I thought Gordon had a terrific time."

"He stormed out of here at four o'clock without a word to any of us."

"Maybe something happened at home—I'm really positive that he loved his party."

Yvonne's face brightened.

As I left the library, a cold wind blasted me. I hadn't been outside since arriving that morning, when the skies were clear and the air was dusky with warmth. I huddled into myself, already cold before I'd got to the end of the block, and I started walking quickly. I was caught up in my thoughts about Aleksi, wondering whether it was okay that I hadn't answered his last E-mail. I certainly wanted to answer it, but I felt funny about doing so since it really hadn't demanded a reply.

I turned down my block and stopped walking. During the day, the leaves had suddenly, or so it seemed to me, changed from dark green to red, and the wind rippled them like a deck of cards. I started to skip down the sidewalk, a real skip like girls do when they're six years old and feeling frisky. Undoubtedly a resident in one of the other buildings on the street was watching me with growing alarm. Had that celibate spinster librarian finally gone cuckoo?

The cuckoo is a male bird who makes a strange, singular cry during mating season. The cry is repeated, over and over, in such an endless fashion that the term *cuckoo* developed in America to mean crazy. So, yes, imagine that I have gone cuckoo as you peer and peek from your windows! The male and female gender boundaries, once so sacred, have slipped. I am the cuckoo, the male bird, crying for my mate. My body flew into the air, front leg cocked and knee lifted. Then down, a quick step, and I was climbing into the sky again, with the opposite leg performing its geometric design, rather like an upside-down four, missing the crosspiece.

My cuckoo's cry soared up and up and up, over and over and over, so that I understood the reason why the cuckoo repeated his call often enough to demand ridicule. It just felt so damn good.

12

For questions about the father-daughter relationship,
go to the 306s (e.g., The Father-Daughter Dance:
Insight, Inspiration, and Understanding for Every Woman and
Her Father; Women and Their Fathers: The Sexual and
Romantic Impact of the First Man in Your Life).

$\mathcal{S}$ince I'm notoriously early for all appointments, I was already seated at the City Tavern on Friday night when I saw my father walk by on the sidewalk and then turn in at the entrance. But here's the thing: I had to look twice before I was sure that the man I thought I recognized as my father was, indeed, Joseph Sheffield.

His gentle, nondescript demeanor had always given him a ghostly presence, almost as if you could see right through him. Yet this man cast a real shadow. This man loomed. This man had wide shoulders, the kind you could imagine crying on. While he waited for the maître d', I examined him, even though I should have been waving him over to the table.

The blue suit had to be new. A starched white collar and knotted rose-colored silk bow tie gave him the appearance of a naughty elf. I leaned forward, not quite believing my own eyes, and stared. Then I sat up a little straighter and wished I'd had the LASIK surgery, though at least I'd worn the fall suit that I knew was becoming on me.

He followed the maître d' across the room and I stood up. His warm kiss on my cheek lingered and I felt him press his lips deeply into my skin for a second longer than usual.

"Dad, you look terrific," I said.

"So do you, sweetie."

We sat down and fiddled with silverware and napkins.

The transformation in him was so obvious that there was no pretending. "Really, there's something different about you." I smiled. "You're handsome!"

"I've been incubating handsomeness," he said.

"I like that concept."

"Just like you're incubating beauty."

I looked across the dining room, my gaze unfocused and shy. I felt him lean toward me.

"You really are," he whispered.

Something tugged in me and I ached to tell him that I'd fallen in love with Aleksi Kullio, and that even though he was married, I was somehow, inexplicably, convinced that I would win the Prince.

"I do have some big news," he said, "but let's get drinks first." He signaled the waiter and placed precise orders for two perfect martinis.

I grinned. "I knew there was some reason I liked you."

We chatted aimlessly until our martinis were placed in front of us.

Dad held his up in the air and then moved it toward mine. "A toast," he said.

Suddenly I felt afraid. Although I wasn't intimately close to my father, he'd always been a grounding of unalterable personhood. That's a mouthful. I mean, probably, that as my father, he could be depended on for two things: he was a man and he never changed. Since I didn't exactly have a clutch of men in my life, he was obscurely—if distantly—important. I suspected something was up.

I was right.

"I'd like to make a toast to the new woman in my life," my father began.

For a moment, I actually thought he was referring to me and my "incubating beauty." Hah.

"Her name is Wendy and we are to be married in two months." He clinked his glass against mine, and icy cold martini sloshed over my hand.

Which was trembling.

I smiled, of that I'm sure. I took a gargantuan gulp of my drink, placed it on the table, and neatly dried off the wet hand with the cloth napkin hidden in my lap.

"That's wonderful," I lied. "Tell me everything!"

His gray eyes gleamed and I noticed that his white hair shone with light. "Wendy Silverstein joined the orchestra over the summer—"

I interrupted, "What instrument?"

"Percussion!"

"Jeepers—a female in percussion."

"Isn't it *great?*" He grinned idiotically and took another halfhearted sip of his martini.

I hated it when people didn't give their full attention to the glory of an excellent martini. It struck me as down-right sacrilegious. Defiant, I gulped at mine.

"She's thirty-two years old, Jewish, stunningly beautiful, brilliant, and—" He stopped talking and I watched, horrified, as he swallowed several times to keep the tears from spilling into sobs of joy.

So, the gist of the story was that my father was engaged to marry a woman eight years younger than his unmarried daughter. I admit that this should not have bothered me. I had urged my father to remarry many, many times over the years, but only because I was convinced that he wouldn't. Actually, now that I think about it, I was pretty obnoxious on the subject. He never urged me to marry, much less remarry, and if he had I would have been furious.

I cast my eyes to the tablecloth, as if to give him time to control himself. Or come to his senses.

"Doesn't she want to have a family?"

"Of course!"

"You're going to be a father again?"

"You betcha! I got cheated out of being near you all those years—I can't wait to have children."

My father was sixty-three years old. I picked up my martini and began figuring in my head. He would be about eighty-two years old when his child graduated from high school. I debated telling him: *First time around, you were cheated. Second time around, the kid is cheated.*

"Is there going to be an actual wedding?" *Please, please, let him say no.*

"She's got an enormous family and her heart's set on the whole shebang. I did try to talk her out of it—you never remember anything about your own wedding and it seems like a colossal waste of money—but she's determined." He sipped at the martini, shaking his head. "Plus, I have to convert to Judaism, which is no joke. The Jews are not proselytizers, as you may know, and it's not like you can just go through a simple ceremony like a baptism."

I swallowed, trying to find my voice. "What do you have to do?"

"Attend classes, learn to read Hebrew—I started last month—all that kind of thing. Thank goodness I was circumcised when I was a baby."

Having recently been somewhat enamored by visions of penises, I felt threatened by this comment. In fact, it seemed as if my father had lost his mind. Since when do I want to hear whether or not his penis has been circumcised?

"Wendy can't wait to meet you," my father said. "We thought about having her come tonight, but she figured it would be better for me to tell you first."

"Where will the wedding be?"

"Boston, at the Four Seasons." He blushed.

"Ooh-la-la!"

He shook his head lazily, apparently stunned by the enormity of events.

By the time we left the restaurant and headed for the hall, just two blocks away, I'd managed to pull myself together a bit. The martini, a delicious osso buco, and sublime chocolate mousse provided significant assistance. The clear night tasted of winter, and I huddled into my black velvet cape.

"You look like you stepped out of a fairy tale," my father said.

I smiled.

"I remember how you loved fairy tales when you were little—I had to read them to you constantly, and then when you could read to yourself, you devoured them, from all different countries."

I was touched and about to say something when he continued.

"Maybe you can read fairy tales to our child—with your background in children's literature, you'll be a wonderful sister."

I'd always dreamed of having a sister. But those dreams were long ago.

My father tipped his head backward, looking at the arching ceiling far overhead. "I've read the major articles assessing the acoustics of this place—I'm curious to hear for myself."

"I think Maestro Kullio is great, so if you don't agree, spare me your opinion."

He gave me a sidelong glance. "I want to go backstage to say hello after the performance."

My stomach stood on its head, its legs kicking wildly. "You *know* Aleksi Kullio?"

"Sure—he guest-conducted at the BSO many times, but I also worked with him quite intensely, one-on-one, when I was playing in Chicago a couple of summers back."

My mind vaulted into outer space. *Should I tell him?*

Then I saw the first violinist walk onstage and begin to tune the orchestra. I settled back, thinking furiously. When Aleksi began to conduct, I watched him as if from a great height, looking directly down at the top of his blond head. I felt a deepened love and sense of connection to him. My father knew him! This was yet another sign, like the fact that his mother was a children's librarian, a sign that we were somehow coordinated. I admit that I barely listened to the music.

As soon as the lights came up during the intermission, I turned my head to look at Dad.

He caught my eye and laughed. "Pretty good," he said.

"I thought so." I laughed back. "Isn't he gorgeous?"

"I don't usually comment on whether men are *gorgeous* or not, but I will admit that I'm glad Wendy didn't come tonight." He stretched his arms out straight and worked the muscles in his hands.

"Were you playing?" I asked.

Sheepish, he nodded. "A little."

After a terrific second half, during which I concentrated on the music, we paraded backstage with dozens of others. "I'm not sure we're going to get anywhere near him," I whispered.

"We'll manage," Dad said, serene.

This Wendy woman certainly had upped his confidence quotient. Quietly, I let my left hand drift to my face. I took off my glasses and tucked them into the pocket of my cape, which I'd draped nonchalantly over my shoulders. I wished I could go to the ladies' room and let down my hair.

I thought Maestro Kullio, surrounded by obsequious admirers, would be tired, and I was sorry that he had to deal with the social obligations of his position on top of everything else. Wasn't it enough that he'd conducted a masterful evening of music?

He and Dad shook hands violently, as if Kullio was grateful for the excuse to ignore the nonmusical public.

"Aleksi, this is my daughter, Alison Sheffield," my father said.

I held out my hand, strangely bold. "Yes, we met down in the archival room last week."

Aleksi's bright blue eyes shot open. Suddenly the fatigue and social boredom disappeared. "My librarian!"

I grinned and nodded.

Aleksi reached out with his right arm and encircled my waist while he gazed at my father. "Did she tell you about the discovery she made?"

Smiling, Dad shook his head.

"A letter between Stravinsky and Stokowski debating questions about the *Rite of Spring*," Aleksi said.

"That premiered in Philly, right?"

"We're actually celebrating that premiere in a gala concert."

Dad smiled at me. "Wonderful."

"How's the new conductor?" Aleksi tried to hide a smirk.

His arm was still around my waist. I was frozen, scarcely breathing.

My father sighed dramatically. "I fear we are not in sync."

Aleksi nodded knowingly.

"Unlike you and this orchestra."

"Thank you," Aleksi said.

He finally let his arm drop from my waist, though I fancied he was reluctant. It was clearly appropriate for him to talk to others now.

Aleksi looked at me. "I would love a tour of the library, as you offered."

"Just name a time." My voice came out hoarse, probably because I was oxygen deprived.

He winked. "I'll drop you an E-mail."

When we had pushed our way back to the edges of the crowd and then down the long corridor leading outdoors, it was my father's turn to drape his arm around my shoulders. Very uncharacteristic.

Outside, I fastened the top button of my cape. Dad squeezed my shoulders, as if to warm me. But, really, it was as if to *warn* me.

"Remember, he's very married."

"I know, Dad," I said.

"Do you."

It was not a question.

After my father walked me back to my apartment, our good-byes were quick. He would take the train home to Boston early the next morning. I made sure to offer my congratulations and I even said that I was anxious to meet Wendy.

I trudged up the three flights, trying to understand why I felt both exhilarated and depressed. My apartment smelled old and musty. Despite the cold night, I threw open two windows on opposite walls so that a fresh current of air would be pulled inside. Then I collapsed on my couch, the black velvet cape still around me.

I tried to accept that my mousy father had turned into a lion. I would have to attend the wedding in two months. I would have to smile and pretend to be thrilled, even though I could hear the whispers about me. *Never been married, a real bookworm, looks like a virgin, poor thing, bet she's mortified. Can't someone tell her to cut that hair?* I fought those whispers, not with tears but with my imagination. My eyes were to be fixed next Friday, and I decided that I would come to my father's wedding dressed as if I were a princess stepping out of the pages of a fairy tale. I would silence the whispers.

Resolved on that, I rose from the couch and began to get ready for bed. I decided that the interaction with Aleksi had been so delicious that it deserved my favorite nightgown. You know what I mean. The flannel nightgown that you've had for fifteen years. It is cozy and gentle against your skin, and it smells like the you of yesterday, today, and tomorrow. Usually the lace is half hanging off and several buttons are missing. I only wear this nightgown on special occasions because it's obvious that one day it will simply fall off my body when the threads give way. Then this nightgown will be gone forever, and no other nightgown can possibly match its aristocratic character.

In bed, I wrapped the flannel around my feet and sighed with pleasure. I closed my eyes and in the liquid darkness I relived every moment with Aleksi. I felt the pressure of his hand on my waist and I heard him exclaiming, *My librarian!*

Never had my existence as a librarian seemed so utterly magnificent.

13

*For questions about eyesight,
go to the 612s and 617s (e.g., The Crystal Clear Guide to
Sight for Life, Your Eyes, 20/20 Is Not Enough:
The New World of Vision).*

I turned over in bed, my eyes screwed so tightly shut that I didn't allow the daylight to even seep beneath the lids. Had the LASIK operation been a success? Would I really be able to open my eyes and see clearly? I clawed at the blankets and brought my hands up to cover my eyes. I allowed the lids to open a mere slit. Light. My fingers splayed and more light shone through. Tears filled my eyes and I blinked to clear them.

I allowed my hands to slink to either side of my face, limp but ready for action. The lids opened without my conscious command and I was momentarily stunned by their aggression. They forced me to test the hypothesis. No more messing around.

I looked toward the windows first. I saw the leaves of the orange trees and the tiny, unripe oranges dangling from branches. The brass curtain rods and rings gleamed suggestively. Dark green velvet covered one window, dull and dusky, but large swaths of morning sun sneaked through cracks. I sat straight up in bed, scrambling to pound pillows into place behind my back, and felt as if I could voraciously swallow the room whole.

I threw off the covers, ran over to the stereo system on tiptoe, and put on a CD of The Chieftains playing rollicking Irish tunes. Then I jumped awkwardly all over, flinging myself around in a way not at all appropriate to a forty-year-old librarian. My new eyes danced with me.

In a paroxysm of ecstasy, I grabbed the cordless phone by the couch, leaped onto the couch, and punched in Suzanne's number.

"It worked!" I shrieked when she answered.

"That's wonderful," she said. "Do you feel any pain?"

"Nope, nada, nada, nada."

I'd already heard that Suzanne hadn't been able to wrest herself away from the bosom of her family to follow Michelle Kullio, and I'd forwarded to her all the E-mails between Aleksi and myself. We were caught up, so it was time for new business.

"Should I cut my hair?" I asked.

"I can't believe you would actually contemplate cutting your hair," she said. "I don't think you've cut it for twenty years or something."

"I had a drastic trim fifteen years ago." I growled. "Those hair people are like Nazis—they just do whatever they want, no matter what you say. I gave express orders to cut only—"

"I've heard this many times," Suzanne interrupted.

"It was very traumatic."

"Uh-huh."

I tucked the phone into my shoulder, freeing up my

hands, and began to measure coffee into the French press. "So maybe I've gotten over it—should I get it cut?"

"How much are we talking about? A whole new hairdo?"

"Just a sec." I filled the kettle with water and put it on to boil. "I was thinking about something still long, but with layers. And maybe even bangs?"

"Don't you dare do bangs!"

"I've been doing an informal study from magazines in the periodicals room and I noticed that models all have bangs."

"That's because they don't have to worry about frizz— some hairdresser blows it out straight and gorgeous."

"My hair doesn't frizz."

"*Everyone's* hair frizzes in bangs."

"That's pure speculation. I could check in the 390s and—"

Her voice became shrill as she interrupted. "If you cut bangs, you will curl up and die."

"Curl up!" I said. "Get it? Curl up, like frizz up?"

I poured boiling water into the French press, stirred three times, then replaced the top to wait the requisite five minutes.

"You should cut your hair a little bit, but no bangs, and nothing drastic."

"Yes, Your Highness."

"You asked me." She was defensive because of her propensity for bossiness.

"I have to do my volunteer hours at the Philharmonic this morning, then I'll get my hair cut, and *then* I'll stake out the Rodin and see if I get lucky with Michelle."

"I'm sorry I haven't been any help . . ." Her voice trailed off.

"You sound depressed." I pushed the plunger through the hot water until the grounds were tightly compressed at the bottom. Then I carefully poured a steaming stream of coffee into my Bryn Mawr mug. It made me crazy with pleasure when I contemplated the perfection of my coffee.

"Being a mother is tough," she said.

"Maybe I could help."

"No one can help, not even John." She sighed. "He tries, but the bottom line is that I'm at home and he's got responsibilities at Haverford."

"Why not at least consider the possibility of returning to work part-time?"

"I'd feel too guilty."

"Then you have to find something to do at home, something that will make use of your mind and make you feel productive." I spoke forcefully because I knew that if she didn't follow my advice, she was going to spiral deeper and deeper into depression.

"Ally, I appreciate that you're trying to help," she said, "but this has always been a problem for women—I don't think I'll be able to solve it."

"Why don't you research how women who are success-ful while staying home with their kids manage it? I bet a study exploring all the different ways mothers have cre-ated for coping would result in some obvious methods. You know, 'How to Find Fulfillment in Family Life,' or 'Managing a Modern Motherhood.' I can tell you this much—I haven't seen anything published on the subject."

"You really think there *is* an answer?"

"I do, yeah." I kept my voice peppy. "I don't have a clue what it is, but I bet there are ways, and it would really be interesting to research what women have done—you could probably even use the Seven Sisters alumnae for gathering data."

A moment of silence ticked by. I sipped my coffee and smiled.

"This may be an inspired idea," she said.

"Librarians are excellent at developing inspired ideas," I said.

"Don't push it."

I sipped more coffee during another companionable moment of silence. The true test of friendship is about silence—can silence fit between the two of you?

"You're going to need an appointment for your hair if you go to a halfway decent place," Suzanne said.

"I've got pull. Remember my mother's best friend, Jerome, the ICU nurse? One of his ex-lovers is a top stylist at Hades. Jerome's been after me to cut my hair for years—he'll get me in."

"Should I grow my hair?" Suzanne said.

She wore her hair cropped close to the head, an easy if not particularly attractive style. "It'll take you years," I warned.

"Maybe that's what I need, a long view and a long goal."

"Remember your long hair in college? It really suited you—I never did understand why you cut it all off right before your wedding."

"I was overwhelmed by the whole veil and hairdo concept. With no hair, I couldn't possibly wear a veil."

I wandered over to the windows and began yanking back all the velvet curtains.

"Is this one of the most boring conversations we've ever had?" Suzanne asked.

"Right up there in the top five."

"Anyway, I have to pee."

"I'll call you after my hair gets cut."

Jerome got me an appointment for two o'clock at Hades thanks to a lucky cancellation. Quickly I yanked on blue jeans, a dark blue turtleneck, and a gray sweatshirt. I arrived at Liberty Hall by ten o'clock.

When I walked into the volunteers' office, Jeffrey whirled around, stuck his fingers in his mouth, and erupted with a shrieking whistle.

My hands jumped to cover my ears, and I pulled a face.

"It's the lady who's brought our office fame and acclaim," he said.

Now Genevieve, one of the secretaries, inserted two fingers into *her* mouth and gave another loud whistle.

"What is wrong with you guys?" I asked. Actually, I was annoyed that they weren't commenting on how great I looked without thick glasses.

"Maestro Kullio stopped by about an hour ago," Jeffrey said.

I started to flush with anticipation, though of what I didn't know.

"Seems you've put us on the map by the discovery of that correspondence in the archives. He was raving."

"Oh, that."

Jeffrey undulated across the office. It occurred to me that if anyone could teach me to dance, it might be Jeffrey. "You look different." His nostrils flared and he sniffed extravagantly.

"I smell fine!"

I'm not going to tell you when I last had a bath. I don't want to discuss it. Suffice it to say that I *knew* I'd be getting filthy dirty when I continued sorting through the archival papers.

He placed a finger on his lower lip and pouted. "Where are the glasses?"

I grinned. "You noticed."

He dipped his head sideways, waiting. I was rapidly beginning to like Jeffrey.

"I had that LASIK surgery done yesterday."

"Oh, my God." He peered into my eyes. "Are you sure you should be out and about?"

"They said if I felt like it, there's no problem."

Genevieve hopped up and came around her desk. "Can you see?"

"Yeah—it's great."

"You look really different," she said.

I tried not to show my disappointment with this hesitant comment.

Jeffrey clucked. "It's an amazing change."

"Thanks."

His large, gangly hand reached out and touched the top of my head. "Now, the hair—"

I interrupted, "I have an appointment at Hades this afternoon."

"With whom?"

"Bertram." I couldn't hold back the smirk.

His eyes blinked. "Bertie?"

"You know him?"

Jeffrey shifted from one hip to another. "Yes," he said primly.

I laughed.

"Bertie will do a good job, no question," he said. "Tell him I said hello."

"Okay." I took off my corduroy jacket, hung it on the coatrack, and then went to pick up the key to the storage room.

Since I felt more comfortable with everyone, I helped myself to a mug of coffee, which I carried down to the archival room. For a moment, I surveyed the wreckage and sipped at the surprisingly good coffee. The week before, I'd sorted through all of the lower shelves, reaching to the back walls of the room. I figured I'd need a stepladder to get higher, but in the end I was able to stand on top of two full boxes. I started at the very highest shelf, laboriously carrying papers down and stacking them on the floor. After half an hour of this ascent and descent, ascent and descent, the load of papers and scores covered every surface below me, looking like the view of farmland from on top of a mountain. I shifted things around to clear a space and settled in, cross-legged.

The odor of the antique documents seemed downright venerable. A feeling of gratitude stole over me. Very simply, it was gratitude at being able to touch the papers, to smell and explore and engage with them. Like books, old or new, they were precious. They held writings and music both. I lifted a single page from a score of Beethoven's, a piece called "Wellington's Victory." Of course this wasn't original to Beethoven's time, but it was dated 1939. I covered my face with the paper and breathed in deeply. If I weren't a fairly confirmed atheist, I might have described its essence as Godlike.

I continued sorting, and I have to admit that I didn't hurry. Somehow I'd unconsciously decided to enjoy myself. Twenty minutes later, when I picked up a Copland score called *Connotations for Orchestra,* I glanced at it somewhat idly because there was no interesting handwritten marginalia. Then I saw the date, 1962, and I started to get a funny feeling in my gut. I'm not sure how or why we know things at certain times. It's quite inexplicable, but I suddenly remembered the existence of the Aaron Copland Collection at the Library of Congress. I opened the score to the second page and then held it up to the light, looking for paper marks and how notes had been printed onto the paper. I immediately felt sure that this was an original document and, possibly, quite valuable.

I cleared a space on a lower shelf and carefully placed it there, with a clean sheet of white paper on top. I thought of leaving Aleksi a note telling him about it, but I decided I wanted the opportunity to send him a private E-mail on Monday morning.

I quit at twelve o'clock because something told me that I should take a bath and make an attempt to look better when I went to my hair appointment. I felt odd taking a bath in the middle of the day, especially since I was eating a peanut butter and jelly sandwich at the same time. I so love soaking in the tub that I figured I could combine soaking with eating lunch. Worked out well, except the sandwich tasted a little damp and gluey. It was probably the close proximity to all that hot, steamy water.

Then, the dilemma: what to wear? I wasn't immune to how fancy women dress when they go to the beauty parlor downtown, but I didn't own anything that could compete, even if I'd wanted to. And I didn't want to. The other

way to go was skintight and sexy. Needless to say, I didn't
have skintight and sexy. I pulled out drawers from the ancient bureau listing in the corner. Beneath the corduroy
pants with elastic waistbands (they're *comfortable*), I dug
out blue jeans I'd never worn. When I held them up, they
seemed very small. I pulled on underpants and then the
jeans.

Phew. I zipped them up, but I couldn't move for five
minutes. After some deep knee bending and then leaning
over from the waist, which nearly sliced me in two, I was
able to strut, stiff-legged, to the full-length mirror that
hung on the back of the door into my apartment. I turned
sideways and assessed.

I looked *rawther* sleek.

I fastened my Sears bra and then rummaged around
some more until I discovered a boy's white undershirt. A
couple of years back, I started avoiding bras whenever I
could. I liked the way soft cotton undershirts felt against
my skin, and they also allowed me to skip antiperspirant.
This particular undershirt had shrunk. I pulled it over my
head, tucked it in, and made another sortie to the mirror.
Not bad. Or, anyway, good enough. I was getting so fed
up that I was about to chuck the whole idea of a haircut;
and I knew Jerome would never forgive me.

At three o'clock, I exited the beauty parlor and blinked
at the afternoon light. My hair. How to explain it?

My hair bounced. It just bounced. That sums it up. I'm
not going to waste any more time on the issue, even
though I now have to admit that hair, whether bouncing
or leaping or jabbing, sighing or screaming or singing, is

an important subject. But someone else can write about it. You have as much as you need.

It bounced.

Next stop: a department store makeup counter. I explained that I did not wish to have my face made up, I did not care about "day" lipsticks and "evening" lipsticks, and I definitely didn't want to try the newest bronzer on my face. I pointed to my eyes. I said that I'd just had LASIK surgery the day before and that after thirty years of wearing very thick glasses, I had pronounced circles under my eyes. According to my ophthalmologist, this was due to the absence of peripheral vision for so long. The muscles under my eyes had atrophied. I bought an expensive cream and practically ran out of the store.

Then I stopped at a drugstore to buy my first pair of normal sunglasses. It was a blustery autumn day, with clouds blocking the sun one minute and sailing off again the next. My tender eyes needed some protection.

I stationed myself in front of the Rodin and watched the doorman's activities for as long as it was humanly feasible to find him interesting. He definitely didn't warrant so much attention. Some doormen do—they hop around like busybody sparrows, chirping and peeping, with body movements and gestures as complex as a ballet. This guy was sleep inducing. So, sure enough, I fell asleep.

When I woke up, my neck ached from the ungodly angle I'd kept it in, and I was chilly. I stood and stretched with an arm-popping exuberance, which caused my eyes to momentarily close. Open, they rested on Michelle Kullio standing right in front of me. This was not by accident. She stared at me with a belligerent expression. I pushed up my sunglasses, buying time, hoping against hope that she thought I was someone else, someone she knew and/or had business with.

"Why are you following me?" she said.

"*¿Perdón?*" I asked in my best Spanish accent. I guess I thought I might fool her.

A torrent of fluid Spanish poured over me. I couldn't understand a word. Well, that's an exaggeration. I understood one out of ten words, which amounted to not being able to figure out even the most general meaning.

I made my voice calm. "I am not following you. I stopped my shopping to sit for a while in the park." I held up my bag from Strawbridge's as proof. "And I fell asleep. I just had my eyes done yesterday, you know that LASIK surgery everyone's talking about?"

"You look different, but you're that librarian."

That librarian. Sums it up. Once a librarian, always a librarian. I could pay thousands of dollars to get my vision fixed, have my hair cut, wear a thong and halter top on the streets of Philadelphia, and I'd still be *that librarian*.

"I'm Alison Sheffield, the director of the research division at the Free Library of Philadelphia." I snapped my fingers. "Aren't you the woman working on a mystery?"

The corners of her mouth, which had been turning down in a dramatic fashion, almost as if they were pulled by some cosmic force, twitched and then angled upward. Personally, I didn't like her smile any more than her frown, but I could see this was a good sign.

"Yes, I am working on a mystery."

I gave her a pitying look. "I can assure you that I'm not following you."

"Actually, you are. You're haphazard about it, and profoundly amateurish, but you certainly are following me."

She stood tall, both hands hanging easily to her sides. Her blond hair was pinned up on the back of her head so that her face, contrasting with a black turtleneck and black leather jacket, pounced like a wild puma or lion across the air between us.

I decided to keep silent.

She shrugged. "You also followed me the week before, so how do you explain that?"

"I'm very sorry, but you must be mistaken." I turned and walked away. I tried to exude an aura of mastery and control, but I probably wobbled a bit. You can imagine how unsettled I was. She knew I was following her, she'd confronted me, and I had lied to cover for myself. I hated the whole thing and I desperately needed to talk to Suzanne.

When I got back to my apartment, I tried to call her for over an hour, but I kept getting a busy signal. I knew why. As usual, she'd gone hell-bent over this idea for a study about motherhood, and she was surfing the 'net. Since they only had one telephone line, I couldn't get through. If I'd had a computer at home, I probably would have had better luck with an E-mail. I left her a message that at precisely five o'clock, I was going to take a nap, so not to call and wake me, but to please keep her line open because I had to talk to her immediately. I let my voice crescendo on the last word, *immediately.*

I threw off my jeans and sweatshirt and dived under the covers. I was asleep *immediately.*

14

*For questions about body language, go to the 153.6s
(e.g., Manwatching: A Field Guide to Human Behavior,
How to Read a Person like a Book).*

$\mathcal{I}$ admit that I was already growing quite fond of my postglasses face. And my bouncy hair. These were worthy changes. I got a particular kick out of thinking about the next time I saw my mother, who had no idea about any of this. She might keel over. Or go cuckoo.

Still, there were obstacles on the road ahead. I was flummoxed by Michelle Kullio. After spending too many hours analyzing our interaction, both with Suzanne and by myself, the only conclusion I kept returning to was that she was involved in an ornate plan to murder her husband. She was, therefore, exquisitely sensitive to people's movements around her. She noticed I was following her because that was just the sort of thing you *would* notice when you were planning to murder someone, and she was coming on strong to warn me off. But why the library research and the conflicting stories about her mystery writing? First she told me that she had finished the book and needed help on how to submit the novel to publishers, and then she asked Yvonne for advice with the plot.

I could only assume that the story of her writing a mystery novel was just that, a story. Her plot killed off the conductor of a major orchestra, and in trying to figure out how to murder her own husband, she needed a cover for doing research. Obviously, to come up with a plot like this, even if she wasn't going to murder him, Michelle Kullio must have had bad feelings for her husband.

Late on Sunday night, I moved beyond conjecture and the what-ifs with which Suzanne and I had been amusing ourselves, and I began to have strong intuitive hunches that this could actually be true. I know the idea seems ludicrous, and I was cautious about letting my imagination conjure up drama simply because I found it satisfying. Yet I thought it reasonable to wonder, given the information we had uncovered. No sooner had I approached this final and conscious acceptance of the idea than I began to fear for Aleksi.

I got to work early on Monday morning, despite another autumn downpour that made you want only to stay in bed forever (and I mean forever), to write my E-mail to Aleksi.

Dear Maestro Kullio,
It was a pleasure to see you with my father at the marvelous concert last week. I wanted to let you know that I did make an interesting discovery in the archive room on Saturday morning, a score by Aaron Copland that looked original to my admittedly untrained eye. (I spent several hours in the Copland Collection of the Library of Congress several years

ago.) I left it in a corner of the room, covered by a piece of plain white paper.

Again, I'd love to take you on a tour of the library whenever your schedule permits.

Best wishes, Ally

Reluctant, I reached for the telephone. Early in the morning, before her workload got too heavy, was a good time to call my mother, and I'd put off telling her about Dad. I wasn't sure why, exactly, but I must have sensed that his engagement to a thirty-two-year-old would create massively destructive vibes. I cringed as I prepared to speak to her.

Her scream sounded as if someone had murdered her ego.

"Mom, come on, it's not that bad."

I knew how she felt, of course, but I'd managed to control myself. That was the story of our life together. I controlled myself, and she didn't.

While she carried on with phrases like *robbing the cradle, disgusting, should be ashamed, erection problems, hair loss, skin like cheesecloth,* I checked my E-mail and made grunting noises to show my solidarity.

"Kuku" beckoned!

Dear Ally,

How terrific to discover that you were the daughter of Joseph Sheffield—thanks for bringing him to the concert. Now he'll say good things to the other BSO musicians . . . !

The first rehearsal for *Rite of Spring* was grueling, particularly since we had to cope with a terrible smell all afternoon. The stage and first few rows simply reeked of vomit. Really awful. Luckily we had no concert scheduled in the main hall for that night. Anyway, despite that, I believe the musicians are intrigued by this pure interpretation of Stravinsky's vision.

Aleksi

My mother's voice broke through. "Did you *tell* him he'd look like a fool?"

"Of course not." I sighed and decided it was time to curtail the histrionics, even though I'd found them so satisfying. "We should be glad for him."

She was silent.

"This is your own frustration," I said without thinking first. Obviously.

"My frustration?" she yelled. "What have *I* got to be frustrated about, pray tell?"

When she starts with the *pray tell*, I'm done for.

"For a sixty-three-year-old professional woman, I'm in GREAT shape! I have no frustration, let me assure you!"

"Uh-huh."

"What's that supposed to mean?"

"I think you're a little jealous, that's all."

"Of what, pray tell?"

"Look, I'll admit that I was jealous when he told me. It's not that I even want to be married, because you *know* I have no interest in marriage—"

She interrupted, "That's an understatement."

"Don't interrupt!"

She sighed.

"But I still felt funny about Dad's engagement, like he

was showing me up. We know you've never wanted to remarry, because you've turned down dozens of proposals."

"Dozens, literally."

"But this can make you wonder about that."

"I do not for a second wonder about that."

A beat of silence ticked by.

"Do *you* wonder about that?" she asked, tentative.

"Maybe."

"We could talk about it."

I wondered why I'd suddenly had one of the most real
conversations with my mother, ever.

"I'm sure you've got to see your first patient," I said. "I
just wanted to let you know the big news."

After we hung up, I immediately reread Aleksi's E-mail.
It was odd that he made no mention of the E-mail I'd just
sent him. Perhaps its delivery was delayed.

But more importantly, I had to decide whether to mention that the library had had a problem with the smell of
vomit just weeks ago, and that I could only assume I
might be the link between library and orchestra, like a
germ that has leaped from one body to another.

Gordon chose that moment to fling open my door and
march in. He stretched both arms out on my desk and
leaned toward me, staring. "You have green eyes!" he said.

"I've always had green eyes," I said patiently, as if he
was an idiot, which, at the moment, seemed likely. "The
operation doesn't change the color of your eyes."

"But you could never really make out the green
through the lenses of your glasses."

I let my glance drift back to the computer screen. Worried that Mr. Notice Everything might decide to peek, I exited from my mail system.

"Did you cut your hair?" Gordon asked.

"Yeah, a little bit."

"I don't think you've ever worn it loose before."

Embarrassed, I yanked it into a ponytail with one hand while the other went searching in my top desk drawer for a rubber band.

"Don't tie it back," he said. "It looks great."

"Thanks."

Since he kept staring and it was unnerving, I spoke. "Do you know if Ed showed up over the weekend?"

"I didn't get any reports about him, but he might have been helping in the basement again." Gordon meandered around my office, peering at some photos on display— they'd been there for years—and at the artwork, mostly posters I got free from BookExpo every year.

"If you see him, or hear anything, let me know."

"How come?" Gordon plopped down in one of my chairs and then tilted backward on its rear legs so that he was balanced precariously. "I thought everything was working out with him helping us."

I decided there was no harm in telling him. "I just heard that Liberty Music Hall had a run-in with a terrible smell of vomit a couple of Saturdays ago and—"

"You're kidding!" he interrupted.

"And," I said pointedly, "I've been volunteering there, in the archives. The Monday before last, Ed and I went shopping for your birthday present, and then to the hall because I needed to give the new conductor some documents I'd unearthed." I paused to take a breath and work on ignoring the simpering expression Gordon's face had shown when I mentioned his birthday present. "I didn't exactly appreciate Ed tagging along with me, and when I came out of the hall, I was quite abrupt in telling him that I wanted to walk back to work alone."

I glanced at Gordon's face and was gratified to see that he'd lost the silly expression. "And I haven't seen him since, even though he managed to drop off your birthday present."

"You think he got pissed, and that he's responsible for the odors?"

I nodded.

He ran both hands through his hair, giving him the look of a rogue. "I'd probably better contact Liberty Music Hall's administrator," he muttered.

"We should talk to Ed first." I stood up and paced. My hair bounced. "It could be a coincidence, or—"

"This is way too bizarre to be a coincidence," Gordon interrupted.

"I agree that it has something to do with me, but 'something' doesn't necessarily equate with Ed."

"I guess it wouldn't hurt to see whether he shows up today."

"And if he doesn't, his continued absence will be really peculiar."

Gordon opened my office door wide and gestured me through the doorway. "Let's get some coffee."

When we got to the small lunchroom, the aroma of recently brewed coffee was positively aphrodisiac.

"You already made the coffee?" I said to Gordon before helping myself.

He nodded and pointed proudly to boxes crowded with round, thick, luscious doughnuts. "And look what else."

I pulled out a chair at the table, sat down, and reached

for one of the plain doughnuts sprinkled with cinnamon sugar. When I held it to my nose, it smelled yeasty and moist. After a gargantuan bite, I moaned out loud.

"You have quite the sweet tooth." Gordon sat opposite me, cradling a mug of coffee with two large hands. He did not reach for a doughnut.

"There's no such thing as a sweet tooth." My words were garbled and thick from the doughnut I was chewing.

"Sure there is." Gordon tilted back in his chair again, this time with his hands laced behind his head and the elbows flying on either side like wings.

"It's a figure of speech with no scientific meaning." I gulped some coffee to help clear my mouth of doughnut.

He shook his head sorrowfully. "You're so anal—things exist whether we can verify them or not."

"If I'm anal, you're ultra-anal, and don't tell me there's no such thing because you will eviscerate your own argument."

"You can't eviscerate an argument." He grinned and teetered on the chair, rocking it back and forth.

"Look it up—I'm profoundly correct."

"How can you be *profoundly* correct? Either you're correct or you're not." He wagged a finger at me. "Sometimes you get tied up in gobbledygook."

"*Gobbledygook* is not a word."

"So what?" His chair rocked, teetering on its back legs like a little girl trying to walk in her mother's high heels.

Suddenly I threw myself across the table at him, both hands flapping at the end of extended arms. "Boo!" I yelled.

The chair keeled over backward, carrying Gordon with it. He might have hit the back of his head with quite a wallop, and terrified that I had been the cause of severe brain damage, I rushed around the table to crouch next to his sprawled body. His eyes were closed and his breath labored.

"Shit," I muttered.

His eyes flew open. "You should be ashamed of yourself." Then he promptly closed his eyes and groaned.

"Are you hurt?" I asked.

"Terribly." He groaned again. One eye shot open and peered at me.

"Get up," I ordered. "You scared me half to death."

He fumbled around until he was sitting. "*I* scared *you?*"

I yanked the chair away and settled it in place at the table, then reached out my hand to pull him up. "Friends?"

Gordon grabbed my hand and rose without needing my help.

I tried to pull my hand out of his huge paw, but he wouldn't let me go. A flush boiled up my neck and exploded, as if grateful for release, out the top of my white turtleneck and across my face.

Without a word, he squeezed my hand.

A squeeze is a funny thing. When you don't want it, you feel constrained, like when your parents are dropping you off at college freshman year and you're panting for them to leave. Although, truth be told, you're quite ambivalent about them leaving. So, in fact, you want them to leave and you want them to stay forever. Uncomfortable. Squeezing is the same. That's all I'll say on the subject.

I did not want my boss, Gordon Jeremy Albright, to squeeze my hand in that silent way. It felt as if he were whispering sweet nothings into my ear, and that utterly discombobulated me. Yet I was flattered. In fifteen years, it was the only time he'd ever—even silently—shown an interest in me.

Also, I had to admit, he had a hand that made you wonder.

I got businesslike fast. "If we don't have the opportunity to question Ed today, I'd like to be the one to call Liberty Music Hall."

He lifted one eyebrow, questioning.

He'd never lifted his eyebrow at me. I'd seen him do it to countless women. I'd even admired it surreptitiously.

"I feel responsible, and I'd like to handle it." My voice was harsh.

"Okay." He put his hands on his hips and rolled back on the heels of his shoes.

What was it with this backward stuff, anyway? Was this a clue, a word, a gesture, I was supposed to understand? If so, I didn't know the language. I had a terrible urge to push him over again.

I turned and walked out. If he was going to communicate in gestures of indecipherable *gobbledygook*, then I wouldn't even attempt to respond.

In my office, I returned to the E-mail from Aleksi while simultaneously calling Suzanne. Too late, at the sound of her weary voice, I realized it was only eight a.m.

"I thought you'd have been awake since dawn," I said.

"I was awake long before dawn," she groaned.

"Oh."

"Then I fell asleep again, with this little monster sucking the life out of me."

"Oh."

"Let me burp him," Suzanne said. "You must have news, so just give me a sec."

I heard the phone plop down, then a lot of rustling and rushing noises, and finally the most unbelievable burp burst like a billion balloons. I started giggling, pleased that I could experience motherhood vicariously through Suzanne.

"All right," Suzanne said, "he's attacking the other breast."

"Surely you overstate."

"No, I don't think so." She laughed, finally awake. "What happened?"

Whenever Suzanne asked that, and it was often, she had this wonderful, breathless quality. At my reply—the actual words and content were irrelevant—she sucked in the same breath she'd appeared to lose just seconds before. It was very gratifying. It made me feel important.

First, I read her Aleksi's E-mail and told her how I believed I was responsible for the episode of vomit vandalism, via Ed. I explained that Aleksi hadn't really answered anything in my previous E-mail, but that I figured he just hadn't got it when he wrote to me. And finally, I described every blessed thing that had transpired between Gordon and myself. Obviously, she had a lot of material to work with.

Her voice was low and pulsated with meaning. "I think Gordon likes you."

"That is ridiculous."

"Sorry, can't change my assessment."

"Back to Aleksi," I said. "Is it okay for me to pursue the Ed connection to the vomit odor with the chief administrator of Liberty?"

"Sure." She yawned. "Unless you want Aleksi to know that you bring vomit smells wherever you go!"

"Thanks," I said dryly.

"I'm more worried about whether his wife intends to murder him, frankly."

"You've been thinking about it?"

"I talked to John, too—at first, as you'd expect, he thought we were nuts."

"And now?"

"He's concerned."

"But I can't say anything without admitting that both of us actually trailed Michelle."

"I think you have a moral obligation to warn him, even if you have to admit what we did."

"I can't tell him the whole truth; you know that!" I couldn't imagine how I would explain anything to Aleksi without also revealing that I'd fallen in love with him. "Can't I go for something semitruthful?"

"Just be serious for a second."

I sighed. Loudly.

"We believe something *may* be going on. I think you need to make him cognizant of that."

"Like that his wife is planning to murder him?"

"Like that, yeah."

"What are you saying, Suzanne?"

"You should tell him the truth."

"I cannot tell him that I followed his wife." I tried to control the anxiety that was beginning to make my voice shake. I respected Suzanne's opinion, and it wasn't often that I actually disagreed. She was my built-in Pinocchio. Without her, my nose would look like Yvonne's.

"Why not just give him the whole scoop?"

My voice went quiet. Otherwise, I would have screamed. "Because I've fallen in love with him, *and* he's interested in me, *and* there's something seriously wrong with his wife, *and* I may actually have a chance with Maestro Aleksi Kullio."

Suddenly, I couldn't stop talking. "Did it ever occur to you that there might be a reason I've been waiting?" My voice slowed and dropped to a whisper. "He's my intended. He's the one I've waited for. He's the love of my life."

Silence.

I know I've said that you can judge a friendship by its ability to flourish within silence. But sometimes silence is wicked. During those times, you know the only reason the other person isn't speaking is that they're gritting their teeth together to keep from exploding with a comment they recognize you will hate. And that's the real test of a friendship. Do you trust the other person so deeply and completely that you're willing to listen to her opinion, even when the last thing you want is to hear her out?

Huh?

I sighed. "Spit it out."

"You can't fall in love, find the man you've always been waiting for, blah, blah, blah, when the man is someone you don't know."

"I may not *know* know him," I said, "but reading between the lines, I think I most certainly do know him."

"No, you don't." Her lawyer voice in full blast.

"Suzanne—" I said.

"You want me to prove it to you?"

Lawyers are altogether too fond of winning arguments. That's what I've always thought and I don't mind saying it right up front.

I expelled a bluster of air through my nose and mouth, lips fluttering. A snort, actually.

"If you 'know' him so well, how do you account for the fact that he would marry a woman like Michelle?"

"And how do you 'know' that Michelle isn't the nicest person in the world?" I asked.

She took a breath, but I jumped in again. "We do this all the time, Suzanne. We judge people by all kinds of outside stuff, even when we don't actually have a relationship with them."

Victory.

"I don't want you to be hurt," Suzanne said.

"I understand your concern, but sometimes—"

"Sometimes you gotta get out and risk being hurt."

"Right."

"This is new for you, Ally," she said gently. "You're not experienced in the fine art of grief."

"Then I guess it's about time."

I heard a rustle of bedding as she squirmed around. I could imagine their brass bed, atumble with pillows and blankets, the whole mess somehow evocative of love.

"You're thinking of a half-truth, then?" she said finally.

We quickly developed a game plan, and as soon as I hung up, I clicked on Aleksi's E-mail to begin typing a reply.

15

*For questions about the epistolary form, in love or out of it,
go to the 808s and 826s (e.g., Love Letters: An Anthology,
Will You Marry Me? Proposal Letters of Seven Centuries),
and the 155s (e.g., Leavetaking: When and How
to Say Good-bye).*

∙ ∙

$\mathcal{I}$'d typed *Dear Aleksi* when Yvonne burst in without so
much as a knock at the door. I could see she'd been crying. Also, though it's indelicate to mention, a drop of
something or other dangled from the tip of her sharp nose.

She crumpled into the chair near my desk as I rose and
moved to her. I crouched down and put an arm around
her shoulders. "What's the matter?" I whispered.

"It's"—she paused to gulp for air—"it's Gordon."

I nodded and tightened my arm.

"I'm crazy in love with him and I thought if I gave him
the birthday party—"

"And he tasted your sour cream chocolate cake," I interrupted.

She peered at me. "It *was* good, wasn't it?"

"Fabulous."

She sniffed with an elaborate sound. Must have something to do with her razorlike nasal passages.

∙ ∙

Her voice, muggy and indistinct, swallowed words. "I know it's old-fashioned, but they do say that the way to a man's heart is through his stomach."

"You tried." I squeezed her shoulders and debated leaving her long enough to grab a box of tissues on the other side of the desk. "But how do you know he's not—"

"I sent him a letter!" she wailed.

Holy shit. I have to confess to beating down a surge of "knowitallitis." The letters I was getting from Aleksi didn't make me cry . . . far from it. "And?" I prompted.

She pulled up the red sweater she was wearing, and for a second I thought she'd really gone nuts and was about to strip naked. Why she would want to be naked didn't cross my mind. It was illogical, I admit. Instead, she wrenched two crumpled pieces of paper from where they were tucked into the waistband of her pants. "Read my letter first." She thrust it into my hand.

This was fun. I mean, I was sorry for her, of course. You couldn't help being moved when someone looked so distraught, but at the same time, I was fascinated by her predicament. Plus, I had the appalling thought that her letter would be poorly written. Sort of gratifying, in a perverse way.

Dear Gordon,
I feel a compelling urge to write to you of my love.
I would not dare to do this except I've seen signs that you love me, too, and that you're too shy to tell me.

Talk about deluding yourself.

I love you with my whole soul and heart and body. I love you more than I've ever loved anyone before, and that includes my mother and father! I do not love you more than God, of course, but I love you as much as I love God.

Thank God for that.

I am thirty years old and it is time for me to get married and start a family. I would keep your house in perfect condition, prepare delicious dinners every night, and raise your children to be wise and strong. I guarantee your complete happiness.

Is this a money-back guarantee?

I await your response. No matter what, remember that I love you.
Love, Yvonne

I swallowed and kept my eyes on the paper, as if I hadn't yet finished reading. Then I reached for the tissue box and handed it to her.

"Isn't it a good letter?" she said.

She wasn't being facetious.

"It's an emotionally powerful letter," I said. Not a lie. It was emotionally hilarious.

She nodded, eyes wide, ready to believe anything I said.

"I guess that's not really the issue," I said gently.

Those big eyes registered doubt.

"You fully expressed yourself, and that certainly took a

lot of courage, but I suspect Gordon didn't respond in quite the way you hoped he would."

Yvonne handed me Gordon's letter, which I was panting to read.

Dear Yvonne,
I am very sorry that I have apparently misled you into believing my feelings are reciprocal to yours.

Slick language, you devil.

I am not sure how you can love someone you've never even dated, but I will not presume to judge or question what you say.

Even though that's exactly what you just did.

I am sure that you will find the right partner if you pursue him in the right way. Have you gone to one of your church's events for singles? Or you might try square dancing . . . I've heard that is effective.

Gordon should be shot at dawn.

And you might consider an exploration of your gender affiliation. Perhaps, unbeknownst to you, a lesbian lifestyle would be appealing. This would open a lot of possibilities for a life of true love and companionship.

No, a bullet to the brain would be too kind. He should have his insides *eviscerated* by a sharp, curved implement.

I hope that this correspondence between us will not cause undue discomfort in our continued professional association.
Gordon Albright,
Director, Free Library of Philadelphia

I was speechless, and not because I was trying to spare Yvonne's feelings. Gordon's letter was arguably the most horrendous epistle ever written. I desperately wanted to make a photocopy of it, but I suspected Yvonne wouldn't allow it. Meanwhile, I had to tell her something, though what one could possibly say was a serious question.

"He's a gigantic asshole," I said.

Her face brightened. She looked at me, eagerness beaming forth.

I continued. "I seriously doubt that he is a human being. Maybe he's one of those androids from Mars or something."

She smiled.

"We should make hundreds of copies and get Ed to hand them out to everyone entering the library."

Yvonne grinned, revealing those pointed teeth.

Suddenly I could see why Gordon had written the letter. She didn't exactly bring out the best in me, either. Why is that, anyway? Some people demand a negative response, or so it seems, and you feel deeply guilty for joining in with everyone else in the human race who also has a visceral dislike of them . . . until, five years later, you run into them at a concert and they're beatifically happy with a reasonably attractive mate.

I decided not to feel guilty.

"I know you want revenge," I said gently.

She shook her head vehemently. "I'm a good Christian—I really don't believe in revenge." She sniffed and blew her thin nose. "I want him to be happy."

I swallowed.

"Do you think I could write him one last time, telling him I understand and that I'll pray for him to find the right woman?"

"I'm not sure that this letter writing has been a particularly good idea, so far."

She sat up and started curling her hair with thin, anxious fingers. "I don't agree! I've really learned something from Gordon's letter."

"Really?"

I saw the red creep up her neck and crawl across her bony cheeks.

"I feel like I can tell you anything," she whispered.

I started to disagree, but she hurtled on.

"I was so mortified when Gordon said that about"—she dropped her voice—"lesbians . . . but then, after the shock wore off, I started to *wonder*."

My eyes wanted to drop and dash for cover, but I knew I couldn't do that. I was probably the first person she'd ever spoken to about this, and I was a woman (which was making me a little nervous, frankly). I had an obligation to listen with enormous empathy to what she said. "Hey, I went to Bryn Mawr," I bellowed. "Lesbians run wild there."

She gave me a weak smile, and that's when I jumped from nervous to terrified.

"Ally—"

I wanted to scream, *Write me a letter! Please, please, write me a letter!*

Instead, I interrupted. "Yvonne, I think you need to have

a day off. You've earned it. Go home and take a nap, or go shopping, whatever your heart desires, and stop thinking about all this. Put it on hold and get a good night's sleep."

"What'll Gordon say?"

"You leave Gordon to me."

I urged her up and out. To my surprise, she actually seemed grateful. She probably did need a day off.

I certainly could have used one.

As soon as she left, I dialed Gordon's extension.

"Gordon, it's Ally."

"Hi!"

You'd think I hadn't seen him for years.

"I've had Yvonne in my office for the last twenty minutes."

"Yeah?"

At least he sounded a little nervous.

"She's very upset, as I'm sure you know, and I told her to take the day off."

"Good thinking."

"It shouldn't count as a vacation day."

"I'm not sure—"

"If I were you, I would comp this day to her. I would strongly advise you to do so."

"Okay, okay."

I hung up abruptly. I had my own affairs to pursue. I hit the space bar on my computer keyboard and waited for the screen saver to bleed into the E-mail I'd begun writing.

Dear Aleksi,
I was pleased to hear that you felt good about the rehearsals. I do know something, though not much, about the development of an orchestra's sound.

174 • Josephine Carr

You've probably received my earlier E-mail, so I'll wait to hear what you want me to do about the Copland score.

I continue to run into your wife from time to time. Has she mentioned her work on the mystery novel to you? I feel a bit of concern because the mystery's plot revolves around the murder of a famous conductor. Surely not you, I would hope?

Take *care*,

Ally

In agreement with Suzanne, I did not mention my suspicion that I could be the link to the unfortunate experience with the odor of vomit that the orchestra encountered.

Then I called Suzanne again, to ask for a favor. Presumably, Michelle Kullio hadn't known that Suzanne trailed her for several hours one afternoon. If Suzanne could manage to get away again, I had a feeling that a watch on Michelle might be profitable. Perhaps we might even prevent a murder. She was eager to help, and in fact, she'd had the same thought fifteen minutes earlier. She'd already arranged for her mother to take care of the kids. She hoped to be on the trail within the hour.

I hung up and immediately checked my E-mail. No reply from Aleksi, though I now noticed that a dozen other E-mails, from fellow librarians and professionals, had piled up. I got to work, my fingers flying on the keyboard. I wanted to get everything tidied and organized in case events somehow came to a head with Aleksi, when he would need me.

Between desk work and prowling the reference section for any problems on the floor, I checked my E-mail every ten minutes or so. When three hours had passed, I started to worry. He'd never kept me waiting so long for a reply. It wasn't like him. Since I needed an excuse to call the Philharmonic—maybe he was traveling, although I thought he'd have mentioned plans to me—I made a concerted effort to thoroughly search the library for Ed. I spoke with all employees, asking when they'd last seen him. It became clear that Ed was avoiding us.

I called Liberty Music Hall and asked to speak to Ellen Yanovitch, the chief administrator. I explained my connection to the Philharmonic as succinctly as possible, and told her I'd been in correspondence with Maestro Kullio about papers I'd discovered and he'd found useful.

"Yes, Ms. Sheffield, the maestro made quite a speech before rehearsal, lauding your find."

I thought she was being kind, but I wasn't sure. Something about the word *quite* in the sentence sounded an alarm.

"Oh, good, I've been anxious about that—I'd been hoping to hear back from him today."

"He called in sick—his wife said it came on suddenly and probably was a twenty-four-hour bug," she said. "But can I help you?"

"Maestro Kullio mentioned that you had to cope with a terrible smell during rehearsal." I coughed. "An odor of vomit?"

"Yes, we certainly did. It was dreadful." She paused, clearly wondering how much to say. "We're assuming it was some sort of vandalism."

"The public library may be able to help." I explained what had happened to us, and that I'd been to the hall with Ed. "I'm afraid I might be indirectly responsible—I got a little worried about his interest in me and I was forceful in explaining that I wanted to be left alone."

"You think he got angry and took out his frustration by doing to us what he'd already done to the library?"

"Right—the best bet would probably be for me to give you a complete description of him so that you can keep an eye out for him. I'll also call the police and share all this with them."

"The good news is that no one was actually hurt—as these things go, it was relatively benign." Her voice had been amused, but now it shifted more to concerned. "It does worry me that we have the gala this coming Saturday night and—"

"Oh, I didn't realize it was so soon," I interrupted. "The maestro is holding two tickets for me."

"I hope you'll be coming."

"Absolutely."

"If I don't talk to you again before then, and I trust there won't be any cause to," she said, laughing, "please find me at the reception and introduce yourself. Since your discovery of those important papers, I've had the thought that we should have an ongoing display of historical documents, relevant to a given performance. And perhaps we might copy them into our Web site and write some articles as explication."

Abruptly, I decided not to mention the Copland score until I'd heard back from Aleksi. "I'll definitely look for you." I betrayed my nervousness. "It's black-tie, right?"

"Yes, and you know how the old guard will handle that. I wouldn't be surprised to see white elbow-length gloves!"

I called the police next and managed to tell them everything over the phone. Naturally, they were familiar with

Ed, since we'd been dealing with him as a nuisance in the library for at least two years. They even seemed to have an idea of where he lived.

I scooched my chair backward and stared at the wall. A poster depicting the Dewey decimal system in all its rational glory hung in a black-and-gold frame. The frame had cost more than the poster, but the effect as you entered my office was satisfyingly regal. The Dewey decimal system deserved prominent billing.

I closed my eyes briefly. I had many things to worry about and sort through. I wondered, for the umpteenth time, whether it was melodramatic to imagine that Michelle could have poisoned Aleksi, and that was why he'd called in sick. I thought about phoning him at home, but the fear that I could be wrong kept me from picking up the phone. I sat there stewing, and that made me think about stewed prunes. Suddenly, like a vision, I decided that Aleksi Kullio just had a stomach virus. His wife was not murdering him with stewed prunes.

On to equally important questions: what would I wear to the orchestra's gala, and who would I take with me?

I called my mother for the second time in one day and got her between patients. I talked fast, finally filling her in on the LASIK surgery and cutting off her gasps of delight. Then I invited her to join me at the performance and reception.

"Darling, how I wish I could," she sighed. "But I promised Jerome I'd spend the weekend in New Hope. He's got some love interest up there, and he needs me along for moral support. If he weren't absolutely *counting* on me, I'd cancel."

She owed him; I knew that. I extricated myself from a

longer conversation by pretending someone had come into my office, but before hanging up, she said, "Come by some night this week and try all my dresses. I've got dozens of black-tie gowns and we're the same size!"

Yeah, dozens of dresses that nipped. I placed both hands at my waist and tightened them. Could I handle something different, more dramatic, sexier . . . nippier?

Possibly.

16

For questions about sleuthing, go to the 809s (e.g., Sleuths, Inc.: Studies of Problem Solvers) and the 327s (e.g., The Ultimate Spy Book, Great True Spy Stories).

At one o'clock, Suzanne called me from a cell phone.

"I didn't know you even *had* a cell," I said, trying to keep the disapproval out of my voice.

"I borrowed my mother's."

"Where are you?"

"Outside Le Bec-Fin."

"Aren't we the fancy one?"

"I'm not *inside*," she said, grumpy. "Michelle is the one who's inside, lunching with three men."

"Is Aleksi one of them?" I asked hopefully.

"Nope."

"What do they look like—banker, lawyer, artist?"

"Nope, nope, nope." She paused.

"What, then?"

"Very rough," she whispered. "Like mobsters or something."

Fear galloped through my body. "Maybe she's hiring a hit man!"

"Why do you think I called you?"

"I don't know what to do—I can't tell Aleksi that my best friend has been spying on his wife for me."

"Let's not get too worked up," she said. "I'll see where she goes next."

The grumbling in her voice was still there. "Are you hungry?" I asked.

"Starved."

"Why don't you head inside Le Bec-Fin for lunch, my treat?"

"In leggings and an oversize T-shirt?"

"Is there some kind of hot dog cart up the street but on the same block?"

"No."

"I could bring you something, but then we run the risk of Michelle seeing me."

"I guess I can probably assume they'll be in there a certain amount of time," she said. "I know lunch isn't prix fixe, but it would have to take at least an hour, don't you think?"

"Yeah, get something to eat—if you make it fast, there's no way you'll lose them."

"Okay, I'm going." Her voice came in panting spurts.

"Don't hang up while you're walking," I said. Then I asked her if she could get away Saturday night and attend the Philharmonic gala with me.

"It's John's sister's surprise birthday—remember talking about what I'd be able to fit into?"

"Yeah, that's right."

"Why don't you ask Gordon?"

"Oh, please, I don't want to start that kind of stuff with him."

"I'm about to turn into a McDonald's," she said, "but listen to me. Gordon is a tall, handsome, erudite guy— Aleksi Kullio will be impressed and maybe even a little jealous."

"I hadn't thought of that."

"This kind of thinking is not your forte," she said kindly.

"Very true."

"You should do it—I know what I'm talking about. I'll call you when I can, okay?"

"Yeah, I'll stay in the library—have them find me if I'm not in my office. I'm getting kind of hungry myself."

In the kitchenette, I opened the refrigerator to contemplate whether I might have brought some food in and then forgotten about it. But I could not legitimately claim ownership to anything. Then I spied Yvonne's paper bag, neatly labeled YVON'S LUNCH-SAND.,YOG.,COOK. She probably could make some man, or woman, very happy, I thought as I grabbed the bag.

I sat down, emptied the contents of the bag, and quickly peeled apart the sandwich to see what kind it was. Roast beef! Wow, this was something. Undoubtedly, she had hoped that Gordon would be sharing lunch with her in an ecstasy of love, so she had brought this manly sandwich, but now she'd gone home and didn't need it. I gobbled happily. I would take her out to a nice lunch next week, and meanwhile, it made no sense to have this lunch go to waste.

Even though I'd been momentarily alarmed by

Suzanne's description of the men she'd seen with Michelle, my gut told me it was unlikely that a woman of Michelle's pedigree and class would hobnob with mobsters.

The door to the kitchenette opened and I turned to see Gordon standing there, irresolute. Somehow I had the feeling he'd actually been planning to nab Yvonne's lunch for himself.

I grinned and held up the thick sandwich. "Beatcha to it!"

With no warning, he took a quick step forward. His hand reached out and snatched the sandwich. I was stunned. My mouth still chewed on the last bite I'd had. It was so *good* and I needed more. In fact, I was furious. I pushed my chair back and stood up. "Give that back to me! You of all people do not deserve Yvonne's sandwich."

Deliberately, he took a huge bite, tearing at it with white teeth.

I knew I couldn't physically get the sandwich away from him. I sat back down at the table, shoved the cookies into my lap and out of sight, then opened the container of raspberry yogurt. "I was going to invite you to something very special, but not now," I said.

He actually spoke with his mouth full of food. "What?"

"Not unless you give me back the sandwich."

Gordon walked around the table and pulled out a chair. The sandwich, looking a little frayed, was placed on a paper napkin and pushed across to me.

Since I hadn't started on the yogurt, I slid the container, a plastic spoon sticking out of the virulent pink stuff, over to him. He just looked at it.

"You don't like yogurt?" I said sweetly. Then I took the biggest bite of sandwich I could manage. The truth was that I no longer felt very hungry. Two bites and my stomach got filled up.

"I'm lactose intolerant." He eyed the roast beef sandwich.

"I didn't know that."

"Lots of things you don't know."

"Okay, you can have the rest." I gave him the sandwich, but he didn't pick it up.

"Are you still going to invite me?"

"Yeah, yeah."

He ate the sandwich in three bites, masticating in a surprisingly delicate manner given the amount of food in his mouth. Then, I have to hand it to him, he showed admirable patience. He didn't bug me about the invitation.

I was having second thoughts, anyway, so instead I told him about the conversations with the administrator at Liberty Music Hall and the police department. Maybe he'd forget.

"Ed must have a love/hate relationship with you," he said.

"He has *no* relationship with me!"

"You did go shopping together," he said smugly.

"I regret that," I said. "At my age, I should have known better than to give him such confusing messages."

A smile played around his lips. "You'll be more careful in the future."

"I will," I said, defiant.

"I know."

I stared at him, baffled by the conversation.

I rose from the table and quickly gathered up the napkins, paper bag, aluminum foil, and cookies. "You want these?"

"What happened to your sweet tooth?"

"It soured."

He took the cookies and began eating immediately. "Homemade chocolate chip," he murmured.

I tossed the trash and started for the door.

"The invitation?" he asked in a calm, deliberate voice.

"Oh, yeah." I kept my hand on the doorknob and my body aimed for departure. "I've got an extra ticket to the gala celebrating the seventy-fifth anniversary of the Philharmonic's premiere of *The Rite of Spring*. There's a black-tie reception afterward."

"You're asking me to go with you?"

"Well, I'm going and I have an extra ticket—neither my mom nor Suzanne can use it, so—"

"—you're offering it to me," he interrupted.

"Uh-huh."

"I'd love to go."

"Okay, great." My mouth was dry and uncomfortable. I needed water. "I'll find out the particulars, the time and stuff, and let you know."

He held out the plastic Baggie in which three cookies nestled. "Sure you don't want one?"

"No, thanks."

Back in my office, I checked my E-mail even though I knew there wouldn't be anything. There wasn't.

I opened the most recent issue of *Library Journal* and began scanning the reviews. My concentration shot, I registered nothing, so I started over with a pen in my hand, determined to get some work done. I have a strong work ethic, which might surprise you given the shenanigans I'd been up to lately. I know it seems as if I never did any real work at all. But one thing I hasten to tell you is that I'd given far more hours to this library than I'd ever been compensated for. We are talking about fifteen years of unpaid overtime. So I figured I was due for a little fooling around on the library's dole. But unfortunately, I still felt guilty. Maybe I should have written a letter to "The Ethicist" in *The New York Times Magazine*, except I had an idea what he'd say.

I focused. I could not continue like this.

Two seconds later, I was checking my E-mail. Okay, I hereby promise to cut my vacation time this year. I would not cheat the library. With that decided, I twirled around in my chair and faced the back wall again.

I thought about Aleksi first, of course. I wondered if he really was sick, and not already dead. I tried to imagine him vomiting into the toilet. Yucky, but that's real life. If you can't deal with your loved one vomiting—and you'd have to be lucky for him to reach the toilet, frankly—then you'd better get out while you can. Listen to the woman of experience speaking.

It occurred to me that I'd never actually *seen* another person vomiting. No, wait, there was the time when Suzanne got obscenely drunk junior year and she was vomiting at three o'clock in the morning. I think maybe I wasn't very helpful, actually. I didn't hold her head. I stood in the doorway of the stall and made reassuring sounds and kept asking if there was anything I could do. I didn't actually see the vomit coming out of her mouth.

This was very disappointing to realize.

And that was it. The moment when I recognized that I

was alone, celibate for fifteen years, not because other people didn't love me, but because I didn't love other people. I'd always believed that I loved Suzanne, but the truth was that I skedaddled when things got messy. I never visited her in the hospital when she had her kids, and I avoided going out to see her until they were at least two weeks old.

And my mother? My messy, larger-than-life mother, who exuded the scent of sexuality like a perfume? I tolerated her. I thought I loved her, but tolerating someone isn't love.

My demure father announced that his life was taking off because he'd found the woman of his dreams, and what did I do? I resented him.

Love is about crouching next to the toilet while your best friend vomits. You place your hand on her forehead, smooth her hair back, and tell her that you will take care of her, no matter what.

Love.

I imagined Aleksi at home, vomiting and sick. His wife was not holding his head, getting ginger ale, smoothing the rumpled bedclothes. He needed me. For the first time in my life, I was thinking about someone else.

Not, *I need him.*

He needs me.

17

For questions about who the hell you are,
go to the 153s (e.g., The Undiscovered Self) and the 155s
(e.g., Down from the Pedestal: Moving Beyond Idealized
Images of Womanhood).

. . . .

"They're gone!" Suzanne wailed.

"I spoke to you half an hour ago—how can they be gone?"

"Don't ask me, but they've left."

"Go home and forget about it, Suzanne."

"What are you talking about? I'll head back to the Rodin and try to pick up the trail."

"I don't want you wandering around town on a wild goose chase."

"Have you been drinking?"

I burst out laughing. "I'm at the library."

"You're not acting like you."

"I just feel guilty having you do all this for me—"

"But I'm having a fine time—siccing the kids on my mother feels great," she interrupted. "I'm genuinely worried that Michelle may have hired someone to murder Aleksi."

. . . .

"You think the poison akee didn't work, so plan B is to have someone else do it?"

"I don't know about the akee part of this, but these guys didn't look very nice. Hunky, but mean."

"Maybe she's having an affair."

"With *three* men?"

"It's called a threesome."

She exhaled a voluminous sigh into the phone. "Three men and one woman makes a foursome, you nincompoop."

"I knew that."

She started to laugh.

I jumped right into the middle of her laugh, nicely ruining the moment. "It was terrible the way I didn't hold your head when you got so drunk junior year and started vomiting."

"What on earth are you *talking* about?"

"Don't you remember when you were—"

She yelled, "Of course I remember, though it's not a particularly pleasant memory, but what I don't understand is why you're bringing it up now!"

"I was feeling bad. I started thinking about Aleksi, possibly vomiting at home alone, and then I remembered that I'd been a real wimp when you needed me."

She was quiet.

"Suzanne?"

"Everyone has their strengths, Ally. You've done plenty for me."

Tears filled my eyes. "I love you and I want to do better."

"Okay, okay." Her voice was gruff.

"You can help me learn."

"I am perfectly happy with how—"

"Just tell me, okay? Promise that you'll tell me."

"I promise—now, can we return to the here and now?"

"I still think you should go home."

"I could go over and—"

"Go home," I interrupted and then sighed. "Aleksi will probably be in touch tomorrow, after he's thrown this bug."

"Why are you backing off?"

"If I don't get an E-mail from him tomorrow, we'll figure out what to do. I feel like I really did warn him about his wife. I've done what I could, under the circumstances." Suddenly I remembered that bathtub of mud, transformed into chocolate, when I'd first started spinning theories. It occurred to me that since a person cannot see through chocolate or mud, I'd had rather an opaque vision for any attempt to figure out the truth. Clear water would have been more effective. In the ecstasy of indulging in the irrational, I feared I may have deliberately obscured things and "muddied the waters."

"Well, if you're sure, I think I'll do some shopping—see if I can find something to perk me up and make me feel less fat."

"You aren't fat, Suzanne."

"I admit I'm not obese or anything, only a bit overweight. The main thing is these gigantic jugs—none of my clothes button without gaping, and you know how I feel about gaping."

I did, too. Suzanne had always been obsessive about the issue. She took offense when women's blouses were so tight that you could glimpse their bras or, worse, their bare breasts. She actually found it insulting and would rant about how this failing indicated class struggle, the lack of a liberal arts education, and/or vegetarian diets. Totally nuts.

"Look for pullover styles," I said helpfully.

When I left the library at five o'clock, a cold wind hurled down Benjamin Franklin Parkway, picking up my unpinned hair and tossing it straight in the air. I stopped walking and gathered the hair together into a makeshift ponytail, which I stuffed down the back of my jacket. I tucked chin to chest and walked home fast.

My apartment was cold. I rushed around, yanking on the old knobs of the radiators. Then I grabbed a large roasting chicken from the refrigerator, turned the oven to five hundred degrees (I don't know much about cooking, except vital things like that chickens should initially be roasted at a high temperature because that seals in the juices . . . it makes for a smoky and messy oven, but the result is well worth it), and plopped it into a pan. I usually roast a chicken every Sunday so that I can eat off it during the week, but with all the excitement and planning I'd been doing, my routine had been goofed up.

I stripped to my underwear and pulled on gray sweatpants, a stretched-out white turtleneck, and a sweatshirt bearing the faded words BRYN MAWR BABES. A little inside joke. The women of Bryn Mawr are not usually considered babes, though they're every bit as babelike as, say, the princesses of Princeton. And the even larger truth is that Bryn Mawr babes, though indeed babes, don't want to be considered babes at all. So, all told, a convoluted inside joke. The kind that women of the Seven Sisters tend to favor.

With the oven preheated, I slid in the chicken. The radiators pinged and ponged, heating up. Below the chicken, I placed two baking potatoes. One for dinner tonight, and one for chopping up and frying with onions and leftover chicken tomorrow night.

Finally, I went into the bathroom to brush my hair and pull it back with a scrunchie. I started brushing, zoned out, not really paying attention, until I had to blink twice. I didn't recognize myself in the mirror. A stranger stared back at me. My arm fell and I looked even harder, searching for me. Slowly, like a baby taking first tentative steps, I found myself.

She had a special face and an interesting one. Pointed like a fox, with wide, watchful eyes. The skin glowed white, and two red slashes cut the cheekbones. This is you, I thought, and my hand reached to the mirror. I touched its cold surface. Now the same hand moved back, as if in slow motion, and I watched it place one finger on my nose, a small nose still cold from the walk home. I smiled.

The phone rang. I sauntered through the apartment to where the cordless resided on a wall in the kitchen area. I didn't really care whether I got the call or not, since I expected it to be Suzanne. Instead, it was a police officer named Joe Calhoun.

"We got Ed in for questioning 'bout forty-five minutes ago," Joe said without preamble.

My stomach flipped. "Do I have to come over?"

"He's denying everything, says he had the flu or something, and since we haven't got any proof, there's not much we can do." I heard him stifle a yawn. "My bet is that he'll get a little nervous and stop playing these games. I'm just calling to let you know and to double-check that nothing else has happened since we talked this morning."

"Nothing at all, which I think is suspicious in itself, don't you?"

"Hard to say—a pattern hasn't been established, so it's impossible to tell if anything's up."

"Well, let's hope."

"Call us if anything else happens."

"All right."

The idea of seeing Ed made *me* nervous. Even though the vomit vandalism was relatively benign, I remembered reading that violence can begin small and then escalate. I hadn't forgotten that it was my office he made stink of farts. I had no doubt that I was a target, even if, as Gordon suggested, it was a love/hate kind of thing.

I wandered around the apartment. Finally, uneasy with my uneasiness, I got out the watering can and gave my orange trees a good dousing. They always had a hard time with a change of season, but most particularly in the transition from summer to autumn. By the time winter hit, they appeared to have accepted the inevitable cold drafts and little light. Then I got a damp cloth and started wiping off leaves. I could never do all the leaves of all the trees, but it was the kind of mindless activity that could be soothing. An enormous silence filled the room, echoing in the corners.

I needed some music, but I had a hard time choosing a composition and performance that fit my mood. I dropped from crouching to sitting on the floor as I perused the choices. Though I'd tried to develop a select collection, it had grown over the years. I figured I had three hundred

CDs. I searched for something I hadn't listened to in a long time and finally settled on some Elgar. I turned up the volume and immediately began to feel better.

The smell of roasting chicken whispered through the air, and the music became entwined with the odor, like tendrils of ropelike clouds twisting together. I lay down on the couch and stared.

I don't know how many people do the kind of mindless, sightless staring to which I'm partial. Maybe there's been a study done—I might check it out. I might not. Anyway, this is something I do from time to time. I'm totally awake, but my eyes are usually fixed in space. They remain open for longer-than-usual stretches, so that when I do blink, I tend to be aware of it. I probably think, or fantasize, or I suspect that's what a cognitive scientist would tell me I do, but I never have memories of anything particular.

It's not that I dream, either. I exist. That's what it feels like, moments of pure existence, of saying, oh, so simply, *I am me; I am alive in this time and place.* And for some reason it renews me. Tension floats into the air above me, and the music wraps around it and draws it away. Then "peace comes dropping slow." My little Innisfree moment.

By the time the chicken was roasted, two hours later, I had lost my appetite from snacking on those ubiquitous baby carrots. I placed the chicken on a platter and left it to cool, then debated about whether to take a bath. It always struck me as a lot of bother to bathe, and as I've already mentioned, I'm not fanatical about personal cleanliness. I'd had a long bath the night before and didn't feel dirty. On the other hand, I'd begun to suffer from an obsession about odor and I certainly never wanted to think that I might smell.

No sooner had I chosen a CD of Pavarotti—his ringing tenor had a energizing effect on me—and lowered myself into the deep bathtub of steamy hot water than the phone rang. In the old days, I would have ignored it. But too much was going on. I leaped from the tub, stamped my feet a couple of times, and raced on tiptoes, grabbing it on the fourth ring (the answering system picks up on the fifth).

"It's me," Suzanne said.

"Hi, you—hold on a sec; I'm just getting back in the tub." I climbed in carefully, the phone held high, and settled my head against the curved porcelain tub. "Okay, I'm all set. Did you buy anything?"

"I actually found a great dress—I'm so excited."

"I'm glad." She knew enough not to start describing it in detail. We rarely discussed clothes.

"It's this wine red velvet, but the fabric has a little stretch to it, and it pulls over my head with a tight turtleneck."

I guess the rules were changing. "That right?"

"I tried it on for John and he loved it."

"Cool."

Belatedly, she remembered that we don't discuss clothes. "So, did you ask Gordon to go with you on Saturday night?"

"Yup—don't say I never follow your advice."

"And?"

"He said okay." I gingerly splashed my feet in the bath, making tiny waves and bubbles. Suddenly I didn't understand why I always found baths a bother.

"Ally."

"It was no big deal. He agreed to go. He was perfectly pleasant about it, but not effervescent or anything."

"What are you going to wear?" she asked, overly effervescent herself.

Clothes again. I would have to nip this in the bud.

Nip. Cinched-in waists, exploding bosoms, blossoming buttocks.

"I haven't given it much thought," I said airily. "My mother said to come try on her three zillion black-tie gowns."

"Can I come, too?"

"You want to watch me try on dresses at my mother's?"

"I haven't seen her in a long time." She gave a gentle burp over the phone. "Excuse me, we had Chinese take-out."

"I guess if you really—"

"I'd love to see you without glasses, anyway, and the image of Alison Sheffield in a ball gown is not to be missed."

"Not a *ball* gown."

Balls, round, dangling, testicles, bulls, boobs.

"Please, please, please?" she said. "I can get John to cover here tomorrow night."

"Yeah, okay."

After the bath, I pulled on flannel pajamas and sipped a mug of sweet green tea while reading *The New Yorker*. An hour later, I climbed into bed and turned out the light. I don't know why, but I suddenly thought of Yvonne.

I resisted.

I argued with myself, *She'll get the wrong idea and think you're interested in a relationship with her.*

Sitting up in bed, I switched on the light, climbed out, and shuffled over to my desk to search for the phone book.

"Hi, Yvonne?"

"Yes?" Her timid voice squeaked.

"It's Ally—I'm just calling to check on how you're doing."

"That is so sweet of you," she whimpered.

"Are you going to be able to come to work tomorrow?"

"I guess."

"We need you, Yvonne—you handle the public so well."

"Thank you."

"I wanted to say, in case we don't have the chance to talk privately tomorrow, that although I myself am not lesbian, nor have I ever had any of those kinds of feelings, I am supportive. We want you to be happy."

She started to cry. "You're not, yourself? I mean, I wondered because you're still single and—"

"I'm quite sure that I'm not," I interrupted, trying to make my voice firm, but not hard, like a crème brûlée with a crusty topping of burnt sugar.

We talked for only a few more minutes, and then I gently managed to get off the phone. Climbing back in bed, I reached for my glasses and groped at my bald eyes instead. Laughing, I rubbed them a bit. Then I laughed some more. I felt, obscure though it might seem to everyone else in the world, that I'd just crouched next to the toilet while my friend was vomiting. My hand had been firmly in place across her forehead, and my voice had been kind.

18

For questions about fashion, go to the 646.3s (e.g., Dress for Less:
A Step by Step Guide to Looking like a Million
Without Spending a Fortune!).

"You're so thin compared to me." Suzanne glared at me.

"I'm a normal, healthy weight." I adjusted the dress across my shoulders to see if I could hide my bra straps.

"Nope." She shook her head violently.

I glanced at the expression on my mother's face, behind Suzanne. Mom looked like she was about to jump in.

"I weigh the same as my mother."

My mother spoke haughtily. "And I am a perfect weight for my height—neither too thin nor too fat."

Suzanne continued. "Well, usually you wear baggy stuff—"

"Excuse me," Mom interrupted, "but the clothes I buy for Ally are not baggy."

"I never see her in work clothes," Suzanne said. "I'm talking about huge baggy pants and sweatshirts. She didn't look so thin because you couldn't see her body."

"I question the concept of *huge*." I tiptoed toward the full-length mirror standing in a corner of my mother's bedroom, with the hem of the skirt picked up.

Night had closed in an hour ago, as we were having drinks in the living room. When you came to my mother's, especially if it was dusk, you had to have drinks. Suzanne never understood why I complained. She boasts of having once offered her parents tickets to a Broadway show if they would have a drink. No go.

My mother had sashayed out of the kitchen, holding a glass pitcher with both hands, and screaming, "I made old-fashioneds!"

We both must have smiled too politely.

"Get it?" she yelled while pouring the alcohol over ice cubes packed into squat crystal glasses. "Old-*fashioneds*?!?"

"'Cause we're having a fashion show!" Suzanne looked like she'd won the lottery.

"I will disabuse you of that right from the start," I said.

"Isn't her face absolutely gorgeous without those glasses?" Mom asked Suzanne.

"Yes."

Worried by the absence of superlatives, I glanced at her. "Don't you like it?"

"You look so different," she said, "it takes getting used to."

With my mother raving and Suzanne not, I wondered whether I'd made a terrible mistake. I wasn't sure, but it was possible that never before in my entire life had I done anything about which my mother so wholeheartedly approved. We may not like to admit it, but we gauge our effect on people constantly, and certain friends or family members have a distinct power over us. Suzanne had always made me feel comfortable with being myself, in all my eccentric glory, while my mother's displeasure worked as a guarantee that I was following a path unlike her own. Definitely the path I had always wanted to be on.

I gulped at the drink and looked first at Suzanne, then at my mother. They had switched places on me and I felt dizzy.

In the bedroom, my mother had released the blinds over the dark-paned windows and switched on little lamps that dabbed the room with hazy spheres of gold light. Suzanne crawled onto the bed without asking permission from my mother—courageous and laudable—and now lolled against the pillows and made pronouncements about each dress. So far, she hated them all.

Me, too.

It may be that a haircut and the shedding of eyeglasses can make a beauty out of a plain Jane, but in case there's any doubt, I am not a beauty per se. And although my petite size and good weight would appear to be an advantage, the truth was much more complicated. My pale skin looked like an albino frog's, and my chest did this funny concave thing right above where the breasts began. Nice breasts, flat and wide and hugging the body, they've always reminded me of those round, freshly baked loaves of Italian bread. Unfortunately, they swell just below the concave thing previously mentioned. I don't know. I looked very weird in those dresses.

My mother must have seen that I was losing heart. She swept over and busily unzipped the latest. "I know what the problem is."

"Surely it's not a single problem."

"Right, it's the problem of being single," Suzanne crowed.

I tried to scowl at her, but she was rhythmically throwing herself backward against the pillows in a paroxysm of joy at her own cleverness, and instead I laughed. Dancing around in my underwear, I began to sing, "*Saturday night and I ain't got nobody!*"

My mother shook her head in mock despair. "I will explain the problem if you shut up."

Somehow, instantaneously, I was ravenous with the need to know. I twirled around. "Tell me!"

"Your neck, and chest, with the color of your skin—"

"That sounds like many problems," Suzanne interrupted gleefully.

Mom frowned and Suzanne clamped her lips tightly together.

"You need a particular neckline," she said.

"I need a particular neckline," I repeated.

"She needs a particular neckline," Suzanne echoed.

"You should wear something high-necked, as you've always done with those damn librarian blouses I've been buying for years," she said, "or you need a plunging neckline." She marched toward me.

"Plunging, as in a plunging knife?" I whispered.

"Plunging, as in plunging into a pool?" Suzanne asked.

I took a step backward.

"Take off that bra," my mother said.

"I really don't—"

"Take it off!" Suzanne insisted.

"Hey, whose side are you on?"

Suzanne stood up on the bed and bounced. "I'm on the side of plunging!"

Mom veered away from me and disappeared into her very walk-in closet. A very walk-in closet meant that, actually, you could drive a sports car in, if you were so inclined. She emerged holding a dress swarming with dry cleaning plastic. Her face became religious.

"This is the dress," she announced. "I know that this is the dress."

"I wouldn't get my hopes up," I muttered.

"My hopes are up, up, up!" Suzanne said.

"These are my rules," Mom said.

"Rules?" I gulped. Frankly, she'd never been much for rules when she should have been. Lucky for her, I wasn't a rebel type.

"My rules are as follows."

Suzanne collapsed, cross-legged, on the bed. I didn't like how serious she'd become.

"You remove every stitch of clothing," Mom said, "and, to be specific, I mean your bra and underpants."

"Calm down," I said.

"Starkers," Mom insisted.

"What's that mean?" Suzanne asked.

"Shorthand for stark naked," I explained.

"Starkers," Suzanne murmured. "Cool word."

"I'm not used to—"

"Oh, for God's sake, we're two females, your mother and your best friend," Mom interrupted. She was enveloped by plastic as she carefully fought her way to the dress.

"This will be good practice," Suzanne said.

I gave her a warning look.

"Good practice for what?" Mom said.

"She has a problem with excessive shyness," Suzanne said. "You know how psychologists take phobic people through a strategic process by which they slowly become inured to the very thing they fear?"

"Yes, yes, I see," Mom mumbled.

I reached behind my back and unleashed my breasts from the bra. I even faced my mother and Suzanne, although I have to admit that I felt extremely uncomfortable. "Why do I have to take off my underpants?"

"Because the panty lines beneath the dress fabric will ruin the effect," Mom said.

The dress, finally free, struck me in the face. It was, well, raspberry. Exceptionally raspberry. Overripe raspberry. The kind of raspberry that when picked squishes into smithereens in your fingers. Still, you lean over and lick the fingers clean, and yes, the raspberry is utterly delicious.

She walked toward me, the dress cradled in her arms. "No underpants."

I saw the gleam of raspberry velvet, alive and undulating, as if anxious to be out of my mother's arms.

And into mine.

I pulled off the underpants.

Scared, truly scared, I glanced at Suzanne.

She smiled.

Tears. I blinked fast.

"Really, you're one of those women," Suzanne chattered, "who looks better out of clothes."

"Not so fast," Mom said.

She held out the dress and I ducked into it. Suddenly I

felt like a child trying on her mother's dresses, dresses that hung like ancient, tattered flags.

The dress slid over me and then down, down, settling across my hips with a blissful sigh before cascading to the floor.

"Close your eyes," Mom said.

I screwed them shut.

I felt it as she ran the short zipper to just above my waist. It nipped. I could tell. Then she moved to the front and adjusted the shoulders. Finally, she turned me.

"Okay," she said.

I couldn't wait. My eyes flew open.

Let's see, how to put this? There was no neckline, plunging or otherwise. The dress hung from the shoulders in two long, skinny triangles until the fabric joined at my waist. My chalky skin, pebbled with red spots, had disappeared. The raspberry color seemed to swallow everything, like a gigantic whale, and my skin. Oh, my skin. This was my skin? It was milky and thick, like a rich Devonshire cream.

The breasts moved beneath the fabric, although I wasn't, in fact, moving at all. I was a statue. Dimly, I heard Suzanne's sharp inhale of breath. And I waited.

"Ally," she whispered.

"Yeah?"

"You look incredible."

Me, incredible. The celibate librarian lady with her Victorian blouses. I rose to tiptoes. "I need high heels," I said.

"Hold on," Mom said. She skedaddled back to the closet and emerged seconds later with strappy, silver high heels. I put them on and moved away from the mirror, testing.

Testing what?

My arms lifted and I cradled my hair at the nape of the neck. Tendrils drifted down.

"Yes, like that." I felt my mother coming close and I didn't shy away. Her kiss landed on my bare shoulder.

"You were right," I said faintly. "This is the dress."

"Plunging," Suzanne said.

My mother nodded sagely, as if agreeing to a diagnosis. "Plunging."

"Does this mean I always have to wear plunging neck-lines?" I asked.

"Always," Mom said.

" 'Fraid so." Suzanne hopped off the bed and advanced. I watched in the mirror's reflection. "She needs earrings."

"I've got earrings," Mom said.

"That's an understatement," I said.

We crowded around an open bureau drawer to ogle the earrings nestled in velvet-lined compartments. I began to feel like a Christmas tree as we dangled them, one by one, from the lobes of my ears. When my mother reached for the platinum pair encrusted with diamonds, an inch and a half in length (not real, I assure you), I rolled my eyes. But she insisted and I held them up. Absolutely great.

"You can wear either my velvet cape," Mom said, "or the mink."

"I'm not wearing a fur coat." I glanced at Suzanne, seeking support. "I've got my own velvet cape."

Her eyes widened and she shook her head. "Fur is out."

My mother packed the dress and cape into an extra-long clothes bag, then found an old jewelry case for the earrings and a shoe box for the high heels. "Maybe you should have a necklace," she pondered aloud, one finger on her lower lip.

"No," I said.

"I have this stunning one that would—"

"If I put on one more ornament, I'll fall asleep for a hundred years."

"What are you talking about?" she said.

I shrugged. "You know, like the fairy tale."

"Ally, wearing a necklace has nothing to do with pricking your finger and falling asleep for a hundred years!" Suzanne grinned at my foolishness.

"I don't want to prick anything."

Prick, penis, prong, plunge, puncture.

Suzanne was right. A necklace wasn't a needle. Still, it felt like a sharp instrument. I simply couldn't wear a necklace.

Mom patted my rear end. "That's okay. I think it's better without a necklace, anyway."

I leaped away. "Can you please stop that?"

"You mean this?" She skipped forward a few steps and flapped dangerously close to my bottom.

"Yes, that!" I ran out of the bedroom and down the long hallway.

The furnace in my building died sometime during the night and I huddled tighter and tighter into my comforter. By the time I opened my eyes at six a.m., I felt like a bear waking up from a long winter's hibernation. I curled into a comma as I dressed and quickly decided that I'd grab a

Starbucks coffee on the way to work. The super confirmed that the furnace was, indeed, dead and he promised to do what he could.

"Buy a new furnace if you have to," I said.

He shook his head mournfully. "Naw, we don't have to
go to that expense—Mrs. Jamison on three is having a
hard enough time making ends meet. I'll fix it fine."

To hell with Mrs. Jamison, I wanted to say but didn't.
Instead, "You remember the furnace is thirty years old. We
might have no choice. How's Mrs. Jamison keeping
warm?"

"I got her a good fire going. Nice and toasty in there."

I unfurled my umbrella and stepped outside into a
steady autumn rain. Though it was only seven o'clock in
the morning, Starbucks throbbed with soaking wet, un-
happy people who barked their orders, poked each other
with umbrellas, sprayed water everywhere, and smelled
dank. I tried to pretend I was on a Caribbean island and
failed miserably.

The library was even darker than usual, given the rain
and early hour. Its cheery odor of books was weighted
with damp and chill. The lights in my office buzzed and
blinked, finally turning on and blasting me. I hung up my
raincoat and propped the soaking wet umbrella so that it
would drip onto a section of newspaper. At my desk, I
pried off the plastic top to the coffee and took a tentative
sip. Nice and hot. I sipped again.

And then, for no reason, I stared out my walls of glass
and imagined how my office shone like a beacon into the
darkness of the library's interior. Goose bumps jammed
my arms and legs. I got up and moved slowly to the door,
where I quickly turned off the lights. It took a few sec-

onds for my eyes to adjust, but I still couldn't see anything untoward. Yet I felt afraid. My hand turned the doorknob with exquisite patience. I opened the door inch by inch, wanting to avoid any telltale squeak.

I walked through the deserted reference section. Suddenly I heard a faint clanging noise. I turned around and headed to the stairs. I kicked off my shoes and ran downstairs on stockinged feet. It felt peculiar to be without shoes in the library, almost like sacrilege. The heavy door opened soundlessly into the basement stacks, but I knew it would shut with a deafening bang if I let it go. Instead, I eased the door back until it gently clicked shut.

A few steps forward, stop, listen. Nothing. I thought about what might be going on and, obviously, deduced that it could have to do with the bad smells. I turned left, edging toward the small wooden desk where Ed would sit and wait for orders to arrive. The dark was thick and palpable, with the periodicals and newspapers emitting a strange, gleaming light. The smell was of musty old paper, wonderfully dry and warm.

I glanced down one of the aisles and saw only black, but then a flash of light through the shelves. The next aisle was empty, yet again I saw a flicker of light, as if beckoning to me. When I looked down the third aisle, I could just discern a black shape huddled at the far end. I picked up my pace, scared. The light came on again, a tiny flicker from a flashlight, and I saw a small figure bent over, training the flashlight at something unseen by me.

My footsteps were silent and went faster. I could see that I was bigger and stronger, and for some reason I wasn't scared. Two feet away from the figure, and the flashlight flicked on. Long hair hung in twisty curls around a tiny, impish face. I dashed forward and wrapped my right hand around her upper arm.

She let out a yelp of surprise, dropping the flashlight, which rolled crazily along the floor, sending arcs of light rippling across the shelves.

"What do you think you're doing?" I said.

Instead of answering, she twisted every which way, trying to get out of my grasp. But her arm was thin and my hand held on tight. With my left hand, I reached out and grabbed her other arm.

"Who are you?" I peered into her face.

Suddenly she stopped moving. It was as if all the fight went out of her in one enormous exhale of breath.

"My name is Louisa May Alcott." She hooted with laughter.

"Uh-huh, and I'm Mark Twain."

I began dragging her back down the aisle and she came docilely. We turned at the end and continued for a few feet, all the time with me walking backward and pulling her along with me. I let go of one hand, groped along the wall, and found the light switch.

Her face was quite bewitching, small and elfin, with green eyes framed by those wild curls. She looked familiar.

My voice became gentle. "Who are you?"

"The Louisa part was true," she said, "but everyone calls me Lou."

"Lou what?"

"McCabe."

"What were you doing back there?"

"Stink bomb."

She actually grinned at me.

"So you're the one—"

"This time, though, I was really going to confuse you guys," she interrupted.

"How's that?"

"It was going to smell like roses."

"Interesting." I couldn't help being charmed by her. Out of self-defense, I thought we should go see if Gordon had arrived. Let him try to be tough with her. Keeping one hand around her arm, I marched her upstairs.

Sure enough, Gordon's office light was on. She moved with a light step and graceful fluidity, and she didn't seem in the least perturbed at having been caught. I opened Gordon's door without knocking because I could see that he was just hanging up his coat.

"Here's the culprit responsible for the horrible odors," I said without preamble.

He whirled around and stared at Lou.

"How old are you?" he asked.

"Fifteen."

"Was this some kind of practical joke?"

"No."

We waited. She stared down at her feet, which made me look down, too. Bright red rubber boots planted on Gordon's green carpet. Faded blue jeans, black turtleneck peeking out of a yellow mackintosh, and then the hair. Always the hair, like a fairy-tale princess. I finally remembered that she was the girl Yvonne had mentioned to me, the one who hung around the library all the time but never checked out any books.

"Can I sit down?" she whispered.

I looked at Gordon and he nodded.

She sat down and I went to stand by the door in case

she decided to make a run for it. At that moment, I remembered Liberty Music Hall. Surely this kid didn't have anything to do with that?

"What about Liberty Music Hall?" I blurted out.

"Since my dad liked you, I wanted you to get in trouble."

"Your *dad?*" Gordon burst out. "Who's your dad?"

"Ed."

I collapsed against the door, my whole body folding in like a piece of paper.

"And your mother?" I asked.

"Joyce McCabe—are you going to call her?"

"Absolutely." Gordon yanked open a desk drawer and pulled out the phone book.

"I can just tell you the number," Lou said.

"Fine." Gordon picked up the phone and waited, ready to dial.

"Only she's going to get pretty upset."

Gordon still waited.

"She doesn't know I've been following Dad around."

For the first time, I saw anxiety flicker across her beautiful face. Lou's voice dropped to a tiny whisper. "I think it might hurt her feelings."

Surreptitiously, I turned the lock in the door and then moved forward. I sat in the other chair, next to Lou and facing Gordon. I shot him a warning look. He slowly replaced the telephone receiver.

"Why don't you tell us what's going on?" I said quietly.

She swallowed. "About a month ago, I overheard my mom on the telephone. I could tell she was talking to someone she didn't want me to know about, because she sounded upset and she kept hissing into the phone. So after she hung up, I snuck downstairs and did *69." Lou pushed both hands into her hair and raked them through the curls. "See, I thought it might be my dad. So when this man answered, I pretended we'd had a wrong number and I got him to tell me his name. Ed McCabe, he said."

Lou shot me a beseeching look.

"Ed who comes to the library all the time?" Gordon asked.

"Yeah," she muttered.

"I was mad because he hasn't come to see me since I was five years old."

"He knew where to find you?"

"He talked to my mom, didn't he?" she yelled.

"That's true." I kept my voice level.

"He could have come to see me."

The wobble in her lip was unmistakable. My eyes filled with tears.

"Maybe your mother kept him away?"

Gordon frowned at my question.

She shrugged, her head dropping lower.

At that moment, Gordon's attention lifted and he stared out his glass wall.

Uh-oh, I thought, turning to look.

Sure enough, there was Ed knocking at Gordon's office door. I glanced toward Lou, but she was oblivious, lost in her own thoughts.

Gordon rose and walked around his desk. He opened the door. "Yes?"

"I wanted to talk to you," Ed said. "The police called me in yesterday and I have to tell you that I had nothing to do—"

"Why don't you come in?" Gordon interrupted, opening the door even wider.

Lou had straightened up at the sound of Ed's voice. Without thinking, I reached over to take her hand. I gave it a big squeeze and she looked at me carefully, as if to say, *Please do this right for me.*

I stood up, pulling Lou with me.

"Ed, may I introduce Louisa McCabe, otherwise known as Lou?" I said.

He took a step backward and for a second I thought his knees would buckle.

"Louie?" he whispered.

She nodded.

"But you're so beautiful," he murmured.

Lou blushed, the red scorching her cheeks.

"Your daughter's been angry that you never came to see her," I said. "So she tried to get your attention."

"*You* made the smells?" Ed said.

She stared at the floor.

He moved toward her. "Louie, I was embarrassed—ever since I got fired from that job on the West Coast, I haven't had a real job."

I felt the trembling from her tight grip in my hand. I let go and quickly placed an arm around her shoulders.

"I'm sorry, Louie," Ed murmured. "I should have known."

She lifted her head and the tears spilled over. "Yeah, you should've."

And then, like a moth to a light, she spread her wings and went to him.

The tears in my own eyes ran down my cheeks and I swiped at them with both hands. A handkerchief dangled in front of my face.

"Blow your nose," Gordon said.

I grabbed the handkerchief and blew like a truck back-firing. His face twitched with pain from the noise and I started to giggle.

I hoped I could get to know Lou McCabe better. She reminded me of someone familiar, yet a someone I didn't know at all.

Back in my office, I twirled the desk chair so that I faced my poster of the Dewey decimal system. My own father's face seemed to be superimposed over the numbering system detailed on the poster. I saw his gentle eyes and I heard his voice murmuring *Sweetie*. I think that in that moment I really saw him for the first time. *He loves me,* I thought. *He's always been there, waiting with open arms.*

But instead of turning to him, I had done a remarkable thing. I had used libraries, and even the Dewey decimal system, to replace my father. I had loved books, and the clever system by which libraries organize books, more than my own father. My primary relationship in this world was not with people at all. Only books. I called that a remarkable thing. Now I understood how remarkably wrong I'd been.

19

*For questions about the science of the heart and how it beats,
go to the 616.12s (e.g., The Cardiac Rhythm,
The Heart Rate Monitor Book), and for questions about the
philosophy of the heart, go to the 700.4s
(Heart: A Personal Journey Through Its Myths and Meanings).*

I left my office, full of resolve, and went to get some more coffee. On the way back, I strode toward my office, from which a powerful pull radiated, like a muscled, grasping Herculean arm. Ed was taking Lou home and it was time for me to check my E-mail.

The doors had opened fifteen minutes earlier, and my eyes swept the Reference Department, scrutinizing that all was in order.

She was standing at one of the computers, her right forefinger clicking away on the mouse. You know who.

Frankly, I was stunned. After the confrontation in front of Michelle's apartment building, I expected her to avoid the library. I stood still and tried to decide whether I should speak to her. Of course, I realized abruptly, I shouldn't. She was going about her business (whatever that was—the question of the century) and I would go about mine.

My business, oddly enough, was to see if her husband had replied to my E-mail. The truth was that her business and my business appeared to overlap. I closed my office door and locked it. Then I released the venetian blinds to cover the glass walls that faced directly into the reference section. I had never put them down before. Dust and dirt flew through the air.

Waiting for my computer to boot up seemed interminable, but I finally reached my E-mail.

"Kuku" had written.

Dear Ally,
In answer to your concerns about my wife, you should understand that she's one of those women with an overactive imagination. I wouldn't worry.
I look forward to seeing to you on Saturday night. There will be quite a crowd of people, but perhaps we will be able to talk a bit more, despite the hubbub.
Aleksi

Briefly, I wondered why he still hadn't mentioned the Copland score, but in my excitement I let my imagination go. I saw my reflection in the mirror, wearing the raspberry velvet dress that plunged to my navel. He would see me in that dress, and he would talk to me. It was clear that he had no respect for Michelle, and it was equally clear from the plotting of her mystery novel that she hated him. The road had opened for me, the most unlikely woman in the city of Philadelphia, to win Aleksi Kullio, the most desirable man in the entire world.

I bounced away from my chair, dashed over to the blinds, and yanked on the cord so hard that the screws gave way. The whole contraption clobbered me across the head and I fell to the floor with a shout.

I heard pounding on the door and the fruitless jiggling of the handle. Then Gordon's voice. "Ally, are you all right?"

I sat up and unlocked the door. He burst inside and stopped abruptly, staring at me where I crouched on the floor, tears of laughter streaming down my face.

"I'm great," I managed to squeak.

Gordon picked up the blinds and leaned them against the wall. Then he reached under my arms (that is to say, my *armpits*) and hauled me to my feet.

I squirmed to get away from him, but his large hands flapped all over my shoulders and arms in an attempt to brush off the dust and dirt.

I stepped back, protesting, "I'm all right."

His right hand rose and touched my brow, carefully scooping a long lock of hair out of the way. My entire body froze. We weren't talking and I thought I could hear his breath heaving in and out, faster and louder than normal.

"I'm fine," I said again.

"Yes."

His hand had dropped to my shoulder where it rested lightly, sending a faint trembling into my skin and bones.

I stepped sideways, leaving his hand in midair.

By the time I'd cleaned up, and the blinds had been hauled away, my coffee tasted very chilly. I left my office, heading for the kitchen for a fresh cup, and I glanced left to where the computers were lined up in a lugubrious vigil. I'm well aware that computers are not of the animal world (just look at their number in the Dewey decimal system, 004s) but to me they are practically human and

I'm sure they will become human sometime in the future. Granted, it may take a while.

When I didn't see Michelle, I got stuck between relief and disappointment. I continued on and turned to look down every corridor of books, a habit I couldn't shake even though the staff teased me about it.

Back in my office, with a hot cup of coffee, I called Suzanne and read her Aleksi's E-mail. Neither of us still believed that Aleksi's life was in danger, and I didn't want to talk about what had happened with Gordon. Actually, I didn't even want to think about it.

I changed the subject. "Have you made any headway on the idea of a book about successful motherhood?"

"That can be the title!"

I thought for a moment. "*Successful Motherhood?*"

"Yeah!" I could practically hear her grinning. "Nonfiction sells really well when you have the word *success* or *successful* in the title."

"Are you making this up?"

"I'm sure I'm right."

"Does your research show that anything like this has been done?"

"Not published in a book," she said. "I sent off a letter to all the Seven Sisters to ask if they'd cooperate in a study."

"Great."

"Meanwhile, your namesake is proving her merit." Suzanne sounded as if she was trying to tone down her excitement.

"What's little Ally done—made a library in her doll-house?"

"She's reading."

"She's only three years old," I said. "Is she really reading or has she memorized the story?"

"That's how you learn to read, but she's also actually reading words."

"I'm going to buy her a present," I said.

"You don't have to do that," Suzanne said.

"I want to—can you put her on the phone?"

For about two minutes, I conversed with Ally about books and reading. When I hung up and checked the time, it was eleven a.m. At this rate, I would have no vacation at all next summer.

Since I'd eaten no breakfast, my stomach rumbled. I couldn't afford to lose weight if I wanted The Dress to stay on. I rang Yvonne at the checkout desk.

"How are you feeling?" I asked.

"I've decided to go on one of those Club Med vacations in Mexico—I'm sure I'll meet someone."

I wasn't so sure, but there was nothing to be gained by saying so. Somehow I had a feeling that Yvonne was going to be a responsibility for a long time to come, but perhaps, ultimately, I'd be able to help. I, who once upon a time had been as hopeless as Yvonne.

"You heard about Ed and his daughter?" I asked.

"I was so glad to find out that she belonged to Ed— remember I mentioned that I was worried about her?"

"You were astute to have noticed, Yvonne."

"Thanks."

"Listen, is it still raining?" I couldn't see outside from my back office.

"Misting."

"I'm going to get some early lunch—can I bring you anything?"

"No, thank you," she said. "I've got another roast beef sandwich for my lunch."

"Remember, next week I'm taking you out."

Suddenly tired, I picked up my umbrella from the corner of the room. I wandered through the library, opened the umbrella just outside the entrance, and began to trot along the sidewalk. Cars had their headlights on, which is always a depressing thing in the middle of the day. I knew I was reacting to Yvonne's situation. I knew my own wasn't really any different.

But I also have a problem with rain.

It's not that I don't know why. I do know.

On the day my mother and I left Boston and, coincidentally, my father, I was five years old and it was raining. I remember the windshield wipers swishing rhythmically and my heart beating out of time. Maybe that's not the sort of thing you can imagine a five-year-old knowing: a heart beating out of time. But I'm certain I noticed because it has continued to this day.

My heart beats out of time.

I am like an orchestra conductor without the necessary sense of tempo. Oddly, this is not so unusual. In the lore of orchestra players, much discussion has transpired about particular conductors' poor beating of the time. And they say, or it's been theorized, that a conductor hammers a cadence according to his own heartbeat.

You couldn't hear the misty rain as it hit the umbrella. The sound was too thin and sketchy, but I felt the damp creep through the umbrella's impenetrable skin and the way its haze coated me like oil.

I began to run, my feet splashing and my heart beating out of time with the rhythm of my feet. Desperate, I ran faster and faster, trying to make my feet and my heart match. I wanted to be in time. For once, I wanted to be able to dance. I wanted rhythm.

It did not happen.

The disappointment was terrible, worse than ever before. Worse, even, than when I'd watched the windshield wipers in my mother's car.

Swish. Beat. Swish, swish. Beat.

I shook my umbrella at the sky and began to cry with silent tears. I made sure the tears would not be out of time. They flowed straight and simple, with no stress or accent. My tears matched my poor, plain beating heart.

20

For questions about Igor Stravinsky, go to the 780s (e.g., Poetics of Music in the Form of Six Lessons) and to Biography, under Stravinsky (e.g., Selected Correspondence).

I picked my way down four flights of stairs, one hand gripping the banister and the other lifting the raspberry velvet hem to my knees. Gordon had rung my bell a few minutes earlier, but I hadn't buzzed him in. I didn't want him to watch my precarious balancing act on the staircase. He'd have insisted on giving me his arm when I wanted the arm of only one man. A man called Aleksi.

Which is not to say that I didn't find it immensely gratifying to watch Gordon's face as I came into view. He made an expression that I'd never seen in fifteen years of friendship. He seemed like one of those little boys who periodically get lost in the library. Frightened and vaguely excited by the experience of being lost. I opened the door and smiled at him.

"Ally?" His blue eyes were worried, almost as though he really didn't know that I was me.

"Hi." I felt a rush of shyness, which I battled to contain.

"I don't know what to say."

"Oh, don't be silly." I marched past him and then stopped to peer down the stone steps leading to the sidewalk. Gordon's black sports car crouched at the curb.

Gordon tried to give me the dreaded hand, but I skedaddled just ahead of him. Three flights of practice stairs had paid off.

He got to the car and whipped open the door. I gingerly lowered myself to the seat, making sure not to destroy anything, and slammed the door just as I heard Gordon say, "Ally, you look—"

After he'd seated himself behind the steering wheel, he tried again. "You look spectacular." His voice seemed to be trembling, and I wondered if something traumatic had happened at his home before he'd left to get me. Maybe his most recent fling had been incensed that he was taking a female friend to this event and she'd refused to satisfy him sexually?

"Thanks, you look nice, too." I'd been so caught up in my own clothing, I hadn't really paid attention to Gordon in his tuxedo, but it was a safe bet he looked good. He always did.

The drive to Liberty Music Hall was short, and we didn't speak. I was too busy controlling the sweat glands under my arms. I'd been horrified to read recently that both men and women were injecting BOTOX into their underarms to repress perspiration. Now I understood.

Gordon had a small box of tissues jammed into the space between our seats. Desperate, I yanked out two tissues and stuck them under each arm. He gave me a wary, sidelong glance.

"If I sweat on this dress, my mother will kill me." I sounded like I was fifteen years old.

"I can understand—it's really beautiful."

"She's got taste; I'll say that much for her."

"I like your mother."

"Me, too."

He shot me another quick look of surprise.

"Now I like her," I said. "Times change."

"They sure do." His smile made me nervous.

We pulled into the hall's underground parking and inched forward. Elegant people teemed.

"This is quite the prominent event," Gordon said. "I hope to get a moment to talk to the mayor about renovating the library."

"That would be opportune."

"Yeah." He paused. "I'm glad you offered me this opportune opportunity."

"You can't say *opportune opportunity*," I said.

"I seem to have just said it."

"It's not correct."

He smiled, confounding me again.

After we parked, I opened my door before he had the chance to get around to my side.

"Could you possibly behave like a lady?" he said as I maneuvered sideways, bringing my legs through the door and to the floor of the garage while my hands clenched at the dress.

"I don't need a man to open my door."

"Actually, you don't need a man at all." Gordon tilted his handsome head backward and roared with laughter. "Celibacy certainly makes that crystal clear."

I glared. "Don't you dare—"

"Okay, okay," he interrupted, both hands held in the air.

As I teetered to the elevator, Gordon took my elbow and I didn't object. My legs had turned jellylike from nerves. This was the kind of thing most women do without even thinking about it, but seducing a man, particularly a married man, and a famous one, for someone as inexperienced as I was . . . I didn't even know how to finish the sentence because the evening's purpose suddenly overwhelmed me.

Before entering the concert hall, I said, "Gordon, I have to go to the ladies' room—why don't I give you your ticket and I'll meet you in there?"

He looked disappointed, but he took his ticket. I picked up the front of my dress and tore to the elevator. I punched the button for the basement, and then clicked open my bag to take out the key to the archival room, which I'd fortuitously discovered in my blue jeans pocket from the previous Saturday.

The hallway, lit only by dim emergency lights, made me even more nervous. When I was turning the key in the door, I thought I heard a sound in the direction from which I'd come, by the elevators. Quickly, I jumped inside and quietly shut the door. When I turned on the light, I blinked for a moment and then looked at the corner of the shelf where I'd left the Copland score. It wasn't there. I picked my way across the floor and searched haphazardly. No sign of the score.

Immediately, I figured out that Aleksi must have retrieved the score and put it in the safe he'd mentioned. I locked the door behind me and flew down the hall, no longer afraid of who might be around.

I spotted the back of Gordon's head easily. He rose to his feet, smiling, as I collapsed into my chair. We were both silent as we stared at all the people. The dresses, the jewels, the glint and glimmer of their skin, the hands undulating, the peals of laughter and deep chortles of refined glee, the odor of mingled perfumes and colognes—it was all profoundly disorienting.

Saturday night. Where were my deep hot bath and icy martini? Where were my book and flannel nightgown? Why was I here?

"There's the mayor," Gordon whispered.

"Yeah."

"His wife has put on a lot of weight."

"You would, too, if you had to be the mayor's wife."

He chuckled. "Very true."

Michelle Kullio twirled and unfurled from person to person along the front row of the hall. Her dress was a burgundy color, sprinkled with little diamonds, or something like diamonds. She sparkled so much that at times she almost blinded me. Blond hair was swept high on the back of her head, like a sleek hood.

Slowly, everyone found their places. The lights dimmed. My breath grew scarce at the thought of seeing Aleksi. The first violinist strode out and tuned with the orchestra. Then he sat down.

Skippity, skippity went my heart.

Maestro Kullio walked out, still the little boy who's learning to match his stride to the new length of his legs. Quickly, he turned and acknowledged his reception from the audience, graciously dipping his head so that the pure blond hair fell forward. When he straightened and tossed the hair back with a flick of the head, I saw that his hair was loose instead of in a ponytail. I considered keeling over, but I didn't want to draw attention to myself.

He was the most beautiful man in the entire world.

"Kind of affected," Gordon whispered.

I swallowed and did not deign to reply.

During the entire concert, I gorged. My eyes never left the sight of him, not for a moment. I confess that after the first five minutes, I didn't hear the music. I imagined touching him, and I gloried in it. It was as if an enormous brick wall had fallen into dust at my feet, and I could step beyond it and experience, without fear, his physical body. In my mind, my lips moved over him, lapping and licking and loving. A tiny moan spilled from my mouth.

"Ally?" Gordon whispered.

I put out my hand and patted his arm to reassure him.

When intermission came and the lights brightened, I stood up right away. "I'm going to speak to Maestro Kullio," I said.

"They won't let you backstage."

"Yes, they will." I eased past Gordon. "I'll be in my seat when intermission is over."

I flew around people, as if they magically knew to get out of my way, until I stood in front of the security guard.

"Maestro Kullio asked that I speak to him during intermission." My strong voice and eyes discombobulated the guard.

He reached for a clipboard. "Name?"

"Alison Sheffield."

One thick finger crawled down the page.

"He may have forgotten, but if you'll just call—"

"Yeah, here it is." He stood back and ushered me through. "He's the very last door at the end of the corridor."

Musicians jabbered in clusters and ignored me.

I knocked on the door at the end of the corridor.

"Who is it?" His voice was harsh.

"Ally."

The door was flung open and he grabbed my hands. Shocked, he stared at me. "God, you're lovely."

He pulled me into the dressing room. "Did you notice in the second movement, when the oboes came in, how I took it? No one's ever done it that way before because we had no record of Stravinsky's intentions . . . until you came along!" He raised my arms into the air, triumphant.

Aleksi dropped my hands and took a step backward. "Are you sure you're a librarian?" he teased. "You don't look like a librarian!"

"I *am* a librarian." I smiled. "I came to tell you it was an extraordinary performance."

He did a little jig in place. Then he whirled and dashed over to a table where he grabbed a bottle of water and gulped it down. "Sorry, but I was dying of thirst."

"I can imagine."

I stared at him. His lips were sleek, and the color of his skin was like the surface of a deep snowfall on a brilliant, sunny day. I remembered how, during the performance, I'd imagined touching him all over with my mouth.

"You found the Copland score and locked it away?" I asked, just to be sure.

"I'm sorry?"

"The Copland score? I wanted to make sure it was safe."

His blue eyes were puzzled. "What are you talking about?"

I told him about the E-mail I'd sent him Monday morning.

"I was sick that morning," he explained, "and I never saw an E-mail from you."

"The score isn't in the archival room where I left it." I tried to keep the panic out of my voice.

"I wonder if my wife read my E-mail that morning—"

"I thought it might be valuable."

He moved closer to me and reached for both my hands. "This is what's valuable," he whispered.

I couldn't speak.

"My little librarian," he murmured.

He lifted my arms out to the side and then pinned them behind my back with gentle hands.

When he kissed me, I closed my eyes and gave myself to every sensation. I was open. I was ready.

I was horrified.

My eyes flew open.

A voice called out, "Three minutes, Maestro."

"I've got to get back to my seat!" I said.

"Go, go, go!" He stepped away, dropping my hands and laughing. "Find me during the reception—I want to dance with you."

I rushed out the door, feeling my body move with a rhythm and grace I'd never known before. I made it to my seat at the last moment. Women in our row, forced to stand up so that I could pass, grumbled and threw me nasty looks. The men smiled and looked at my breasts.

"Hi," I said breathlessly to Gordon.

The lights went out completely and the first violinist walked on stage.

I could tell Gordon had turned to look at me. In a strange voice, he said, "What's going on?"

"Sssh." I placed a finger to my lips and nodded to the orchestra.

He continued to stare at me until, finally, he faced forward again.

Aleksi walked onto the stage and bowed to the audience, and then to the musicians.

As the music began, I closed my eyes tight. I tried to crush every feeling and thought that welled inside me. No good. I must face it. His kiss felt like the bullet from a gun. His voice, murmuring *My little librarian*, tasted incestuous and dirty.

My body was telling me something, and I understood that my body had the truth buried inside. I had to dig. And then, coincidentally, the music Maestro Kullio was conducting, Sibelius' *Finlandia*, gave me the beginnings of an answer.

This man, Aleksi Kullio, wanted something from me, and that something had something to do with Finland. That's a lot of somethings without any substance. If I'd told anyone this, even Suzanne, I would have been met with skepticism. *What are you talking about?* It didn't matter. I knew what I knew. And what I knew had also been buried deep within the secret.

For the moment, as I sat through the rest of the concert, I could do nothing except grapple with my humiliation. I now grasped the full and flavorsome meaning of the

phrase *I'm so mortified*. *Mortification*, in its religious connotation, means "the subjection of one's appetite and passions by the practice of austere living" (*Oxford English
Dictionary*). Or it means death. I saw that, paradoxically,
when I believed I was finally living with passion and appetite, I was actually toying with a process that would result in my mortification.

Why is it in life that if you try to change and go in a different direction, you get hit by the very thing you were
trying to change in the first place? It makes no sense
whatsoever, yet it happens all the time.

My shame at having fallen in love with a man like
Aleksi Kullio, after years and years of protecting myself
from *all* men, grew huge and monstrous. I wanted more
than anything else to simply walk away and ignore it. I
wanted to turn around and go back.

And I knew, what with life being so absurd, that was
the very last thing I was going to be allowed to do.

21

*For questions about the physiology of sexual excitement,
go to the 612s (e.g., The Alchemy of Love and Lust:
Discovering Our Sex Hormones and How They Determine Who
We Love, When We Love, and How Often We Love)
and the 306s (e.g., Extraordinary Togetherness:
A Woman's Guide to Love, Sex, and Intimacy).*

"What can I get you to drink?" Gordon asked, leaning toward me so that I could hear him over the thunderous sounds from the ballroom's crush of people.

"Vodka martini, shaken, up, and with an olive." I glanced at him and felt a bit guilty for not having given him even a modicum of attention all evening. "You look really handsome in a tuxedo."

He flushed. "Thanks."

I allowed the throngs to squeeze me this way and that until my back was cornered into the wall on the outer fringes. I didn't bother to try to spot Aleksi or Michelle.

Gordon threaded his way carefully, two martinis held high above his head to keep them from spilling. I waved.

When he passed the drink to me, the liquid shivered at the top of the glass but did not splash over. "Good job," I yelled.

He grinned and gulped at his martini.

I sipped mine.

"Are you having an affair with that conductor?" Gordon asked.

The martini stuck halfway down my gullet and I coughed violently, my entire body convulsing so badly that the drink swung in an arc and poured across my hand.

When I finally caught my breath, I frowned at Gordon. At least I wouldn't be lying. "Of course not!"

He arched his eyebrows. "Something's going on—I can tell."

As a distraction, I fluttered my hand around to shake off the droplets of martini. He smiled benignly.

My eyes had filled with tears and I was blinking rapidly, trying not to give way. Hazily, through the skein of tears, I saw three men walking toward me. They wore black tie, but they looked uncomfortable and out of place. I noticed that Gordon turned and followed my line of sight.

"Ms. Sheffield," one of the men said when they were very close, "we're with the FBI. May we have a word with you privately?"

I stared at the man, focusing on the way his cheeks quivered as he spoke. He was a little plump.

"Excuse me," Gordon said, "I'm Ms. Sheffield's boss— what do you want to speak to her about?"

The man kept his eye on me, ignoring Gordon.

"I don't want to speak to you privately," I said, suddenly realizing it was true. What I felt like saying was, *Does this have anything to do with Finland?*

"Do you have the Copland score?" the man said.

I swallowed, not fully believing what I'd heard. "What?"

The second man, standing slightly behind the first, spoke. "Where's the Copland score?"

"I have no idea!"

"That right?"

"Ally, what's going on?" Gordon asked.

"I'm not sure."

"I must remind you that *the FBI* stands for *the Federal Bureau of Investigation*," the man lectured. "You are under obligation as a citizen of this country to answer all our questions fully and honestly."

"I found a score by Copland that looked original to me, though I'm no expert, in the basement archival room of this building," I said. "I haven't a clue how you know about it. I went down there before the concert to check that it was still there and it wasn't. I assume—" I stopped talking abruptly because my mind was scampering all over the place.

"What do you assume?" barked the second man. He pronounced *assume* like a dirty word.

I shrugged. "Actually, I don't know what to assume. I can only tell you the facts. My assumption would be that someone in the Philharmonic's administration must have found it and thought it needed to be put away for safe-keeping."

The three men stepped backward while the plumpish man spoke. "I want to warn you that your activities this week appear suspicious. If you have any information to share with us, please do so immediately."

He held out a card, which I took with a shaking hand.

"I will."

To think that I had believed I knew the meaning of mortification. Turns out I'd barely touched its essence.

The men were gone within seconds. I waited until I saw them leave the celebration from a back entrance. In my mind, I begged Gordon not to ask me anything. He must have caught on, because he kept quiet until I turned and ran out of the room.

Gordon tore after me, catching me just as I pushed through the concert hall doors onto the sidewalk.

"Let me drive you home," he said.

"No." I rushed along the sidewalk and, furious, bent over to yank off my high heels. I continued walking in my stocking feet.

"Ally, come on."

I whirled on him. "Leave me alone—I mean it, Gordon—if you don't get the hell away from me I'm going to start screaming."

He stopped dead.

I turned and began a slow jog. Crunchy bits of stone and debris bit at my feet, and cold seeped up my ankles. Tears dried on my face in salty, tight lines. I picked up my pace and flat-out ran, clutching the gown high and moving to tiptoes.

At my house, breath heaving in my chest, I dashed up the stone steps and crammed the key into the lock. When I went through the door, I saw Gordon's arm holding it open from behind me.

"Leave me alone!"

"I'm not going to leave you alone."

He followed me inside.

And then I wanted him with me. I needed someone to help me, to take care of me, and I realized that Gordon would do that. We trudged up the three flights of stairs.

Inside my apartment, I tossed the shoes wildly across

the room and threw myself into a corner of the couch. The furnace was still limping along, and the apartment was chilly. Without a word, Gordon went over to the fire-place and began laying a fire.

"There's a fake log in that closet over there," I whis-pered, pointing.

He nodded.

Soon the fire caught and drew me to its flames.

Time faltered until Gordon handed me a mug of some-thing hot. Steam billowed.

"Drink," he said.

I blew on it and then slurped some of the liquid, which turned out to be a potent mixture of apple cider and bour-bon. "Thanks," I muttered.

He settled into an opposite corner of the couch with his own mug.

"Tell me," he said.

So I did.

I left nothing out, nothing at all. (Okay, so I didn't ex-actly reveal that Aleksi had kissed me in his dressing room—I couldn't get the words to form.) I even admitted that I was convinced Aleksi Kullio had been the man I'd been waiting for all these years.

Finally, I said, "I suspect he's doing something illegal, but I really don't know what happened to the Copland score—maybe his wife, Michelle, read my E-mail and stole it herself."

I gulped at the concoction. "This is good."

"Ally?"

"Umm?" I looked at him.

His eyes were thoughtful and still danced with amuse-ment. "I think you and I may be the dumbest two people who ever lived, especially considering the fact that we both work in a library, where we have all those books around us."

"I'm the dumb one, not you."

He leaned forward and set his empty mug on the coffee table, then rose to go poke at the fire. It didn't really need poking. I noticed that he had taken off his tuxedo jacket earlier. When he leaned over the fire, the back of his cummerbund rode up and his white shirt was all bunched and wrinkled.

"Want some music?" he asked.

I sighed, wondering whether I would ever feel the same about classical music. Maybe not the same. Different.

"Yeah, music would be good."

He spent a few minutes perusing my CDs. Then I heard my father's oboe.

"That's my dad," I said.

"I know."

Gordon was walking around the apartment behind me.

When I turned to look at him, he was pulling down the sheets and comforter on my bed. "What are you doing?" I asked.

"Putting you to bed."

And then I knew why we were two of the dumbest people in the whole world.

"Get your nightgown on in the bathroom," he said gently.

I did.

When I came out, he asked whether I had brushed my teeth.

I looked at him reproachfully. He cocked an eyebrow. The most exquisite feeling rushed through my body. At

first, I didn't know what it was. I stopped in the middle of
the room, on my way to the bed, relishing it and wondering what it was.

"Is something wrong?" he asked.

"I have this feeling—"

"What kind of feeling?" Gordon walked toward me
slowly.

I held up my hand. "Stop!"

Now he really looked alarmed. "Are you sick?"

I tipped my chin toward my chest and slowed my
breathing so that all my concentration could be directed
away from my mind and to my body. My precious body.
The tingling was tender, like a flower drifting up my bare
legs, across my belly, stroking my breasts.

"Gordon?"

"What, baby?"

He stood in front of me. And then we were moving together and I was engulfed by his hug. I rested my head in
the space where his arm joined the rest of his body. My
head fit perfectly.

Baby. A delicious word, almost as delicious as the sen-
sations sweeping over me. I was embarrassed, but I had
to tell him.

"I think I just felt sexual excitement," I said into his
chest.

"Is this the first time?"

Would the mortification never end?

"As crazy as it sounds, yes," I whispered.

"Can I come closer?" he said in the gentlest voice imag-
inable.

I nodded. I couldn't meet his eyes.

He touched my shoulder. "Get in bed."

I started to walk. Still without looking at him, I said, "It's a miracle feeling."

He didn't say anything, which was good. Miracles don't bear too much talking about.

After he tucked me in, he sat comfortably on the edge of the bed.

"I have something I need to confess," he said.

"This sounds serious—and I don't want to hear anything serious right now."

"My confession is—"

"Did you understand what I said?"

He wrapped his arms around me. My head rested on his chest and I could hear the hammering of his heart.

"I understood, but I'm still going to tell you," he said.

I laughed.

"I didn't sleep with all those women I dated."

I reared up and out of his arms. "What?"

"I've only slept with a handful of women in my life."

His brown curly hair looped ferociously around his head.

My right hand dived in and grabbed a handful. "This many?" I shook it.

He grinned and tucked his head toward my hand so that it wouldn't hurt. "About that many."

I let go. "Yvonne actually told me she didn't think you had sex with all those women."

"Really?"

I stared at him. "Exactly how many lovers have you had?"

"More than you, but I'd have to be a real loser not to beat your record."

"No insults."

He leaned forward, his mouth curved into a warm, wonderful smile. Then he shook his head sadly. "I can't believe we wasted fifteen years," Gordon said.

I started to say that it wasn't a waste, but then I had to wonder. "We're not that old," I said instead.

He punched me lightly. "Speak for yourself."

For the next half an hour, I tried to convince Gordon to spend the night, but he refused to stay.

He also refused to kiss me or do anything physical. See, here we went again. Life was ridiculous. I know you're wondering why he wouldn't kiss me. I wondered, too. Finally, when I started to cry with frustration, he tried to explain.

"We have to take tiny steps, Ally." His voice whispered as if we were sharing a special secret. "Do you agree that I have more experience than you do?"

"Yes." I sighed.

He picked up my hand and turned it over. Then he gently kissed the palm. "Trust me," he said.

So I did.

22

For questions about Finland, go to the 948s (e.g., Of Finnish Ways, Finland: A Country Study).

On Monday, my phone rang at six thirty in the morning. I groped wildly, first for the glasses I no longer needed, and then for the telephone.

"Wake up, beautiful!" Gordon's voice exuded vigor, as did all the rest of him. (I distinctly remember mentioning his vigorous testicles earlier.)

"Hi."

"What a welcome."

"I was asleep."

"That's why I called to wake you up, goosey girl."

Goosey girl?

He continued. "Actually, I called so that you'd get to the library early. I have a surprise for you."

That perked me up, even though I was still in that stage of not truly believing that Gordon liked me. Since we'd talked over the telephone for five hours on Sunday (I also spent two hours talking to Suzanne), I should have begun to have faith. I certainly liked him.

You're probably thinking it was weird for us not to spend Sunday together. But this felt right. I couldn't get rid of my bashfulness immediately, and talking on the phone was a good way to relax. I liked listening to his voice and not having to concentrate on all the other parts of him. Those glorious, unmentionable parts.

"I can probably get there by eight o'clock," I said.

"Do so!"

I hung up and shook my head. He was going to be a challenge, no question. He would probably be a challenge for any woman, but for a woman with my depths of inexperience it could be profound. Then again, I'm all for profundity.

I wore a long, navy blue skirt and a white "librarian" blouse buttoned high up the neck. I'd already reverted to twisting my hair into its familiar french twist. When I looked in the mirror, my hair was poufy and shiny, my cheeks were like pink little flowers, and my swollen lips pouted. Gordon would say I was in love.

When I emerged from my building, I discovered the kind of autumn morning that makes you crazy. Light splashed everywhere, giant puddles of sunshine, and the crisp air gyrated with particles of energy (I know those particles have a scientific name, but at the moment I can't quite remember). I started to trot, and then to run. In amazement, I saw my feet fall rhythmically in tune with the dancing photons—that's it!—of light.

My heart was beating in time.

Gordon was pacing up and down in front of the checkout desk, and he rushed over when I came through the door. I was overwhelmed with embarrassment. Absolutely disabled by it.

Unfazed, he grabbed my hand and yanked me through the library to his office. I looked around, searching for a gaily wrapped package—large or small, I didn't care—but his office revealed nothing exciting and mysterious. He settled me in the chair for visitors, patted his jacket exper-imentally, and pulled out a white sheet of paper.

"I've written you a poem," he said.

Maybe you would have felt the way I did? A little let down? A little anxious? The difficulty is that in some key ways, I am quite like other women. I adore presents and I really don't get enough of them in my life. It's not a big deal, nothing I'd ever complain about, but just one of those wee facts that I'd change if I had my druthers. I also happen to adore poetry. For that reason, I can be critical of it. Bad poetry is almost as heinous as television.

Gordon cleared his throat dramatically.

I melted. Not that I want to be cloying, but he looked adorable. Bad poetry, bring it on!

He recited,

"Alison's the one,
yum, yum, yum!
Into my tummy,
I swallow her whole.
Into my heart,
and through my blood
she swims.
Alison's the one
and I'm all done!"

He grinned at me.

"That was really something," I said bravely.

"I thought it was kind of cute." He sidled toward me.

I was feeling more timid than ever, but suddenly I knew what I had to do. I leaped to my feet and ran straight at him. He caught me and lifted me up in the air.

"I love you!" I said.

"I love you more!" he said louder.

At that moment, as we were about to kiss for the first time, his door flew open.

I turned around and saw Yvonne as she opened her mouth to scream.

I waved at her desperately, and she clamped her lips together. She was wonderfully biddable.

"What is it?" Gordon said.

"There's a woman asking for"—she swallowed hard— "for Ally."

"Where is she?" I asked.

"Right out front."

As I went through the office door, I saw Michelle Kullio. Gordon and Yvonne were several steps behind me.

"Good morning," I said to Michelle.

She glared at me. "How dare you?" she hissed.

"Now wait one minute," Gordon said, stepping forward.

"Are there *no* decent librarians in this country?" she shouted.

We all blinked in disbelief and confusion.

"Every city we go to, there's a luscious librarian ready to give my husband whatever he wants—Philly was no exception!"

I flushed.

"Are you suggesting—?" Gordon said in a loud voice.

"You were her date Saturday night, weren't you?" Michelle said. "Did you know she was kissing my husband in his dressing room during intermission? That's lovely behavior, huh?"

Now, at last, I truly understood the definition of *mortified*.

Gordon turned and stared at me.

"I was going to tell you—"

"You said you told me everything."

"Almost," I whispered.

Michelle stepped forward, so that she was a foot away from me. "As you may have noticed, he's got a *thing* for librarians. You could probably start a Web site for librarians who have fucked Maestro Kullio! But *you* took the cake!" Spittle flew through the air. "You actually combined two passions into one: you could screw him and steal musical scores. What a perfect little package."

"I have never stolen anything in my life, and I have no idea what you're talking about!"

"Remember your little chat with the FBI?"

"I told them I didn't know what had happened to the Copland score."

"Let me fill you in, then, by all means." Michelle took a deep breath. "Your lover, my husband, had the score overnighted to Mommy in Finland, who just happens to be . . . a librarian!"

She gazed triumphantly around the room, where I now realized a small crowd had gathered.

"A children's librarian, right?" I said feebly.

"Oh, that was years ago. Now Mommy is the head librarian of the music section of Finland's state library.

Mommy keeps all the precious musical documents, scores and other memorabilia, organized and safe."

I could not say a word.

"Finland has an exceptional dedication to music, of course, but they lag a bit in some areas. Their collections are weak."

"Aleksi has been stealing documents and sending them to his mother, is that right?" I said.

"Bingo!"

"Why can't the FBI find them in the library and—"

"Mommy the librarian isn't stupid! Mommy the librarian is a very, very good librarian—those documents will be hidden away for a hundred years, and then Finland can simply claim that they've always had them."

I breathed in deeply, trying to gather my resources. "Michelle, I have to tell you that your husband was *not* my lover—"

Before I could finish, she had whirled around and marched out the door.

I turned to find Gordon, but he, too, was gone. Without a word to anyone, I walked to my office and slammed the door behind me. I went right to the telephone and called Suzanne.

After I'd told her the entire story, I wasted no time. "I think I kept the FBI's card."

"What are you planning?"

"Hold on."

I plunked the phone down on the desk and then up-ended my purse so that everything spilled out. I grabbed my wallet and searched in the money section. There it was.

"I've got it," I said into the phone. "I'm going to call them immediately and tell them I'm willing to set up a sting to catch the bastard."

"Ally, are you sure—"

"I have to convince Gordon that I'm capable of doing the right thing. I'm going to let my actions prove it."

Her voice was tender. "It's going to be all right—I'm sure of it. Just get strong and follow your gut. Let me know what's happening when you can."

After I'd called the FBI, I sat still for a moment. Then I reached for the phone yet again. "Dad, I'm calling to invite myself to Boston. I want to meet Wendy."

It felt good to do this thing called *right*.

23

*For questions about redemption, go to the 291s
(e.g., The Cat: A Tale of Feminine Redemption) and to the 158s
(e.g., Secrets About Life Every Woman Should Know).*

I recited my lines into the telephone. "Hi, may I speak to Maestro Kullio? It's quite urgent." I glanced at the plump FBI man, whose name I now knew was Malcolm.

He nodded, telling me that my voice was good.

"I'm sorry, but the maestro is extremely busy," his secretary cooed into the phone.

"Tell him that Alison Sheffield needs to speak to him about an exciting and valuable development." I emphasized the word *valuable*.

"One moment."

"I'm on hold," I hissed.

"You're doing fine," Malcolm assured me. Then he rubbed his hands together gleefully and grinned.

Aleksi's voice exploded suddenly. "Ally, what a wonderful surprise! From now on, tell my secretary you're returning my call and there won't be any problem."

"Oh, great, I'll do that." I hoped he couldn't hear the

buzz of my body's vibrations. I gripped the telephone receiver. "I thought it was important I let you know about something I found in the archives, and I was afraid to use E-mail because of what happened with the last one."

"Of course—you made another discovery?"

"I can hardly believe it—I mean, I had to call you. I think I've found an original Beethoven score."

His gasp was audible to Malcolm across the room.

"Are you serious?" Aleksi said.

"I could be wrong, but somehow I doubt it—I'm pretty excited!"

Malcolm gave me the thumbs-up.

"Where is it?"

"I have it here in the library, the main branch on Vine. I didn't dare leave it where just anyone might come across an original Beethoven score—"

"I'll be right over."

Surprised by how quickly he'd fallen into the trap, I faltered momentarily. Malcolm made rapid rolling motions with his hands.

"My office is behind the reference desk."

"Okay. I'm coming."

I hung up the phone and stared at Malcolm. "That sure was easy."

Ten minutes later, I sat behind my desk, ramrod straight, and touched the wires hidden beneath my blouse. Malcolm was in the closet at the back of my office, and the two others were stationed at computers in the reference section. The library staff, including Gordon, knew nothing. Seems that the fewer people who knew, the fewer chances of the secret leaking.

Aleksi came into view. He was hard to miss, with that flowing white blond hair, magisterial stride, and arrogant aura. Suddenly, to his right, I saw Gordon. He kept his distance, but it was obvious he wanted to know why Aleksi Kullio was heading toward my office.

Don't mess this up, Gordon; please don't mess this up!

When Aleksi circled behind the reference desk and aimed for my door, Gordon stopped and pretended to be using the computer. His eyes rose above the screen, watching.

Aleksi closed the door behind him. His handsome face glittered with a glorious smile. "Can I kiss you?" he mock whispered.

I plastered on a fake smile. "Absolutely not." I stood up and carried a white 8½-by-11 envelope around the desk.

He grabbed it out of my hand and opened it immediately.

The FBI had borrowed an original Beethoven score from the Albrecht Music Library at the University of Pennsylvania.

"Careful," I said unintentionally.

Aleksi gave me a sly sideways glance. "Don't worry." He placed the score on my desk and tipped my desk lamp over it.

I waited, trying not to worry whether Gordon might burst through my door. Sweat flowed from my armpits like twin waterfalls. The biggest concern was that Aleksi might know of the university's holdings, especially one so rare.

His bleached skin glowed with a paranormal sheen.

I swayed on my feet, hoping I wouldn't pass out. I saw the pronounced Adam's apple in his throat bob, and I realized he was trying to swallow his excitement.

"By George, I do believe she's got it," he said lightly.

"You think it's an original Beethoven score?"

He slid the score back into the envelope without answering. "I've got to run—I'm meeting with the mayor in twenty minutes. I'll lock this up safely; don't you worry. Sure I can't kiss you?"

The expression on his face made me sick.

I shook my head.

He pretended to be disappointed. "At least promise to meet me tonight for a drink?"

"I'd love that," I gurgled.

"Come by my place—the wife is out of town." He winked.

At that moment, Malcolm opened the closet door and said, "Aleksi Kullio—I'm with the FBI. May I have a word with you?"

To my amazement, Aleksi pushed me out of the way so hard that I went sprawling onto the floor. I decided to stay there until things calmed down. He literally ran for the door, where the other two FBI agents were waiting. Malcolm hadn't expected that they would have enough proof to truly catch him, but they'd decided a good scare might be the best bet. Obviously, Aleksi must have more to hide than the FBI knew, given the way he'd reacted.

They grabbed his arms and escorted him back into my office. Aleksi was demanding that he be allowed to call his attorney when Gordon suddenly flew through the door.

He knelt next to me. "Are you okay? Should I call an ambulance?"

I collapsed backward with my arms flung out on either side. "Depends," I gasped.

"On what?" A small smile skipped over his face.

"Maybe I just need some CPR—are you trained to give CPR?"

His two warm hands nestled under my left breast and pressed gently. His mouth moved closer until his lips touched mine. His breath blew into me.

I breathed deeply. Saved.

Josephine Carr lives in Washington, D.C. During high school, she studied at Loreto Convent in Nairobi, Kenya, and Collège du Léman in Geneva, Switzerland, before graduating from an American high school. Her B.A. degree from Mount Holyoke College and M.A. from Bryn Mawr College were in English literature. Her children, Rachel and Daniel Sussman, attend Yale University. For more information, visit her on the Web at www.josephinecarr.com.

The
Dewey Decimal
System of *Love*

JOSEPHINE CARR

A CONVERSATION WITH
JOSEPHINE CARR

✽

Q. Your novel, The Dewey Decimal System of Love, *can be laugh-out-loud funny. Have you always been a funny person?*

A. I'm not in the least bit funny. In fact, when I told my eighteen-year-old son that I was writing a comic novel, his head whipped around and he stared at me in disbelief. "But *you're* not funny!" he said. Unfortunately, this was so true that I could only stare back at him and wonder whether I was making one of those fatal mistakes that writers are wont to make. As luck would have it, I've discovered that I was always meant to write funny. My next challenge is to be as funny as I write.

Q. Your previous novel, Monday's Child, *was in the suspense genre. What made you change to humor?*

A. I have to confess that it was partly out of desperation. After *Monday's Child*, I'd written another thriller/suspense novel on the intriguing subject of mad cow disease, set at Harvard University. It appears that others didn't find the subject nearly as intriguing as I did! One day, I picked up a pad of paper and asked myself, Well, what do you love? Immediately I thought of libraries. The desire to write funny came from my belief that women's lives are often full of pain and challenge. It simply occurred to me that what women need, most of all, is a good laugh. My mission was born.

Q. Because this novel is written in the first person, it's tempting for the reader to believe Ally is based on you. Is there any truth to that idea?

A. Yes and no. How's that for an answer? I think every story a writer tells is in some way, shape, or form a reflection of themselves. The tricky part is defining and understanding what role the fictional personality plays in the writer's psyche. Why have I chosen to write about this character? Since I am quite opposite from Ally in terms of my outer behavior, it's particularly interesting for me to reflect on this question. My best guess is that a part of me would like to be Ally, with her perpetual innocence and eccentricity. Certainly, in other ways, we are similar. I love martinis, for example, and I enjoy solitude. Finally, we both adore and worship books.

Q. Ally's character is very unusual—after all, she was celibate for fifteen years! Did you wonder whether your readers would find her so quaint as to be unbelievable?

A. I think that when we read fiction, we are looking for a dramatic experience, a heightened sense of the way life seems to have an uncanny ability to throw fastballs, slow balls, curves, and twists. Indeed, we may want to experience a particular reality, without actually "experiencing" it, because the character's story line is so formidable or frightening. So, yes, I wondered whether the reader would be willing to go along for the ride. As the writer, I can't know for sure whether I've gone too far until someone else reads the story and gives me his or her opinion. That's when having an agent and editor whose opinion you truly respect can be invaluable. You can count on them to let you know.

Q. Did you plan the structure and plot of the novel before you began writing?

A. For the first time in my career, I made no notes or consciously shaped the plot. I knew for a certainty how it would end, and I hadn't a clue how I was going to make it happen. I wrote by the seat of my pants, and it was both a scary and an exhilarating ride. Interestingly enough, the very thing about which I was so confident—the ending—turned out to be as wrong as could be!

About midway through the novel, the characters began to leave me little hints that things weren't going to turn out as I had expected. Many writers have commented on this process, when a book's characters seem to direct the action, rather than the writer. I imagine this is hard for readers to understand. The explanation comes from a very real fact: "my" characters in "my" novel are no more mine than they would be yours or anyone else's. They exist as themselves. You can compare this to the way we think about God as our Creator. S/he creates each of us, and the world in which we live, but we are given free will to make the choices and decisions as we see fit. Just so, I create a story and its characters, but I give them the freedom to, in turn, create their existence.

Q. Are you going to continue writing funny, or will you return to the more serious suspense genre?

A. I guess nobody should ever say never, but I sincerely doubt that I will want to write a suspense or thriller novel in the future. I feel as though I've experienced a true epiphany about why I write. Earlier in this interview, when I mentioned that I'd found my mission, I was being serious about being funny! Humor allows me to write deeply about important themes, but with a light touch. The purpose of fiction is to open our eyes so that we may see a part of the world—or ourselves—in a new light. Sometimes our eyes open wider and see more clearly when the truth comes sideways, sneaking up on silent feet and making itself known in an explosion of laughter.

QUESTIONS FOR DISCUSSION

❧

1. In the opening pages of *The Dewey Decimal System of Love*, Ally declares that she has suddenly fallen in love with the new conductor of the Philadelphia Philharmonic. Do you believe it is possible to fall in love in the way Ally claims? Have you ever experienced a similar event?

2. As you get to know Ally in the first half of the novel, you may notice that she has a definite case of Peter Pan syndrome. What about the act of growing up does she seem to be afraid of, and why?

3. Ally has a unique and memorable way of speaking. How does her use of language, in this first-person narrative voice of the novel, reveal her personality?

4. In our society, we do not condone an unmarried woman's pursuit of a married man. How did you feel about Ally's attempt to woo and win Aleksi? Was your moral conundrum eased by the fact that his wife, Michelle, appeared to be a destructive person?

5. Ally is obviously passionate about the Dewey decimal system, which is used to organize the library's collection. Are you

familiar with how the Dewey decimal system works? Have you ever used it to find books in the library, and can you understand or share Ally's fervor for the system?

6. Although Ally is definitely a true eccentric, it might be argued that she is also Everywoman. What kind of evidence would you find to support this idea? Or do you believe that she is simply a unique, quirky character with no relevance to most women of the twenty-first century?

7. What imagery is used at the midpoint of the novel to capture Ally's pivotal turnaround moment? How might you analyze and discuss this image? Is it an experience that you've had or yearn to have, and if so, why?

8. Ally's relationships with her mother and her father are troubled, albeit in different ways. In discussing those relationships, how would you characterize them? Is the root of her difficulty in growing up, even at the ripe age of forty, a result of her emotional attachments to and disconnection from her family?

9. A recurring motif in the novel is Ally's sense that she is "beating out of time." This concept obviously has parallels with her obsession for Aleksi Kullio. In what ways is Ally's tempo wrong, and what is the discovery she needs to make in order to get in step? Have you ever felt that you were beating out of time in the way that Ally describes?

10. By the end of the novel, it appears that Ally has discovered the man she was always destined to love. Do you believe this love will survive and result in marriage? And, to be even more visionary, will the marriage be happy and fruitful?

CONTENTS

For Helena Caroline

1

INTRODUCTION TO THE STUDY OF MEDIA ECONOMICS

Media economics is concerned with how media operators meet the informational and entertainment wants and needs of audiences, advertisers, and society with available resources. It deals with the factors influencing production of media goods and services and the allocation of those products for consumption. This chapter explores these factors and the development of the principles of the market economy in which media operate.

This book is concerned with the economic aspects of mass media. It is intended to help find answers to such questions as: How could *USA Today* be established when hundreds of daily newspapers have died nationwide? Why have Home Box Office, Showtime, USA Network, the Family Network, and other cable channels significantly diminished broadcast network affiliates' audiences but not as strongly affected independent stations' audiences? Why does the videocassette market bear more resemblance to the book market than the television programming market? Why doesn't raising prices of newspaper subscriptions influence publishers the same way that raising cable television subscription prices affects cable systems? Will producing more record albums increase or decrease a company's financial return?

In order to consider such questions fully, it is necessary to understand the economic milieu in which the media operate. This requires knowledge of the nature of economic study and the development of economic principles and market capitalism. This book is intended to help develop that knowledge by focusing on media in the United States, a western capitalist nation. Although the fundamental principles and concepts can be applied in other settings with different economic systems and industrial structures, the U.S.-based examples presented in this book are not intended to be indicative of media situations in those settings. This chapter is intended to introduce basic elements in the study of economics to help provide a base for specific concepts and

issues that will be discussed further in later chapters that relate more
directly to media.

Economics is the study of how limited or scarce *resources* are
allocated to satisfy competing and unlimited *needs* and *wants*, and of
the forces that direct and constrain that activity. Scarcity exists because
resources are finite, whereas wants tend to be infinite, exceeding available resources.

Economics is the study of the production and consumption of resources and products, as well as the choices made to meet needs and
wants. *Production* is the creation of goods and services for consumption. *Consumption* is the use of goods and services or resources to
satisfy wants and needs. Individuals and firms are both producers and
consumers in that they consume resources and produce goods and
services.

In order to consider the ways in which these activities take place and
the effects that these activities have, economists have divided the study
of economics into two major branches, macroeconomics and microeconomics. *Macroeconomics* studies and analyzes the operation of the
economic system as a whole, usually at the national level, to understand
its relationship to issues such as economic growth, employment, and
inflation. Macroeconomic studies often focus on political economy,
that is, the public policies toward the economy, aggregate production
and consumption of goods, employment and income, and policies to
stimulate or retard growth or promote social welfare.

Microeconomics departs from the large scale and considers the
market system in operation, looking at the economic activities of producers and consumers in specific markets. It considers the behavior of
individual producers and consumers, as well as of aggregate groups of
producers and consumers in those markets.

There is an interplay between macroeconomics and microeconomics. Government actions and policies affect the decisions of producers
and consumers, and the performance of various product markets in turn
stimulates government action or inaction. The predominant focus of
this book will be microeconomic, that is, looking at the activities of
consumers and producers in media markets. These activities are influenced by macroeconomic factors, and so these concepts will be introduced as well.

NEEDS AND WANTS

Needs and wants are both public and private. Individuals and societies must make decisions about which needs and wants get satisfied and

to what degrees. *Private wants and needs* include subsistence, convenience, and individually determined wants and needs. Subsistence needs include those basic elements necessary for survival, such as food, clothing, and shelter. Human beings are not satisfied with mere subsistence, however. Once those needs are met, they have convenience wants that they seek to satisfy. These include the goods and services that make life easier, more comfortable, and more convenient, such as washing machines, automobiles, and prepared foods. In addition to such wants, individuals usually have psychologically motivated wants, such as fame, belonging, and status, that can be partly satisfied through the acquisition or use of resources.

Each society also has it own wants and needs that leaders attempt to satisfy. These *public wants and needs* include such items as military forces to protect against foreign aggressors, police forces to protect individuals and property from criminals, highways and transportation infrastructures, public education, and social services. Each of these public wants and needs competes with the others for scarce resources, and the public sphere competes with the private sphere for resources as well.

Media organizations function in the economic system to meet both private and public needs and wants. Media serve the wants and needs of four distinct groups: 1) media owners, the individuals or stockholders who own media outlets; 2) audiences, those who view, listen to, or read media content; 3) advertisers, those who purchase time or space to convey messages to audiences; and 4) media employees, those who work for the firms.

In general terms, each of these four constituencies has the following wants and needs: Owners want the preservation of the firm and its assets, high rates of return on their investments, company growth, and increase in value of the firm and, thus, their investment. Audiences want high quality media products and services, at a low cost if the product or service is purchased, and they wish to be able to acquire the media product with ease. Advertisers want access to their targeted audiences, at a low price, and high quality service from media employees. Employees want good compensation, fair and equal treatment, safe and pleasant working conditions, and psychic rewards for their labor. As will be shown later, media, audiences, advertisers, and employees are all involved in both consumption and production.

Media also serve public wants and needs by providing forums in which ideas and issues may be conveyed that are necessary for the maintenance of social order and progress. Public wants for media include multiple stable media outlets, organized use of resources, and content diversity.

ALLOCATION

The resources available to produce goods and services to satisfy private and public needs and wants are scarce, and meeting all the wants is impossible. As a result, choices are made among the wants and available resources to determine which and how many of the wants will be satisfied. This process is called *allocation* of resources. Allocation involves determining what is produced, how it is produced, and who consumes the products made. Allocation involves three major choices in using available resources: 1) what good should be produced; 2) how should it be produced; and 3) who gets to consume the good or service.

The first issue involves answering the questions of *what* should be produced and made available to meet wants and, secondarily, *how much* should be produced to meet those wants. In the public sector, for example, this decision involves questions about whether government funds should be directed to pay for "Star Wars" or to provide housing for the homeless. In the realm of media, it involves public choices over whether the government should allocate available broadcast frequencies for more local television stations or for mobile telephone communications. In the private sector, this type of decision involves choices of whether a company should make calculators or adding machines, or in media whether a recording firm should use its money to record ten artists or only five, but to produce more of the latter's recordings. It also involves the question of whether the firm should produce the recordings as records, cassettes, compact discs, or a combination of the three products.

The second allocative issue involves *how* the goods are made. That is, who or what will do that work? Will human or machine labor be used? What type of tools and technology will be employed? The issue of where the goods will be made must also be answered. In media these allocative issues are addressed by answering questions such as whether live disc jockeys or automated playback equipment should be used in radio stations, and whether a television program should be filmed in a studio in Hollywood or Toronto.

The third major issue is *who* will consume the goods and services. That is, how will they be distributed among people and industries? The answer to this question is based on the pattern of decision making adopted in a society. Four major allocation patterns are common: 1) *traditional decision making*, in which choices are based on repetition of earlier decisions, socioeconomic or class status, and other factors; 2) *market decision making*, in which the amount of supply and consumer demand determines prices, which in turn influence production and who is able to receive goods and services; 3) *centralized decision making*, in which choices are made by authorities and planning boards; and 4) *mixed decision making*, which combines elements of market and centralized decision making.

Allocation in the United States and most western nations is done by mixed decision making, with a great reliance on the market but some central planning. Most communist nations in Eastern Europe, Asia, and other parts of the world are also using mixed decision making, but with great reliance on central planning and some reliance on the market economy.

DEVELOPMENT AND PRINCIPLES OF THE MARKET ECONOMY

The market economy, that is, a system in which allocative decisions are made on the basis of the economic forces controlling operations of the market, is the primary basis of the capitalist or free enterprise economic system. This system emerged when production and distribution of goods and services moved outside the control of state authorities through the decline of the feudal system. Political and economic systems then developed that led to the accumulation of wealth that could be used for production of additional goods and services. These basic elements were then combined with a concurrent development of technology that increased production and led to a greater division of labor and the general rise of living standards in the eighteenth and nineteenth centuries.

The major political, social, and economic upheaval caused by the transition from feudalism to mercantilism to the market economy was watched with interest during the seventeenth and eighteenth centuries by a number of observers, who attempted to understand and explain the new market-based order that was emerging in England, Germany, and France. Their observations were synthesized and rearticulated in a comprehensive form by Adam Smith in 1776 in *The Wealth of Nations*. Smith argued that the market system's operation was based on several major principles. These include:

1) Competition between different producers and competition between different consumers are the central elements of the system.

2) Consumers and producers have equal strength in the market.

3) Economic self-interest of producers and consumers will be used as a guide in all production and consumption decisions.

4) The market is its own regulator and will operate in an orderly fashion, producing what is needed and wanted by consumers, in the amounts needed and wanted by consumers, at prices consumers are willing to pay and at which producers are willing to sell. The market constantly readjusts to meet changing needs and wants and the demand of consumers of products. (Smith, 1776/1952)

Smith argued that if the market was left alone ("laissez-faire") to operate according to these basic principles, capital would be accumulated that could be used for new production, resulting in growth in the national economy. This would improve the quality of life for all men and women, and society as a whole would be improved. Smith saw this process as inevitable, continuous, and orderly.

A corollary theory of the marketplace of ideas followed, based on the economic marketplace and the argument that an ideal market allowed to operate without constraint would provide the public the opportunity to select from among the most meritorious of the ideas and information offered. In such a system, it was argued, truth would ultimately emerge and the individuals and society would benefit.

As the capitalist market-based system continued to develop during the eighteenth and nineteenth centuries, economists began observing differences between the way it had been described by Smith and others, and the way it actually operated. A number of observers began questioning Smith's view that the marketplace was orderly, and that the results would inevitably, by continuous growth of the economy, improve the quality of life of all members of society. These critics included capitalists such as Robert Owen and members of the nobility such as Henri de Saint-Simon, who believed that the market must be tempered by Christian ethics lest it become an immoral quest for accumulation that impoverished and enslaved workers. Socialists, such as Gracchus Babeuf, William Godwin, and Pierre J. Proudhon, argued that the market system created inequalities that must be eliminated.

David Ricardo, Karl Marx, and other nineteenth-century economists further described the economic mechanisms that created these problems. Marx put forth his views and synthesized others' observations to add additional understanding of how the market system worked. Among the principles he laid out were the following:

1) Consumers' demands for and producers' supplies of goods and services are never perfectly matched. There is a mismatching of production and consumption that creates lag times in responses to demand and misreadings of demand by producers. As a result, there is a regular cyclical expansion and contraction of the economy in what is now called the business cycle.

2) Accumulation of capital leads to the creation of bigger firms that have unequal power over smaller firms. This diminishes competition between producers, creates unequal power between producer and consumer, and thus diminishes or removes the benefits of the market system.

3) The use of machinery instead of human labor permits producers to provide goods and services at lower prices, but at lower profit margins as well. As profit margins decline, weaker firms are unable to survive and are closed or merged with other firms. This diminishes competition and its benefits. (Marx, 1867/1952)

The bases of the development of economic thought are well outlined in such classic works as J. F. Bell's *A History of Economic Thought* (1967), Charles Gide and Charles Rist's *History of Economic Doctrines* (1979), Joseph F. Schumpeter's *Ten Great Economists* (1965), and Lewis H. Haney's *History of Economic Thought* (1949), as well as Robert L. Heilbroner's more popular work, *The Worldly Philosophers* (1980).

The market system problems described by both capitalists and socialists led to the development of large business enterprises throughout the developed world. Concurrently, the idea of *the firm* as a separate economic entity with its own self-interest emerged. Larger firms purchased small firms and merged to create even larger firms. Producers formed trusts and cartels whereby they could control supply of raw materials, production of goods, and price of products. Capitalist nations responded by creating laws supporting the market system that outlawed many anticompetitive actions and the creations of trust and cartels. In the United States the Sherman Antitrust Act of 1890 and the Clayton Antitrust Act of 1914 were enacted to outlaw activities that undermined the system.

The large firms that developed by the latter half of the nineteenth and early twentieth centuries also used their economic power in ways that disadvantaged laborers, did not share the wealth accumulated through the market system as Smith had envisioned, and kept many persons in untenable social conditions. In response, workers organized labor unions, and governments enacted legislation throughout the capitalist world to promote better working and living conditions by regulating job safety, minimum wages, and hours worked, and by providing mechanisms of basic social welfare for workers harmed in depressed periods of market operation.

The basic principles of the market system have remained the same since the early twentieth century, but the changes sparked by government intervention have resulted in mixed economies rather than pure market economies. New theories to explain operations within the broad principles of the market economy have appeared since that time, but these have tended to focus on government activities at the macro-economic level or on specific elements of microeconomics that develop understanding based on the broad principles outlined above.

MEDIA AND THE MARKETPLACE

Media in the United States are for the most part capitalist ventures, operated by private parties for the purpose of generating profit, and are thus subject to the operational principles of the market system. Even not-for-profit media — such as public broadcasting or organization-operated media — are influenced by the principles of the market system and are thus affected by its operations.

Because these principles affect the operations of media, one needs to understand how they apply to media. It is also necessary to under-stand the issues that are raised in media operations as individual and aggregate firms produce media goods and services for consumption by individual and aggregate consumers.

Communication firms use scarce resources — electricity, paper, equipment, skilled labor, programming, information — to satisfy their wants to produce media goods and services and gain profit. Consumers use scarce resources — time and money — to satisfy their wants and needs to acquire information and be entertained by media products or to get their message carried in media. Because the resources of pro-ducers and consumers are scarce, producers of media goods and ser-vices and consumers of media goods and services are constrained in their abilities to meet all the wants and needs they have for media products. Thus, each turns to allocation to determine what and how media products will be produced and how and by whom they will be consumed. Media economics focuses on these basic issues, concentrat-ing on the operations of economic principles in media markets.

Media cannot be considered separately from the economic system in which they operate because the economic forces of the system direct and constrain the choices of those who manage media, just as they do the choices of managers of any other industry. This book is concerned with those forces and how they affect media, and provides a framework for understanding the underpinnings of the economic system affecting media and the specific issues that arise in media economics. The approach is what is called positive, or applied, economics, which concentrates upon what actually happens and can be shown to occur. From time to time allusions will be made to the more theoretical branch of economics, which proposes what might occur under given circumstances or attempts to structure broader operations within a larger framework. This book will not concentrate upon these ideas, however, but upon those that will be most useful to students of media and to media managers in analyzing and making economic decisions.

2

THE CONCEPT AND ROLE OF THE MARKET

The economic behavior of media is impelled and constrained by the characteristics of and influences on media markets. This chapter discusses how markets are defined, how similar and dissimilar media compete, and how different market structures affect that competition and the products available to consumers in the market.

Every industry has different characteristics, but they all participate in markets that can be analyzed using similar concepts. It is important for media personnel to understand these concepts because the nature and structures of markets significantly affect their work. Such knowledge is essential for advertising sales personnel at the Los Angeles *Times* to understand whether they are in the same market as the *Daily News*; it is crucial for the circulation manager of *Atlantic Monthly* to know whether his magazine is competing with *Reader's Digest* for readers; and it is necessary for the programmer at WBZ-TV in Boston to know whether the station is competing with videocassette rentals for its audience and to what degree.

Although there are some similarities, media industries differ from many other industries in terms of the markets in which they operate, the amount and nature of competition in those markets, and their unique concentration and monopoly characteristics. Media serve public interests that have resulted in regulatory control of the structures of some media industries and at the same time media have special constitutional protection in order to carry out their public interest role. This chapter outlines the structure of the good and service markets in which media participate, the nature of the geographical markets in which they operate, and the availability of substitute goods and services within those markets, as well as the effects that these factors have on media operations.

the sellers' *good or service* — the commodity or labor available for trade — the geographical locations of sellers and buyers, and the willingness of the buyers and sellers to engage in trade. There are many markets for goods and services because the availability of these resources is influenced by geographic areas in which various sellers and buyers are willing and able to conduct their transactions. A *market* consists of sellers that provide the same good or service, or closely substitutable goods or services, to the same group of consumers. The geographic market determines the boundaries in which these sellers offer the same good or service to the same buyers. In economic discussions of markets, it is necessary to define a specific market in which such activity takes place. This is especially true when discussing media markets, because they are somewhat more complex than those of many other industries. Defining a market involves specifying the *good/service markets* involved and *combining* that description with a specific *geographic market* description.

THE MEDIA GOOD/SERVICE MARKET

In economic terms, media industries are unusual because they operate in what is called a *dual product market*. They create one product but participate in two separate good and service markets (Figure 2.1). Performance in each market affects performance in the other.

The first market in which media participate is that for the *good*, the media product. This good (sometimes called the content product) is the information and entertainment packaged and delivered in the form of a printed newspaper, magazine, or book, a radio or television broadcast, cable service, or a film or video production. This product is marketed to media consumers. Performance in this market is measured in a variety of ways. For newspapers and magazines, it is measured by circulation statistics for subscribed and single copy sales circulation or revenue from that circulation. For books and videos, performance is measured by the number of books or videocassettes sold or revenue from those sales. Broadcast performance is measured by audience ratings, and films are judged by tickets sold.

Marketing content to consumers involves attracting their attention to the product so that they will exchange either their time and/or time and money for the product. Not all media require that consumers pay money for the content product, but all consumers must pay with their time, a scarce resource. Daily newspapers, magazines, books, videocassettes, cable television service, and films typically require a purchase by

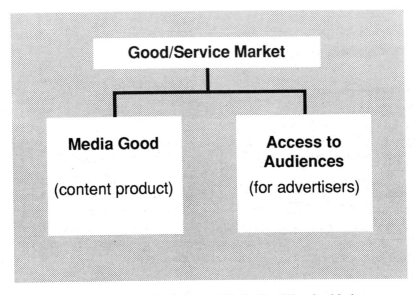

Figure 2.1 Elements in the Definition of Media Good/Service Markets

consumers, but radio and television broadcasters offer their services without charge to consumers.

Differing characteristics of goods affect demand for goods and consumption of goods. A good is considered to be a *private good* if its use by one consumer diminishes its availability to others. A *public good*, however, does not diminish the availability of the good to others. Media are both private and public goods, depending upon their attributes (see Table 2.1). A consumer who purchases a copy of a newspaper diminishes the number of available copies; thus a newspaper is a private good. A consumer who views a television broadcast, however, does not consume it in a fashion that diminishes its availability to other viewers, so it is a public good.

The second market in which many media participate is the advertising market. Although some observers may casually conclude that media sell space or time to purchasers of advertising, a more precise and descriptive explanation is that media sell *access to audiences* to advertisers. The amount charged for bringing readers and viewers into contact with advertisers' messages is more dependent upon the sizes and characteristics of audiences to which access is provided than the sizes or lengths of the advertisements themselves. Not all media participate in this advertising market, however; some rely solely on revenue from sales of the content product and others are funded by contributions. Examples of media that do not participate in the advertising-based

TABLE 2.1 Public and Private Goods in the Media

Medium	Private Good	Public Good
Books	x	
Cable programming		x
Films		x
Magazines	x	
Newspapers	x	
Radio broadcasts		x
Recordings	x	
Television broadcasts		x
Videocassettes	x	

market include public radio and television, adless publications such as *Consumer Reports* and *Mad* magazine, books, and film and video productions. Media that provide access to audiences to advertisers do so in a variety of ways and provide access to subcategories of the advertising market — including local advertising, classified advertising, insert advertising, and national advertising — in varying degrees.

Media, then, participate in the dual markets differently. Some participate in both markets and some participate in only one, and the degree to which they compete in each market differs as well (see Table 2.2).

THE GEOGRAPHIC MARKET

Media units operate in specific geographic markets and are inextricably linked to those markets by the product content and advertising services they provide within those markets. Some media operations compete nationwide, including nationally circulated magazines and newspapers (such as *USA Today*, the *Christian Science Monitor*, and the *Wall Street Journal*), radio, television and cable networks and syndication firms, national magazines, and book, videocassette, and film companies. Most individual units of media, such as individual newspapers, television and radio stations, cable operators, and regional and local magazines, are linked to specific local geographic markets.

The standards and means of determining local geographic markets vary among media industries, based upon inherent differences in the media and ways in which audiences of various media are analyzed. For newspapers, the retail trading zone (RTZ) is the relevant geographic market in most situations because this is the zone in which the primary business for retail and classified advertising lineage and circulation is

TABLE 2.2 Markets in Which Media Participate

Medium	Content Paid	Market Nonpaid	Local Ads	Advertising Class. Ads	Market Inserts	Nat'l Ads
Books	*					
Cable						
networks	(some)	*				*
local service	*		*	+		
Films	*					
Magazines						
local	*	(some)	*	+		
national	*	(some)		+		*
Newspapers						
daily	*		*	*	+	+
weekly	*	(some)	*	+	+	
shoppers		*	*	+	*	
Radio						
networks	*					*
local-comm.		*	*			+
noncommercial		*				
Recordings	*					
Television						
networks	*					*
local-comm.		*	*			+
noncommercial		*				
Videocassettes	*					

* = primary market + = secondary market

conducted. In some situations, the metropolitan area (metro area) may be the appropriate geographic market; in other cases, papers limit their markets to a designated primary market area (PMA).

Television and radio stations operate on electromagnetic frequencies within geographic markets specified by the Federal Communications Commission (FCC). Because of variances in geographic markets defined by the FCC for stations in the same location, the broadcast and advertising industries have developed standardized geographic areas defined by the Arbitron Co. as the Area of Dominant Influence (ADI) or by the A. C. Nielsen Co. as the Designated Market Area (DMA).

The geographic markets of cable television systems are specifically designated within their franchise agreements, but many other local media — including weekly newspapers and local and regional magazines — select and specify their own geographic markets. In some unique situations, the location in which a medium is produced is much smaller than the geographic market in which trade is conducted. This is sometimes the case for newspapers and broadcast stations that domi-

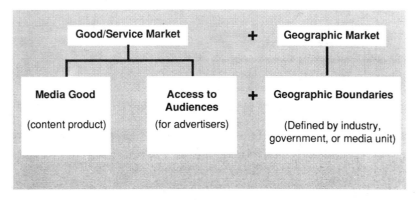

Figure 2.2 Elements in the Definition of Media Good/Service Markets

nate a large portion of a single state, an entire state, or several states, such as the Des Moines *Register*, the Salt Lake City *Tribune*, KFI-AM in Los Angeles, WSM-AM in Memphis, KOA-AM in Denver, and WBBM-AM in Chicago. In such situations a case can be made for expanding the relevant market into a regional market with designated boundaries. When this is done, however, it is often necessary to separate the geographic market for the content product from the geographic market for audience access because they do not always coincide.

Definitions of media markets, then, are created by combining the geographic and good/serve market definitions into a specifically defined market for a specific media unit or portions of its media products (see Figure 2.2).

ISSUES INVOLVING MARKETS

Understanding and defining the concept and role of markets is crucial to managers of media and to those who make public policy because market issues are central to issues of competition and concentration. Many of these issues will be addressed more fully in subsequent chapters, but we must first consider the role of markets in determining whether and how different types of media, and different units of the same medium, compete with each other, and the nature of market structures and market power.

INTERMEDIA COMPETITION

The issue of whether different media compete with each other is inextricably linked to the concept of the market, the dual markets in which media participate, and specific geographic markets in which competition takes place. At the core of this discussion is whether all media products are similar and the degree to which they are *substitutable*, that is, whether media goods and services are interchangeable with each other. To understand the degree of substitutability and, thus, competitiveness among media, one must consider the dual products of media separately and then consider whether the geographical markets for the media are interchangeable as well.

In the broadest sense, all media compete in the content product market by providing information and entertainment. Although media have these content similarities, newspapers, television, radio, magazines, books, films, videocassettes, and other media products serve distinctly different needs and are used in distinctly different ways by audiences. They are not fully interchangeable products any more than football games are interchangeable with ballet performances as leisure time spectator activities.

For audiences, newspapers and magazines serve primarily information and idea functions while broadcast media, film and videocassettes, and cable television serve primarily entertainment functions. Even magazines, which most closely approximate the content provided by newspapers, clearly are not substitutes because of differences in frequency and approach to information. Television, radio, cable, and other media do not provide the range or amounts of information provided by newspapers, and their formats, frequencies, and usage differ.

These differences affect the way in which content is conveyed and the times and formats in which it is available. For instance, television and radio carry news and information, and thus compete with newspapers, but they carry only a limited amount of news and only at specified times. Premium cable television services convey films to audiences, but only after they have appeared in theaters and with a limitation of the visual perspective provided viewers.

Because of content differences, day-to-day substitution of different media as a source of information is limited. Substitution of different media as a source of entertainment is much less limited, however, but is somewhat constrained by the originality and freshness of the material presented. Nevertheless, there appears to be a significant amount of long-term substitution of different media resulting from the development and diffusion of new media technology. McCombs (1972) has shown the willingness of consumers to substitute new media for existing media; this results in significant intermedia competition for audience attention among similar media, such as film, television, and video. Levy and Pitsch, for instance, have shown that audiences are willing to substitute VCRs and cable television (1985). That one medium is not

| Production Form | Communicative Form | | |
	Aural	*Visual*	*Aural & Visual*
Inscribed		books magazines newspapers	
Recorded	recordings radio		cable film television video

Figure 2.3 Media Product Characteristics

ing media; this results in significant intermedia competition for audience attention among similar media, such as film, television, and video. Levy and Pitsch, for instance, have shown that audiences are willing to substitute VCRs and cable television (1985). That one medium is not necessarily substitutable for another has been shown by Lacy (1987), whose research reveals that the development and diffusion of radio nationwide had little impact on newspaper competition throughout the country. Similar results were found by Fullerton (1988), who remarked that the diffusion of television induced consumers to make temporary diversions of resources from nonmedia uses to purchase TV sets but that expenditures for media and nonmedia uses returned to their normal pattern immediately thereafter.

The ways in which different media are used and messages internalized by audiences are also affected by the differing communicative and productive characteristics of media (see Figure 2.3). Exposure to aural communications, such as radio broadcasts and sound recordings, usually coincides with other audience activities, and the communications rarely receive the full attention of listeners. This problem is also found with aural-and-visual media, particularly television, video, and cable. Exposure to visual media such as books, magazines, and newspapers is generally voluntary and audiences focus attention on the content to a much greater degree than do users of other media.

The relationships of audiences and different media are not defined merely by use. Important differences also exist in the financial relationships between media and audiences, and these affect the significance placed upon them. Newspaper, magazine, and book readers, as well as and attachment to the product than they do for media products procured at no direct cost, and attend to their content (including advertising) to a greater degree than to those for which no monetary exchange is made.

More substitutability is evident in the market for advertising than in the content product market, as has been argued by Rosse (1980) and Owen (1975), but that interchangeability is limited. Although there are similarities among media that rely upon sales of access to audiences for income, these media are not completely interchangeable because they provide significantly different types of access to audiences. The major reason that media are not fully interchangeable in the advertising market is that their audiences differ widely in terms of product usage patterns as well as in geographic, demographic, and psychographic terms, all of which are key elements in advertisers' choices of media. Variations in the penetration of different media into homes in communities, the length of time that different media receive the attention of audiences, and the types of people using different media create differences in the ways media are utilized by advertisers.

In addition, the various media have unique qualities that make them suitable or unsuitable for various messages (see Table 2.3). For example, the media needs of grocery and department stores, whose managers wish to display their products in ads, are best met by the inherent properties of newspapers. Companies wishing national brand name recognition, such as McDonald's and Procter and Gamble, find television most suitable for conveying their message to meet that need. Firms wishing to provide discount coupons to lure customers use newspaper and magazine advertising, advertising inserts, and mail delivery.

The differences between media products are often not recognized by media personnel, but they have been recognized in legal decisions and public policies regarding media, although there has been some government confusion and disagreement over how to separate the dual products — content and access to audiences — when defining markets. In several cases, courts have ruled that newspapers and broadcasting stations do not operate in the same product markets (see *United States v. Citizen Publishing Co.*, 1968; and *United States v. Times Mirror Co.*, 1967). In 1975, when the FCC promulgated its rule against cross-ownership of broadcasting enterprises and newspapers in the same geographic market, the agency accepted a definition of media markets that blurred the distinction between newspapers and television stations in the advertising market, but specifically excluded other media from evaluations of the availability of diversity in specific geographic markets. The FCC argued: "According to the Department of Justice, newspapers and television stations are in many ways engaged in the same business, namely attracting audiences and selling them to adver-

TABLE 2.3 Strengths and Limitations of Different Media for Advertisers

Medium	Strengths	Weaknesses
Newspapers	intense coverage	short life
	flexibility	hasty reading
	prestige	moderate to poor
	dealer/advertiser coordination	reproduction
Magazines	market selectivity	inflexible area coverage and time
	long life	
	high reproduction quality	inflexible to copy changes
	prestige	low overall market penetration
	extra services	wide distribution
Television	mass coverage	fleeting message
	impact	commercial wear-out
	repetition	lack of selectivity
	prestige	high cost
	flexibility	
Radio	audience selectivity	fragmentation
	immediacy	transient quality of listenership
	flexibility	
	mobility	limited sensory input

Source: from *Managing Media Organizations* by John M. Lavine and Daniel B. Wackman, copyright 1987 by Longman. Reprinted with permission.

tisers. . . . Since Justice sees newspaper and television advertising as interchangeable, it would define the product market so as to include newspapers and television stations" (FCC, 1975, para. 35). The FCC also stated, "the Justice Department would only include local television and newspapers in evaluating diversity since in its view these are the only effective competitors for local advertising. Weekly newspapers and other periodicals as well as broadcast signals originating outside the market on this basis should therefore not be counted" (FCC, 1975, para. 48).

The fact that there are differences between media and that these intermedia differences are recognized in law and public policy does not mean there are no similarities among media product markets and that advertiser demand will never be satisfied by substituting one medium for another. However, switching advertising from one medium to another would be based on unusual rather than usual decision making and would take into account a wide variety of factors in a specific market, including the impact of the differences discussed above, the cost for reaching targeting audiences, and differences in the geographic, demographic, and psychographic characteristics of the media audiences in the specific market served by the media. Advertising plans take these differences into account, seeking a mix of media that best serves an advertiser's needs.

Most advertiser decisions about placing advertising in media are predetermined before advertisers seek specific media outlets in which to place the advertising. Because of this preselection of what types of media will receive what percentage of available advertising dollars, most media are not in direct competition and are not seen as direct substitutes by advertisers. It has been noted that

> Advertisers and advertising agencies will usually select the media types within which an advertising campaign will run prior to the negotiation process to purchase time and space. This is because it is believed that there are other more important factors in determining advertising effectiveness than the cost efficiencies between various media outlets. (Busterna, 1988b, p. 41)

If an advertiser determines that a choice exists between two media outlets for the specific advertising message he or she wishes to convey, then an analysis of the geographic market served by the two types of media will be undertaken before determining their substitutability. Although the media may both operate in the same location, their separate geographic markets might preclude finding a substitute. The generally larger markets of broadcast media might extend well beyond a newspaper or cable system operation, but not as far as a regional magazine. These types of considerations, as well as the higher costs of the media serving a larger market, would keep different media from being substitutable for many advertisers.

Some competition among different media in the same geographic market exists, but it is limited. Although all media compete for the attention of audiences in the content product market, each provides varying gratifications to audience members, who tend to use a variety of media rather than a single medium to receive the content products of their choice. Competition for advertising revenue also exists but is significantly limited except among media with similar qualities and content delivery forms. In the same market, television, cable, film, and video compete most directly for audiences. Television and cable compete most directly for advertising dollars, and there is competition for some advertising dollars between newspapers of different frequency.

Despite their differences, advertising-based media compete somewhat in the long run as new media enter the market and alter the types of media available. Expenditures on advertising remain relatively constant as a portion of the national economy (Scripps, 1965), and the addition of new media results not in increased spending but in a reallocation of the existing expenditures among media (McCombs, 1972).

The existence of such intermedia competition over time has been shown in an application of the theory of niche to media. That theory, drawn from the natural sciences, argues that organisms adapt to their environments by developing separate niches from which they compete and coexist with each other in uses of resources. When the theory has been applied to media, increasingly diffuse competition, particularly for national advertising, has been shown to follow shifting use of different media by audiences. Competition was shown to be greatest among media that provide similar types of audience access or message form (Dimmick and Rothenbuhler, 1984).

The breakdown of traditional boundaries between media, such as classified advertising now being carried on cable channels as well as in newspapers, makes it more difficult to define markets that had previously been defined solely by format or production process distinctions. Compaine has argued that "the economists' approach of looking at a specific medium, such as newspapers, is becoming less valid — if it ever was valid — as the technologies of alternative media forms merge with one another" (1985, p. 82).

The answer to this criticism lies in defining good and service markets precisely, and in recognizing that a medium competes in several different good and service markets and that different media compete in such markets to different degrees. Thus, market definitions must include the subcategories of markets in which different media compete.

INTRAMEDIA COMPETITION

Different units of the same medium operating in the same or portions of the same geographic market generally compete with each other to provide content to audiences and access to audiences to advertisers, and can be substituted. This is not to say that there are no differences in the content product or the audience that is accessible to advertisers, because product differentiation and market segmentation result in variance, but that the substitutability of units of the same medium is much greater than that between different media.

If a half dozen commercial television stations compete in the same market — as is the case in many mid-sized markets — the inherent qualities of the content product and type of access afforded advertisers will be substantially similar, although specific programming will differ. As a result, substitution can take place with minimal sacrifice of the attributes that make any one station attractive to viewers or advertisers. If a dozen radio stations exist in the market, however, they will exhibit greater content differences. Normally, they each will have different music and program formats and their audience segmentation and shares of the available audience will be highlighted as they seek advertisers wishing to gain access to the different audiences of each station. Some substitution of stations with different content and audience access products can be made without giving up the attributes that make radio advertising attractive.

The types, sizes, and number of geographic markets for broadcasting stations have been the subject of significant policy debates, but it is now the policy of the FCC to have as many local geographic markets as possible (Noll, Peck, and McGowan, 1973, esp. pp. 97-107). In addition, the FCC is using newly available spectrum and technology to increase the number of potential stations in each of these markets to promote more choices for viewers, listeners, and advertisers.

Units of the same medium that operate from the same location do not necessarily compete directly with each other within the same geographic market, however. It is quite common for RTZs, metro areas, ADIs, and DMAs to include media that compete in only a portion of the market.

This situation is illustrated in Figure 2.4, which shows a metropolitan area that includes three separate cities — Metropolis, Suburbia, and Outskirt City — and an unincorporated area. Three daily newspapers are published within the metro area: the *Daily Times*, which serves the entire metro area and is based in Metropolis; the *Suburbia Gazette*, which is based in Suburbia; and the *Globe*, which is based in Outskirt City. The suburban papers are available to subscribers within the city limits of the towns in which they are published, and single copy sales are available within those cities and some surrounding areas. Thus, their geographic markets are much smaller than that of the metro daily.

In this situation competition is limited. Although both the *Gazette* and *Globe* compete with the *Daily Times* within their primary markets — Suburbia and Outskirt City — they do not compete with the metropolitan paper in the city of Metropolis or the unincorporated suburban area. Neither do the two suburban papers compete with each other. Rosse (1975) has described this style of market structure as *umbrella competition*, in which suburban dailies, weekly papers, and other

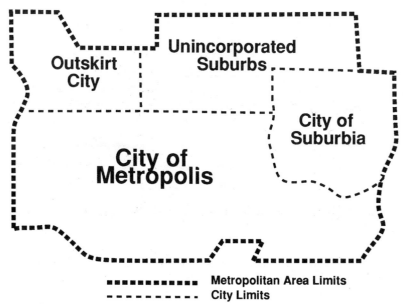

Figure 2.4 Metropolis and Its Metropolitan Area

Rosse (1975) has described this style of market structure as *umbrella competition*, in which suburban dailies, weekly papers, and other publications compete in different layers under the umbrella of a metropolitan daily (see Figure 2.5).

In umbrella competition, the first layer is that of the metropolitan daily newspaper, which reports on and circulates throughout the metro area and sometimes throughout the state or region. In a few situations the first layer includes more than one metropolitan daily, but that situation is found in fewer than two dozen metropolitan areas in the U.S. today. The second layer is that of satellite city dailies. Satellite cities were usually established long before the metropolitan area expanded to include them and have local identities separate from the metropolitan identity and well-established local daily newspapers. The third layer of competition is suburban dailies. These papers operate in metropolitan suburbs created by the growth of the metropolitan area; these metropolitan suburbs have a local identity but closer ties to the major metropolitan city because many residents work, shop, and seek entertainment in the city. The fourth layer of competition includes weekly newspapers and shoppers that circulate in all or part of a suburb or satellite city. Competition for readers and advertisers occurs within and between layers, but great differences in the levels of competition exist.

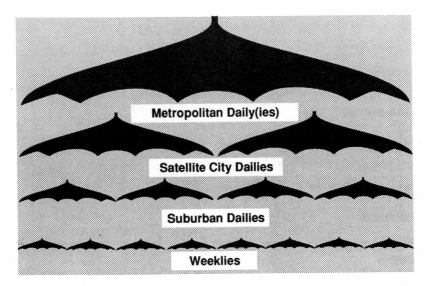

Figure 2.5 Umbrella Competition

cities or metro areas within an ADI or DMA experience more competition from the different layers of competition. A station may identify strongly with one community and limit its operations to that area, especially its advertising sales activities. The delineation of a smaller market is more difficult for broadcasters than for newspapers, however, because their ability to keep distribution of their content product in a specific geographic area is limited because broadcast signals do not stop at city limits, at the boundaries of metro areas, or at RTZs.

For a unit of a medium to be directly substitutable for another, it must be substantially similar in format and content, garner a similar audience, and operate in the same geographic market as the other unit does. In the newspaper industry, for example, a directly substitutable content and advertising product for a local daily newspaper exists only when another daily newspaper produced and distributed primarily in the same geographic market is present. Such situations exist in fewer than two dozen U.S. cities, including New York, Boston, Chicago, Los Angeles, and Dallas. Daily newspapers from outside the locality provide some limited substitutability if they are available within the geographic market, but that substitutability is limited. In such cases the interchangeability involves content originating outside the local area, such as state, national, and international news, features, and national advertising. Papers from separate geographical markets differ substantially in terms of the provision of local information and advertising, however. Local daily newspapers can be substituted in a limited way by weekly or other nondaily papers that also provide local, but not national and international, information. In cases where a local daily exists, however, it is rare for consumers to substitute the nondaily as an information source. Instead, it is usually used as a supplementary source of information. Advertisers, however, find that nondailies provide some substitutability. This is particularly true of advertisers who produce inserts and who may be willing in certain circumstances to sacrifice access to the daily paid-newspaper reader for access to a larger audience provided by a free circulation total-market-coverage paper.

Competition among units of broadcast media is far greater than that existing for newspapers. Because of the existence of multiple stations, many with overlapping audiences, a greater degree of substitutability exists among television stations or radio stations for advertisers. Some similar situations exist in the magazine industry, but the audiences tend to be segmented to a much greater degree and appeal to specific advertisers.

Intramedia competition in broadcast television is also influenced by the assignment of frequency and affiliation with programming networks. Levin (1980) has shown that stations with VHF frequencies and those with network affiliations have competitive advantages over stations assigned to UHF frequencies and those not affiliated with the major networks.

MARKET STRUCTURES AND MARKET POWER

The number of producers in a given market is important because it is an indication of the market power that firms possess and their ability to control and influence the economic operations in that market. The industrial organization model provides a method for analyzing markets based on four major market structures: perfect competition, monopolistic competition, oligopoly, and monopoly (see Figure 2.6).

The model states that the structure of a market is dependent upon a variety of factors, including the number of buyers and sellers present, differences in their product, and barriers to the entry of new competitors in the market.

Perfect competition exists when there are many sellers of a good or service that is not differentiated and no firm(s) dominate(s) the market. In such a situation the economic forces operate freely.

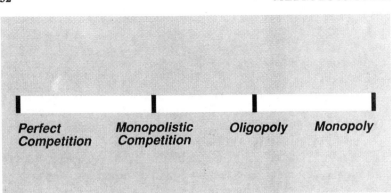

Figure 2.6 The Market Power Continuum

Monopolistic competition exists when there are a number of sellers of similar goods or services, but the products are differentiated and each product is available only from the firm that produces it.

If there are only a few sellers in a market but some competition exists for their products, either homogeneous or differentiated, the market structure is described as *oligopoly*. In such a situation, a greater degree of control over the economic forces exists than in the perfectly competitive or monopolistically competitive situations.

Monopoly market structures are characterized by situations in which a single seller of a product exists in the market and has great control over the economic functions of the market.

Determining which structure fits a given media market involves defining a specific market, analyzing the number of firms within it, and assessing their control over the economic functions to determine the market's location on the market power continuum. If one considers the average markets in which major media industries operate nationally, the industries fall upon the continuum shown in Figure 2.7.

That cable television should be a monopoly is not surprising because it operates somewhat similarly to a utility. Cable systems generally have a monopoly franchise within their areas of operation; that is, they are granted the exclusive right to deliver cable service to a town, city, or metropolitan area. Newspapers tend to operate between oligopoly and monopoly on the market power continuum because the number of newspapers published or available in a given geographic market is limited. The market for television programming, which once was an oligopoly and then in monopolistic competition, has in recent years moved closer to the competitive end of the spectrum because of the expansion of outlets for programming through syndication and cable television channels. No media industries operate in a perfectly com-

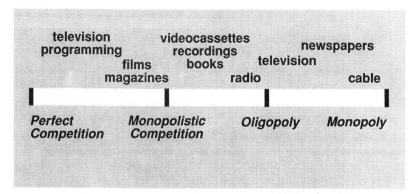

Figure 2.7 Media Industries on the Market Power Continuum

moved closer to the competitive end of the spectrum because of the expansion of outlets for programming through syndication and cable television channels. No media industries operate in a perfectly competitive situation because most media differentiate themselves and try to segment their audiences. The magazine industry exhibits the most competitiveness, but is clearly operating in the monopolistic competition market structure.

Studies applying the industrial organization model to media markets are beginning to appear, including an explanation and application of the model to newspapers by Busterna (1988b) and an examination of barrier to entry into various markets by Wirth (1986), which found barriers higher for the newspaper industry than for broadcasting industries.

Related to determination of market structure is the idea of market concentration. Economic concentration in specific markets provides an indicator of the ability of the marketplace for goods and services to operate efficiently. In economic terms, *concentration* is a measure of the degree to which the largest companies control production, employment, or other indicators of size in an industry in a market. In media industries the degree of concentration in the content product market is calculated using circulation or ratings information. Concentration in the advertising market may be measured in terms of advertising linage or time, or by using revenue figures that are a better measure.

Concentration is measured by observing within specified markets the ratio of total sales or assets of the top companies to the total sales or assets of the industry as a whole. Commonly used measures include the ratio of the top four or eight firms to all firms. Traditional thresholds for concern that concentration is leading to oligopolistic or monopolistic activities that will harm the economic marketplace have been when the top four firms control more than 50 percent of a market or the top eight firms more than 70 percent of a market.

Recent studies of concentration in the daily newspaper industry revealed that local markets are highly concentrated and that even the most competitive markets are well above the levels at which monopolistic behavior is problematic (Picard, 1988a), and these studies have argued that economic pressures in local markets, combined with poor public policies for newspapers, have promoted market concentration and monopoly (Picard, Winter, McCombs, and Lacy, 1988). The television programming and syndication markets have been shown to be concentrated (Owen, Beebe, and Manning, 1974). Chan-Olmsted and Litman (1988) have shown that the cable system market is unconcentrated, but that horizontal and vertical integration are giving great power to a few firms. Other evidence indicates that the book publishing and film distribution markets are concentrated.

A related area of concern, *concentration of ownership*, considers the amount of an industry controlled by individual firms. This type of concentration is usually considered only in aggregate, national terms rather than in relation to specific local geographic markets. Important contributions to this area of inquiry have been made by Baer, Geller, Grundfest, and Possner (1974), Bagdikian (1987), and Compaine (1979), whose data reveal information such as that the four largest newspaper firms control about one quarter of newspaper circulation and that 20 companies receive half of all magazine revenues. This type of information has important implications in terms of diversity of information available to the public and the ability of media to serve the functions ascribed to them in a democratic society. In the economic approach with which this book is concerned, concentration of ownership is considered significant in terms of its concurrent concentration of specific geographical and product markets and the limitations on the market forces that accompany such concentration.

3

CONSUMER CHOICES AND MARKET RESPONSES

Consumption decisions of media audiences and advertisers are influenced by economic choices. This chapter reviews the factors that determine these choices and how they can be measured. Issues such as the value and satisfaction of consuming media products and how prices affect these choices are explored using the concepts of utility, indifference, and demand.

Because we are concerned with how audiences and advertisers choose and use media, and the amount of different media products and services that these audiences and advertisers consume, understanding the activities of consumers in markets is crucial. The choices made by consumers to subscribe to one magazine over another, to watch a videocassette movie rather than broadcast television, or to advertise in a daily newspaper rather than on television are dependent upon the value of the media commodities and services to consumers.

Knowledgeable media managers make decisions based on their understanding of consumers' preferences and willingness to buy, and the value of media to audiences and advertisers. The same forces that affect media consumers also affect media managers when they consider purchases of their own. When the publisher of the Kansas City *Star* considers whether to raise circulation prices and what effect it might have on newspaper sales, when executives of Cablevision of Baton Rouge decide whether to place 9, 12, or 15 channels in the basic cable subscription package, and when the general manager of KGO-TV in San Francisco decides whether to replace a microwave truck with a mobile satellite unit, the choices are based on economic considerations of value and utility.

Value is a measure of the worth of a good or service, indicated by its ability to command money or other goods in exchange for the good or service in the market. The amount of value represents the importance placed on the good or service by consumers. The value is not intrinsic to the good or service but is rather imparted to the good or service by consumers' perceptions of the degree to which their wants and needs

Utility	*Indifference*
Total utility is a function of quantities of various goods consumed.	
Consumers select goods to maximize utility within budget available.	
Utility is measured on a *cardinal* scale.	Utility is measured on an *ordinal* scale expressing preferences.
Marginal utility of each additional unit of a good/service declines.	Marginal rate of substitution diminishes at any given level of utility.

Figure 3.1 Assumptions of the Approaches

are satisfied by it. As a result, the value of any good or service fluctuates and changes over time.

Value is thus linked to intangible consumer satisfaction, which economists call *utility*. Consumers maximize their utility when making choices in the market and using their resources to acquire commodities and services. Two basic approaches are used in exploring consumer choices and the satisfactions achieved in making selections among goods and services. These consumer choice models are called the *basic utility model* and the *indifference model*. Although both approaches are based on the assumptions that consumers' satisfactions are based on the amount of goods consumed and that consumers maximize their satisfaction by balancing the goods and services they consume with the resources available to them, the models differ regarding how the satisfaction should be measured and how decisions are made by consumers (see Figure 3.1).

The utility approach uses cardinal measurements, assuming that the satisfaction obtained by consumers can be measured using a ratio scale measurement. Such measures have a true zero and a standard interval between the values. Thus a utility measurement of 100 is twice as large as a utility measurement of 50.

The indifference curve approach, however, assumes that no one can truly measure utility but can only gain a relative ranking of that satisfaction. This view is based on the idea that consumer choices cannot be considered only as choices of whether to consume a product and how much of that product to consume, but as choices involving multiple products and differing amounts of consumption of each. The indif-

TABLE 3.1

Activity	Utils
Reading a book	35
Watching a television show	78
Listening to the radio	45
Going out to a movie	86
Staying in and watching the same movie on a VCR	47
Listening to an audio recording	51
Reading a magazine	42
Talking to a friend on a telephone	89
Reading a letter	92

ference curve approach uses ordinal measurement on the assumption that consumer utility has no true zero and that the intervals between values may vary and are not additive. As a result, a consumer with an ordinal utility of 100 can be said to have more satisfaction than a consumer with an ordinal utility of 50, but this does not necessarily mean that the person is twice as satisfied. Thus the indifference approach provides a relative ranking of utility. It concentrates on the satisfaction, or utilities, that consumption of a product brings consumers and can thus give an answer to the question of how much satisfaction is obtained by consumers who use different media.

THE UTILITY APPROACH

In considering and analyzing the abstract concept of utility, economists use a measure of each unit of consumer satisfaction that is called a *util*. This unit of measurement is used under the utility approach to study consumer choices to establish indicators of cardinal utility and marginal utility.

Cardinal utility assigns util value based on some numerically measurable factor. In studying media use we could assign cardinal utility based on average amounts of time devoted to different media daily or weekly. Or, using a survey of the public nationwide, we might determine that listed communication activities have the average utils shown in Table 3.1.

Cardinal utility thus provides a measure of the satisfaction brought consumers by goods and services. But it does not provide an indicator of whether having more of those goods or services brings more pleasure. That function is calculated by what is called *marginal utility*,

TABLE 3.2

Number of Channels	Total Utility (Utils)	Marginal Utility (Utils)
1	100	100
2	185	85
3	255	70
4	310	55
5	350	40

a measure of the additional satisfaction of having more units of a commodity. Marginal utility thus indicates the increments of satisfaction provided by consumption. Thus it answers questions such as "If listening to an audio recording brings you 51 utils, will listening to two audio recordings bring you 102 utils? Or somewhere between 51 and 102?"

Calculations of marginal utility are made by subtracting the total utility obtained before adding the additional unit from the total utility obtained including that unit. Marginal utility can also be calculated by dividing the change in total utility by the change in number of units consumed:

$$MU = \frac{\text{Change in total utility}}{\text{Change in units consumed}}$$

Using such a calculation can answer the question "What is the marginal utility of having more than one television channel available?" Such a question is, of course, crucial to someone considering starting a new television station in a market, or to understanding why most cable subscribers choose only basic cable services.

If we determine that having one channel brings viewers 100 utils of satisfaction, having two channels brings 185 utils, having three channels creates 255 utils, and so forth, we calculate marginal utility as shown in Table 3.2.

This reveals that the marginal utility (satisfaction) of having access to each new television channel diminishes as the number of available channels rises. It is possible for marginal utility to increase in the short run, but in the long run, marginal utility diminishes as each new unit of the good or service is added.

Another way of observing this diminishing marginal utility is to view it graphically, showing utils obtained by each new channel as shown in Figure 3.2.

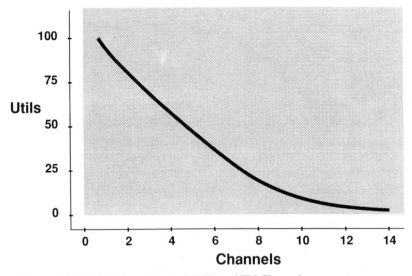

Figure 3.2 Diminishing Marginal Utility of TV Channels

Because of this phenomenon most cable TV viewers are content with access to fewer than two dozen channels rather than increasing their access to as many as the 120 channels that some television sets will accommodate. For the same reason, magazine readers choose only a few of the thousands of titles available nationwide.

UTILITY AND PRICE

Utility thus provides a measure of what worth goods and services have to consumers, that is, a means of establishing value. It must be noted, however, that utility and the price of a good or service are not directly correlated. Water, for instance, is a necessity and has great utility in its satisfaction of wants and needs, but the normal price of water is lower than the normal price of diamonds. This would change, of course, if a person were lost in the desert and the utils of having water overcame the utils of having a diamond. The price of goods and services is determined not only by utility but by the labor necessary to produce commodities and services and other costs associated with the production. And price is also determined by diminishing utility for multiple units of a commodity or service, which is one reason why many products are available in multipacks at a price significantly less than the cost for the units of the product separately.

TABLE 3.3

	Marginal Utility (Utils)	Price	Marginal Utility Per Dollar
Seeing film today	86	$5.00	17.2
Seeing film on bargain night	86	$2.00	43

When making choices in the market, consumers consider both utility and price. For example, if you really wish to see a new hit movie you can go today and pay $5 to see the film or you can wait until bargain night when you can see the same film for $2. When you choose to wait until the less desirable night and pay the lower price, you have decided that the extra cost of going today is not worth it. In analyzing the decision, we can combine utility and price to yield a measure of marginal utility per dollar. Assuming that the marginal utility of viewing the film is 86 utils, we can make the calculation as shown in Table 3.3.

This example reveals that the decision is one of rational choice. The marginal utility per dollar of seeing the film on bargain night (43) is two and one half times that of seeing the film today (17.2).

This example, however, assumes that the marginal utility of seeing the film today or on another day is the same. But this may not always be the case. Suppose that seeing the film today is part of a date with someone or an evening with friends. Such factors might induce you to pay the higher price by raising the marginal utility of seeing the film today through the additional utils associated with these additional factors.

The allocative decisions made in life are rarely as simple as choosing between two alternatives, however. In fact, consumers make thousands of decisions among goods and services. In doing so they seek to maximize their satisfaction. Such maximizing behavior occurs when consumers spend more on goods and services that bring more marginal utility per dollar and less on goods and services that bring less marginal utility per dollar. This is why consumers are willing to spend more of their income on food, clothing, and housing than on purchasing media products. The marginal utility per dollar of satisfying the basic needs far exceeds the marginal utility per dollar of satisfying the wants and needs for information and entertainment.

Although consumption creates utility, this satisfaction is also created by nonconsumption or by saving resources until a later time.

TABLE 3.4

	Marginal Utility of Consuming Now	Interest Rate	Price of Consumption Now	Marginal Utility per Dollar
Example 1:				
paper A	150	7%	535,000	.00029
paper B	100	7%	535,000	.00019
Example 2:				
paper A	150	10%	550,000	.00027
paper B	100	10%	550,000	.00018

Individuals and firms save resources for future use or to accumulate wealth. In determining the marginal utility of such savings, one must take into account changing values for commodities held and interest rates or investment dividends that add to the value of money saved and invested.

Just as marginal utility and price combine to help determine *what* is consumed at present, the two are combined to determine *whether* to consume at present or save for future consumption. For example, assume that two newspaper companies are planning to purchase new printing presses and that they can acquire the presses immediately or sign agreements to acquire and pay for the presses next year. The price for the presses is $500,000. If the papers buy the presses immediately, the cost of consumption will be $500,000 plus the *opportunity cost* of buying now instead of later. In this case the opportunity cost, that is, the cost of the best foregone alternative, is one year's interest that will be lost because the money is not left in the bank. Whether newspaper companies A and B decide to purchase now or to delay purchase for a year will be decided based on the different marginal utilities per dollar for the companies.

Let us consider two different examples in which this might occur. In one example, the interest rate for the money held in the bank is 7 percent. In the second example, the interest rate is 10 percent. In both examples, paper A gains the most satisfaction from purchasing the press immediately. This could be because the current press needs immediate replacement or because the purchase is part of a modernization program that is raising morale and improving the image of the company. As a result of the additional utility of purchasing now, the paper will gain more satisfaction per dollar by making the purchase immediately than will paper B (see Table 3.4). Notice, however, that the

TABLE 3.5

	Marginal Utility of Consuming Now	Interest/ Inflation Rates	Price of Consumption Now	Marginal Utility per Dollar
Example 1:				
paper A	150	7/10%	465,000	.00032
paper B	100	7/10%	465,000	.00022
Example 2:				
paper A	150	10/10%	500,000	.00030
paper B	100	10/10%	500,000	.00020

marginal utility of making the purchase immediately diminishes for both papers in example 2. This occurs because the higher rate increases the interest lost through purchasing now, thus increasing the cost of making the purchase immediately, thus lowering the marginal utility per dollar.

The decision to consume or to save is also influenced by changes in prices. If inflation occurs, goods and services cost more and may reduce any advantage of saving resources for future use. Drawing from the above examples, assume that a purchase of the press today will cost $500,000 but because of 10 percent inflation the cost will be $550,000 next year. Thus the price of consuming now is $50,000 less than it would be after waiting a year, which alters the marginal utility per dollar. In both examples, paper A's marginal utility per dollar is higher for purchasing now than is newspaper B's (see Table 3.5).

Paper A still has greater marginal utility for making the purchase immediately than has paper B, but because its money will be worth less a year from now due to inflation, the marginal utility per dollar of making the purchase now increases for both papers.

THE INDIFFERENCE APPROACH

Although agreeing with the basic assumptions about how consumers behave and that consumer satisfaction can be measured using utils, some economists believe that the utility approach does not approximate reality as well as it should because consumers are rarely faced with merely a choice of whether to consume only one type of good or service, but instead face choices among many types of goods and services. This is particularly true in choices among media products and between media products and those of other industries. The indifference approach argues that every consumer has a different set of preferences that assigns utility to goods and services and to different quantities of those goods and services. These preferences can be ranked by consumers, and economists can study them using ordinal utility.

Ordinal utility is based on the assignment of util value based on rank ordering of consumer preference. An example of creating ordinal utility occurs if one orders by rank the following communication activities in terms of the satisfaction they provide you on a scale of 1 to 100. The numerical value then represents the number of utils of satisfaction each provides.

Reading a book
Watching television
Listening to the radio
Going out to a movie
Staying in and watching the same movie on a VCR
Listening to an audio recording
Reading a magazine
Talking to a friend on a telephone
Reading a letter

If talking to a friend on the telephone receives the score 100 and going to a movie receives the score 80, each activity is worth 100 and 80 utils, respectively, and talking on the phone can be said to provide more satisfaction than going to a movie does.

Indifference, then, uses the idea of consumers maximizing utility by considering what must happen when choices are made involving more than one consumption. Consumers always seek maximum satisfaction and will accept balanced consumption of different amounts of different products to achieve total maximum utility. Indifference is a measure of the point at which the preference between different quantities of different goods and services disappears because the level of satisfaction (utility) is the same for the two.

Assume that you have enough money to purchase 10 tickets to performances at a movie festival as well as coupons for 10 video-cassette rentals. If you purchase both, you have the total satisfaction associated with example 1 below (see Table 3.6). But if you are able to purchase only 8 movie tickets, how many more video rentals would be needed to reach that same level of satisfaction? The answer, of course, depends on how much you will enjoy going to the movie festival

TABLE 3.6

	Movie Tickets	Video Rentals
Example 1	10	10
Example 2	8	12
Example 3	4	20
Example 4	2	25

presentations compared to how much you will enjoy viewing the videos. If you will enjoy each equally, you might find that 2 extra video coupons would make up for the lack of the 2 movie tickets, as shown in example 2. In other words, you are indifferent as to whether you have 10 of each or 8 movie tickets and 12 video rentals.

But what if you could acquire tickets to only a few of the movie festival performances? How many video rentals would it take to achieve the same level of satisfaction? In such a situation, illustrated in examples 3 and 4, the additional rentals of videos provide less and less satisfaction and you need more videos to make up for your inability to go to the movies. You might require 10 video rentals to make up for the loss of 6 festival tickets or 15 video rentals to make up for the loss of 8 festival tickets. This is the idea of a diminishing marginal rate of substitution. That is, at some point, consumers are less and less willing to accept substitutes because the satisfaction received is lower.

Indifference is plotted on what are called indifference curves to provide a better view of the relationships between the satisfaction achieved by different quantities of goods and services. The indifference curve for the above example is seen in Figure 3.3.

This figure illustrates that as the quantity of the one good decreases, the quantity of the other must be increased to achieve the same satisfaction. The shape of an indifference curve is thus determined by the substitutability of goods or services involved. If, however, perfect substitutes were involved, a straight downward line would appear on the graph. If no substitution were possible, a curve of right angles would occur (see Figures 3.4A and 3.4B).

CONSUMER DEMAND

Consumer demand for goods and services is affected by their utility to consumers and the price at which the goods and services are available. *Demand* is a measure of the quantity of goods and services that

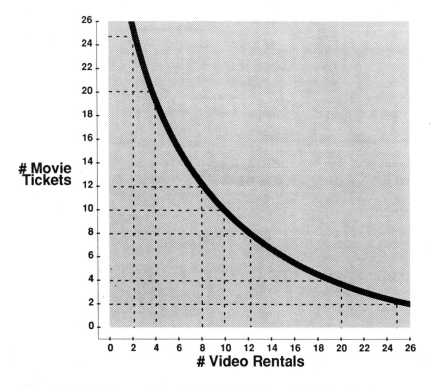

Figure 3.3 Indifference Curve for Movie Tickets and VCR Rentals

consumers are willing to purchase at a given price. Thus, demand is dependent upon the willingness and ability of buyers to pay particular prices for goods and services.

Using the concept of demand, we can estimate what will happen to the number of copies of a magazine sold if we raise the cover price from $1.75 to $2.50 per copy, or how many minutes of advertising we will sell if we raise the price of ads on a TV station from $2,000 to $3,500 per minute. This interplay between price and amount of a good or service consumed is illustrated on a demand curve shown in Figure 3.5.

The graph illustrates that consumers will purchase more of a good or service if the price is low than if it is high. As price for the good or service *decreases*, the quantity demanded by consumers *increases*. Conversely, if price *increases*, the quantity demanded *decreases*. This demand curve holds true for both individual consumers and market demand overall, that is, consumers in aggregate.

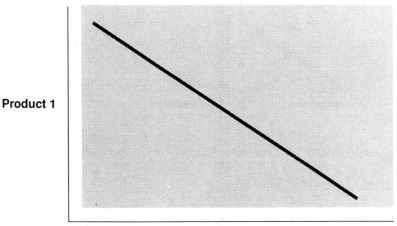

Product 1

Product 2

Figure 3.4A Indifference Curve for Perfect Substitutes

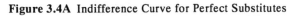

Product 1

Product 2

Figure 3.4B Indifference Curve for Nonsubstitutes

The amount that demand changes when price is changed is called *elasticity of demand.* Demand can be elastic or inelastic, or unit elastic. When it is *elastic,* a change in price is accompanied by a greater change in quantity demanded. Demand is said to be *inelastic* when a change in price is accompanied by no significant change in quantity demanded. If a change in price results in an equal change in quantity, *unit elasticity* exists.

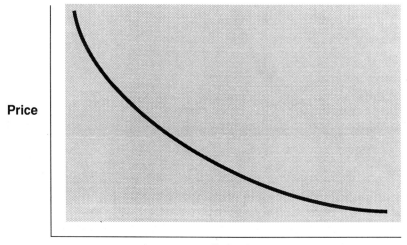

Figure 3.5 A Demand Curve

Elasticity is calculated by dividing the change in quantity by the change in price:

$$\frac{\text{Percent change in quantity}}{\text{Percent change in price}} = \text{Price elasticity of demand}$$

With regard to the elasticity statistic, a negative or positive sign preceding the statistic indicates the direction of demand. This is disregarded in determining elasticity per se. Elasticity is shown if the statistic exceeds 1.0. Unit elasticity is shown if the statistic is 1.0, and stats that are less than 1.0 reveal inelasticity.

Although price is normally the single most important factor influencing demand at any given moment, demand is also influenced by the availability of substitute products and their prices. Over time, a variety of factors influence continuing demand for a good or service, including: changes in consumer income, changes in taste and preference, changes in expectations for the future, and changes in population.

The use of elasticity to measure effects of price on demand can also be applied to substitution of a different product or service when the price of the product or service studied changes. This is called *cross-elasticity of demand*. This concept is useful in discussions of media because it can be used to determine the extent to which different media compete for different portions of media product and service markets.

As a general rule, cross-elasticity increases when there are many good substitutes.

Cross-elasticity is also affected by the amount of a consumer's income required to acquire a good or service. When the proportion of income required to consume a good or service is high, cross-elasticity increases.

ISSUES OF MEDIA UTILITY, VALUE, AND DEMAND

The concepts of utility, value, and consumer demand manifest themselves in major issues when dealing with media: 1) demand for the media product by audiences; 2) demand for access to the audience by advertisers; and 3) demand for units of media available for sale.

Despite the importance of the concepts of utility, value, and demand to media marketing, relatively few studies have been undertaken on the subject. In recent years, utility and value have been indirectly addressed by uses and gratifications studies of media, and some utility indicators can be extrapolated from descriptive audience surveys. Demand studies are more readily available, but their number is limited because most of the information needed is proprietary data held by media companies and industry research firms. Nevertheless, the available data and information provide some important understanding of these issues.

Media Product Demand

The issue of consumer demand for media products is most often considered in terms of media for which audiences pay a fee for acquisition. This includes subscriptions and single sales. Media products that are sold in this manner include newspapers, magazines, films, videos, recordings, and cable service. Although there are similarities among these media, consumer demand for the different products varies.

Demand for newspapers, for instance, is generally inelastic relative to price. That is, a rise in price will not cause a significant decline in consumption. This inelasticity was noted by Landau and Davenport (1959, p. 272) when they found that "the sales price of a newspaper . . . is expressed neither by the interaction between Supply and Demand nor by a relationship to production cost facts. Price determination is purely arbitrary." Several more recent studies have come to similar conclusions. A study of 213 papers over a 25-year period found that demand for daily newspapers by media consumers fluctuated slightly but was inelastic over time (Field, 1978). A similar study of price effects on circulation in 239 papers over a 10-year period also found price inelasticity and found that newspaper circulation rose despite increases in subscription rates and single copy rates (Clark, 1976). A study by Grotta (1977) also concluded that consumer demand for newspapers is inelastic and that only insignificant decreases in circulation will occur at the time prices are raised.

Demand for motion pictures has been shown to be elastic. Pigou (1932) revealed that variations due to price differentials for time of day, whether a film is in exclusive or general distribution, location of screening, and other factors showed that demand is transferable among submarkets for motion pictures.

Demand for cable television subscriptions was a significant concern as cable companies began making extensive investments in operating systems in the 1970s. Predictive studies of demand by Comanor and Mitchell (1971), Park (1970, 1971), and Noll, Peck, and McGowan (1973) based their estimates on available broadcast channels, media use, demographic information, and subscription price estimates. They also argued that the cross-elasticity of demand between network television and pay television (cable) would result in audience losses as high as 50 percent in markets with one and two network-affiliated stations and declining audiences for broadcast television. Their study provided a useful model for studying the cross-elasticity of demand between television and cable.

Many of the early estimates of cable demand have been supported by recent studies. Ducey, Krugman, and Eckrich (1983) have shown that there is a difference in demand for basic cable service and for pay/premium cable service; this difference has resulted in basic service reaching about 50 percent of U.S. households, but pay/premium service reaching only about 25 percent. Bloch and Wirth (1984) showed that demand for both pay and basic cable services is affected by price, household demographics, and programming quality. Childers and Krugman (1987) revealed the direct competition between pay-per-view cable programming, other cable programming, and VCR rentals, which indicates that there should be significant cross-elasticity of demand between those media markets.

In media in which consumers do *not* pay for the product monetarily, issues related to demand still arise, but they tend to focus upon determining the preferences and utility of various media products and programming for audiences. Research by Steiner (1952), Rothenberg (1962), and Owen, Beebe, and Manning (1974) has shown how utility for radio and television programming can be measured as a component for determining consumer demand for certain types of broadcast content.

Highlight 3.1 The Principle of Relative Constancy

"The level of spending on mass media by consumers and advertisers is determined by the general state of the economy. Any change in the level of the economy causes a parallel change in spending on mass media."

(Scripps, 1965)

"What Americans spend on mass communication has not increased with the advent and spread of new media such as radio and television. The money to create two ubiquitous broadasting systems, first radio, later television, seems to have come more from changing media habits and general economic growth than from any fundamental shifts in consumer habits — such as allocating mass media a larger share of personal income. This close relationship between general economic conditions and spending on mass communication media suggests we are dealing with a behavioral principle, the Principle of Relative Constancy. . . . . This principle appears to hold under a wide variety of historical conditions and communication technologies."

(McCombs, 1972, pp. 18-19)

Consumers' overall demand for media products appears to be relatively stable. According to the *principle of relative constancy* proposed by McCombs (1972), media spending tends to be constant over time relative to the general performance of the economy and accounts for approximately 3 percent of total consumer spending. Consumer expenditures for media have the same characteristics as expenditures for staples such as housing and clothing. Thus, new media must attract consumer spending from other media spending, rather than attracting spending from other goods and services in the long run.

Advertisers' Demand for Access

Demand for advertiser access to audiences varies, depending on the medium, but few studies of the differences and their importance are available.

Noll et al. (1973) argue that demand for television advertising time is highly elastic for individual advertisers, but that it is less elastic overall. They also note that increasing the number of stations in a market, and thus increasing available advertising time, does not change the quantity of time desired by advertisers. "Demand for viewer minutes is unlikely to be affected by an increase in the number of stations," they argue (p. 36). This occurs because the additional quantity of advertising time supplied to the market by the new stations results in the marginal cost for the advertising time and its price growing closer together, thus reducing the profit each produces for broadcasters.

Picard (1982) revealed that newspapers pay little attention to economics when setting prices for advertising space and that prices are set with more attention paid to industry trends than to consumer demand. Research by Busterna (1987) has shown that there is no cross-elasticity of demand for national advertising between newspapers and television, radio, magazines, newspaper supplements, or outdoor advertising. Norris (1982), after studying the interplay between circulation and advertising in magazines, argued that prices for advertising are based both on actual circulation and estimates of demand elasticity in the advertising market. A study by McGann, Russell, and Russell (1983) found great variability in prices for advertising space in metropolitan editions of national consumer magazines. The absence of price equilibrium suggests that the magazines are setting prices based on consumer demand factors rather than cost or target profit factors.

Demand for Media Units

Several studies of television station transactions have found that demand for stations is affected not just by price but by a variety of market and station characteristic factors that are closely related to the interests of advertisers. Levin (1971, 1975, 1980) found that market size, audience size, network affiliation, age of station, and VHF band frequency affected the demand and price for stations. Levin's findings were matched in a study by Cherington, Hirsch, and Brandwein (1971). Blau, Johnson, and Ksobeich (1976) concurred that the previously identified factors affected demand but found that the price that purchasers were willing to pay for stations was greatly influenced by the annual revenues of the television stations. Bates (1988) explored the impact of federal deregulation efforts on demand for stations and found that it had little impact on demand or on the price of stations.

Factors influencing demand for TV stations have also been found to influence the demand for radio stations. Cheen (1986) identified the market and financial factors contributing to demand for and value of radio stations and noted the important effects of the following on the value of a station: whether a station broadcasts on the AM or FM bands, what its market size is, and what its audience characteristics are.

4

PRODUCER CHOICES AND MARKET RESPONSES

The production decisions of media companies are affected by economic forces. This chapter discusses how production takes place, how inputs are changed into outputs, and how media decide how much of their product to supply. Central to these decisions are the concepts of cost, profit, economies of scale, and diminishing returns.

Those who create products behave rationally in the market and make decisions based both on the costs of goods and the profits they receive from making products. Producers are those individuals who create goods or services for consumers. Production takes many forms, ranging from factory work to housework, from producing feature films to publishing books. All production involves altering or reconfiguring some good or goods for use by others.

Producers make choices based on the costs of production and the financial benefits that result from production and sale of their product or services. These decisions involve the amount, the type, and the price of the goods and services. Thus, executives of Columbia Records consider the additional costs of producing additional copies of an album that has just won a Grammy award in comparison with the additional revenue they may be able to generate. Similarly, Sage Publications weighed the costs of producing this book in hardback and paperback and projections of sales for each in order to determine how many of each to produce. This type of analysis can only be done fully if one understands the nature of the production processes, the use of resources, and the implications of different types of costs for production.

In the production process, *inputs* are transformed into *outputs*. In other words, some resource(s) or factor(s) of production is (are) utilized to produce some product or service or other form of the good used. In media industries, inputs are goods such as information, scripts, newsprint, videotape, and film stock, and services offered by reporters, editors, producers, directors, and performers. Outputs in media are such products as films, records, newspapers, magazines, and broadcasts.

Two main categories are used to describe inputs: fixed inputs and variable inputs. *Fixed inputs* are those which are necessary for production but which cannot be changed to increase or decrease output. In media industries, these include buildings and land, printing presses, transformers, satellite stations, and so forth. *Variable inputs*, however, directly affect the amount of output when their quantity is varied. These include labor, newsprint, plastic for record albums, videotape, and so forth.

Every industry has its unique inputs and production processes required to produce its outputs, and some companies produce similar outputs with different inputs and processes. Most industries require many inputs to produce a single output. The inputs of media industries vary widely because of the variety of production and distribution forms for media goods and services, and the amount and variety of components necessary to produce these products.

HOW MUCH SHOULD BE PRODUCED?

A major issue in production involves the question of how much output a producer should create and what will happen to that output when inputs are increased. This is a crucial issue because producers wish to locate their production levels at points at which their firms operate most efficiently in terms of the inputs required to get their outputs. Although various industries differ in the amount and types of inputs needed, all industries — including media industries — can be considered using an input-output approach, and the analysis of different situations follow similar patterns.

By considering a production situation in which a single input is considered, one can more easily understand the economic issues surrounding inputs. Let us consider the example of a television news director who is considering how many news crews are needed to produce a newscast. The TV crews' labor (the input) is used to produce news packages (the output) and the news director wants to know what number of crews will be most efficient for the station. Obviously, if no crews work, no output is created. Likewise, if the number of crews working increases, the amount of output changes (see Table 4.1).

The *additional output* resulting from the *additional input* of each day of crew labor is called the *marginal physical product* (MPP). This measure provides an indication of what contribution the last unit of

TABLE 4.1 Effect of Input on News Package Output and MPP

Days of Crew Labor Input	Package Output (Total Product)	Marginal Physical Product
0	0	—
1	1	1
2	3	2
3	5.5	2.5
4	7	1.5
5	8.25	1.25
6	9.25	1
7	10	.75
8	10.5	.50
9	10.25	.25
10	10.25	0

input added made to output. In the example in Table 4.1, the size of the marginal product increases at first, to a high of 2.5 with three days of crew labor, but then begins to decline. The area in which marginal physical product increases is known as the area of increasing returns, and the area in which marginal product decreases is known as the area of decreasing returns.

This decline in MPP occurs because of what is known as the *law of diminishing returns*. This law states that at some point the output resulting from each new input begins to decline. This occurs because the increasing amount of input is ultimately used inefficiently. In some situations, it can become so inefficient that MPP not only diminishes but actually becomes negative. Because of the law of diminishing returns, the amount of additional product that can be produced by increasing input can be expected to rise at first but then begin falling. Thus, a producer cannot expect to increase output continually by increasing input.

In the example of the news crews, the MPP begins declining at four days of news crew labor. This inefficiency could occur because some equipment production would need to be shared and the demands of the large number of crews would be expected to cause news crews to wait to use some equipment. This, of course, would diminish the efficiency of the crews and their productivity, and reduce the output benefits of having additional crews.

In situations in which the input and output units are larger and not as easily calculable as those indicated in the example above, the following formula is used:

TABLE 4.2 Effect of Input on News Package Output, MPP, and APP

Days of Crew Labor Input	Package Output (Total Product)	MPP	APP
0	0	—	—
1	1	1	1
2	3	2	1.5
3	5.5	2.5	1.83
4	7	1.5	1.75
5	8.25	1.25	1.65
6	9.25	1	1.54
7	10	.75	1.43
8	10.5	.50	1.31
9	10.25	.25	1.14
10	10.25	0	1.14

$$\text{MPP} = \frac{\text{Change in output}}{\text{Change in input}}$$

Another means of determining what happens to output when input is altered is to consider what is called the *average physical product* (APP). This measure is concerned with the average output, rather than the amount of additional output achieved by adding input that is shown by MPP. It averages the contribution of input across all output. Average physical product is calculated as follows:

$$\text{APP} = \frac{\text{output}}{\text{input}}$$

Using the example of how additional days of television news crew labor affect the number of news packages produced, we see that APP rises, plateaus, and then declines (see Table 4.2). Thus, as with the marginal physical product, average physical product also has an area in which it increases and decreases due to the law of diminishing returns. But although MPP can decline into a negative situation, the APP will remain positive because it deals not with change but with actual output.

The relationship between total product (the output), MPP, and APP, is shown graphically in Figure 4.1, using the news crew example.

Producers obviously want their combinations of input and output to result in a return of the best possible level of output. To accomplish this goal, producers try to add input as long as increasing returns remain possible and to stop adding input before they reach negative returns. In practice, this usually means not adding more input once diminishing returns are evident.

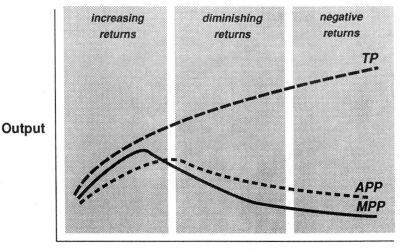

Figure 4.1 Returns on Inputs Showing TP, MPP, and APP

This discussion of input and output has focused on how variations in a single input affect output. As mentioned earlier, however, most outputs require many inputs, ranging from labor to raw materials and supplies. The general principles for understanding the relationships between an input and output are applicable to situations in which multiple inputs are involved. It is, of course, further complicated by the necessity of combining variations in different proportions of specific inputs to achieve the output level desired.

COST, PROFITS, AND PRODUCT SUPPLY

In addition to being affected by changes in input, the *product supply* of a good or service is affected by its production costs and the profitability of producing the product. Producers wish to get the largest quantity of product for the lowest cost as a means of generating a high financial return.

Because of that orientation, a significant amount of attention is paid to understanding the cost of producing various levels of output. The costs of production fall into the categories of monetary and nonmonetary costs. Monetary costs, sometimes called explicit costs, are those for which the company expends money. These include costs for procuring labor, supplies, raw materials, buildings, and equipment. Nonmonetary costs, sometimes called implicit costs, include opportunity costs and the value of uncompensated use of labor or equipment.

The concept of profitability involves two definitions of profit. The first is what are called *normal profits*. Normal profits are the minimal return to inputs that must be available to keep a company or individual producing. Included in this category are nonmonetary costs for one's own labor and psychic rewards for doing the work. The second type of profit, *pure profit*, is the return that exceeds both the monetary and nonmonetary costs. This is the kind of profit most people think of when they consider the term profit in a business sense.

Producers are rational and make decisions based on cost and profitability so that the amount of output produced, the product supply, is based on achieving the lowest possible costs and highest profits.

A primary element in determining product supply is *marginal cost* (MC). Marginal cost is the added production cost for making more output or, conversely, the lowering of costs that occurs when there is a reduction in the output.

This type of analysis involves calculating the costs associated with the two main types of inputs, fixed inputs and variable inputs. The costs associated with fixed inputs are called *fixed costs* and the costs associated with variable inputs are called *variable costs*. Fixed and variable costs can include both monetary and nonmonetary costs. In calculating marginal cost, one combines both fixed and variable costs.

Continuing with the news crew example considered earlier, it might be determined that the fixed costs of maintaining a camera crew are $100 per day and that the variable costs for the crew (their labor) are $300 per day.

Total variable cost (TVC) is then calculated by multiplying the days of labor input by the variable labor cost of $300 per day. *Total cost* (TC) results from adding the fixed cost of $100 per day to the TVC. To calculate marginal cost, one divides the change in total cost by the change in output:

$$\text{MC} = \frac{\text{Change in total cost}}{\text{Change in output}}$$

The resulting calculation of marginal cost provides a measure of the cost of gaining one more news package for each day of crew labor (see Table 4.3). If no crew labor is used, the total cost is $100 because the fixed costs exist whether or not any work is done. If one crew is employed for one day to produce one news package, the TC increases to $400 and the marginal cost is $300 ($400 − $100).

TABLE 4.3 Marginal Costs for Additional Input and Output

Days of Crew Labor Input	Package Output	Total Variable Cost	Total Cost	Marginal Cost
0	0	$ 0	$ 100	$ —
1	1	300	400	300
2	3	600	700	150
3	5.5	900	1,000	120
4	7	1,200	1,300	200
5	8.25	1,500	1,600	240
6	9.25	1,800	1,900	300
7	10	2,100	2,200	400
8	10.5	2,400	2,500	600
9	10.75	2,700	2,800	1,200
10	10.75	3,000	3,100	1,200

If two crews are employed, the change in TC, $300 (derived by subtracting $400 from $700), is divided by the change in output, 2 (derived by subtracting 1 from 3), to yield a marginal cost of $150. The MC varies significantly given the different input days and TVCs. It begins moderately high, declines as output begins to increase, and then increases rapidly as output moves upward.

There is an important relationship between marginal cost and the marginal physical product discussed earlier. If they are graphed simultaneously, it becomes quickly apparent that MC reaches its low point at the output level where MPP is at its peak and vice versa (see Figure 4.2). This occurs because when labor is most productive, it is less costly to get another unit of output.

Although marginal cost provides an important indicator about the relationship between alterations in costs that are altered by changes in marginal product, it does not measure the changes in costs overall by such changes. That function is provided by *average costs* measures that indicate the mean costs for each unit of output produced.

There are three measures of average cost: 1) *average fixed costs* (AFC), 2) *average variable costs* (AVC), and 3) *average total costs* (ATC). Each provides an important indicator of the contributions of inputs to costs. Average fixed costs are calculated by dividing total fixed costs by output:

$$AFC = \frac{Total\,fixed\,costs}{Output}$$

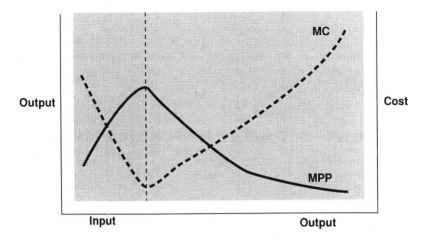

Figure 4.2 Relationship Between Marginal Cost and Marginal Physical
          Product

Average variable costs are calculated by dividing total variable costs by
output:

$$\text{AVC} = \frac{\text{Total variable costs}}{\text{Output}}$$

And average total costs are calculated by dividing total costs by output:

$$\text{ATC} = \frac{\text{Total costs}}{\text{Output}}$$

ATC can also be calculated by adding average fixed costs (AFC) and
average variable costs (AVC). Given the television news crew example
used before, in which total fixed costs were $100 and total variable
costs were $300 per day of crew labor, the three measures of costs
across the various examples of input are found in Table 4.4.

Upon examination, it becomes clear that average fixed costs (AFC)
decrease as the output *increases*. This occurs because the fixed costs
are distributed among the increasing output so that each output unit is
responsible for only a small portion of the fixed costs. The average
variable costs (AVC) also decline as output increases, but they then
increase as the inefficiencies of production diminish the return. The
average total costs do the same, but ATC reach their lowest point after
AVC because of the influence of the AFC decline. Thus, when more of

TABLE 4.4 Average Costs for Output

Days of Crew Labor Input	Package Output	AVC	AFC	ATC
0	0	$ – – –	$ – – –	$– – –
1	1	300.00	100.00	400.00
2	3	200.00	33.33	233.33
3	5.5	163.64	18.18	181.82
4	7	171.43	14.29	185.72
5	8.25	181.82	12.12	193.94
6	9.25	194.60	10.81	205.41
7	10	210.00	10.00	220.00
8	10.5	228.57	9.52	238.09
9	10.75	251.16	9.21	260.37
10	10.75	279.07	9.21	288.28

a product is produced by increasing input, the costs for the additional input decrease for a time but ultimately must rise because return for the additional input diminishes.

There is a relationship between average cost and marginal cost. The marginal cost intersects ATC and AVC at their lowest points. This occurs because the marginal cost pulls the average down to meet it as long as it is below the average, as shown in Figure 4.3.

Average variable cost has a special relationship with average physical product. Average physical product is at its height when the AVC is at its lowest point because the APP gets higher when labor is most productive, and thus the average cost of the unit declines as shown in Figure 4.4.

Producers wish to generate output at the point where both APP and AVC are optimal and the amount produced will be regulated to keep it in that range.

The price set for output by producers is related to the marginal cost. A general rule is that producers will maximize their profit by seeking a level of output at which the marginal cost equals price.

In deciding whether to make extra output to sell, MC and price are considered jointly. If price is higher than MC and MC is rising, producers will increase output until price and MC are equal. If MC goes higher than price, producers lose money on each new unit produced and, thus, cut back output to bring it to the optimal level.

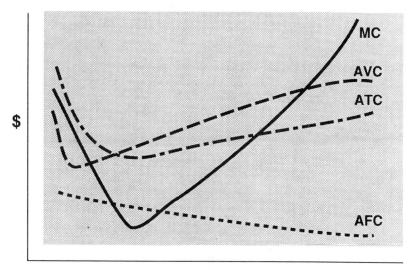

Figure 4.3 Relationship Between Marginal and Average Costs

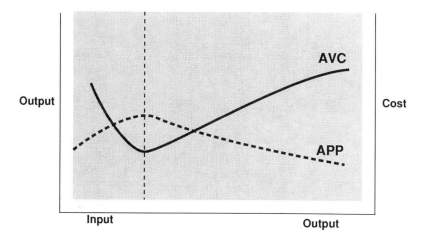

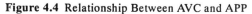

Figure 4.4 Relationship Between AVC and APP

LONG-RUN COSTS

Until this point, the subject of discussion has been what are called *short-run costs*. In the grander scale and over time, one must consider *long-run costs*, in which all inputs are considered variable. Thus fixed variables such as land, buildings, and manufacturing equipment enter the picture. This type of analysis is particularly useful in considering the impact of new products, manufacturing plants, and so forth. In the long run, producers seek a *long-run average cost* (LRAC) in which profit is maximized for the entire operation of the firm. In such a situation, the LRAC is paired with output to determine the most efficient point of operation, and firms try to optimize their profit by operating at that point.

Important to this discussion is the idea of *scale*. Scale economies relate to advantages inherent in the size of a firm or the quantity of output produced. Several important types of scale economies exist: 1) those occurring due to production efficiencies and technology that result in declining average costs, 2) those occurring due to economies of scope, and 3) those occurring due to distribution density.

The scale economies inherent in production efficiencies and technology that result in declining average costs are especially germane to industries with high start-up costs because of capital expenditures for equipment. In such industries, including several media industries, expensive equipment and facilities are necessary whether one produces one unit or many units of output. As the quantity of output increases, the cost for producing each unit — that is, the average cost — drops, and thus large-scale production is more efficient than small-scale production. This advantage of scale is not without end, however, and at some point scale itself introduces inefficiencies, and the advantage disappears.

Economies of scale related to production efficiences of size are sought by developing and maintaining production facilities and equipment of optimal sizes and configurations, and developing and maintaining individual companies at optimal sizes. This concept of economies of scale is easily seen in newspaper production, where the start-up costs, sometimes called first-copy costs, are the same whether one uses the presses to print 1, 2, 50, or 10,000 copies. As the number of copies produced increases, however, the average costs drop rapidly. Related economies of scale are also found in broadcast and cable television, which are also somewhat equipment driven by comparison to other media industries, but the output must be measured in a different manner because there is no tangible product for these public goods. Substitute

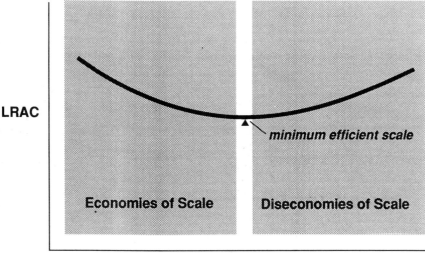

LRAC

minimum efficient scale

Economies of Scale   Diseconomies of Scale

Output

Figure 4.5 LRAC Curve

measures that can be used in analyzing such economies of scale are the amount of programming broadcast or cablecast or viewer or listener time generated.

As illustrated in Figure 4.5, a firm wishes to set its output at a level at which at least the *minimum efficient scale* exists but, preferably, to operate where *economies of scale* exist. At all costs, firms attempt to avoid *diseconomies of scale*.

The LRAC curve is typically a flat U-shaped curve. It begins to decline because production factors, especially technology, bring economies of scale that reduce costs as output quantity increases. In addition, LRAC curves decline when economies of scope exist. Such economies occur when the production of one product lowers the production costs of another product because they share inputs and spread the cost between them. The curve can also be affected by efficiencies from the size of the firm, such as those resulting from bulk purchases of inputs or tax incentives given to locate or keep a firm in a city or state. Further, LRAC curves can decline because of distribution factors known as economies of density, in which a product is distributed densely in a market. Such distribution is cheaper than when distribution is sparse in a market and the costs of reaching customers is higher.

Changes in the curve of any firm can be affected by new technologies that reduce the inputs required to produce a good or services (especially labor-saving equipment), by external factors that increase the costs of inputs, by ineffiencies that enter use of facilities, and by high debt that develops from takeovers of public companies or defenses against takeovers.

Considering production in the long run also allows one to consider the effect of increases in inputs. When these factors are increased, three possible outcomes can occur: 1) a proportionate increase in output—that is, scale is constant; 2) an increase in output, disproportionately low to the increase; or 3) an increase in output, disproportionately high to the increase.

Studying the results of such outcomes, and the long-run costs of operating a firm, provides important insight into the economic situation of producers. Three types of measurements of LRAC are normally encountered. The first is engineering estimates. These are estimates of the LRAC of equipment and facilities that are normally made in the course of considering new technology or plant expansion. The second measurement is based on past costs. This method requires access to proprietary information but can be made within firms. The third measurement is a technique called survival analysis, which attempts to identify distinguishing elements between firms that survived and those that failed.

Both short-run and long-run factors affect the supply of a good or service made available. But price still plays an important role. How price affects the quantity of a good or service made available by a producer is illustrated in a supply curve (see Figure 4.6). Product supply will increase if price is high because producers will want to receive the income from the high prices and the pure profits that will presumably accrue. The supply curve applies to both individual producers and the market supply of all producers as well.

As with demand, the interaction of price and supply is measured using the concept of elasticity. If a change in price results in a greater change in quantity supplied, product supply is said to be elastic. If the change in price results in no significant change in quantity supplied, supply is said to be inelastic. Unit elasticity of supply is shown if there is an equal change in price and product supply. Calculation of elasticity is made as follows:

$$\frac{\text{Percent change in supply}}{\text{Percent change in price}} = \text{Price elasticity of supply}$$

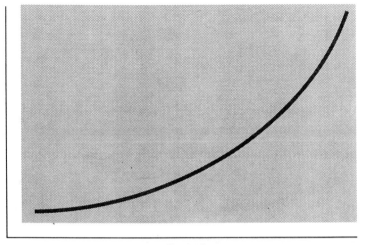

Price

Quantity

Figure 4.6 Supply Curve

A variety of factors in addition to price can affect supply. These include the price of inputs, price of other substitutable products, changes in producer expectations for the future, changes in technology, and changes in the number of producers.

DISTRIBUTION ECONOMICS

Throughout this chapter, discussion has focused on the production of tangible outputs and the effects of changing input quantity on output and costs. Although this discussion matches the settings in which the newspaper, magazine, recording, and video industries operate, it does not approximate well the setting in which broadcasting, cablecasting, and films most often operate. This occurs because the latter industries create public goods, and their operations do not approximate production economics but can best be considered using distribution economics.

When dealing with public goods, it becomes immediately clear that the cost of production is not affected by the number of users. Production costs of a television show, a radio broadcast, or a feature film remain the same whether many or few individuals comprise their audiences. There are no significant production cost advantages related to scale when the product is a public good being distributed.

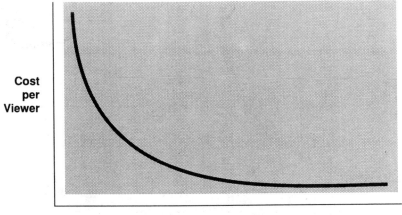

Figure 4.7 Effect of Audience Size on Cost per Viewer

Once a program or production is complete, the costs of getting it to a larger audience by making it available nationally or internationally are small and incremental. This additional cost is all that must be covered by distribution. As a result, great profits are possible in these industries by syndication, networking, and general distribution. By reaching these larger audiences with the product, the cost per viewer drops remarkably (see Figure 4.7).

There are cost differences between programming produced for large audiences and small audiences, but these are inherent in the costs of getting better writers, performers, directors, and technicians to increase the quality of the production. Low-cost productions can, and have, been made available to large audiences without additional production costs. Networks usually increase the production costs of prime-time productions by hiring popular performers and increasing production budgets because the cost will be spread over a large national audience by simultaneous broadcasting through affiliates.

Public goods are also not affected by supply and demand in the same way that private goods are affected. Providing a public good to a consumer does not diminish its availability to others. If a viewer watches a TV broadcast, this action does not keep others from watching. In such a situation, the broadcaster receives income from advertisers and thus seeks profit-maximizing audiences. This generally means the largest possible audience because income increases with audience size (see Figure 4.8).

When dealing with such public goods, setting a price on the product cannot be done with the same type of efficiency found when tangible

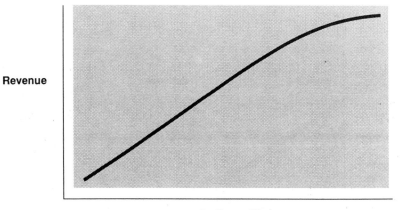

Revenue

Audience Size

Figure 4.8 Effect of Audience Size on Revenue

private goods are involved. No single price will lead to an efficient equilibrium because any price above zero will exclude some customers, and the potential revenue from them will be lost and cannot be replaced with higher income from other customers. The most efficient price in terms of generating the largest audience is zero, but this removes the incentive for a producer to do anything more than pander to mass tastes.

When audiences begin to pay for public goods, as in the case of cable TV, pay TV, and feature films, the price element begins to affect demand by losing viewers who would watch only if the price were lower. This is particularly true in cablecasting for premium channels.

PRODUCERS MEET CONSUMERS

There is a point at which producers depart from the abstract world of economic projects and enter the concrete and very real world of the marketplace for goods and services. When this occurs, forces promoting or constraining the supply of the good or service come into contact with the forces promoting or constraining the consumer demand for the good and service that were discussed in the last chapter.

Equilibrium is the point at which supply and demand meet and equalize the price and quantity produced. This is the optimal point for consumers and producers (see Figure 4.9). Related to the concept of price and supply is the issue of revenue, that is, income, received from the sale of the output. Determining the impact of revenues on supply decisions is made using the same concepts employed in exploring costs. As a result, on the income side of the ledger one deals with *marginal*

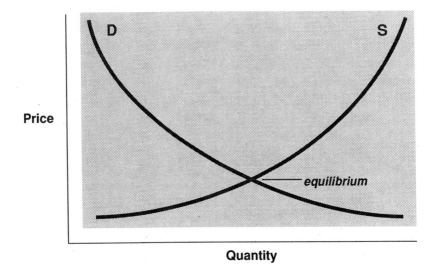

Price

Quantity

Figure 4.9 Supply and Demand

revenue, the additional revenue received from producing each additional unit of output, and *average revenue*, the revenue averaged over all units.

If a competitive situation exists with many small producers, the supply curve for any one producer would allow it to produce as much of the product as possible and continue to receive the same price and additional revenue for each. This is shown in the following example of what happens to revenue for a magazine. As the output increases, both marginal and average revenue stays the same as the price and total price rises linearly (see Table 4.5). If this situation were displayed on a graph, it would appear as Figure 4.10. In reality, the firm could not continue producing into infinity as a means of increasing revenue and profit because at some point the law of diminishing returns will make the costs per unit rise and thus marginal return would diminish into a negative zone.

In most production situations, producers do not operate in perfect competition so the marginal and average revenue curves are not at right angles as in Figure 4.10, but slant or bow downward.

In making production decisions, producers obviously must balance the issues of cost and revenue, and they seek to reach the optimal point where MC and MR intersect, as shown in Figure 4.11. In making production decisions, marginal cost — not average cost — is used in making production decisions.

TABLE 4.5

Output	Price	Marginal Revenue	Total Revenue	Average Revenue
1	$2.50	$2.50	$ 2.50	$2.50
50,000	2.50	2.50	125,000.00	2.50
100,000	2.50	2.50	250,000.00	2.50
250,000	2.50	2.50	625,000.00	2.50
500,000	2.50	2.50	1,250,000.00	2.50

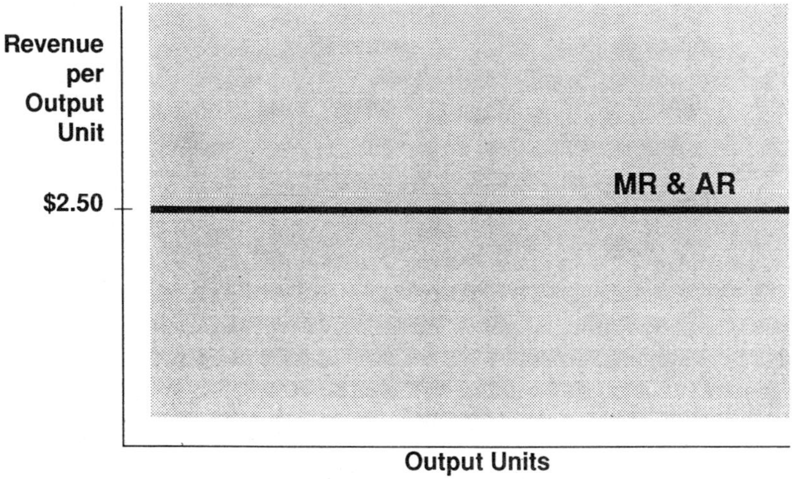

Figure 4.10 Marginal and Average Revenue in Competition

Having established the optimal output level for the price, one can now consider how the firm is doing in terms of profit. In order to do so, average costs and marginal costs are added to the analysis (see Figure 4.12).

Under some circumstances, a producer may deliberately seek to establish disequilibrium. In situations where elasticity of demand exists for a good or service, not all increases in prices will be damaging to a firm, and some may be helpful. An example of this occurs when total revenue increases if prices are raised despite a decrease in the quantity that consumers desire.

A record company, for example, may wholesale 100,000 copies of an album at $4 each, yielding $400,000 in revenue. If the price were raised to $5, the firm would not be expected to receive $500,000 in revenue because some consumers would probably not buy the record

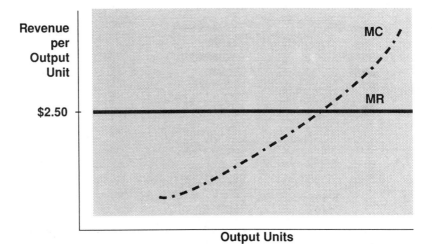

Figure 4.11 Optimal Output

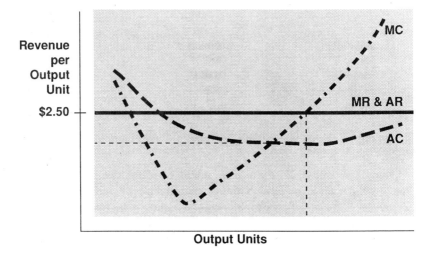

Figure 4.12 The Relation of Revenue to Output and Cost

since a retail price increase would be expected to follow. As a result, the company might sell only 90,000 albums at the $5 wholesale price, yielding $450,000 in revenues. Although the firm sold fewer albums, it is better off because it has an additional $50,000 in revenue.

Thus, firms can attempt to reach a point at which optimal revenue is received by manipulating price and quantity.

ISSUES OF MEDIA PRODUCT SUPPLY

Scholarly and trade literature contains little analysis and discussion of issues related to product supply, such as costs and scale economies. That which exists is generally brief but is noteworthy because of its originality and import.

Levin (1971) has used product supply concepts as a means of analyzing average and marginal costs for using broadcast frequencies and the public policy implications of such costs for expansion of the spectrum. Jane Henry (1985) has provided an analysis of costs in the context of pay TV and revealed that the costs for multichannel microwave distribution service are more favorable than those for direct broadcast satellite service and are competitive with cable television.

Corden (1952-53) used equilibrium analysis to consider the issues of cost, revenue, and output in newspapers. He argued that in considering newspaper economics, quality rather than price is variable for the nonadvertising portion of the newspaper product and that price, quality, and quantity are variable on the advertising product portion.

Economies of scale in cable television have been addressed by Noam (1985a), whose research revealed that few cost advantages occur because of the size of a firm and that economies of scale arise in the packaging and marketing of cable services by large cable systems. Thus, large cable companies have cost advantages when they do more than merely distribute programming through their systems.

Economies of scale in newspaper production have been the focus of Owen (1975, pp. 34-37) and Barry Litman (1988), who significantly explored the issue of long-run average costs and efficiencies and their impact on newspapers. They show that the high first-copy costs are rapidly spread over the printing of additional copies, so that average costs and marginal costs decline. Their work supports important evidence developed by Rosse (1967) that scale economics may be the single most important contributor to concentration and monopoly in newspaper markets.

A few attempts to analyze the effect of economies and diseconomies have been made. Dertouzous and Thorpe (1982) found that economies of scale are not created equally across all sizes of newspapers by the acquisition of new technology, that group ownership does not create significant economies of scale, and that even such economies in newsprint acquisition are not created by group ownership unless accompanied by vertical integration. A survival analysis of the newspaper industry by Norton and Norton (1986) suggests that electronic typesetting technology and offset printing have reduced first-copy costs and lowered the minimum efficient scale. As a result, papers with circulations between 10,000 and 100,000 have survived and grown in terms of market share and number of firms, while firms in the 250,000 to 500,000 circulation range, and those below 5,000 circulation, have been experiencing declining market shares and number of firms.

A study of the survival of new magazines indicates that the scale of the firm is not a factor in survival. The research showed that publications started by leading media companies were much less likely to survive than those started by smaller firms (Husni, 1988). This would indicate that there are few cost advantages in the magazine industry related to size of firm.

Little research on price elasticity of supply has been undertaken, but it has been shown that television programming supply is elastic (Owen et al., 1974, pp. 17-36). Blankenburg (1982) studied how disequilibrium in supply and demand may be used by newspaper firms to increase revenue and profit. In a study of newspaper circulation, he found that some newspapers deliberately manipulate price and circulation into disequilibrium — and lose some circulation — in order to increase total revenue.

5

MONOPOLY AND COMPETITION IN THE MARKET

How media firms behave influences the kinds and amounts of choices consumers and competitors can make in markets. The behavior of firms is, in turn, influenced by the structures of the markets in which they operate. This chapter explores how product, price, and competition policies are affected by market structures and how they influence choices in markets.

The choices that consumers and producers have in the market are significantly influenced by the *market conduct*, that is, how the market operates and conducts its exchange. Various markets operate differently because of the structures under which they operate and it is important to understand the differences in market conduct that are typically found under different *market structures*.

In precise terms, conduct refers to the policies of a firm or firms regarding market decisions and policies in dealing with competitors. Conduct includes 3 major issues: 1) product policies; 2) pricing policies; and 3) responses to competitors. Thus, when Cable News Network decided to add continuous stock prices to its Headline News channel, it made a product decision and a competition policy decision to compete with the Financial News Network by providing a similar product. If the St. Louis *Post-Dispatch* considers raising its single copy price to 50 cents or to stay at the industry standards of 25 and 35 cents, it is making a price policy decision.

Product policies involve the strategies employed by firms in deciding how to position their product in the market and how the products will be marketed. Policy decisions in this area involve issues of product differentiation; product qualities such as durability, size, and colors; product options; preference building through advertising; and new product lines. In media, such policies involve decisions about whether a radio station's format should be top-40, album-oriented rock, classical, or talk; whether a motion picture should also be released for video sales; whether a newspaper should be printed as a broadsheet or tabloid; and whether a cable network should program classic films or contemporary motion pictures.

Pricing policies involve setting price levels for products and decisions regarding discounting, multiple packaging, and price setting orientation. These orientations include: 1) demand-oriented pricing, in which prices are set solely based upon market forces; 2) target return pricing, in which prices are set based on the amount of pure profit desired in return; 3) competition-oriented pricing, in which prices are based on those charged by competitors; and 4) industry norm pricing, in which prices are based not on market or return issues but on whatever the industry as a whole is charging.

Responses to competitors as a form of market conduct involve decisions as to whether a firm will choose to compete, engage in price competition, or attempt to keep potential competitors out of the market. Policies of competition or noncompetition involve decisions about what product lines to produce, whether prices will be competitive with those of competitors, and whether the firm will advertise heavily for certain products. Such decisions are faced when a daily newspaper considers whether to start a total market coverage free-circulation paper to keep mail advertising services from penetrating a market, when a video manufacturer decides whether to price a video at $79 or $39, and when a magazine company decides whether to use television to advertise its weekly issues.

The issue of responses to competitors in the price area involves whether a firm will engage in price wars with other producers or distributors or whether it will engage in predatory pricing, in which the price of a product is set below its marginal cost as a means of harming a competitor who must likewise lower his costs. Thus losses are forced upon that competitor. A large firm using this tactic is able to absorb losses longer and can force a smaller firm out of business or can force it finally to raise its price at a loss of market share. This tactic is illegal under antitrust law, but it is hard to prove intent and predatory pricing, so some firms use the strategy.

A third policy toward competition involves increasing barriers to entry in the market to discourage potential competitors. One strategy involves observing the price limit — that is, raising the price of one's product as high as one can go without encouraging other companies to enter and gain a share of the market by selling at a lower price. A second strategy is to integrate the firm vertically. When this is done a company acquires other firms that serve other sectors of the industry. For example, a newspaper company might purchase a paper mill and manufacturer or a newspaper distribution firm. The end result is that supplies become less costly to the integrated firm and more costly to

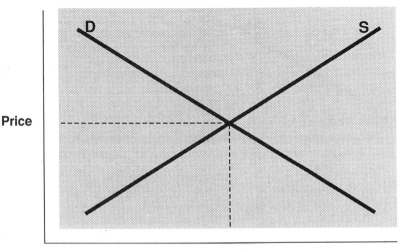

Figure 5.1 Demand and Supply Curves Under Perfect Competition

competitors or potential competitors doing business with the firm, so barriers to entry are increased.

MARKET CONDUCT UNDER
VARIOUS MARKET STRUCTURES

In a market structure of perfect competition, there are many firms and each has only a small market share. In nearly every case, perfect competition involves undifferentiated, homogeneous products for which buyers have no brand name preferences.

In this type of market, the output by each firm is relatively low, production is labor — rather than capital — intensive, and wages are also low. There is also a tendency toward overcrowding because of the ease of entry.

In such situations price is set by the market alone. The firms are thus called "price takers"; that is, they accept and must conform to the existing market price. As a result, prices are constrained downward. Because producers do not control price, the only production choice that producers have to make is the quantity of output produced. The demand and supply curves under perfect competition are thus straight (see Figure 5.1). The producer accepts the set price level and then decides how much of the quantity demanded the firm will provide or attempt to provide.

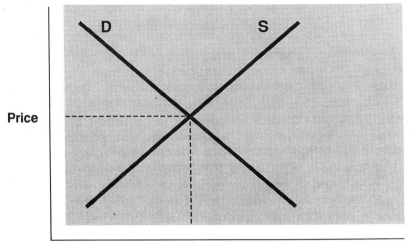

Figure 5.2 Demand and Supply Curves Under Perfect Monopoly

No media industries operate under the perfect competition market structure. This is not particularly surprising, however, because few industries operate in perfect competition — including manufacturing industries. The market for agricultural products most approximates perfect competition.

Perfect monopoly, the market structure at the other end of the spectrum, exists when only one firm provides the product, when barriers to entry are high, and when there are no ready substitutes. Typically in such situations, the capital requirements for entry are high, the industry is capital rather than labor intensive, output is high, and wages are high. The supply and demand curve for a perfect monopoly is shown in Figure 5.2.

Under this market structure, prices are set by producers seeking a combination of price and quantity that optimizes their return. The producer is a "price maker"; that is, the firm has great control over price and sets the price it wants. The producer also controls production by increasing quantity produced by adding input until marginal revenue intersects with marginal cost, and optimal levels of price, quantity, and return are achieved (see Figure 5.3).

Producers under perfect monopoly conduct themselves by making three choices: what price to charge; how much to manufacture; and whether to maximize output and revenue. In some cases, producers will

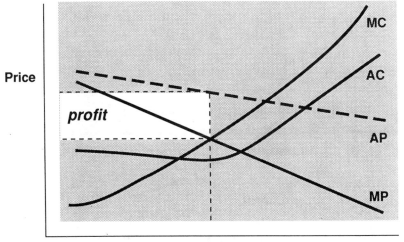

Figure 5.3 Equilibrium Under Perfect Monopoly

choose not to maximize but rather to help communities or serve the public welfare; this, however, is rare in unregulated perfect monopolies.

No media industries operate in perfect monopoly market structures but several come close. Cable television systems are the nearest to perfect monopoly, but perfection is limited because some substitution is possible. If there is only one motion picture theater in town, a near perfect monopoly exists, but some substitution is possible if consumers are willing to give up leaving home and instead view entertainment on a smaller screen. Newspapers have nearly perfect monopolies in some aspects of their product markets if they are the only local newspaper, but some limited substitution is possible.

The oligopoly market structure is found between perfect competition and monopoly but is closer to the monopoly structure. This tends to be a relatively stable structure in which a few firms, typically three to six, share the market, know each other, and watch each other's conduct. Barriers to entry are typically high in oligopoly markets and the products are not typically highly differentiated. The supply and demand curves for oligopoly are shown in Figure 5.4.

In such structures firms tend to have product policies that promote extras and quality differences through heavy advertising and positioning in the market. The firms are able to control price and quantity to a great degree, and decisions on those issues tend to be made interdepen-

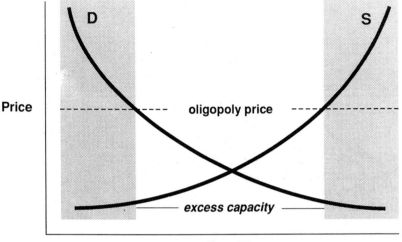

Figure 5.4 Demand and Supply Curves Under Oligopoly

dently with other firms. In other words, the firms have a tendency to cooperate in terms of price and output levels and to set them by watching each other and jointly seeking stability in price and quantity. If one firm cuts prices, others will follow suit, and if one raises them, others will follow. This is called price leadership. Other firms do not have to follow, and some may hold out in the short run to increase market shares slightly. In the long run, however, most producers stick together in oligopoly market structures. A number of media firms operate under oligopoly structures, including many television stations, radio stations, and some categories of magazines.

Monopolistic competition is a structure that lies between perfect competition and oligopoly. In such a situation there are typically a number of firms in the market with some differences in terms of production capabilities and location. There is usually some product differentiation, and the prices and quantity decisions are set both by the market and the firms. The supply and demand curves for monopolistic competition are shown in Figure 5.5

Some price differences are evident in monopolistic competition market structures, but these usually occur within a price range that is determined by competitors' prices. As a result, the actual price is set by the individual firm with an eye on market. In monopolistic competition, a firm's optimal price comes when product quantity yields a marginal cost that equals market price. Monopolistic competition is seen in the motion picture exhibition and magazine publishing industries.

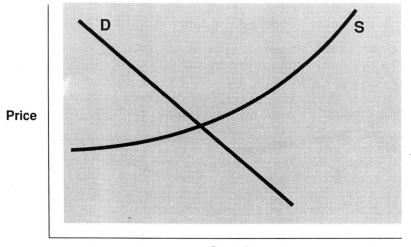

Figure 5.5 Demand and Supply Curves Under Monopolistic Competition

MEDIA CONDUCT ISSUES

How media firms behave in general and how they behave under different market structures is a concern of media economists, and has also been a great concern of media scholars concerned with the important social and political roles ascribed to media. Studies on media conduct have typically concentrated upon product issues (including content), pricing issues, and other management issues. Other studies have explored whether different market structures affect the quality of content or if the structure of one media market affects the structures of adjacent media markets.

Given demand theory and market structure expectations, one would expect consumers to benefit economically from competitive situations and to be harmed by monopolies. One would expect competition to improve the media content and monopoly to harm it. The evidence in this regard is mixed. Owen, Beebe, and Manning (1974) found that network programming and price decisions were influenced by oligopolistic interdependence rather than economic decisions because of time lags between decisions and airing of programming and because advertising prices were also determined prior to knowledge of the actual size of the viewing audiences. This, of course, is a result that fulfills our expectations.

The newspaper industry, however, provides little evidence that market structure has any significant effect on news and editorial content.

Most studies that have compared papers of each type and found few differences have concluded that professional norms and journalistic standards are more important in determining content than economic structure is, and that because of these social factors, the marketplace is not getting diverse ideas and content from different papers.

The development of this line of inquiry can be seen in the work of Bigman (1948), Nixon and Jones (1956), Grotta (1971), Ardoin (1973), Weaver and Mullins (1975), Niebauer (1984), Litman and Bridges (1986), McCombs (1988), Candussi and Winter (1988), and Lacy (1988a and 1988b). Their research has shown that when compared as groups, competing and monopoly papers have not shown important differences in news or editorial content, and local monopoly papers created by the demise of a competitor have been shown generally to continue the news coverage and editorial practices used before the monopoly developed. Papers with joint operating agreements provide news coverage similar to that of papers which compete with each other. Thus, it appears that the presence or absence of competition is again less of a factor in determining content than are professional norms and industry standards.

Chain and nonchain papers resemble each other in the coverage of national and international news and vary little in the type of coverage found on editorial pages, but there is some indication that chains that require the use of their own news services do so at the expense of some local coverage. Not surprisingly, locally owned papers tend to do a better job of covering community controversies as news, but there is evidence that chain-owned papers — perhaps because they are less affected by adverse local reactions — take more editorial positions on local issues than do local papers.

Busterna has significantly explored the effects of cross-ownership of television stations and newspapers in the same market and multiple ownership of television stations on the quality of television news content. He found that neither was related to the size of news staffs of television stations (1978) and that neither was related to local news expenditures (1980), but that cross-ownership was related to more local programming and that multiple station ownership was related to less overall local programming but more local news and public affairs programming (1988d).

Price

Market structure would also be expected to be related to prices charged for products, with media on the monopoly end of the continuum charging more for products than media at the competitive end.

Levin (1971) found some support for this view in his study of the radio industry. Broadcasters operating in monopoly and oligopoly structures used their market power to push advertising prices — and profits — upward until the 1950s, when the number of stations increased and television began creating intermedia competition for audiences. At that point the financial conduct and performance began to move away from what was expected in monopoly situations.

Wirth and Wollert (1984) found that prices charged for television news advertising time were not affected by group ownership of stations, but that cable penetration in markets resulted in lower prices and that higher prices existed in highly concentrated television markets.

Picard (1982) found that the newspaper industry paid little attention to economics and marketing knowledge in making decisions about advertising rates and relied more on hunches than data in making price decisions. This problem leaves newspapers at a disadvantage when dealing with advertisers. In analyzing newspaper market structures, one deals with local daily newspaper monopolies and local daily newspaper competition, which is actually oligopoly.

This pricing behavior of newspapers under competition and monopoly has yielded interesting results. Richard Brown (1967) studied the market behavior of daily newspapers, found differences in the ad rate-setting conduct under different structures, and concluded that the chain-owned papers used target return pricing models and that large papers and papers facing other local daily competitors use profit maximizing models for rate setting. Ferguson (1983) found that competing papers have higher advertising rates than do monopoly papers, a result similar to the finding of Blankenburg (1980) that weekly papers with competition are correlated with slightly higher prices.

Picard (1986), however, found that competing papers had higher actual rates than monopoly papers had, but, when adjusted for circulation, the rates were lower. The results indicated that competing papers raised rates more rapidly than did monopoly papers. High production and distribution costs, lower price resistance, higher salaries in metropolitan areas, and cooperative oligopolistic structures have been suggested as causes for these unexpected results (Picard, 1985c).

Since the 1960s studies have regularly found that newspaper monopolies result in higher advertising rates than do other competing papers of similar size. Grotta (1971) found that when a competitor died, leaving a monopoly, the monopoly newspaper did not pass on the benefits of its economies of scale but instead increased advertising prices, a result replicated in a different study by Charette, Brown-John, Romanow, and Soderlund (1983). Mathewson (1972), Kerton (1973),

Picard (1986), and Candussi and Winter (1988) also found higher advertising rates in monopoly newspapers.

Mixed results have been observed when comparing circulation prices in monopoly and oligopolistic situations, with a tendency toward higher prices in monopoly situations but with the sizes of papers apparently affecting results.

Until the early 1970s, studies of the effects of multiple ownership of newspapers found that chain-owned newspapers were not associated with higher prices. After newspaper groups began to become public companies and began aggressive acquisition strategies, those results changed. Kerton (1973), Bloomfield (1978), Blankenburg (1982, 1983), and Ferguson (1983) have all found that group ownership leads to prices higher than those generated through independent ownership.

Research by Mathewson (1972), Busterna (1978), Ferguson (1983), and Wirth and Wollert (1984) on cross-ownership of different media in the same market has yielded mixed results that lean toward the conclusion that cross-ownership does not affect prices.

Response to Competitors

Few studies have considered the responses that media companies have made to competitors or potential competitors, but there is evidence that many media companies turn to government regulation to raise barriers to entry in electronic media industries. For example, Levin (1971) showed that media companies were responsible for much FCC broadcasting policy that limited competition. Efforts were also made by members of the film and television industry in the 1970s and 1980s to regulate or tax videotape sales. Current efforts are being made by the recording industry to regulate digital audiotape.

Structural Effects

A growing body of literature is concerned with the effects of market structures in one market on the structures of adjacent markets, and most of this research has focused upon the newspaper industry. Lacy (1984), in a study of umbrella competition, found that competition was more intense downward through the layers and was threatening to small dailies in lower layers, but that competition between small dailies and weeklies was not very strong or threatening. A subsequent study found that the umbrella competition model applies well to competition for circulation sales but not for advertising sales (Lacy, 1985).

Niebauer (1984) considered the effects of the monopoly market structure of joint operating agreement newspapers on suburban newspapers, and found no significant evidence that these legalized monopolies have harmed papers in adjacent suburban cities.

The current state of this developing line of research is compiled in an excellent review article by Lacy (1988c).

6

MEDIA PERFORMANCE AND CAPITAL MARKETS

The creation and use of capital are crucial in a market economy. This chapter discusses the processes and issues of capital accumulation, lending, and investing. It also explores how the ownership forms of media firms in their financial performances affect relations with capital markets and the values of media companies.

The performance of media and their ability to gain funds for expansion and growth are critical factors in the management of a media firm and managers need to comprehend the nature and operations of capital markets. It was the existence of capital markets that made it possible for the Media News Corp. to purchase the Houston *Post*, for the Disney company to build new studios in Florida, and for the Little Rock *Gazette* to purchase new printing presses.

The process by which such funds are made available is a relatively recent development in economic history. Throughout recorded history the world's population has created and exchanged goods for consumption, and the leftover wealth created through the exchange was consumed in the creation of individual and national palaces, monuments, and cathedrals. Capitalism developed, however, when the proceeds of exchange transactions began to be accumulated by individuals and groups as a means of creating more wealth rather than as a means of display. The accumulated proceeds — that is, the financial sum of wealth — are called capital.

Capital is created and increased when resources are not consumed but saved for use in the creation of goods and services. Adam Smith argued that through the use of capital to mechanize industry, additional wealth and capital would be created, which would in turn be used for more economic growth and development that would benefit society. Karl Marx agreed with Smith that the marketplace for goods and services was the driving force in the creation of capital. The process by which additional wealth was created by the market became the focus of his economic study on the issue of accumulated wealth, *Das Kapital* (*Capital*). Marx (1867/1952) showed that capitalists use their capital to purchase raw materials, goods, and labor to transform these commodities into new goods and services.

Individuals and firms wishing to carry out productive activities must have access to capital to procure the goods, services, and labor necessary for that process. If individuals have previously accumulated capital on their own by consuming less wealth than they receive, the capital can be used for that purpose.

This is, of course, the situation found in the establishment of many small businesses. In this setting an individual uses money saved, his or her own capital, to buy goods or services to set up and operate his or her business. Because most individuals' capital is small, the resulting business's facilities, equipment, and size are small. The ability of such a firm to expand and grow is low because available capital is low. Many small newspapers, radio stations, magazines, and book publishers have been established by an individual's capital. If such a firm wishes to grow, additional capital must be obtained. The firm can save its pure profits for this purpose, but a lengthy time will be required to accumulate capital for expansion purposes.

In some cases, several individuals will create a larger pool of capital for such a business by joining into a partnership in which each shares the business and its proceeds. In such situations the amount of capital may still be low, and additional sources of capital may be sought to permit growth. Situations of this kind are often found in mid-sized publications, radio and television stations, and book firms.

The needs of capitalists for additional sources of capital for growth led to the development of two important mechanisms that accumulate capital and make it available to capitalists: capital lending and direct capital investing. Both mechanisms involve accumulating capital by individuals and making it available to other individuals or firms for productive uses in capital markets.

In capital lending, pools of capital are created by single individuals or groups of individuals and are loaned by capitalists for a fee. Traditional forms of this mechanism include loans from individuals and from thrift institutions such as banks, savings and loan associations, and credit unions. In direct capital investing, groups of individuals are brought together who contribute their capital to a firm in exchange for shares, that is, partial ownership of the firm. During the three-hundred-year development of capitalism, these lending and investment mechanisms have matured into large, well-established sources of capital represented by thrift institutions and stock exchanges. The availability of large amounts of capital through these sources has made it possible for huge firms with high productive capacities to develop in a way that an individual or small group of individuals could not have made possible through its own capital alone.

These two major sources of capital operate in separate capital markets and compete with each other in attracting financial resources to be used as capital and in making capital available to those who wish to use it for production and personal consumption. The amount of capital available in each market changes over time as those who save financial resources move them between the capital markets in order to gain the best return for the use of their money. General economic conditions, business trends, interest rates, and stock earnings affect decisions of where resources are placed by those with money available and decisions about price and other terms at which the accumulated capital is made available in the markets.

Capital obtained through loans is used by firms to create goods and services. When borrowing the capital, firms agree to repay the *principal*, that is, the amount borrowed, and to pay *interest*, that is, the cost for borrowing the capital. The borrower uses the capital to purchase raw materials, goods and services, and labor to produce a good or service and to sell that product to buyers. The revenue obtained is used to pay production costs, including the cost of the loan of capital, and, if the company is successful, to create pure profit and additional wealth that can be accumulated for the firm. The repayment of the principal and interest to the lending firm increases the wealth of the lender as well.

In a lending situation, lenders obviously are best served by receiving the highest possible interest on the capital that they lend and borrowers are best served when that rate for borrowing capital is as low as possible. If the price of capital rises too high, quantity demanded will diminish because many producers will not be able to pay the price and produce and sell their products at a price that will result in a profitable return. Likewise, if the price is too low, lenders will receive a small return and the opportunity costs for that use of the capital may lead them to use it in other ways.

The quantity of capital demanded and the supply of capital available at given prices are subject to the forces of supply and demand just like any good or service. The supply and demand for lent capital is thus based on price forces and also on other possible uses for capital, the state of the general economy, and government fiscal and monetary policies.

Nearly all media firms, large and small, borrow capital from thrift institutions as a means of stabilizing cash flow and purchasing new equipment and facilities. Larger firms regularly use such borrowed

Highlight 6.1 Public Media Companies
with Market Capitalization Exceeding $2 Billion

American Television and Communications
Capital Cities/ABC
Coca Cola
Columbia Broadcasting System
Disney
Dow Jones & Co.
Dun and Bradstreet
Gannett
Gulf and Western
Knight-Ridder
LIN
MCA
McGraw-Hill
News Corporation
New York Times Co.
Reuters
Tele-Communications Inc.
Time-Warner
Tribune
Times Mirror
Washington Post Co.

capital to finance expansion and to integrate their activities horizontally or vertically through the acquisition of other media firms.

When capital is directly invested in firms by individuals and other firms with accumulated capital, it is done with the desire to have the value of that capital increase through the profit and growth in the value of the firm in which it has been invested. Investment can be made in firms of all sizes, and the process is dictated by whether the firm is a *privately owned* or *publicly owned* corporation. Investments in private firms are made directly with the firm, and investments in public firms are made using brokerage houses that purchase shares in a stock market.

Privately owned firms tend to be smaller than publicly owned firms are because the former do not have high capital requirements or because they operate in limited product or geographic markets in local markets. In some cases they remain small because private firms' abilities to attract investment capital are lower than are those for public firms.

Investors purchase shares of firms that they believe will increase in value and will yield high dividends, that is, payments for profit earned.

The price at which investors are willing to purchase shares of a company is influenced by that company's financial position as well as market trends, technological developments, general economic developments, and other factors affecting perceptions of the state of the economy.

In such direct investment, investors purchase stock or shares in firms and select corporate directors and officers to manage the firms. Two major categories of stock are available: *common stock*, the largest category and primary type of stock, and *preferred stock*, which typically has no voting rights in the firm but has a guaranteed fixed rate of return or preference to assets over common stockholders if the company fails. Preferred stock is often purchased by persons who want a better return on capital than is available in thrift institutions but do not want the larger risk associated with common stock.

The value of a particular type of stock is indicated by three measures. The first measure is *par value*, which is the face value placed on the company shares when they are issued. The second indicator is *book value*, which is the accounting value of the stock to the firm, obtained by dividing a firm's net worth minus preferred stock by shares of common stock. Finally, there is *market value*, which is the actual price of one share if the share is purchased or sold. This value may be above or below book value depending upon investors' confidence, although it is normally close to or higher than book value.

In analyzing the value of firms based on their financial conditions, both direct investors and lenders pay particular attention to indicators of current growth and economic performance as well as past growth and economic performance of individual firms. Growth measures concentrate on growth of revenue, operating income, and assets over time, as well as consider what has happened in a firm in the past quarter or half year, or the past one, three, five, or ten years. Performance measures deal with profits, cash flows, and measures of the financial strength of firms, as well as *return on sales* (ROS), *return on assets* (ROA), and *return on investment* (ROI).

Indicators used in such financial analyses include measures of growth of revenue, cash flow, and assets. Performance measures include operating measures such as profit margins and sales-to-assets ratios, broader long-term analyses such as ratios of assets to liabilities, liquid assets to current liabilities, capitalization, and indicators of the return on investment such as return on equity and price-earnings ratios. Media companies have done very well in terms of growth and performance in recent years, typically exceeding or even doubling the growth and return rates of nonmedia firms (Table 6.1).

The general financial efficiency of a firm is displayed by its *operating profit margin*, which indicates the firm's profit as a percent of sales

TABLE 6.1 Average Growth Rates in the Mid-1980s

Industry	Revenues	Assets
Book publishing	9	16
Broadcasting (TV & radio)	13	24
Cable & pay TV	31	27
Entertainment programming	18	17
Magazines — consumer	8	24
Magazines — business	7	10
Newspaper publishing	11	14
Audio recordings	3	7

Average Performance Measures

Industry	Op. Income Margin %	Return on Total Assets %
Book publishing	10	14
Broadcasting (TV & radio)	18	18
Cable & pay TV	17	9
Entertainment programming	11	9
Magazines — consumer	10	23
Magazines — business	12	26
Newspaper publishing	17	26
Audio recordings	7	14

before accounting for interest payments and taxes. *Current ratio* reports the current assets to current liabilities, a measure that provides a view of the current financial strength of the firm. Generally a firm likes to have a two-to-one ratio. *Liquidity ratio* indicates the amount of cash, securities, and other liquid assets on hand, that is, assets that can be turned into cash without significant loss of value, in comparison to the current liabilities of the company. When firms acquire other firms or make capital expenditures for new facilities or equipment, the liquidity ratio can be expected to be lower than normal.

Capitalization ratios indicate the percentage of capital represented by preferred and common stock and long-term debt. *Sales to assets* ratios provide an indicator of how well company revenues are being used. *Inventory turnover* indicates how many times the inventory of a firm has turned over during a year. This measure is most often used in dealing with retail businesses, but also has bearing on the activities of book and audio and visual recording firms.

Financial analyses also consider the *return on investment* provided by firms. Such measures consider the pure profits, sometimes before and sometimes after reinvestment, that accrue to company owners. *Return on equity* is an important indicator that reports the net income

Highlight 6.2 Calculation of Growth and Performance Measures

Growth Measures

Annual Growth of Revenue (expressed as percentage)

$$\frac{\text{Latest Year's Revenue} - \text{Previous Year's Revenue}}{\text{Previous Year's Revenue}}$$

Annual Growth of Operating Income (expressed as percentage)

$$\frac{\text{Latest Year's Operating Income} - \text{Previous Year's Operating Income}}{\text{Previous Year's Operating Income}}$$

Annual Growth of Assets (expressed as percentage)

$$\frac{\text{Latest Year's Assets} - \text{Previous Year's Assets}}{\text{Previous Year's Assets}}$$

Annual Growth of Net Worth (expressed as percentage)

$$\frac{\text{Latest Year's Net Worth} - \text{Previous Year's Net Worth}}{\text{Previous Year's Net Worth}}$$

Liquidity Measures

Current Ratio
$$\frac{\text{Current Assets}}{\text{Current Liabilities}}$$

Acid Test Ratio
$$\frac{\text{Liquid Assets}}{\text{Current Liabilities}}$$

Profitability Measures

Return on Sales
$$\frac{\text{Operating Income}}{\text{Revenue}}$$

Return on Assets
$$\frac{\text{Operating Income}}{\text{Total Assets}} \quad \text{or} \quad \frac{\text{Operating Income}}{\text{Fixed Assets}}$$

Return on Equity (expressed as percentage)
$$\frac{\text{Operating Income}}{\text{Net Worth}}$$

Price-Earnings Ratio
$$\frac{\text{Market Price of a Share}}{\text{Earnings of the Share}}$$

Highlight 6.2 (continued)

Financial Strength Measures

Operating Profit Margin (expressed as percentage)

$$\frac{\text{Operating Income (Before Taxes and Interest Payments)}}{\text{Operating Revenue}}$$

Cash Flow Margin (expressed as percentage)

$$\frac{\text{Operating Income (Before Taxes and Interest Payments)} + \text{depreciation and amortization}}{\text{Operating Revenue}}$$

Capitalization Ratio (expressed as percentage)

$$\frac{\text{Preferred Stock}}{\text{Common Stock}} \text{ or } \frac{\text{Long–Term Debt}}{\text{Common Stock}}$$

Debt to Equity

$$\frac{\text{Total Debt}}{\text{Total Equity}}$$

of a firm as a percentage of the net worth of a firm. This yields a measure of how much the company is earning compared to the value of the investors' shares. The *price-earnings ratio* indicates the relationship of the price of the firm's shares in the stock market to the earnings per share.

ISSUES OF MEDIA PERFORMANCE AND CAPITAL MARKETS

Although media owners have always been concerned with financial performance and the availability of capital from thrift institutions, it has only been in recent decades that they have entered the market for direct investment capital as publicly owned corporations. This new form of capitalization has resulted in significant changes in the management and size of firms.

Prior to the development of television and cable systems, the number of public companies was low. Even after the development of television broadcasting, public companies tended to be limited to networks and television programs and motion picture companies. The development of cable television with its high capital costs for equipment and installation resulted in the formation of large firms with public corporate ownership to accumulate the capital necessary to build and operate such firms. In the 1970s, newspaper firms that had typically operated under proprietorships and private corporation structures began to turn to public corporate ownership as a means of expansion. The Gannett Co. became the leading newspaper firm and a model of how privately owned newspaper companies could go public and use the additional capital for rapid expansion.

The literature about these developments and analysis of their effects has been limited for the most part to anecdotal and popular studies of media developments. Contributions in this regard include studies by Michael Leapman (1984) and Thomas Kiernan (1986) of Rupert Murdoch's News Corporation, and Edward Scharff's study of the *Wall Street Journal* (1988). Broadcast studies have included one on the role of William Paley in the development of CBS (Paper, 1987), and another on how the financial takeover of CBS affected that firm's news operations (McCabe, 1987). There have also been reviews by McClintick (1982), Litwak (1986), and Yule (1988) of the influence of firms, markets, and individuals on motion picture industry financing. Another of this type of study explored Time Incorporated's disastrous attempt to start a broadcast and cable television magazine (Byron, 1986). Broader studies of the impact of major public companies on media industries have been made by Bagdikian (1987) and Schiller (1981).

It has only been in recent years that a more specialized scholarly and applied literature on the financial performance of, and capital markets for, media companies has developed. Methods for analyzing media company performance and value have been the focus of Wolpert and Wolpert (1986), and studies of financial performance of communications firms such as *Communications Industry Report, Broadcast Stats, Duncan's Radio Market Guide, Radio Financial Report, Investing in Radio, Investing in Television,* and *Kagan Cable TV Financial Databook* are available.

Use of financial growth and performance data for management and investment decisions became a significant topic of media management books in the last part of the 1980s, reflecting the new importance attached by the industry and capital markets to financial performance. Exploration of the importance of profit-and-loss statements, balance sheets, and market information, as well as discussions of how to use such data, has been made in texts by Marcus (1986); Fink (1988); O'Donnell, Hausman, and Benoit (1989); and Lavine and Wackman (1988). Some industry associations and investment firms have produced materials on how to use such data in making investment and management decisions as well, including the National Association of

Broadcasters (1978) and the Institute of Newspaper Controllers and Finance Officers (1975).

A study by McGann and Russell (1988) of publicly owned broadcast firms found that, despite fears fueled by the CBS takeover and the sale of ABC to Capital Cities Communications in the mid-1980s, broadcast firms were well defended against unwanted takeovers, and that their financial performance was better than that for companies in nonmedia industries.

7

GOVERNMENT INTERVENTION IN THE MARKET

Government regularly intervenes in media markets to promote social goals and influence the market conduct of media firms. This chapter reviews the concepts of efficiency, equity, and externalities and how they affect government decisions to intervene. Intervention occurs through regulation, advantages, and subsidies.

Governments intervene in markets to put into place public policies that override or supplement the allocative decisions of market mechanisms, promote competition, and protect emerging industries. These policies are intended to protect producers and consumers or to meet social needs, or to be political responses to pressures brought to bear by producers and consumers. Media companies regularly encounter government intervention. When WIVB-TV applied for a renewal of its license to broadcast in Buffalo, it was because the government had intervened in the structure of the broadcast market. When the Environmental Protection Agency issued regulations requiring newspapers to analyze their ink waste for hazardous chemicals and to dispose of such chemicals properly, the government was intervening in the market. When the Detroit *Free Press* and *News* applied to the Justice Department to form a joint operating agreement, they did so because the government had intervened in the market with antitrust laws that normally prohibit such joint operations.

At the macroeconomic level, capitalist governments intervene to provide currency and raise taxes for economic and social infrastructures, to respond to economic and social ills (such as inflation, unemployment, and poverty) and to stimulate or retard their economies. At the microeconomic level, governments intervene to promote industries and commerce and to respond to market problems in industries by instituting policies that promote desirable outcomes and inhibit undesirable outcomes.

All capitalist nations, despite their market-based economies, intervene and engage in economic planning activities, but not to the extent of centrally planned economies. There are no market capitalist nations that adhere to laissez-faire policies with regard to the economic market. Capitalist nations intervene by engaging in *simple monopoly capitalism* or *state monopoly capitalism*. Simple monopoly capitalism is a condition in which the state engages in low levels of central planning and directs most of its intervention as a means of promoting economic activity. State monopoly capitalism exists when governments override the operation of the market through taxes, public ownership, and monetary policies that provide them extensive control over the market.

Capitalist government decisions to intervene or leave markets alone are made on the basis of *welfare economics*. Welfare economics focuses on the behavior of firms or industries and how it affects their performance. Welfare economics is concerned with the issues of *efficiency, equity,* and *externalities.*

Efficiency is concerned with whether the actions of firms maximize total wealth, measured in terms of *allocative efficiency* and *technical efficiency*. Allocative efficiency deals with the market decisions involving allocation and seeks to ensure that excess profits are not earned by producers and that the pressures of consumers and producers on the market function so that the market can operate at optimal points that spread its benefits between producers, between consumers, and between producers and consumers. Technical efficiency deals with whether the inputs used are used most effectively to maximize output.

Equity is concerned with the manner in which the total wealth is distributed among producers and consumers. In a market-based system, the wealth needs to be distributed among all producers and consumers in a fashion that promotes the interests of both groups and the interests of the society as a whole. If distribution is too equal — as in centrally planned economies or market economies with unduly high taxes used to redistribute wealth — a loss of incentive for producers to produce wealth beyond what one would receive can be expected since that surplus would be taken away and given to others.

Externalities involve results of activities in the market that affect society outside the market itself. These include environmental and social effects of production and consumption.

In making decisions to intervene, governments are influenced by the interaction of efficiency and equity and the externalities that are present. If significant inefficiencies exist, government may intervene. This often occurs when monopolies and oligopolies are present and create allocative inefficiency that also harms equity. Under such conditions producers can restrict output and thus increase price or fix price higher than output would normally produce. Thus the producers receive excessive profits. This, of course, redistributes the wealth from consumers to producers in a way that does not maximize economic well-being. Technical inefficiencies that occur when output is not maximized result in higher cost to consumers and redistribution of wealth toward producers that is harmful, so governments sometimes intervene by making bulk purchases of goods beyond what the market demands in order to improve technical efficiency.

If externalities exist, governments may intervene to stop harmful externalities, to ameliorate the damage caused by harmful externalities, or to protect and promote beneficial externalities.

The issues of efficiency and equity, and government intervention to promote the two, are especially important in terms of media because of the important social roles that media play in a democratic society. Although it may be desirable for government to promote these purposes, it becomes undesirable when the intervention inhibits media activities that carry out those social roles. As a result, there is a tension created whenever government intervenes, as well as concern over its potential impact on society.

When governments decide to intervene in economic markets, they do so with four major types of intervention: 1) regulation; 2) advantages; 3) subsidies; and 4) taxation.

Regulation of industry occurs in three ways. First, there is technical regulation, such as the setting and maintenance of industry standards and control of commonly used thoroughfares in order to ensure compatibility, quality, and safety. Second, governments intervene with market structure regulation. They do so in order to control the number of producers and sellers and to attempt to diversify market structure. Among the methods used for structure regulation are franchises and licenses in which certain types of structures are permitted or protected. Third, governments use behavioral regulation that controls the acts of firms, such as preventing anticompetitive action that might harm the market, controlling rates and prices in efforts to achieve macroeconomic goals, or controlling harmful externalities.

When in place, regulations have economic effects. These involve increases or decreases in costs, revenues, or profits caused by the addition of nonmarket requirements and forces.

Advantages are preferred treatment by government or the provision of reduced prices for government services, those provided by government-regulated industries, or agencies related to government. Advantages may be given to all industries or may target specific industries that governments wish to aid. Included in this category of intervention are tax breaks and exemptions from regulation. The economic effect of advantages reduces the costs of production, thus increasing profit for a firm or raising it to the point where the additional profit is an incentive for production.

Subsidies are cash transfers from government to industries to promote an industry or type of production. They can also be provided as an incentive to halt harmful externalities or to pay for equipment that will halt them. Subsidies increase revenue, thus increasing profit or creating incentives for production.

Taxation involves cash transfers from producers or consumers to government to pay for government activities, but it is also used as a means of penalizing firms for undesirable externalities and providing government money to ameliorate such problems.

Subsidies and advantages can be classed as direct or indirect aid. They are *direct* when they involve specific assistance to an individual media unit, such as a firm subsidy or grant given to a production company. Intervention is considered *indirect* if it is provided across a class of media or other business units, such as tax advantages that are enjoyed by broadcasting and newspaper groups and other media firms for acquisition of new properties.

Intervention may also be *specific*; that is, it may be undertaken by government to promote a clearly stated goal or to help achieve a specified output, as in the case of research grants provided to support newspaper industry efforts to replace wood pulp in newsprint with kenas. Other intervention is considered *general*, that is, aid to promote generally the health or development of a media industry or industry as a whole, such as tax advantages that exempt advertising sales from sales or professional taxes in most states.

Finally, intervention may be mandated or selective. *Mandated intervention* is authorized by law, and government administrators do not have a choice in granting or withholding the intervention, such as in the case of regulating electromagnetic spectrum or providing a tax credit on a tax return. *Selective intervention* involves intervention that is made at the discretion of an official or officials, such as decisions of state or federal antitrust agencies to prosecute anticompetitive actions by firms, or loans can be provided to media by agencies such as the Small Business Administration.

INTERVENTION IN MEDIA ECONOMICS

Government intervention in media economics occurs through all the mechanisms discussed above: regulation, advantages, subsidies, and taxation.

The three types of regulation — technical, market structure, and behavioral — are justified as means of protecting the public welfare and ensuring that the market can operate effectively. Technical regulation occurs in the setting of broadcast and cablecast technical standards — mechanical standards for equipment used in printing and production of video and audio products. It occurred when Congress required television sets to be built with both UHF and VHF channels on them. It also occurs in the assignment and protection of electromagnetic frequencies.

Market structure regulation occurs in the granting of broadcast licenses and cable franchises; in antitrust actions aimed at controlling vertical and horizontal integration and the development of monopoly in specific markets; and in the provision of loans, grants, and other funding to promote media and diverse ownership that would not exist or survive if left to market forces alone. Structural regulation is seen in rules prohibiting cross-ownership of certain media and limiting multiple ownership of broadcasting stations, and in antitrust laws prohibiting motion picture producers from owning exhibition houses.

Behavioral regulation occurs through the determination of acceptable practices for broadcasting and cablecasting, including efforts to halt externalities that result in regulation of offensive speech in television and radio broadcasts, and regulation of sexual content of films, videos, books, and magazines. Regulations are used to control the externalities of pollutants resulting from chemicals, ink, and petroleum products used in printing newspapers and magazines. Regulations are also evidenced by antitrust laws regulating conduct such as price fixing, predatory pricing, and market allocation that harms the ability of media markets to operate effectively.

Much writing and research on the regulation of media has focused upon its real and imagined conflicts with libertarian ideals. Only a few studies have significantly explored its economic bases.

Government intervention through antitrust enforcement and judicial decisions in antitrust litigation present significant issues. Busterna (1988a) has shown that in the 1980s little federal enforcement of antitrust statutes involving newspapers has occurred; rather, antitrust activity has tended to be litigation between newspapers over each other's practices, mainly in the area of advertising pricing and practices. Antitrust enforcement has traditionally been much more vigorously exercised in the motion picture industry than in other media industries and has resulted in an early splitting of production and exhibition activities (Conant, 1978).

Recent acquisitions have begun again to integrate vertically the motion picture industry through acquisition of cable and theater firms by conglomerate owners of production companies. Concurrently, there has been increasing concentration in the motion picture exhibition portion of the industry, but these developments have not yet resulted in strong antitrust intervention by the government (Guback, 1987).

The use of antitrust laws to keep program producers out of joint ventures with cable operators and the need for concern about vertical integration of the cable television industry have been asserted by White (1985), but antitrust enforcement has been minimal in the 1980s, according to Chan-Olmsted and Litman (1988). Their research indicates that horizontal acquisitions in the cable industry have been generally ignored by the Justice Department and that as the result of horizontal and vertical mergers, cable programming companies have gained significant ownership of local cable systems representing the exhibition stage of the industry. As they have done so, the companies have begun exercising significant market power.

The effects of government regulatory policies on broadcasting economics have been of significant interest, especially in terms of the control of local and national audiences that regulation has provided to certain broadcasters and networks. Levin (1971) argued that government licensing and control of the electromagnetic spectrum unduly limited the development of broadcasting and other spectrum-based communication services and provided abnormal financial returns to broadcasters between the 1930s and 1950s. He argued that the market constraints should be limited, thus opening up competition that benefits consumers; that the government should provide incentives to develop use of the spectrum; and that the subsidy of free spectrum use should be eliminated. Owen (1975) argued that broadcasting companies had managed to direct government regulation of broadcasting to promote and protect their profit. In both broadcasting and cable, government regulation was used to limit competition and available spectrum space, and no incentives were provided to improve performance or to promote operating in the public interest. Owen's argument was underscored by Noll et al. (1973), who argued that government policies toward broadcasting needed alteration because they have provided undue economic advantages to broadcasters that have harmed the public welfare, particularly by shielding them from competition and making them unduly profitable.

A later study by Owen (1978) considered the dominance of television networks in terms of programming and suggested that regulatory policies promoting alternative programming sources and reducing network control over the television market could be achieved by altering the industry structure set up by existing government regulation. Levin (1980) concurred in his exploration of the history of government regulation of television and its effects. He supported changes in policies to encourage the availability of multiple channels in broadcast markets, to improve the quality of programming, and to promote diversity.

Disputes over policies that regulate other market structures, such as the FCC's prohibition of ownership of a newspaper and broadcast property in the same geographic market, have also resulted in significant discussion but little research. Owen (1975) has noted that cross-ownership prohibitions are a form of antitrust enforcement in regulated industries.

Advantages involve a variety of public policy decisions that help promote media industries. Included are tax advantages, such as the exemption of advertising from sales taxes on services in most states, and postal rate advantages under which newspapers, magazines, books, and advertising material can be mailed at special reduced rates. Also included in this category are provisions such as the Newspaper Preservation Act, that has exempted some newspapers from antitrust laws. Advantages are often requested and extended because they promote the beneficial externalities of free flow of information and an informed public, and the attendant social benefits that are presumed to arise from these externalities.

The major advantage, made early in the United States, was to reduce the cost of sending newspapers and other printed material through the mail. This fiscal advantage was a means of promoting the health of publishers and public welfare by keeping the cost of acquiring information low, but, according to Kielbowicz (1986), was also made as a means of currying publishers' favor in the late nineteenth century.

Government intervention caused by the exemption of joint operating newspapers from antitrust laws by the Newspaper Preservation Act has been a significant area of concern. Worries about its potential impact were raised by Barnett (1969) and Malone (1969) prior to its passage. Since that time, its actual economic impact has been studied by a number of observers. In order to determine failure in a paper, five major economic and financial tests have been applied under the Act, according to Picard (1987). These arrangements have also created significant concern that public welfare is being sacrificed for the sake of a few newspaper producers. That concern has been well-articulated by Barnett (1980) and Carlson (1982) — who argued that the Act created extensive barriers to entry and allowed harmful anticompetitive acts — and by Barwis (1980), who asserted that the preservation of separate voices was not dependent upon granting such a monopoly and that it unduly shields newspapers from economic forces. More recently, Busterna (1988c) argued that the broad antitrust exemption provided by the Act is harmful to consumers, a view agreed upon by Picard (1988c), who has argued for revision of the act to remove the most flagrant anticompetitive actions in order to protect the public, while at the same

Highlight 7.1 Four Propositions about State Intervention in Press Economics

---

1. The character of state intervention in press economics depends upon the nature of the relationship between the state and its citizens. When citizens are subservient to the state . . . intervention will be authoritarian and seductive and will be used to gain the press's acquiescence. As states become more democratic and individual liberty increases, the intervention becomes less coercive.

2. State intervention expands and contracts in accordance to the economic needs of the press. The amount of intervention is determined by the press's financial stability. Intervention will increase to meet the press's minimum financial requirements and will decrease when these requirements are satisfied by outside sources.

3. The types of state intervention are shaped by the political-economic tenets accepted in a particular nation. The dominant political and economic philosophies, or their accepted interpretations, will determine the nature and forms of intervention in a given state, regardless of the forms of intervention selected by other states at comparable levels of economic and democratic development.

4. In any given nation, state intervention in press economics will parallel intervention in the economy as a whole. State press policies will be consistent with economic policies pursued in other industries and in the general economy.

(Picard, 1985b, pp. 124-125)

---

time allowing the economies of scale from joint operations to continue as a means of cost sharing between joint operating papers.

Subsidies to media in the United States are not as great as in other nations but include research grants to improve journalistic and production techniques and to fund research on improvements in the use of basic resources. Subsidies also include purchases of media products by government, such as broadcast programming for armed services and bulk purchases of newspapers and magazines for government employees.

Smith (1977) and Hollstein (1978) explored increasing government subsidies to newspapers in European nations during the 1970s, arguing that the policies were based on the need to improve access to media, reduce newspaper mortality, and halt concentration of ownership. Picard (1985a) found four main patterns of intervention in newspaper economics among Western nations and asserted that the patterns were related to the general macroeconomic policies of the nations, suggesting propositions that link press policies to the macroeconomic policies and political relationships of the society (Picard, 1985b).

Mayer (1973) revealed how many nations, especially Western European countries and Canada, have provided subsidies to motion picture producers as a means of promoting their national film industries. In many cases, these subsidies are funded with taxes on theater admissions.

Taxation has not been a significant form of intervention in U.S. media because taxes that are not general taxes levied on all businesses have usually been found to be unconstitutional if applied only to media. Much discussion, however, has focused on the application of tax advantages as a means of promoting desirable industry structures. In recent years, concern over video and audiotape has led to efforts to tax these products as a means of providing compensation pools for producers of video and audio recordings who are not compensated when consumers record available copies for their own use. Breenan (1988) has argued against taxation of home audiotapes as a means of compensating record companies and recording artists whose work is copied by individuals for personal use, maintaining that a tax would not provide sufficient benefits to warrant the intervention.

In a study of tax policies affecting newspapers, Dertouzous and Thorpe (1982) found that inheritance and capital gains taxes, combined with tax advantages for the acquisitions of newspapers, are the primary causes of the decline of independent newspaper ownership. Their research revealed that existing tax policies provide economic incentives to both independent newspaper owners and newspaper groups — incentives that promote acquisition of papers by groups. For the trend away from independent ownership to be slowed, changes in tax laws would be required.

8

LABOR IN THE MARKET

Media could not exist without the contributions of employees and managers. This chapter discusses how media become consumers when they employ labor, the influences on labor supply and demand, and the contributions that labor makes to production. It reviews how labor supply is affected by compensation offered, work type, and labor organization.

Labor is an important factor in production. Media industries that rely heavily on human resources must pay a significant amount of attention to their role. Economic issues, including the amount of labor available, wages paid, the quality of labor, and how additional labor increases output, are particularly important in understanding the economics and management of media firms.

Media are labor intensive. Labor is one of the most expensive inputs in media production. The resource is available from an independent labor market made up of individuals selling their labor and companies willing to purchase the labor. Media companies seek labor from a general market for basic, unskilled labor, as well as from markets for labor with specialized technical and creative abilities. When the Minneapolis *Star & Tribune* hires a printer, or Universal Studios hires a carpenter, or ABC News hires a news producer, each enters one of these labor markets as a consumer.

Like other markets, the labor market is influenced by basic economic laws such as the law of supply and demand. The supply of labor available for a given job and overall is influenced by the wages or salaries that employers are willing to pay, and the demand for that labor is influenced by the price at which the labor is made available.

LABOR SUPPLY

The quantity of labor available in the market is also affected by two major nonprice factors: the number of workers in the labor force and the amount of time each laborer works. The number of workers in the labor force varies over time depending upon the size of the population,

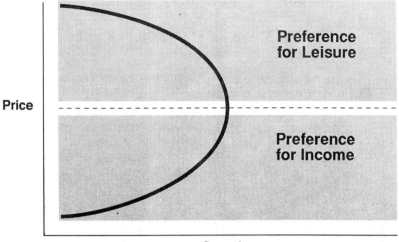

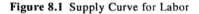

Figure 8.1 Supply Curve for Labor

the average age of the citizens, and social changes that influence the number of individuals willing and able to work. When a nation's population increases or decreases, one can expect the pool of workers to vary proportionately. Changes in the average age of a population also affect the number of workers. If the average age of the population changes, more or fewer of the population will be of working age and this will affect the size of the labor force. When society forbade child labor, the work force size was reduced, just as acceptance of women into the general labor market increased the pool of laborers. The number of hours of work in which workers will engage also affects labor supply. A reduction in the length of the average workday and workweek thus decreases the number of hours of labor available.

In broad terms all workers choose whether to enter the labor market and the amount of time they will contribute in the market. The supply curve for labor is different from the supply curve of other goods and services, but the supply of labor is strongly affected by price (see Figure 8.1).

The backward-bending supply curve occurs because workers are not willing to increase continually the number of hours of work they contribute to the labor market. Although increasing the number of hours of labor increases the total income workers receive, the additional income is more desirable than leisure time only up to the point that the marginal utility of income begins diminishing.

Labor itself involves inherent disutility for most individuals and is undertaken merely as a means of gaining income that can be used for consumption of goods and services that provide utility. As a result, when labor is increased the disutility increases and marginal disutility increases rapidly. Because of this, the number of hours of labor made available in the market will increase as price increases only to the point that the desire for income outweighs the desire for leisure. At that point the number of hours of labor available at even higher prices stabilizes and then diminishes into the backward-bending curve. Thus, a newspaper editor cannot expect that his reporters will be willing to work long overtime hours continually even if they receive additional pay and the general manager of a radio station cannot expect an engineer to do the same thing on a regular basis.

In addition to quantitative factors, the productivity of labor obtained from the market is influenced by qualitative factors. These include human capital, shifts in occupational choices, and worker motivation. Human capital includes the skills and knowledge of workers in the labor force. When workers are highly trained and schooled, their ability to produce productively — that is, their human capital — is increased. Thus, their productive *capacity* is higher and the amount of labor needed to produce the same output is lower than it is for less skilled workers. Firms recognize the impact of trained personnel on productivity and thus seek such skilled labor when hiring, and many conduct internal training to raise the skills and abilities and, consequently, productivity of labor.

Increases in the quality and quantity of labor available elevate the potential productivity of firms, as seen in Figure 8.2. This potential productivity assumes that the labor will continue to be used efficiently and that the marginal physical product will increase proportionately. Because of the law of diminishing returns, however, the productivity will at some point reach a plateau and even decline.

The labor market is also affected by the nonmonetary income, that is, psychic income, that workers receive or do not receive from specific labor. Some occupations provide psychological rewards or satisfactions — such as prestige, power, camaraderie, or a feeling of serving society — that may influence the supply of labor for those occupations by increasing the amount of labor available despite the price paid for the labor. Such is the case in the labor market for actors and journalists, where a high supply of workers exists despite the low price paid for labor.

The amount and quality of labor available are also influenced by the geographic location of available employment and workers and the

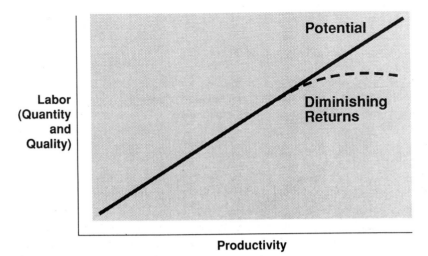

Figure 8.2 The Influence of Increase in Labor Quantity and Quality on Production

degree of mobility to other occupations. For example, a television station in Bozeman, Montana, is a less desirable location for reporters than is a television station in Washington, DC. As a result, the amount and quality of reporting labor in the labor pool for the Bozeman station will be lower than that for the Washington station.

DEMAND FOR LABOR

Demand for labor is, as mentioned above, affected by the price of labor, but it is also affected by decreasing demand for the product produced caused by changes in the price of the product or changes in consumer preferences or tastes. This is illustrated, for example, by the decreasing demand for labor in network television as audiences for broadcast television have shifted to cable television.

Changes in the inputs of production that alter productivity can also affect demand for labor. The introduction of technology that increases the productivity of labor reduces the need for labor. This has been clearly shown by Dertouzous and Quinn (1985), who studied the impact of electronic technology on newspaper labor requirements and found that it reduced the amount of production labor required by at least half. They concluded, however, that few employees were laid off as a result of the transition, but that most of the excess labor was reduced through attrition, buyouts, and retraining.

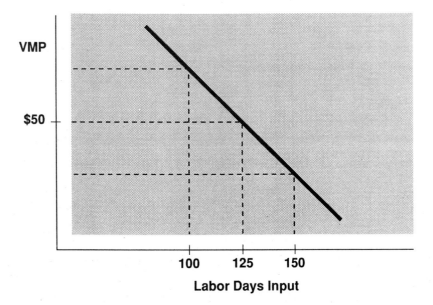

Figure 8.3 Labor Demand Curve Calculated by Value of Marginal Product

When a product and labor market is operating most efficiently under perfect competition, the supply and demand for labor equalize as indicated above. In order to calculate demand for labor in such a situation, one establishes the value of the marginal product (VMP), that is, the value of the additional output achieved by adding a unit of labor. This value is calculated as follows:

$$\begin{array}{l}\text{Value of} \\ \text{marginal product}\end{array} = \text{Price} \times \begin{array}{l}\text{Marginal physical product} \\ \text{of labor}\end{array}$$

A firm will continue adding labor to the point that the value of the marginal product no longer exceeds the price of the input. If a newspaper had an MPP of 200 newspapers that could be delivered by carriers daily and the price of the papers was 25 cents each, the VMP would be $50 a day. Assume that the paper pays carriers the $50 to deliver the papers. Figure 8.3 illustrates that the VMP of the 100th carrier hired would be well above $50 and the firm would get more income than the cost of delivering the papers. This firm would thus wish to hire at least 100 carriers and possibly more. A firm will normally add units of labor until the VMP decreases to the price of the input. If more carriers were hired, the VMP would decline because of the law of diminishing returns. Because the VMP of $50 for the 125th

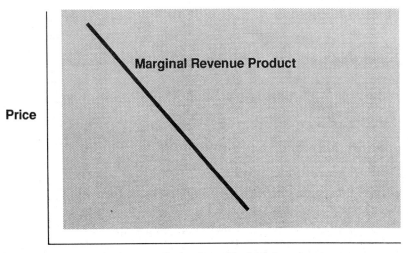

Quantity of Labor Input

Figure 8.4 Labor Demand Curve for Firms in Imperfect Competition
(Indicated by Marginal Revenue Product)

carrier still meets labor cost, the firm would be expected to hire 125
carriers. If it stopped before that point, it would lose the additional
profits indicated by the shaded area. If more than 125 carriers were
employed, however, the VMP would decline below cost and the firm
would lose money by adding labor.

In situations where product competition is imperfect, the product
demand curve slopes downward and the marginal revenue received
from each additional product unit is less than the cost of the unit itself
because producers must lower their price in order to sell additional
units produced, with the cost of the losses on marginal product spread
across all units produced. In such imperfectly competitive situations,
the demand curve for labor is analyzed by calculating the value of the
additional product, using marginal revenue product (MRP):

$$\text{MRP} = \text{Marginal revenue} \times \frac{\text{Marginal physical}}{\text{product of labor}}$$

Marginal revenue product declines rapidly because of diminishing
returns, and the marginal revenue is lower than cost (see Figure 8.4).
As a result, the demand curve for labor in firms in imperfect competition declines more rapidly than that for firms in perfect competition and
the benefits of additional labor disappear more rapidly.

THE PRICE OF LABOR

In a perfectly competitive market for labor, the price paid for labor will be determined by the law of supply and demand, and the price is determined just as the price is for any product in such a market.

Some firms will be willing to pay more for less than the equilibrium price set by the forces of supply and demand. This occurs because some firms wish to acquire the most experienced and skilled workers, while others are willing to provide entry-level jobs at low pay in which workers gain or improve their skills. This is clearly the case in the broadcast and newspaper industries where young or new workers begin work in small stations and papers that pay very low wages; on the other end of the spectrum are stations such as KABC-TV in Los Angeles and newspapers such as the New York *Times*, which pay far above the price for the nationwide media labor market.

At times the labor market can be imperfect and tilt in favor of sellers or buyers. This occurs when the market contains a limited number of workers with necessary skills or when buyers have advantages because of high unemployment or because few other employers exist in the market.

Trade unions and professional societies bring important forces to bear on the economic marketplace by altering supply and demand for labor. The major goals of such groups are to improve working conditions and increase wages or salaries of employees. To do so, industrial and craft unions and professional societies attempt to influence labor supply and demand to increase the price paid for the members' labor.

Such efforts are undertaken by two major strategies. First, unions and similar societies strive to increase the price paid for labor by reducing labor supply. This is usually done by limiting entry into the labor market by requiring apprenticeships, specialized training, and licenses, and by limiting entry into such programs. Newspaper press unions and electrical workers in motion picture and broadcasting industries often limit labor through these tactics. Second, some labor groups work to increase demand for labor by increasing job specializations, by overmanning, and by increasing labor productivity by improving the quality of labor. This strategy is employed by printers' unions and certain broadcasting unions.

Related to these strategies is collective bargaining, in which unions work to achieve wages that are higher than would normally be achieved by supply and demand alone. Under collective bargaining, workers attempt to limit labor in an industry to members of unions, thus requiring all producers to employ higher-priced labor and thus equally increasing the cost of labor inputs so that no firm gains an advantage by using lower-priced labor. Collective bargaining has been effectively used by groups such as the Screen Actors' Guild, the Writers' Guild, the American Federation of Television and Radio Artists, and the Newspaper Guild.

Unions, too, pay close attention to economics in their collective bargaining effects, cognizant that if the price of labor is artificially raised too high, producers will be forced either to reduce labor hired because the price paid to workers for marginal output will exceed the value of the output or to move production to other nations where labor can be obtained cheaper or without collective bargaining. As a result, the ability of labor groups to bargain is somewhat constrained because members of these groups do not wish to risk significant layoffs as a result of demanding increasing raises.

The strategies employed in collective bargaining in media and the impact and development of broadcasting unions in the U.S. have been explored by Koenig (1970), and studies of British unions by Beharrell and Philo (1977) and by Seglow (1978) provide comparative views. This literature, while dealing with economic issues, concentrates on bargaining and managerial issues.

Few important economic studies of the role of labor in media industries have been made, and the scholarly literature is nearly devoid of such contributions. Literature relating to managerial issues of labor is abundant but, for the most part, ignores economic analysis and is concerned primarily with issues such as different educational and training methods, comparative salary surveys, and management of personnel.

SOME FINAL WORDS

This book has provided an introduction to the concepts that are basic to an understanding of media economics and a review of some of the issues and research in the field. It is by no means complete because researchers and practitioners have only recently begun to study the field significantly and recognize the need for understanding of the principles and issues.

It is hoped that this book will help stimulate that understanding as well as more research and analysis of issues in the field. Such interest can only lead to improved decision making in the operations of media, a greater understanding of the economic forces that affect media institutions, and an improved base of knowledge to apply in the making of public policy decisions about media.

This book is intended to provide a starting point for such interest and analysis. There is much to be done in terms of the economic study of media. As the reviews of recent research in each chapter have revealed, there are large gaps in the literature and great opportunities for both applied and theoretical research in the field.

The literature reviewed here has focused on the recent developments in the field and the current state of knowledge. Scholarship about media economics is clearly incomplete and significant work needs to be undertaken to add to the literature of consumer demand for media, media supply, cost issues, market structure effects, and financial and labor issues.

If the readers of this book, however, merely use the information conveyed to understand what differences exist in media markets, how media compete, how audiences and advertisers select media and the economic factors that influence their selections, what the cost and revenue factors are that need to be considered when media managers make production decisions, how government activities influence media economics, how to analyze the economic performance of media, and what factors influence the availability and price of labor, they will have a much stronger comprehension of the forces that shape media industries and a greater ability to make knowledgeable choices should they be placed in decision-making positions in media.

Those who wish to find contemporary data and information about media economics to improve their understanding as media professionals, critics, or scholars should find the various trade, labor, and media service firms and publications in the resources listing at the rear of this book useful. Also of interest should be the listing of early contributions in the field of media economics, the references, and the glossary.

RESOURCES FOR MEDIA ECONOMICS DATA

TRADE AND LABOR GROUPS AND MEDIA SERVICE FIRMS

American Advertising Federation, 1400 K Street, N.W., Suite 100, Washington, DC 20005 Tele.: (201) 898-0089

American Association of Advertising Agencies, 666 Third Avenue, 13th Floor, New York, NY 10017 Tele.: (212) 682-2500

American Business Press, 205 E. 42nd Street, New York, NY 10017 Tele.: (212) 661-6360

American Federation of Television and Radio Artists, 1350 Avenue of the Americas, New York, NY 10019 Tele.: (212)265-7700

American Newspaper Publishers Association, P.O. Box 17407, Dulles Airport, Washington, DC 20041 Tele.: (703) 648-1247

American Video Association, 557 E. Juanita, #3, Mesa, AZ 85204 Tele.: (602) 892-8553

Arbitron Co., 1350 Avenue of the Americas, New York, NY 10019 Tele.: (212) 887-1300

Association of Alternative Newsweeklies, 2 NW Second Avenue, Portland, OR 97209 Tele.: (503) 243-2122

Association of Business Publishers, 205 E. 42nd Street, New York, NY 10017 Tele.: (212) 661-6360

Association of Independent Television Stations, 1200 18th Street, N.W., Suite 502, Washington, DC 20036 Tele.: (202) 887-1970

Association of National Advertisers, 155 E. 44th Street, New York, NY 10007 Tele.: (212)697-5950

Audit Bureau of Circulations, 900 N. Meacham Road, Schaumburg, IL 60195 Tele.: (312)885-0910

Birch Radio, Inc., 44 Sylvan Avenue, #2D, Englewood Cliffs, NJ 07632 Tele.: (201) 585-7667

Broadcast Financial Management Association, 701 Lee Street, Suite 1010, Des Plaines, IL 60016 Tele.: (312) 296-0200

Broadcast Promotion and Marketing Executives, 402 East Orange Street, Lancaster, PA 17602 Tele.: (717) 397-5727

Business Publications Audit Bureau of Circulations, 360 Park Avenue S., New York, NY 10010 Tele.: (212) 532-6880

Cable Television Administration and Marketing Society, 219 Perimeter Center Parkway, Suite 480, Atlanta, GA 30346 Tele.: (404) 399-5574

Cable Television Advertising Bureau, 757 Third Avenue, New York, NY 10017 Tele.: (212) 751-7770

Canadian Community Newspapers Association, 70588 University Avenue, Toronto, Ontario M5J 1T6 Canada Tele.: (416)598-4277

Canadian Daily Newspaper Publishers Association, 8980 Yonge Street, Suite 1100, Toronto, Ontario M4W 3P4 Canada Tele.: (416) 923-3567

Council for Cable Information, 126 E. 56th Street, New York, NY 10022 Tele.: (212) 308-7060

Directors Guild of America, 7950 Sunset Blvd., Hollywood, CA 90046 Tele.: (213) 656-1220

Inland Daily Press Association, 777 Busse Highway, Park Ridge, IL 60028-2462 Tele.: (312) 696-1140

International Circulation Managers Association, P.O. Box 17420, Dulles Airport, Washington, DC 20041 Tele.: (703) 620-9555

International Newspaper Advertising and Marketing Executives, P.O. Box 17210, Dulles Airport, Washington, DC 20041 Tele.: (703) 648-1168

International Newspaper Financial Executives, P.O. Box 17573, Dulles Airport, Washington, DC 20041 Tele.: (703) 648-1160

International Newspaper Marketing Association, P.O. Box 17422, Dulles Airport, Washington, DC 20041 Tele.: (703) 648-1094

International Typographical Union, P.O. Box 157, Colorado Springs, CO 80901 Tele.: (303) 636-2341

Magazine Publishers Association, 575 Lexington Avenue, New York, NY 10022 Tele.: (212) 752-0055

Motion Picture Association of America, 522 Fifth Avenue, New York, NY 10036 Tele.: (212) 840-6161

National Academy of Television Arts and Sciences, 110 W. 57th Street, New York, NY 10019

National Association of Broadcasters, 1771 N Street, N.W., Washington, DC 20036 Tele.: (202) 429-5386

National Association of Video Distributors, 1800 M Street, N.W., Washington, DC 20036 Tele.: (202) 452-8100

National Cable Television Association, 1724 Massachusetts Avenue, N.W., Washington, DC 20036 Tele.: (202) 775-3550

National Newspaper Association, 1627 K Street, N.W., Washington, DC 20006 Tele: (202) 466-7200

Newspaper Advertising Bureau, 1180 Avenue of the Americas, New York, NY 10036 Tele.: (212) 704-4525

Newspaper Guild, 8611 Second Avenue, Silver Springs, MD 20981 Tele.: (301) 585-2990

Newspaper Research Council, 1000 Two Ruan Center, Des Moines, IA 50309 Tele.: (515) 245-3828

Nielsen Marketing Research, Nielsen Plaza, Northbrook, IL 60062 Tele.: (212) 599-6666

Recording Industry Association of America, 888 Seventh Avenue, 9th Floor, New York, NY 10106 Tele.: (212) 765-4330

Screen Actors' Guild, 7750 Sunset Blvd., Hollywood, CA 90046 Tele.: (213) 876-3030

Standard Rate and Data Service, 3004 Glenview Road, Wilmette, IL 60091
    Tele.: (312) 256-6067
Television Information Office, 745 Fifth Avenue, New York, NY 10022
    Tele.: (212) 759-6800
Video Software Dealers Association, 1008-F, Astoria, NJ 08034
Writers' Guild of America, 8955 Beverly Blvd., Los Angeles, CA 90048
    Tele.: (213) 550-1000

PUBLICATIONS

General Media

Advertising Age. Chicago: Crain Communications, weekly.
    Advertising trade publication; annually publishes special issues on top
    media companies and top advertisers, and the state of advertising in
    various media.
Communication Industries Report. New York: Veronis, Suher & Associates,
    annual.
    Financial performance data for public companies in various media in-
    dustries.
CPI Detailed Report. Washington, DC: Department of Labor, Bureau of
    Labor Statistics, monthly.
    Reports consumer prices for products nationally and by state.
Marketing and Media Decisions. New York: Decisions Publications, monthly.
    Contains articles on changes in media trends and relates them to market-
    ing issues. Regular articles on the economy, advertising, sales, and man-
    agement issues.
Media Industry Newsletter. New York: Media Industry Newsletter, weekly.
    Reports developments in media and advertising industries, financial re-
    ports, mergers, acquisitions, closings, and ratings.
Producer Price Index. Washington, DC: Department of Labor, Bureau of
    Labor Statistics, monthly.
    Data on production prices for industries and products.
Standard Rate and Data Service. Wilmette, IL: Standard Rate and Data
    Service, monthly.
    Reports data on advertising rates, media market penetration, and so forth
    for a variety of media types.
State and Metropolitan Area Data Book. Washington, DC: Department of
    Commerce, Bureau of the Census.
    Provides demographic and economic data for states, metropolitan areas,
    and major cities.
Christopher H. Sterling and Timothy R. Haight, *The Mass Media: Aspen
    Institute Guide to Communication Industry Trends.* New York: Praeger
    Publisher, 1978.
    Historical and trend data for books, newspapers, magazines, motion
    pictures, sound recordings, radio, television, cable.

Survey of Buying Power. New York: Sales & Marketing Management, annual.
Economic and demographic data on states, metropolitan areas, and major cities.

Audio and Visual Recordings

Billboard. New York: Billboard Publications, weekly.
Reports developments and trends in music and home video industries.
Radio & Records. Los Angeles: Radio & Records, weekly.
Covers the radio and recording industries and the interplay between the two media forms.
Video Forecaster. Cherry Hill, NJ: Video Software Dealers Association.
Reports demand for sales and rental of video products, the status of competition among dealers, and sales figures.
Video Marketing Newsletter. Hollywood, CA: Video Marketing Newsletter, twice monthly.
News of the video product industry, including trends, new products, and so forth.

Books

Publisher's Weekly. New York: Cahners Publishing, weekly.
News of book publishing, trends, sales, and marketing strategies.

Broadcasting

Arbitron Ratings. New York: Arbitron Ratings Co., quarterly.
Audience data for television and radio markets.
Birch Ratings Data for Radio Markets. Englewood Cliffs, NJ: Birch Radio, quarterly.
Audience data for radio markets.
Broadcast Stats. Carmel, CA: Paul Kagan Associates, monthly.
Reports monthly financial data on broadcast properties.
Broadcasting/Cablecasting. Washington, DC: Broadcasting Publications, weekly.
Reports regulatory and other aspects of broadcast industries including station sales and industry trends.
Broadcasting/Cablecasting Yearbook. Washington, DC: Broadcasting Publications, annual.
Reviews programming suppliers, broadcast and cablecast markets and stations, sizes of markets, and demographics.
Duncan's Radio Market Guide. Kalamazoo, MI: Duncan's American Media, annual.
Provides financial histories and information on competitors in 200 radio markets, as well as geographic and demographic information.

Electronic Media. Chicago, IL: Crain Publications, weekly.
Reports development in television, radio, and cable, including sales, programming, and ratings data.

Investing in Radio. Washington, DC: Broadcast Investment Analysts, Inc., annual.
Market and station information including sales, formats, rankings, power, and ownership, as well as cross-market analyses of growth including demographic and financial growth rates and revenue statistics.

Investing in Television. Washington, DC: Broadcast Investment Analysts, Inc., annual.
Market and station information including sales, formats, rankings, power, and ownership, as well as cross-market analyses of growth including demographic and financial growth rates and revenue statistics.

A. C. Nielsen Co. Ratings Data for Broadcast and Cable Media. Northbrook, IL: A. C. Nielsen Co., quarterly.
Audience data and characteristics in broadcasting and cablecasting markets.

Radio & Records. Los Angeles: Radio & Records, weekly.
Covers the radio and recording industries and the interplay between the two media forms.

Radio Facts. New York: Radio Advertising Bureau, annual.
Reports data on radio audiences, advertising sales, and radio markets.

Radio Financial Report. Washington, DC: National Association of Broadcasters, annual.
Reports revenues and expenses for radio stations by market, station size, frequency, programming type.

Ratings Report and Directory. Los Angeles: Radio & Records, annual.
Directory of radio-oriented firms, top stations in various formats, and market information.

Television Digest. Washington, DC: Television Digest, weekly.
Trade journal that covers finance, ownership, ratings, and other developments in television and electronics industries.

Television and Cable Factbook. Washington, DC: Warren Publishing, annual.
Authoritative reference for TV, cable, and electronics industries. Contains directory of and information on all TV and cable facilities in the U.S.

Television/Radio Age. New York: Television Editorial Corp., biweekly.
Data on television and radio industries including reports on programming and station changes and trends.

Cable

Broadcasting/Cablecasting Yearbook. Washington, DC: Broadcasting Publications, annual.
Reviews programming suppliers, broadcast and cablecast markets and stations, sizes of markets, and demographics.

Cablevision. Denver, CO: International Thomson Communications, biweekly.
Information on sales, marketing, advertising, and cable firms for cable
television managers.

The Kagan Cable TV Financial Databook. Carmel, CA: Paul Kagan
Associates, annual.
Data on cable television firms and programmers, including financial
records, growth rates, ownership and debt data for private and public
firms.

Multichannel News. New York: Fairchild Publications, weekly.
Covers cable, pay cable, and broadcast television, including financial
news, costs, franchising information, and programming developments.

Television and Cable Factbook. Washington, DC: Warren Publishing Co.,
annual.
Authoritative reference for TV, cable, and electronics industries. Contains
directory of and information on all TV and cable facilities in the U.S.

Magazines

ABC Magazine Trend Report. Chicago: Audit Bureau of Circulation, annual.
Reports circulation and cost trends for consumer magazines.

Circulation: Annual Circulation and Penetration Analysis of Print Media.
Malibu, CA: American Newspaper Markets, annual.
Reports by state, county, and market areas the circulation and penetration
of major newspapers and monthly magazines.

Folio. Stamford, CT: Hanson Publishing Group, monthly.
Reports on publishing issues, problems, and trends aimed at magazine
managers.

The Gallagher Report. New York: Gallagher Report, weekly.
Focuses on marketing, advertising, sales, and management issues for
magazine executives.

Motion Pictures

Hollywood Reporter. Hollywood: Hollywood Reporter, daily.
Covers business developments and entertainment aspects of film and
television production.

Variety. New York: Cahners Publishing, weekly.
Reports sales and receipts data for current films as well as information on
motion picture industry developments and trends and some developments
in TV and music industries.

Newspapers

Audit Bureau of Circulation Audits. Chicago, IL: Audit Bureau of Circulation,
quarterly and annual.
Audited newspaper circulation data for individual markets nationwide.

Circulation: Annual Circulation and Penetration Analysis of Print Media.
Malibu: CA.: American Newspaper Markets, annual.
Reports by state, county, and market areas the circulation and penetration
of daily newspapers.

Editor & Publisher. New York: Editor & Publisher, weekly.
Weekly summary of legal, economic, technological, and other developments in the newspaper industry.

Editor & Publisher International Yearbook. New York: Editor & Publisher,
annual.
Provides annual summary of newspaper statistics and listings of papers
and their staffs, news services, suppliers.

Editor & Publisher Market Guide. New York: Editor & Publisher, annual.
Provides economic, business, and demographic data on daily newspaper
markets.

Facts About Newspapers. Reston, VA: American Newspaper Publishers
Association, annual.
Compiles circulation, advertising, ownership, labor, and other statistics
for the U.S. and Canadian newspaper industries.

Inland Daily Press Association Cost and Revenue Study. Park Ridge, IL:
Inland Daily Press Association, annual.
Contains survey data on operating costs and revenues for 300 news-
papers.

Key Facts: Newspapers, Consumers, Advertising. New York: Newspaper
Advertising Bureau, annual.
Compiles data on newspaper advertising readership, costs, effects, and
volume.

Presstime. Reston, VA: American Newspaper Publishers Association, monthly.
Reports on industry trends and data on specific problems and issues
related to topics of articles.

GLOSSARY

Advantages A type of government intervention in economics, such as preferred treatment for a company or industry by government agencies or reduced prices for government services.

Allocation The process of determining who gets the resources, goods, or services that are available in a society.

Average Physical Product Indicates the average contribution that any one unit of input makes to overall output.

Capital The financial sum of all wealth that is increased when resources are used for the creation of goods and services. *Capital Lending* The process of lending capital to firms and individuals for a fee that will be repaid in addition to the capital that is lent. *Capital Investing* The process of contributing capital to a firm for part ownership of that firm.

Centrally Planned Economy An economic system in which allocative decisions are made by centralized authorities.

Competition Rivalry of buyers and sellers in the market. Buyers compete with sellers, buyers compete with buyers, and sellers compete with sellers. *Intramedia Competition* Competition between units of the same medium. *Intermedia Competition* Competition between units of different media or between media industries.

Concentration The degree to which the largest companies in the same product/service and geographic market control the economic activities in that market.

Concentration of Ownership The degree to which activities of an industry or related industries are owned or controlled by leading firms.

Consumption The use of resources, goods, or services to satisfy wants and needs.

Corporation A business firm organized with limited legal liability for the owners of its shares. *Publicly owned corporations* are firms whose shares are sold on stock exchanges. *Privately owned corporations* are those whose stock is not publicly traded; they tend to be owned by a smaller number of shareholders.

Cost The value that is given up for producing a good or service. This value can be measured in terms of both financial expenses and opportunities not selected. *Average cost* is cost of output spread evenly across each unit of input. *Marginal cost* is the cost of the last input made as a means of increasing output. *Long-run cost* encompasses both fixed and variable inputs and analyses of full cost and output over time. *Short-run cost* focuses on inputs and output in the short-term, with a particular emphasis on variable inputs. *Opportunity cost* is the implicit cost of the best forgone alternative to producing the product chosen.

Demand A measure of the quantity of a good or service that consumers are willing to purchase at a given price. See *Elasticity of Demand.*

Distribution Economics A type of economic analysis in which distribution rather than production factors are the focus. Used in analysis of distribution of public goods and a few private goods.

Dual Product Market A situation in which a good is two separate products that the producer sells to more than one type of buyer.

Efficiency An indicator of whether the actions of firms maximize total wealth. Actions that maximize wealth are said to be efficient, while actions that do not optimize wealth result in inefficiency. *Allocative Efficiency* A condition that occurs when the market operates at optimal points that spread its benefits evenly between consumers and producers. *Technical Efficiency* A condition that exists when inputs are used most effectively to maximize output.

Elasticity of Demand A measure of the amount that demand changes when price for a good or service is changed. *Elastic demand* occurs when the change in quantity demanded is greater than the change in price. *Inelastic demand* occurs when no significant change in quantity demanded accompanies a change in price. *Unit elasticity* occurs when the change in price and quantity are the same. *Cross elasticity* measures the substitution of another similar product that occurs when price changes occur in one product.

Elasticity of Supply A measure of the amount supply changes when price for a good or service is changed. *Elastic supply* occurs when the change in supply provided is greater than the change in price. *Inelastic supply* occurs when no significant change in quantity supplied accompanies a change in price. *Unit elasticity* occurs when the change in price and quantity supplied are the same.

Equilibrium The point at which the quantity of a product available and the price at which it is available meet on both the supply and demand curves.

Equity A welfare economics concept that describes the distribution of total wealth among producers and consumers so that it provides the greatest social benefit. The term is also used to describe the value of the ownership of a firm.

Externalities A term used to describe the results of market activities outside the market itself. Such results may be beneficial or harmful.

Geographic Market Defines the boundaries in which producers or sellers conduct trade for the products/services they offer.

Goods Commodities produced and exchanged for trade in the marketplace. *Private goods* are those that are purchased and consumed by a single individual or firm and diminish the supply of the goods available to others. *Public goods* can be acquired by many individuals or firms without diminishing the availability to others, such as a television broadcast.

Good/Service Market Distinguishes the type of good or service offered for trade by producers or sellers.

Growth An increase in output or value.

Income A financial term indicating funds available to the company after basic operating expenses are paid. Contrast with *Revenue.*

Indifference A consumer choice model based on the idea that consumers make choices among a variety of products and services and maximize satisfaction in creating a mix of consumption. Consumers are said to be indifferent to each good or service, and the quantity of each product may be varied to achieve maximum utility.

Inputs Those factors necessary to create a product or service. *Fixed inputs* are those whose quantities cannot be varied but must be present, such as equipment and buildings. *Variable inputs* are varied to achieve different levels of output. These inputs include labor and raw materials.

Interest The cost of using lent capital.

Intervention Government activities in economic markets, both at the macroeconomic level and the microeconomic level. Intervention in industries generally occurs through regulation, advantages, and subsidies.

Labor A factor of production contributed by the work of humans.

Land A factor of production that encompasses real estate and natural resources such as minerals.

Macroeconomics The branch of economics devoted to studying the economy as a whole and major aggregate issues such as employment, growth, and inflation.

Marginal Physical Product The additional output that results from the last input added.

Market Group of sellers and buyers wishing to engage in trade for products or services. See *Geographic Market* and *Good/Service Market.*

Market Conduct The policies of firms regarding their products, prices, and competitors.

Market Economy An economic system in which allocative decisions are made based on the operations of the market.

Market Performance The results of a firm or industry's activities considered in terms of efficiency, equity, and externalities created.

Market Structure The economic features of a market, including such elements as number of buyers and sellers, product differentiation, barriers to entry, and concentration.

Microeconomics The branch of economics concerned with economic activities at the market level.

Mixed Economy An economic system that combines elements of market and centrally planned economies.

Monopolistic Competition A market structure in which there are a number of sellers of similar, but differentiated, products and services competing.

Monopoly A market structure in which a single seller of a product exists and controls the market.

Needs Items that individuals and society must satisfy to ensure subsistence and survival or that are required to produce a good or service.

Oligopoly A market structure in which competition exists among a small number of producers of similar products and services.

Outputs The end good or service created by producers for consumers.

Perfect Competition A market structure in which there are many sellers for a homogeneous product or service.

Principal The actual amount of money provided or received by a firm as lent capital.

Product Supply The amount of a good or service made available for consumption by a producer or producers. See *Supply*.

Profit The return received by a producer. *Normal profit* is the minimal financial and individual reward that keeps a producer operating. *Pure profit* is the return beyond the minimum necessary to keep a firm operating and represents the return beyond expenditures that is commonly called "profit."

Regulation A type of government intervention in which market structure, conduct, or performance is determined by state apparatuses.

Resources Inanimate and animate items that can be used for producing goods and services.

Return The profit received from operation. Used as a financial performance measure, usually in comparison to overall sales, assets, investment, or equity.

Revenue Funds received from the sale or rental of goods and services. Contrast with *Income*. *Average Revenue* The average amount of revenue that the sale of any one unit of output made to overall revenue. *Marginal Revenue* The additional revenue that resulted from the last output sold.

Scale Relates to the size of a firm or its output. *Economies of scale* exist when long-run average costs (LRAC) decline as output and plant size increase. *Diseconomies of scale* occur when LRAC increase as output and plant size increase. *Returns to scale* indicate the relationship between proportionate changes in all inputs and output in the long-run. These returns may increase, decrease, or remain constant.

Services Work done for others to serve their needs.

Stock Shares of a corporation that are sold.

Subsidy A type of government intervention in which cash transfers are made to firms.

Substitutability The ability of one product or service to be substituted for another if consumers choose to for reasons of price, quality, or availability.

Substitute A product or service that can be used in place of another product or service to satisfy a want or need.

Supply The quantity of a product that producers will sell at a given price.

Surplus Value The additional value imparted to goods and services through labor.

Taxation A type of government intervention in which additional costs are added to market transactions to fund government activities or to penalize for externalities.

Theory of Relative Constancy Asserts that consumers' spending for media remains a constant proportion of total consumer spending and that new media induce consumers to reallocate funds spent for media rather than to reallocate total spending patterns.

Umbrella Competition A market structure in which different layers of the same medium exist in the same market, claiming smaller markets under the umbrella of a large unit of the medium that covers the entire market (typically a metropolitan area).

Util A unit of measure used in determining the utility of goods and services.

Utility Intangible consumer satisfaction from goods and services that is a component in the determination of value. *Ordinal utility* is based on a rank ordering of consumer preference. *Cardinal utility* is a measure of satisfaction based on some numerically measurable factor. *Marginal utility* indicates the additional satisfaction achieved by consuming additional units of a good or service.

Value The worth of a commodity or service, indicated by its ability to command money or other goods in exchange for the commodity or service in the market. Values change and fluctuate over time.

Wants Items that individuals and society desire to improve the quality of their lives or to gain nonsubsistence goods or services.

Welfare Economics A type of analysis concerned with public welfare as evidenced by market performance in the study of industries and firms.

EARLY CONTRIBUTIONS
TO MEDIA ECONOMICS
LITERATURE

BELSON, W. A. (1961) "Effects of television on the reading and buying of newspapers and magazines." *Public Opinion Quarterly* 25 (Fall): 366-381.

CORDEN, W. M. (1952-53) "The maximization of profit by a newspaper." *Review of Economic Studies* 20: 181-190.

CURRIER, F. (1960) "Economic theory and its application to newspapers." *Journalism Quarterly* 37 (Spring): 255-258.

FERGUSON, J. M. (1963) *The Advertising Rate Structure in the Daily Newspaper Industry.* Englewood Cliffs, NJ: Prentice-Hall.

GERALD, J. E. (1956) *The British Press Under Government Economic Controls.* Minneapolis: University of Minnesota Press.

GERALD, J. E. (1958) "Economic research and the mass media." *Journalism Quarterly* 35 (Winter): 49-55.

HELLMUTH, W. F. (1961) "The motion picture industry," pp. 393-429 in W. Adams (ed.) *The Structure of American Industry: Some Case Studies* (3rd ed.). New York: Macmillan.

KREPS, T. J. (1961) "The newspaper industry," pp. 509-532 in W. Adams (ed.) *The Structure of American Industry: Some Case Studies* (3rd ed.). New York: Macmillan.

LEVIN, H. J. (1958) "Economic structure and the regulation of television." *Quarterly Journal of Economics* 72 (August): 445-446.

MALONE, J. R. (1951) "Economic-technical bases for newspaper diversity." *Journalism Quarterly* 28 (Summer): 315-326.

PETERSON, T., J. W. JENSEN, and W. RIVERS (1965) *The Mass Media and Modern Society.* New York: Holt, Rinehart and Winston.

RAY, R. H. (1951) "Competition in the newspaper industry." *Journal of Marketing* 43 (April): 444-456.

RAY, R. H. (1952) "Economic forces as factors in daily newspaper concentration." *Journalism Quarterly* 29 (Winter): 31-42.

REDDAWAY, W. B. (1963) "The economics of newspapers." *Economic Journal* 73: 201-218.

SIEBERT, F. S. (1952) *Freedom of the Press in England, 1465-1776.* Urbana, IL: University of Illinois Press.

SMITH, C. (1977) *The Press, Politics and Patronage: The American Government's Use of Newspapers, 1789-1875.* Athens, GA: University of Georgia Press.

SMYTHE, D. W. (1960) "On the political economy of communications." *Journalism Quarterly* 37 (Autumn): 563-572.

SMYTHE, D. W. (1962) "Time, market and space factors in communication economics." *Journalism Quarterly* 39 (Winter): 3-14.

TIJMSTRA, L. F. (1959-1960) "The challenge of TV to the press: The impact of television on advertising revenues and circulations of newspapers." *Journal of Broadcasting* 4 (Winter): 3-13.

REFERENCES

ARDOIN, B. (1973) "A comparison of newspapers under joint printing contracts." *Journalism Quarterly* 50 (Summer): 340-347

BAER, W. S., H. GELLER, J. GRUNDFEST, and K. POSSNER (1974) *Concentration of Mass Media Ownership: Assessing the State of Current Knowledge.* Santa Monica, CA: Rand.

BAGDIKIAN, B. H. (1987) *The Media Monopoly* (2nd ed.). Boston: Beacon.

BARNETT, S. R. (1969) "Statement of Stephen R. Barnett." U.S. Congress, House committee on the Judiciary, Newspaper Preservation Act. Hearings before the Antitrust subcommittee on H.R. 279 and related bills, 91st Congress, 1st session, 247-267.

BARNETT, S. R. (1980) "Monopoly games — where failures win big." *Columbia Journalism Review* (May/June): 40-47.

BARWIS, G. L. (1980) "The newspaper preservation act: A retrospective analysis." *Newspaper Research Journal* 1: 27-38.

BATES, B. J. (1988) "The impact of deregulation on television station prices." *Journal of Media Economics* 1: 5-22.

BEHARRELL, P. and G. PHILO (eds.) (1977) *Trade Unions and Media.* London: Macmillan.

BELL, J. F. (1967) *A History of Economic Thought* (2nd ed.). New York: Ronald House.

BIGMAN, S. (1948) "Rivals in conformity: A study of two competing dailies." *Journalism Quarterly* 25 (Summer): 127-131.

BLANKENBURG, W. B. (1980) "Determinants of pricing of advertising in weeklies." *Journalism Quarterly* 57 (Autumn): 663-668.

BLANKENBURG, W. B. (1982) "Newspaper ownership and control of circulation to increase profits." *Journalism Quarterly* 59 (Winter): 390-398.

BLANKENBURG, W. B. (1983) "A newspaper chain's pricing behavior." *Journalism Quarterly* 60 (Spring): 275-280.

BLAU, R. T., R. C. JOHNSON, and K. J. KSOBEICH (1976) "Determinants of TV station economic value." *Journal of Broadcasting* 20: 197-207.

BLOCH, H. and M. WIRTH (1984) "The demand for pay services on cable television." *Information Economics and Policy* 1: 311-332.

BLOOMFIELD, E. (1978) "Media cross-ownership, newspaper chains, competition, and daily newspaper advertising rates." Ph.D. Dissertation, University of Rochester.

BRENNAN, T. (1988) "An economic look at taxing home audio taping." *Journal of Broadcasting and Electronic Media* 32 (Winter): 89-103.

BROWN, R. D. (1967) "Market behavior of daily newspapers." Ph.D. Dissertation, University of Illinois.

BUSTERNA, J. (1978) "Ownership, CATV, and the quality of local television news." Paper presented to the annual meeting of the Association for Education in Journalism, Seattle, WA (August 15).

BUSTERNA, J. (1980) "Ownership, CATV, and expenditures for local television news." *Journalism Quarterly* 57 (Summer): 287-291.

BUSTERNA, J. (1987) "The cross-elasticity of demand for national newspaper advertising." *Journalism Quarterly* 64 (Summer-Autumn): 346-351.

BUSTERNA, J. (1988a) "Antitrust in the 1980s: An analysis of 45 newspaper actions." *Newspaper Research Journal* 9 (Winter): 25-36.

BUSTERNA, J. (1988b) "Concentration and the industrial organization model," pp. 35-53 in R. G. Picard, J. P. Winter, M. McCombs, and S. Lacy (eds.) *Press Concentration and Monopoly: New Perspectives on Newspaper Ownership and Operation.* Norwood, NJ: Ablex.

BUSTERNA, J. (1988c) "Newspaper JOAs and the logic of predation." *Communications and the Law* 10 (April): 3-17.

BUSTERNA, J. (1988d) "Television station ownership effects on programming and idea diversity: Baseline data." *Journal of Media Economics* 1 (Fall): 63-74.

BYRON, C. (1986) *The Fanciest Dive.* New York: W. W. Norton.

CANDUSSI, D. and J. P. WINTER (1988) "Monopoly and content in Winnipeg," pp. 139-145 in R. G. Picard, J. P. Winter, M. McCombs, and S. Lacy (eds.) *Press Concentration and Monopoly: New Perspectives on Newspaper Ownership and Operation.* Norwood, NJ: Ablex.

CARLSON, J. H. (1982) "Newspaper preservation act: A critique." *Indiana Law Review* 46: 392-412.

CHAN-OLMSTED, S. and B. R. LITMAN (1988) "Antitrust and horizontal mergers in the cable industry." *Journal of Media Economics* 1 (Fall): 3-28.

CHARETTE, M. F., C. L. BROWN-JOHN, W. I. ROMANOW, and W. C. SODERLUND (1983) "Effects of chain acquisitions and terminations on advertising rates of Canadian newspapers." Paper presented to the annual meeting of the Canadian Communication Association, University of British Columbia, B.C., Canada (June).

CHEEN, B. B. (1986) *Fair Market Value of Radio Stations: A Buyers' Guide.* Washington, DC: National Association of Broadcasters.

CHERINGTON, P. W., L. V. HIRSCH, and R. BRANDWEIN (1971) *Television Station Ownership: A Case Study of Federal Agency Regulation.* New York: Hastings House.

CHILDERS, T. L. and D. M. KRUGMAN (1987) "The competitive environment of pay per view." *Journal of Broadcasting and Electronic Media* 87 (Summer): 335-342.

CLARK, J. (1976) "Circulation increase despite higher subscription rates." *Editor and Publisher* (February 4): 32.

COMANOR, W. S. and B. M. MITCHELL (1971) "Cable television and the impact of regulation." *Bell Journal of Economics and Management Science* 2: 154-212.

COMPAINE, B. M. (1979) *Who Owns the Media? Concentration of Ownership in the Mass Communications Industry.* White Plains, NY: Knowledge Industry.

COMPAINE, B. M. (1985) "The expanding base of media competition." *Journal of Communication* 35 (Summer): 81-96.

CONANT, M. (1978) *Antitrust in the Motion Picture Industry.* New York: Arno.

CORDEN, W. M. (1952-53) "The maximization of profit by a newspaper." *Review of Economic Studies* 20: 181-190.

DERTOUZOUS, J. N. and T. H. QUINN (1985) *Bargaining Responses to the Technology Revolution: The Case of the Newspaper Industry.* Santa Monica, CA: Rand.

DERTOUZOUS, J. N. and K. E. THORPE (1982) *Newspaper Groups: Economies of Scale, Tax Laws, and Merger Incentives.* Santa Monica, CA: Rand.

DIMMICK, J. and E. ROTHENBUHLER (1984) "The theory of niche: Quantifying competition among media industries." *Journal of Communication* 34 (Winter): 103-119.

DUCEY, R. V., D. M. KRUGMAN, and D. ECKRICH (1983) "Predicting market segments in the cable industry: The basic and pay subscribers." *Journal of Broadcasting* 27 (Spring): 155-175.

DUNCAN'S AMERICAN MEDIA (published annually) *Duncan's Radio Market Guide.* Kalamazoo, MI: Author.

FEDERAL COMMUNICATIONS COMMISSION (1975) Second report and order: 50 FCC 2nd 1046, 32 RF.R. 2nd 954, Docket No. 18110.

FERGUSON, J. M. (1983) "Daily newspaper advertising rates, local media cross-owner-ship, newspaper chains, and media competition." *Journal of Law and Economics* 28: 635-654.

FIELD, R. W. (1978) "Circulation price inelasticity in the daily newspaper industry." M.A. Thesis, University of Oklahoma.

FINK, C. C. (1988) *Strategic Newspaper Management.* New York: Random House.

FULLERTON, H. S. (1988) "Technology collides with relative constancy: The pattern of adoption for a new medium." *Journal of Media Economics* 1 (Fall): 75-84.

GIDE, C. and C. RIST (1979) *History of Economic Doctrines.* Wilmington, DE: Interna-tional Academic.

GROTTA, G. (1971) "Consolidation of newspapers: What happens to the consumer." *Journalism Quarterly* 48 (Summer): 245-250.

GROTTA, G. (1977) "Daily newspaper circulation price inelastic for 1970-75." *Jour-nalism Quarterly* 54 (Summer): 379-382.

GUBACK, T. (1987) "The evolution of the motion picture theatre business in the 1980s." *Journal of Communication* 37 (Spring): 60-77.

HANEY, L. H. (1949) *History of Economic Thought* (4th ed.). New York: Macmillan.

HEILBRONER, R. L. (1980) *The Worldly Philosophers* (5th ed.). New York: Simon and Schuster.

HENRY, J. B. (1985) "The economics of pay-TV media," pp. 19-55 in E. M. Noam (ed.) *Video Media Competition: Regulation, Economics, and Technology.* New York: Columbia University Press.

HOLLSTEIN, M. (1978) "Government and the press: The question of subsidies." *Journal of Communication* 29 (Autumn): 46-53.

HUSNI, S. A. (1988) "Influences on the survival of new consumer magazines." *Journal of Media Economics* 1 (Spring): 39-49.

INLAND DAILY PRESS ASSOCIATION (published annually) *IDPA Cost and Revenue Study.* Park Ridge, IL: Author.

INSTITUTE OF NEWSPAPER CONTROLLERS AND FINANCE OFFICERS (1975) *Profitability Analysis for Newspapers.* Morristown, NJ: Author.

KERTON, R. R. (1973) "Price effects of market power in the Canadian newspaper industry." *Canadian Journal of Economics* 6 (November): 602-606.

KIELBOWICZ, R. B. (1986) "Origins of the second-class mail category and the business of policymaking, 1863-1879." *Journalism Monographs* 96 (April).

KIERNAN, T. (1986) *Citizen Murdoch.* New York: Dodd, Mead.

KOENIG, A. E. (ed.) (1970) *Broadcasting and Bargaining: Labor Relations in Radio and Television.* Madison: University of Wisconsin Press.

LACY, S. (1984) "Competition among metropolitan daily, small daily, and weekly newspapers." *Journalism Quarterly* 61 (Autumn): 640-644.

LACY, S. (1985) "Monopoly metropolitan dailies and inter-city competition." *Jour-nalism Quarterly* 62 (Autumn): 640-644.

LACY, S. (1987) "The effect of growth of radio on newspaper competition, 1920-1948." *Journalism Quarterly* 64 (Winter): 775-781.

LACY, S. (1988a) "The effect of intermedia competition on daily newspaper content." *Journalism Quarterly* 65: (Spring) 95-99.

LACY, S. (1988b) "Content of joint operation newspapers," pp. 147-160 in R. G. Picard, J. P. Winter, M. McCombs, and S. Lacy (eds.) *Press Concentration and Monopoly: New Perspectives on Newspaper Ownership and Operation.* Norwood, NJ: Ablex.

LACY, S. (1988c) "Competing in the suburbs: A research review of intercity newspaper competition." *Newspaper Research Journal* 9 (Winter): 59-68.

LANDAU, E. and J. S. DAVENPORT (1959) "Price anomalies of the mass media." *Journalism Quarterly* 36 (Summer): 291-294.

LAVINE, J. M. and D. B. WACKMAN (1988) *Managing Media Organizations.* New York: Longman.

LEAPMAN, M. (1984) *Arrogant Aussie: The Rupert Murdoch Story.* Secacus, NJ: Lyle Stuart.

LEVIN, H. J. (1971) *The Invisible Resource: Use and Regulation of the Radio Spectrum.* Baltimore: Johns Hopkins University Press.

LEVIN, H. J. (1975) "Franchise values, merit programming and policy options in television broadcasting," pp. 221-247 in R. E. Caves and M. J. Roberts (eds.) *Regulating the Product: Quality and Variety.* Cambridge, MA: Ballinger.

LEVIN, H. J. (1980) *Fact and Fancy in Television Regulation: An Economic Study of Television Alternatives.* New York: Russell Sage.

LEVY, J. and P. PITSCH (1985) "Statistical evidence of substitutability among video delivery systems," pp. 56-92 in E. M. Noam (ed.) *Video Media Competition: Regulation, Economics, and Technology.* New York: Columbia University Press.

LITMAN, B. R. (1988) "Macroeconomic foundations," pp. 3-34 in R. G. Picard, J. P. Winter, M. McCombs, and S. Lacy (eds.) *Press Concentration and Monopoly: New Perspectives on Newspaper Ownership and Operation.* Norwood, NJ: Ablex.

LITMAN, B. R. and J. BRIDGES (1986) "An economic analysis of daily newspaper performance." *Newspaper Research Journal* 7 (Spring): 9-26.

LITWAK, M. (1986) *Reel Power: The Struggle for Influence and Success in the New Hollywood.* New York: William Morrow.

MALONE, J. R. (1969) "Statement of John R. Malone." U.S. Congress, House committee on the Judiciary, Newspaper Preservation Act. Hearings before the Antitrust subcommittee on H.R. 279 and related bills, 91st Congress, 1st session, 337-344.

MARCUS, N. (1986) *Broadcast and Cable Management.* Englewood Cliffs, NJ: Prentice-Hall.

MARX, K. (1952) *Capital* (Friedrich Engels, ed.; Samuel Moore and Edward Aveling, trans.) Chicago: Encyclopedia Britannica. (Original work published 1867)

MATHEWSON, G. F. (1972) "A note on the price effects of market power in the Canadian newspaper industry." *Canadian Journal of Economics* 5: 298-301.

MAYER, M. F. (ed.) (1973) *The Film Industries.* New York: Hastings House.

McCABE, P. (1987) *Bad News at Black Rock: The Sell-Out of CBS News.* New York: Arbor House.

McCLINTICK, D. (1982) *Indecent Exposure: A True Story of Hollywood and Wall Street.* New York: William Morrow.

McCOMBS, M. E. (1972) "Mass media in the marketplace." *Journalism Monographs* 24 (August).

McCOMBS, M. E. (1988) "Concentration, monopoly, and content," pp. 129-137 in R. G. Picard, J. P. Winter, M. McCombs, and S. Lacy (eds.) *Press Concentration and Monopoly: New Perspectives on Newspaper Ownership and Operation.* Norwood, NJ: Ablex.

McGANN, A. F., J. F. RUSSELL, and J. T. RUSSELL (1983) "Variable pricing in advertising space for regional and metro magazines." *Journalism Quarterly* 60 (Summer): 269-275.

McGANN, A. F. and J. T. RUSSELL (1988) "Are broadcasters especially vulnerable to takeovers?" *Journal of Media Economics* 1 (Fall): 29-40.

NATIONAL ASSOCIATION OF BROADCASTERS (published annually) *Radio Financial Report.* Washington, DC: Author.

NATIONAL ASSOCIATION OF BROADCASTERS (1978) *NAB Guide to Investment in Broadcast Properties.* Washington, DC: Author.

NIEBAUER, W. E., Jr. (1984) "Effects of Newspaper Preservation Act on the suburban press." *Newspaper Research Journal* 5 (Spring): 41-49.

NIXON, R. B. and R. L. JONES (1956) "The content of non-competitive vs. competitive newspapers." *Journalism Quarterly* 33 (Summer): 299-315.

NOAM, E. M. (1985a) "Economies of scale in cable television: A multiproduct analysis," pp. 93-120 in E. M. Noam (ed.) *Video Media Competition: Regulation, Economics, and Technology.* New York: Columbia University Press.

NOAM, E. M. (ed.) (1985b) *Video Media Competition: Regulation, Economics, and Technology.* New York: Columbia University Press.

NOLL, R. G., M. J. PECK, and J. J. McGOWAN (1973) *Economic Aspects of Television Regulation.* Washington, DC: Brookings Institute.

NORRIS, V. (1982) "Consumer magazine prices and the mythical advertising subsidy." *Journalism Quarterly* 59 (Summer): 205-211.

NORTON, S. W. and W. NORTON, Jr. (1986) "Economies of scale and the new technology of daily newspapers: A survivor analysis." *Quarterly Review of Economics and Business* 26 (Summer): 66-83.

O'DONNELL, L. B., C. HAUSMAN, and P. BENOIT (1989) *Radio Station Operations.* Belmont, CA: Wadsworth.

OWEN, B. M. (1975) *Economics and Freedom of Expression: Media Structure and the First Amendment.* Cambridge, MA: Ballinger.

OWEN, B. M. (1978) "Structural approaches to the problem of TV network economic dominance." *Center for the Study of Business Regulation Paper Series* 27. Durham, NC: Duke University, Graduate School of Business Administration.

OWEN, B. M., J. H. BEEBE, and W. G. MANNING, Jr. (1974) *Television Economics.* Lexington, MA: D.C. Heath.

PAPER, L. J. (1987) *Empire: William S. Paley and the Making of CBS.* New York: St. Martin's.

PARK, R. E. (1970) *Potential Impact of Cable Growth on Television Broadcasting.* Santa Monica, CA: Rand.

PARK, R. E. (1971) *Prospects for Cable in the 100 Largest Television Markets.* Santa Monica, CA: Rand.

PAUL KAGAN ASSOCIATES (published annually) *Broadcast Stats.* Carmel, CA: Author.

PICARD, R. G. (1982) "Rate setting and competition in newspaper advertising." *Newspaper Research Journal* 3 (April): 23-13.

PICARD, R. G. (1985a) "Patterns of state intervention in western press economics." *Journalism Quarterly* 62 (Spring): 1-9.

PICARD, R. G. (1985b) *The Press and the Decline of Democracy: The Democratic Socialist Response in Public Policy.* Westport, CT: Greenwood.

PICARD, R. G. (1985c) "Pricing behavior in monopoly newspapers: Ad and circulation differences in joint operating and single newspaper monopolies, 1972-1982." *LSU School of Journalism Research Bulletin.*

PICARD, R. G. (1986) "Pricing in competing and monopoly newspapers, 1972-1982." *LSU School of Journalism Research Bulletin.*

PICARD, R. G. (1987) "Evidence of a failing newspaper under the Newspaper Preservation Act." *Newspaper Research Journal* 9 (Fall): 73-82.

PICARD, R. G. (1988a) "Measures of concentration in the daily newspaper industry." *Journal of Media Economics* 1 (Spring): 61-74.

PICARD, R. G. (1988b) "Pricing behavior of newspapers," pp. 55-69 in R. G. Picard, J. P. Winter, M. McCombs, and S. Lacy (eds.) *Press Concentration and Monopoly: New Perspectives on Newspaper Ownership and Operation.* Norwood, NJ: Ablex.

PICARD, R. G. (1988c) "It's time to revise the Newspaper Preservation Act." *Editor & Publisher* (September 24): 48+.

PICARD, R. G., J. P. WINTER, M. McCOMBS, and S. LACY (eds.) (1988) *Press Concentration and Monopoly: New Perspectives on Newspaper Ownership and Operation.* Norwood, NJ: Ablex.

PIGOU, A. C. (1932) *Economics of Welfare.* London: Macmillan.

ROSSE, J. N. (1967) "Daily newspaper monopoly, competition and economies of scale." *American Economic Review* 57: 522-533.

ROSSE, J. N. (1975) "Economic limits of press responsibility." *Studies in Industry Economics* 56. Stanford, CA: Stanford University, Department of Economics.

ROSSE, J. N. (1980) "The decline of direct newspaper competition." *Journal of Communication* 30 (Spring): 65-71.

ROTHENBERG, J. (1962) "Consumer sovereignty and the economics of TV programming." *Studies in Public Communication* 4 (Fall): 45-54.

SCHARFF, E. (1988) *Worldly Power: The Making of the Wall Street Journal.* New York: New American Library.

SCHILLER, H. I. (1981) *Who Knows? Information in the Age of the Fortune 500.* Norwood, NJ: Ablex.

SCHUMPETER, J. A. (1965) *Ten Great Economists.* New York: Oxford University Press.

SCRIPPS, C. E. (1965) *Economic Support of Mass Communication in the United States, 1929-1964.* Cincinnati: Scripps-Howard Research.

SEGLOW, P. (1978) *Trade Unionism in Television: A Case Study in the Development of White Collar Militancy.* Farnborough, U.K.: Saxon House.

SMITH, A. (1952) *An Inquiry into the Nature and Cause of the Wealth of Nations.* Chicago: Encyclopedia Britannica. (Original work published 1776)

SMITH, A. (1977) "Subsidies and the press in Europe." *Political and Economic Planning* 569.

STEINER, P. O. (1952) "Program patterns and preferences, and the workability of competition in radio broadcasting." *Quarterly Journal of Economics* 66 (May): 194-223.

UNITED STATES V. CITIZEN PUBLISHING CO., 280 F. Supp. 978 (D. Ariz. 1968), aff'd, 394 U.S. 131 (1969).

UNITED STATES V. TIMES MIRROR CO., 274 F. Supp. 6060 (C.D. Cal. 1967), aff'd per curiam, 390 U.S. 718 (1968).

VERONIS, SUHLER & ASSOCIATES (published annually) *Communications Industry Report.* New York: Author.

WEAVER, D. H. and L. E. MULLINS (1975) "Content and format characteristics in competing newspapers." *Journalism Quarterly* 52 (Summer): 257-264.

WHITE, L. J. (1985) "Antitrust and video markets: The merger of Showtime and the Movie Channel as a case study," pp. 363-383 in E. M. Noam (ed.) *Video Media Competition: Regulation, Economics, and Technology.* New York: Columbia University Press.

WIRTH, M. O. (1986) "Economic barriers to entering media industries in the United States," pp. 423-442 in M. McLaughlin (ed.) *Communication Yearbook 9.* Beverly Hills, CA: Sage.

WIRTH, M. O. and J. A. WOLLERT (1984) "The effects of market structure on television news pricing." *Journal of Broadcasting* 28 (Spring): 215-225.

WOLPERT, S. A. and J. FRIEDMAN WOLPERT (1986) *Economics of Information.* New York: Van Nostrand Rheinhold.

YULE, A. (1988) *Fast Fade: David Putnam, Columbia Pictures and the Battle for Hollywood.* New York: Delacorte.

INDEX

ABOUT THE AUTHOR

ROBERT G. PICARD is editor of the *Journal of Media Economics* and associate professor and director of the Communication Industries Management Program at Emerson College in Boston.

He was senior editor of the book *Press Concentration and Monopoly: New Perspectives on Newspaper Ownership and Operation* (Ablex, 1988), and the author of *The Press and the Decline of Democracy: The Democratic Socialist Response in Public Policy* (Greenwood, 1985) and *The Ravens of Odin: The Press in the Nordic Nations* (Iowa State University Press, 1988). He has written more than 100 articles on media issues for publications such as *Journalism Quarterly, Political Communication and Persuasion, Journal of Communication Inquiry, Newspaper Research Journal, Journal of Media Economics, European Studies Journal, International Press Institute Report, Gazette, Index on Censorship, The Press, Editor and Publisher, The Quill* (Society of Professional Journalists), and *The Bulletin* (American Society of Newspaper Editors).

Picard is a member of the editorial boards of *Newspaper Research Journal, Political Communication and Persuasion, American Journalism,* and *Journal of Mass Media Ethics.*

He received his Ph.D. from the University of Missouri School of Journalism, after completing an M.A. at California State University, Fullerton, and a B.A. at Loma Linda University. Picard was formerly publications editor of the Freedom of Information Center (the national research center on controls of information), and editor of the *Ontario* (California) *Daily Report,* editor of the *Riverside* (California) *Community News,* and a reporter for the *Morning Advocate* in Baton Rouge, Louisiana.

His awards and honors include selection as one of the Outstanding Young Men in America and inclusion in *Men of Achievement, Contemporary Authors,* and the *International Who's Who in Education.* He received the Clinton F. Denman Freedom of Information Award, the Frank Luther Mott Historical Research Award, a Herrick Fellowship, an East/West Foundation Scholarship, and numerous grants for research and study from organizations including the Gannett Foundation, the Association of Alternative News Weeklies, the Council for the International Exchange of Scholars, and the Southern Regional Education Board.

He has been a consultant on media economics issues for newspapers and magazines and media labor organizations, has testified before Congress on issues involving the Newspaper Preservation Act, and has provided advice and expert testimony in cases involving antitrust issues in the newspaper and broadcasting industries and joint operating agreements in the newspaper industry. He is often consulted by the popular press and media industry publications covering issues involving media economics and public policy.